THE DISAPPEARANCE OF GENERAL JASON

THE DISAPPEARANCE OF GENERAL JASON

The advertisement ran:

"Five Hundred Pounds Reward for Information as to the whereabouts of General Sir Reginald Jason or, otherwise, as to his fate."

When Mr. Palsover arrived to claim the reward, Lady Jason didn't know what to believe. Her woman's intuition told her that Mr. Palsover's story was true, but her common sense told her it couldn't be. The General, according to Mr. Palsover, had been murdered by his best friend, a fellow British officer, in a place which wasn't exactly in South America or exactly in Africa but which was certainly at the back end of the world.

All she really knew was that her husband had announced one day that he-was going off on a mysterious expedition of his own. And, when nothing had been heard of him for a long while, Colonel Henry Carthew had set out to look for him.

The fate of General Jason and the adventures of Colonel Carthew – and, in the end, what happened to Mr. Palsover – were woven together into a story more exotic, more horrifying, more extraordinary, perhaps even (according to your point of view) more romantic, than Lady Jason could have imagined. Very strange things indeed were waiting for them all in that terrible place at the back end of the world. But there was gallantry there, too, and love.

P. C. Wren's marvellous story-telling skill, which made *Beau Geste*, deservedly, one of the world's most famous books, is displayed again here to the full.

*   *   *

Other books by P. C. Wren available in this series:

Action and Passion
Fort in the Jungle
Spanish Maine
Port o'Missing Men

THE DISAPPEARANCE OF GENERAL JASON

by

P. C. Wren

TOM STACEY

First published in Great Britain 1940
by John Murray (Publishers) Ltd

This edition published 1973 by
Tom Stacey Reprints Ltd
28–29 Maiden Lane, London WC2E 7JP
England

ISBN 0 85468 473 5

Printed in Great Britain by
The Garden City Press Ltd, Letchworth

To DAVIS AND GERTRUDE,
NORAH, MAUREEN AND BILL:
ALSO MICKIE AND BONNIE
AND BARKIS WHO WILL,
SOMETIMES.

PART I

LADY JASON'S butler summed up her visitor, Mr. Samuel Palsover, at a glance. Bowler hat, wrong shape ; big face, on the sloppy-chops side, with big heavy moustache, wrong shape ; stiff white collar, wrong shape ; tie brilliant and deplorable, wrong in every way ; thick brown suit, wrong for the country ; thick blue overcoat, wrong for the time of year ; thick-soled heavy boots, wrong for anyone who wished to pretend he was not a country policeman in plain clothes.

Yes, that's what he would be, detective or rural policeman in mufti. Come about this queer business of the General's disappearance.

"Name of Jones. Davie Jones," observed Mr. Samuel Palsover in answer to the butler's correct if cold look of enquiry. "To see Lady Jason. Got an appointment for three o'clock."

Yes, Her Ladyship had said that a person would call that afternoon, and that he was to be shown into the library.

"Come this way, please," said the butler, and forthwith conducted Mr. Samuel Palsover to the room that had been General Sir Reginald Jason's study.

Seating himself on the edge of a small chair, Mr. Samuel Palsover gazed round the handsome room, book-lined and spacious, much used, slightly shabby, and very comfortable.

So this was where the old bird used to put in his

time, read his books and smoke his cigars. Well, he wouldn't smoke any more. Not here, anyway, and very doubtful whether he would where he was now. No Smoking in Heaven, or wherever he might be. Hope for the best about that, anyway. A good sort, if on the hard short-and-sharp side, and a bit of a martinet. A proper gent, though, and the handsomest fine figure of a man that Mr. Samuel Palsover had ever clapped eyes on. Not his fault that he hadn't brought home the bacon, but someone else would do that all right, and for Mr. Palsover too. Meanwhile, there was this five hundred quid for the picking up, or Mr. Palsover's name wasn't Samuel or his nickname Soapy Sam.

A pity he didn't know more about Her Ladyship, but there, women were all alike, and Sam was the man to handle them, Judy O'Grady or the General's lady. Used to be a lovely fine piece, but that was about all he knew of her, hundreds of times as he had seen her and dozens of times as he had heard her talk. There shouldn't be any trouble about it really. She had made the offer, fair and square, in the newspapers, and if there was anyone who could fill the bill, it was Samuel Palsover. She wouldn't wrangle or show a mean suspicious mind. She'd be too thankful for the news. Full of gratitude she'd be, not only because the General was her own lawful wedded husband—and so far as he had ever heard there had never been a word of any disagreement between them—but because it must be a rotten position, not knowing whether you were married or single, a wife or a widow.

For example, she couldn't marry again, not if it was ever so, until she knew one way or the other. There would be money trouble too. She couldn't do business properly, sign cheques on his bank-account and such,

4

or sell anything, until she knew whether he was dead, good and proper, or still wandering about somewheres.

Yes, she'd be easy enough to handle, and if . . .

The door opened and a tall stately woman entered, dignified, aristocratic and still beautiful. Obviously she had been very lovely, with her almost perfect features, statuesque figure and easy graceful carriage.

Mr. Samuel Palsover sprang to his feet and stood at attention.

" Mr. Jones ? " said Lady Jason.

" Yes, Your Ladyship. Name of Davie Jones," replied Mr. Palsover.

Cor ! What a lovely piece she still was. Hardly looked a day older than when he had last seen her in India. She had never seen him, though. Not to notice. Not the sort that takes much interest in the dirt beneath its feet.

In that assumption Mr. Palsover was entirely correct, for never to her knowledge had Lady Jason seen this man before. Was he just another impostor, or might there be something in it, this time ? As her butler had done, and with equal inaccuracy, she summed Mr. Palsover up, at a glance.

That large face, with the yearning trustful eyes, humble and steady, like those of a faithful hound ; that general expression of benevolence, kindness and simplicity belonged to an honest man, or she was no judge of physiognomy and character. He looked like one of those nice big policemen who are so obliging, kindly and helpful. He reminded her of those splendid sergeants whom her husband had always admitted were the backbone of the regiment. This was the sort of man who would love children, be adored by his wife and be the generous prop and stay of his aged parents. A pity his face was so—well—puddingy, and that his huge moustache, like a buffalo's horns, completely hid his mouth. Anyhow, he was a very different type of person from some of those greasy ingratiating creatures, rat-like and cunning, who had tried to swindle her before. Nothing of the tricky rogue about this fine specimen of the plain British man. Besides, he professed to have documentary evidence, which none of the others had done ; and that would very soon settle the matter. She would be able to tell at once whether it were genuine or not.

" Yes," she said. " I have your letter here," and from her hand-bag she took the curious and intriguing document which she had received two days ago.

" Do sit down Mr. . . . Davy-Jones . . . did you say ? "

" Yes, Ma'am. Davie Jones."

And sinking gracefully into an arm-chair, Lady Jason read the letter through once again.

White Hart Inn,
Crossford.

LADY JASON.

Your Ladyship, dear Madam,

I am writing this in answer to your par in the Papers, and am very glad to be able to do my Duty. I don't do this because of the £500 Reward you offer for anyone giving you information as to the fate of your husband General Sir Reginald.

I can do this and give you proofs. In writing. Which no-one else can do, as I am the sole witness except the One Concerned in it.

Your Ladyship, it will be a melancolly occasion, and for me as well as for you. I'll say no more at present, except that unless I hear from you to the contrary at the above, I shall do myself the pleasure of waiting on your

6

Ladyship at your house at three p.m. on Thursday afternoon.

Ever your most respectful
DAVIE JONES.

Yes, the letter tallied with the man ; straightforward and respectful ; and it offered documentary proof. Could it be possible that this person really was an eye-witness of . . . Could it be possible that she was going to learn, here and now, the real truth for which she had waited for years ? Those dreadful years through which she had watched and worried and wondered in an ever-increasing state of cruel uncertainty and suspense, a most wearing, agitating time of anxiety and trouble. Terrible.

" Well, Mr. Jones, first of all—tell me. . . . And then produce proof of the truth of what you say."

" Well, Ma'am," replied Mr. Palsover, as he took a fat amorphous wallet from some capacious inner pocket, " did you ever hear of the Irish Sergeant-Major who undertook to break to Mrs. Brown the news of the death of her husband, Sergeant Brown, accidentally killed by the discharge of a rifle ? Announce it in the married quarters, to the poor wife of the deceased. They let him do it because, besides having an Irish tongue, he had *tact*. . . . He pushed open the front door of the quarters, and hearing deceased's missus singing about her work, he called out in a loud voice, ' *Is the Widow Brown at home ?* '"

Mr. Palsover paused, fixed his hearer with a large and liquid eye, soulful, yearning and benevolent, and with solemn mien added the words,

" Ma'am, you are a widow."

Tact.

Lady Jason suddenly sat upright.

" My husband is dead ? " she whispered.

" Dead, Ma'am. *And* buried," replied Mr. Palsover, and seemed to brush away a tear. Certainly he produced a colourful handkerchief and with its aid blew two or three notes which offered to a sensitive mind quite a strong suggestion of the Last Post.

Lady Jason undoubtedly displayed great self-control.

" You are absolutely *sure* ? " she asked quietly. " You positively *know* ? "

" I had ought to, Ma'am. I saw it done."

" Saw what done ? "

" His death, Ma'am."

" Done ? What do you mean ? Tell me ! . . ."

Mr. Palsover thrust finger and thumb, both extremely thick and stubby, into one of the compartments of the bulging wallet.

" One moment, your Ladyship, before we go any further. Now it's like this. You are a Lady, a perfect Lady, and I trust your word without scrape o' pen or sign o' signature. But I'm a poor man, and I couldn't afford for there to be any misunderstanding. What I want to ask you, straight and simple, and get your answer fair and square, is whether I am eligible for the reward mentioned here in plain print. Five Hundred Pound. It says ' *For information as to the whereabouts of General Sir Reginald Jason or, otherwise, as to his fate.*' Well, Ma'am, if I can satisfy you that I have full and complete information as to both whereabouts and fate, do I get the said reward and receive same ? "

" Certainly," replied Lady Jason. " Of course you do, provided you can assure me as to your *bona fides*, and convince me that what you tell me is true."

" *Bone a fidees !* Ma'am, do you know where the General went when he left here ? Did he write to you

8

from any place, giving name and address of same ? Did he tell you the name of any place to write to ? "

" No, he didn't. He was extremely secretive about both his object and his destination ; but he did write to me once from what he called the jumping-off place for—wherever he was going. The letter was deliberately vague, since secrecy, he said, was most essential ; and he said that if at any time I thought he was overdue, as he called it, there would be no point in my writing to the British Consul, as there wasn't one there. This jumping-off place was . . ."

" Stop, Ma'am. Stop, I beg Your Ladyship. Let it come from me as partly showing the truth of my— what you said. Might the name of that place be Santa Cruz ? "

" Yes. It was Santa Cruz. How did you know ? "

" Well, Ma'am, just an accident. Strange how these things turn out. I happened to be on the ship in which the General went to Santa Cruz. And I had the good fortune, Ma'am, to do him a service, a good turn, as you might say. Very oppreciative, the General was. And very pleasant and friendly. Well, to make a long story short, I went ashore at Santa Cruz."

" And stayed there, with Sir Reginald ? " asked Lady Jason, as Mr. Palsover paused and appeared to ruminate.

" Well, in a manner of speaking, Your Ladyship. Yes and no. With him, as it were, and then again, not with him, so to say."

" And you know where he went from Santa Cruz ? And why he went and what happened to him ? "

" All of it, Your Ladyship."

" Well, where did he go ? "

Mr. Palsover looked up from the wallet in which he

9

was still rummaging, gave Lady Jason a swift searching glance, and looked down again.

He thought quickly. How much did she really know ? Things were going nicely, and he mustn't get himself in wrong with her. He wasn't going to give anything away, but if he told her a lie now she might have him shown out, and there would go five hundred quid. On the other hand, if she contradicted him, he could take it back and say he was only being a bit careful and secretive, like the General himself.

With a scarcely noticeable pause,

" Up-country," he said. " What they call the hinterland. Inland, you know, Ma'am. A bit back o' beyond."

" And what was the name of this place ? "

" Well, that I couldn't hardly tell Your Ladyship. You see it hadn't hardly got any name. It was just country. The *mofussil*."

" Oh, you've been in India ? "

" Er, yes, Your Ladyship. I've bin in India."

" Is this place Santa Cruz in India ? "

" Oh, no, Your Ladyship. No."

" South America, I suppose."

" Well, that way. In a manner of speaking. Or Africa. More or less."

" And did my husband tell you why he was going to this place ? And what he was after ? "

" Well, no. I want to be strickly truthful with Your Ladyship, in act, word an' deed. He didn't. Very close about it all, 'e was. But it was money. *Big* money."

" A concession of some sort ? "

" Ar ! And you can lay to that, Ma'am. Worth millions."

" Diamonds ? Gold ? That sort of thing ? "

" Ar ! That's right. That sort of thing. Only more valuable."

" Oh ? Is there anything more valuable than gold and diamonds ? "

" Yes, Ma'am. Lots of things. Platinum is more valuable than gold, I believe ; and there's sumpthink more valuable than diamonds. Ten times more ! "

" And did the General get this concession ? "

" He did not, Your Ladyship. He got sumpthink else, and he got it in the neck."

" What . . . ? "

" He got *his*."

" D'you mean he was killed ? . . . By natives. . . . Savages ? "

" No, Ma'am. He was killed by another gentleman."

" Why ? "

" The concession."

And as Lady Jason stared aghast, Mr. Samuel Palsover bowed his head, shook it sadly to and fro, and lowering his voice, added in a portentous whisper,

" And somethink else."

" What ? "

" A woman."

" You mean to tell me, Mr. Jones, that General Sir Reginald Jason quarrelled with another white man over this amazing concession and a woman, and that the other man killed him ? . . . I don't believe a word of it ! It's fantastic ! Absurd ! "

" Yes—*and* it's true, Ma'am," murmured Mr. Palsover, the deep diapason of his muted voice rich with tragedy. Obviously he spoke in great sorrow, sadness and regret.

" You mean they . . . *fought* ? "

" No, Your Ladyship. That would have been bad enough but . . ."

Mr. Palsover appeared to swallow a lump ere he added,

" He was murdered, Ma'am."

" Shot ? "

Oh, why was she asking these foolish futile questions ? What did such stupid details matter ? She wanted the truth. The truth. To know the worst and get it over. What were the right questions to ask him ? Why should her brain fail her now ; now that she was, as she felt, really on the track of the actual truth ?

" No, Ma'am. Worse than that, I'm sorry to say. He was . . . poisoned. Poisoned by one as he thought to be his friend."

And at this point Mr. Palsover again produced the handkerchief and the mournful musical tribute.

" How do you know ? "

" Because I were there, Ma'am, present and corr . . . I mean, present at the end."

" And who was the man with whom he quarrelled ? Some foreign prospector ? Some half-caste Dago person as in a novel, Spanish or Italian or . . ."

How she was babbling on. She of all people. She must control herself.

" No, Your Ladyship. Believe it or not, it was an officer and a gentleman, a British officer, as done it."

" *What ?* Nonsense ! This is really too much. Utterly ridiculous."

Mr. Samuel Palsover raised his large face, sad and sympathetic ; his earnest, yearning eyes, all but tearful.

" Name of *Carthew*, Ma'am," he whispered.

Lady Jason sprang to her feet.

" *Bosh !* . . . *Nonsense !* You must be mad. I won't hear any more of such . . . I was going to say lies. Rubbish ! Lunacy ! "

12

Mr. Palsover sighed as again he gently shook his head.

"Yes. I was afraid Your Ladyship would look at it like that. I expected it. It's natural. But fac's is fac's, Ma'am. An' fac's is stubborn things."

"But it's incredible. It is . . . I have no words for it. To come here and tell me a tale like that, and with no sort of proof or evidence of any kind. Why, I wonder you *dare* to . . ."

Mr. Palsover picked up the wallet from where he had laid it on the floor beside him, and again fumbled in it.

What huge powerful hands he had, and how curiously he used them when talking. Cupped, beseeching. He was like some great animal with enormous flippers. He was like the Mock Turtle, what with his great calf's eyes, huge bulk and enormous flapping flippers. . . . He was like a great bear with mighty paws. . . . Beseeching. . . . How idiotically her mind was behaving, but they were amazing hands, and he really did use them in the most astonishing way. It was as though the subject of conversation were a baby which he dandled, holding it out before you, beseeching, begging, imploring you to look upon it reasonably, kindly, if not with an actually loving eye. He metaphorically handed things to you all the time.

Terrible great hands. Strangler's hands.

Oh, come! This really would not do. He was an honest man and he was telling her the truth.

But no, it was lunacy; sheer midsummer madness. Henry Carthew quarrelling with Reginald over a concession and a woman, and killing him. *Poisoning* him! It was just about the silliest absurdest utter idiocy that she had ever heard. It was nightmare stuff.

Mr. Palsover produced a sheet of paper. Rising and

13

offering it to her, he said in his persuasive sympathetic voice,

" There, Ma'am. You will recognize that as the General's handwriting, I believe, though it might differ slightly from such as he would write at that desk, sitting up to do it and in full health. He was far from it when he wrote that. Lying on a camp-bed, he was. Shaken with fever—and worse—and writing with the pocket-book in his left hand as he lay on his back."

Yes, it was a leaf from the sort of field-service pocket-book that Reginald used ; and the writing was undoubtedly his. Not, as the man said, exactly like his usual writing ; but, allowing for the fact that it was written in pencil while on a sick bed, she was sure that it was really his.

Yes, every ' s ' was as he always wrote it, like a small capital ; and each ' r ' was of the shape that he always made ; and that was his ' g,' looking almost like a ' q.' And the initials, which he always wrote as signature, were undeniably his. The R and the J with the down-stroke in common, the curl of the J at the bottom to the left, and the back of the R to the right, and with that little flourish.

This was genuine. It was a note written by her husband in his pocket-book. The only curious thing about it was that it began " *My dear wife* " which was unusual. She would have expected him to write " *My dear Tony.*" But then Reginald had really written her very few letters, and had not by any means always begun in the same way. It had sometimes been " *My dear Antoinette* " and occasionally " *Toinette.*"

But that was nothing. Being lonely and sick and neglected, he might have felt more affectionate than usual, and put " *My dear wife* " as looking more loving. Well, obviously he had, for there it was,

14

My dear Wife,

You can trust this man. What he tells you will be the truth. I don't want to write it here. But he knows all about it and can tell you everything. I am very ill and have had a lot of fever and dysentry and I feel as though I have been poisoned. I should think it was dysentry except for the horrible pain. In fact, I know it, though I couldn't prove it. I don't want to say too much, but the only food or medecine I have had has been given me by Carthew. I will write more if I can. I would write plainer if I could post the letter somewhere safe. I'll write again later if I can, but I doubt it.

And then the initials in the curious way in which he always wrote them, like a monogram.

But no, this wouldn't do. Reginald, the purist, was absolutely incapable of saying " *I would write plainer,*" or of mis-spelling a word, and surely there were two ' *e*'s ' in " dysentery." But perhaps she was wrong about that. And weren't there only two ' *e*'s ' in " medicine " ? She'd look the words up by-and-bye.

But how absurd of her to quibble over the style and spelling of a letter written by a man incoherent, almost delirious, with fever. As well expect him to talk with the utmost accuracy and lucidity when unconscious under an anæsthetic, or when in a complete state of delirium at the height of a bout of malarial fever. She was being absurd. What further proof did she want than Reginald's own writing and signature ? She would have been suspicious at once if it had been signed ' R. Jason,' a form which he never used. He might have done so on official documents, but he never did so in private correspondence, and how would this man know that ?

No. The letter was genuine and this man was genuine.

But Henry Carthew!

It was unthinkable.

On the other hand, what wouldn't men do when they were poor, and the prize was, as this man put it, millions. Gold, diamonds and something more valuable still—whatever that might be.

And a woman!

Surely neither Reginald nor Henry Carthew was the kind of man who did that sort of thing? But there again, you never knew. Thousands of miles in space, and years in time, away from home; no feminine companionship; no restraining public opinion; and some more-or-less-coloured Venus.

Well, men were like that, she supposed, but . . . No. Nonsense.

" And has Colonel Carthew got this marvellous concession ? " she asked.

" Not yet, Ma'am. Not as I knows of. But now the poor General's gone, there's nothing between him and it, in a manner of speakin'.

" Except me," he added ; and there was a faint note, as of a growl, in his voice.

" Except you ? How do you mean ? "

Again the enormous powerful hands fumbled clumsily with the wallet, and Mr. Palsover withdrew another folded paper from its recesses.

" Will you read that, please, Your Ladyship ? "

Reginald's handwriting again. Undoubtedly his—though different.

What was this ?

" I hereby give and bequeath all my rights in the concession of which Major Carthew and Mr. Davie Jones

*know, to the said Mr. Davie Jones, as is his right. No-
body whatsoever, especially Colonel Carthew, has any
rights in it whatsoever. I hereby request and direct my
wife not to give the said Colonel Carthew any document
that may be in my safe or desk bearing on the same. Any
such document is the rightful property of the bearer of this
paper, Mr. Davie Jones. Please see without fail that
such document does not fall into the wrong hands, but only
those of the said Mr. Davie Jones. Beware of Colonel
Henry Carthew who I firmly believe is poisoning me, that
he may get what belongs to me and the said Mr. Davie
Jones—to whom I leave ALL my rights in the concession."*

And then again the unmistakable monographic
initials.

Somewhat vague, not to say incoherent. But then
again Reginald was ill, of course. Dying, according to
Mr. Jones. Dying of fever and of *poison.*

Henry Carthew. To think of it !

And then again, common sense rebelled, and she
refused to think of it, refused to entertain such an idea
for another moment.

Henry Carthew of all people !

" This certainly appears to have been written by my
husband," she said, " but I know nothing of any document referring to any concession. There is none in my
possession."

" Well, Ma'am, I would not press that, for I would
be very sorry indeed to give you any trouble. Never
mind about the concession, except . . ."

And here again, Mr. Palsover, looking up, shot a
quick glance at her face.

" . . . *except* that, as the General says there, no such
document should ever be given to Colonel Carthew.
Never ! On no account whatsoever.

17

" Not that he'd ever have the face to come here and ask for it, surely, the wicked murderer ! " he added.

" But, my good man, I cannot *possibly* believe such a thing. Why, Colonel Carthew was my husband's oldest and best friend. Do you know that he went out to Santa Cruz especially to look for him ? After he had been missing for over two years."

" Ho ! He did, did he ! "

" Yes, he went to Santa Cruz with the sole object of trying to find out what place it was for which the General used Santa Cruz as a starting-point, a jumping-off place, as he called it. I wrote to him myself. To Colonel Carthew, I mean, and begged him to try to find my husband, as I was getting desperate about him. . . . At least a couple of years, without a word. . . . The papers were talking about it. Full of it. I never picked one up without expecting to see the heading cropping up again—' *The Disappearance of General Jason* ' or ' *Where is Sir Reginald Jason ?* ' or ' *Strange Disappearance of famous British General* ' or ' *Is General Jason lost ?* ' That sort of thing. Colonel Carthew had just retired and was free ; and when I asked him, he said at once he'd be only too delighted to go and look for him."

" Well, he found him all right," sneered Mr. Samuel Palsover, if the word sneer could be used with regard to the vocal and facial expression of so kindly and benevolent-looking a person.

" Yes," he continued, " he found him all right. And he stayed with him too, when he found something else —that he was on to a concession that meant a thundering big fortune ! Not to mention the woman. A kind of princess, she was. What they'd call a princess in such Gawd-forsaken 'oles at the back o' beyond. . . . Found him, stayed with him, and done him in."

18

" Bosh ! I don't believe it," snapped Lady Jason who was not given to snapping. " I can't believe it. Have you any other sort of proof ? "

" Well, Your Ladyship. I have proved to you that I knew that Sir Reginald went to Santa Cruz. I've proved to you that I knew him there. I've proved that I knew all about Colonel Carthew going to find him I've brought you letters written by the General himself. . . . And there's this, Ma'am."

Fumbling at the massive silver chain which adorned his waistcoat, Mr. Palsover hauled a large silver watch from his pocket, detached the watch from the chain, and released a ring through which the chain had passed.

" There, Your Ladyship ! " said he, with an air of modest triumph, as he gave her the ring. " What's that ? "

Even before she took it she recognized it as her husband's signet-ring, ancient and worn, bearing the Jason crest, a ring that had belonged not only to him but to a dozen Jasons before him. There was the half-obliterated crest, suggesting the wilted carcase of a sheep, but intended to represent the Golden Fleece.

Yes, this was most undeniably her husband's ring. About that there could be no possible shadow of doubt.

Lady Jason never wept, and had a profound contempt for women who did—save with some excellent purpose in view—but there was a faint suspicion of tears in her eyes and of a break in her voice as she asked,

" Where did you get this ? "

" He gave it to me, Your Ladyship.

" ' *Take that, my dear friend,*' he said in his dyin' voice ; and almost his very last words they were, ' *and give it to her Ladyship, with my love, so that if she has any doubts about you whatsoever, or of the truth of your story,*

19

this will prove it.' And as he took the ring from his little finger of his left 'and, he said, ' *This is the first and last time this ring leaves the 'and that has worn it all me life.'* "

Mr. Palsover did not break down, but he ceased speaking, in the manner of one who can speak no more, his heart too full for words.

With another searching glance at Lady Jason's face, as she regarded the ring lying on the palm of her hand, he decided that the moment was ripe. Obviously she was deeply affected, and surely would be in no mood for unseemly bargaining. He rose to his feet.

" You 'ave my proofs, Your Ladyship," he said, with a quiet dignity, " and, as a poor man who has travelled all the way from South—er—all the way from Santa Cruz to set your mind at rest, I respectfully claim the Five Hundred Pounds Reward offered to him as should give you ' evidence as to the whereabouts of General Sir Reginald Jason or, otherwise, as to his fate.' I have proved to you that I knew his whereabouts ; and I have proved to you that he is dead, by bringing you the ring which never left his hand until dying. Also letters from him begging you to trust me and do as I says."

Lady Jason also rose to her feet, her mind a tumult, her notable poise, aloofness, and *sang froid* disturbed.

Her woman's intuition told her that this nice man, so kindly and sympathetic, so patently honest, simple and straightforward, had told her the truth, the whole truth and nothing but the truth.

Her common sense, likewise notable, told her that it was also perfectly impossible that Henry Carthew should have done such a thing as this. It would be a dreadful deed even to believe so appalling an accusation, brought against him by a stranger, and completely

20

unsupported. Although this Davie Jones had provided satisfactory credentials and what really amounted to proof of her husband's death—for how otherwise would the man have been in possession of this ring—she had only his bare word as to the means, manner and cause of his death.

That Reginald was dead she did not for one moment doubt.

That Henry Carthew had killed him she did not for one moment believe.

But that had no bearing on the right or wrong of this claim for the offered reward. She glanced at the letters, her husband's handwriting, his ring, and felt that to demand more in the way of proof would be absurd, unjust, and something like a mean and despicable piece of evasion. The man had brought the desired information and proofs of the truth of his story.
. . . If only he had not mentioned Henry Carthew ! But that again was a form of proof. What should any impostor know about Henry Carthew going to Santa Cruz ?

Yes, she must accept this man's evidence, give him his reward, and henceforth regard herself as a widow. But wait a moment, would a Court of Law allow her to presume her husband's death ? It was, after all, only circumstantial evidence—convincing, and bearing the stamp of truth—but was it proof, legal proof ? Would not the Court require something more than this ?

" Where is the General buried ? " she asked, looking up and seeming to see the large face that loomed above her, distorted with avarice, cupidity, avid hunger for . . .

But how absurd ! She was getting positively distraught. It was a benevolent face. The eyes that for a second had seemed hard as marble, fierce and terrible as those of a hungry tiger, were gentle, smiling and friendly. Hard? They were limpid, soft and child-like.

" In the jungle, Ma'am. Up-country, behind Santa Cruz. I buried him meself with me own 'ands.''

He held them out to her as though tenderly supporting the body.

" Yes, Your Ladyship, though there was only me, the poor General had Christian Burial. I knew the drill and . . . done everything correct. All as laid down in the book. . . . That must be a relief to Your Ladyship's mind.''

" And where was Colonel Carthew then? ''

" Gone, Ma'am. Gone. D'rectly he knew that the General had passed over, he hurried on. The concession . . .

" And the woman,'' he murmured, with obvious distaste.

Lady Jason was a realist. Business and sentiment are bad partners. Incompatibles. Poor Reginald was gone, and that was that. The story about Henry Carthew she rejected. Mr. Davie Jones she accepted —but there was something wrong somewhere. What poor Reginald used to call " fishy.'' She must pull herself together and be business-like.

" Listen, Mr. Jones,'' she said. " Up to a point I don't doubt your story. I don't question that my husband is dead. But I cannot, and do not, believe that Colonel Carthew had anything to do with his death.''

More in sorrow than in anger, Mr. Palsover made with his hands a wide and sweeping gesture more eloquent than words.

" No. Listen,'' interrupted Lady Jason, as his mouth opened, while the great hands offered her, as it were, the solid concrete truth. "I shall not pay you the reward—not the whole of it, at any rate—at once. I shall try to get into communication with Colonel Carthew."

"But Your Ladyship," expostulated Mr. Palsover, and the voice was now possibly a shade less deferential, sympathetic and benevolent. "I have brought you proofs, and it ain't likely that Colonel Carthew is goin' to say anythink that will get himself into trouble, is it ? "

"I shall try to get into touch with Colonel Carthew," continued Lady Jason, ignoring the outburst, "and if he confirms your statement that my husband is dead, I shall at once accept it, and pay you the balance of the reward."

"And suppose you can't get into communication with him ? " asked Mr. Palsover.

"Well, we will fix a time limit. I will give you . . . a hundred pounds . . . now, and the balance when I get confirmation of my husband's death."

Mr. Palsover smiled tolerantly and with a touch of amusement, the kindly smile of one humouring a child.

"Come, come, Your Ladyship ! As I said before, you are a perfect Lady, and would never squibble with a poor man when it came to the payment of a promised and well-earned reward. You say there, plain and clear, in the paper, that you will pay Five Hundred Pounds Reward ' for information as to the whereabouts of General Sir Reginald Jason or, otherwise, as to his fate.' I've give you that information, and I've brought proofs, and all I ask of Your Ladyship is that you will now fulfil your promise and keep your word.

"But of course you will," added Mr. Palsover with a sort of chuckle, as at one who will have her little joke.

"I will do exactly as I say, Mr. Jones," replied Lady

23

Jason. " I will write you a cheque for a hundred pounds now ; and I'll pay you the balance, another four hundred, six months from to-day, or directly I hear from Colonel Carthew—whichever may be the sooner."

Mr. Palsover's hands expressed resignation but not defeat. An excellent judge of character and no mean judge of women, he knew when to wear the velvet glove, when to bully and when to wheedle. This was a thoroughbred with a snaffle mouth. No good trying curb or spurs and whip here.

" Very good, Your Ladyship," he sighed. " I admit I had expected to have pleased you more than I seem to have. 'Owever, I done me best. I can wait six months, for I doubt if you'll ever get 'old of Colonel Carthew. If you do, he'll have to admit that the General is dead. Prob'ly say he died of malaria, or pitch some other yarn. Any'ow, he can't and won't pretend that General Sir Reginald Jason is still alive."

It was perhaps fortunate for him that Lady Jason was unable to see Mr. Samuel Palsover's face as she sat at the desk and wrote the cheque.

" There you are," she said, handing it to him. " An open cheque which the Bank will cash across the counter. Where shall I send the other cheque ? To the address on your letter ? "

" Thankin' you kindly, Ma'am, the same. It will be forwarded to me quite safe, if I am not there. But I hope I shan't have to wait that long. Not after all the trouble I've taken and the expense I've been at."

" I hope not, Mr. Jones," agreed Lady Jason coldly. " I shall naturally do my best to get a cable from Colonel Carthew. What I do not understand is why I haven't had one from him before."

"*I* understand it all right, Ma'am! So'd you, if you'd seen what I've seen," was the grim reply.

What was it that had been at the back of her mind as she wrote the cheque ? What was it she had been going to say to this man ? . . . Yes.

"Look here, Mr. Jones. If what you say were true, and Colonel Carthew actually did murder my husband, are you prepared to give evidence against him in a Court of Law: to stand up and be cross-examined by defending Counsel ? "

Mr. Palsover's large features settled in a firmer mould as a look of righteous indignation hardened his ingenuous countenance.

"Ma'am, I'd give anything for the oppertunity. Yes, anything. But where's me proofs ? Just my word against his. Me, a poor ordinary common man ; him a British officer and gentleman. Who'd believe me ? Where's me witnesses ?

"Even if you cared to run 'im in, Ma'am," he added.

And, indeed, Lady Jason entirely failed to visualize herself bringing an action concerning the murder of her husband against his life-long friend and brother officer, Colonel Henry Carthew, on the unsupported testimony of Mr. Davie Jones.

Crossing the room she touched a bell.

"I must thank you very much indeed for what you have done, Mr. Jones," she said formally, "and you must not think me suspicious or over-cautious about the paying of the reward. Five hundred pounds is a large sum of money, and I am quite sure that my lawyer and man of business will approve of what I have done."

Privately Mr. Palsover doubted that Her Ladyship's man of business would approve anything about the whole affair—save the withholding of the four hundred pounds.

25

" Well, Your Ladyship, I shall hope to hear from you soon. Thanking you, and my best respects, yours most sincerely, Ma'am," he said as he backed away, bowing.

As the butler opened the door, he turned and bowed again in Lady Jason's direction.

" Most sincerely, Ma'am," he repeated.

And indeed he looked the very essence of sincerity.

PART II

I

O^N a day some years previous to that of his visit to Lady Jason, Mess-Sergeant Palsover superintended with special care the work of his subordinates, the servants of the Officers' Mess of the Royal Wessex Fusiliers—then stationed at Sitapur in India. For this evening was a special occasion and what he himself would term a melancholy occasion, the last appearance at dinner in that Mess of Lieutenant-Colonel Jason, up to that day commanding the Regiment.

So, not only was it Guest-night, but a kind of farewell dinner to the Colonel, to-night almost a guest in his own Mess.

Mess-Sergeant Samuel Palsover, a little distrait, ran an experienced professional eye over the set dining-table, with its snow-white crest-enwoven Regimental linen ; its wonderful array of silver trophies, some of them over two hundred years old ; its beautiful glass, tankards and cutlery ; looked upon the handiwork of his staff of mess-servants, and found it good. Nevertheless, he sighed, for not only would the departure of the Colonel mean the going of the man whom he admired and approved, but the stepping into his place, temporarily, if not permanently, of a man whom Sergeant Palsover could neither admire nor approve.

That Major Cárthew . . .!

He'd have it in for Sergeant Palsover. . . . There'd be no pleasing him . . . Nothink wouldn't go right no more. . . . Why, almost from the day Samuel Palsover joined the Royal Wessex, Carthew had had it in for him, whether as Private, Lance-Corporal, Corporal or Sergeant.

Fact was, Major Carthew didn't like him, and made no secret of the fact.

On the other hand, Sergeant Palsover didn't like Major Carthew, though he was constrained to make something of a secret of the fact. At any rate, as far as the Major was concerned.

Picked on him, the Major had. Always picked on him, from the time Palsover had been a young recruit and Carthew a subaltern. Always trying to catch him out and crime him. . . . As though it weren't a good thing for the men to have a quiet gamble, a bit on a horse, a flutter at the Crown and Anchor game, and such. Kept 'em happy, 'specially in the hot weather when there was nothing to do, and all day to do it in. And wasn't it a good thing for a man who had run short, or who was in difficulties, to be able to know where he could borrow a bit to tide him over ? . . . Calling him a shark and a sharper, a corrupt influence, and a— what was it—u-su-ry-ous Shylark. All right for him to go to a bloomin' bazaar *sowcar*, *chetti*, *bunnia*, *shroff*, or whatever you like to call 'em, and borrow a hundred pounds at twenty per cent, as no doubt he had done many a time and oft, when he was a subaltern. That was all right ; but for poor old Palsover, the soldier's friend, to lend 'em a bob and charge a penny for the accommodation, oh, no, that was all wrong and wouldn't do at all. The Officer could have his native money-lender and borrow till he was broke, but Other Ranks couldn't even have a kindly Sergeant they could go to and ask to help 'em along. What was it the old devil had called him, only the other day ? A bloated blood-

30

sucker. And said that a penny a week on a bob was interest at the rate of *four hundred and thirty-three and a third per cent per annum* ! What a silly way to talk. " Other ranks " didn't want no per cents nor per annums. They wanted a bob, and were glad to pay a penny for the accommodation, when they were thirsty —and broke.

Interfering old devil ! What had it got to do with him ? Wasn't it better to keep the boys at home, instead of letting 'em go borrowing from some greedy native rascal who'd skin 'em alive. . . . Too fond of pickin' on people.

And now he was going to command the Regiment.

Well, there wasn't so long to go now, and Mess-Sergeant Palsover hadn't done so bad. Far from it. Be a damned sight better off than the Major himself when they retired ; for, from the time he had joined, the silly beggar had only just kept his head above water. There wasn't much Mess-Sergeant Palsover didn't know about the Officers' financial affairs, and while the Colonel wasn't rich, Major Carthew was definitely poor. His man Jackson knew it too. Practically no pickin's at all. Jackson himself had to borrow from Sergeant Palsover more weeks than not.

Well, well, when he commanded the Regiment, Carthew would have plenty to keep him busy. Keep him out of mischief ; picking on people and poking his nose into their private affairs.

Huh ! What would the new Colonel say if he knew that Mess-Sergeant Palsover held the careers of at least two of his promising young Subalterns in the 'oller of his 'and. . . . Thinking of which, they'd have to pay up, in the course of the next two or three years. Pay up or be sold up, when Sergeant Palsover retired. Pity, too, for the way the interest on them nice little debts mounted up was surprisin'. Go off the deep end proper, Carthew would, if he knew. But there again, where was the 'arm? Young Officer wants a polo pony—well, he's got to play polo, hasn't he? Young Officer has a bad day at the Races—well, he's got to pay his bookie, hasn't he? Better a young Officer should go to a good honest Briton than to some rascally ol' vulture of a native *bunnia*. Those bazaar money-lenders were just robbers and thieves. Why, Mess-Sergeant Palsover had been a boon and a blessing to many, saving them from the clutches of them merciless vampires.

Have a lot to say about discipline, Carthew would, too. . . . Oh, an 'orrible thing for discipline, that a Subaltern should let a Mess-Sergeant get him out of dangerous trouble. . . . Tripe! As if Mess-Sergeant Palsover didn't know his place, or would ever presume on having lent half a dozen fivers, or five hundred rupees, to young gentlemen in difficulties. Never. Treat 'em more respectful than ever. Friendly. More like a kind father, so to speak, than one of those stony-'earted grasping money-lenders. . . . P'raps he'd rather a young Officer went borrowing from the Parsi mess-contractor or the Hindu bazaar furniture-wallah?

There went the massed bugles playing the Regimental Call. . . . Now the Officers' Mess Call. He'd better go and 'nounce dinner ready.

Then they'd be comin' out of the ante-room in good time. Ol' Carthew'd be fancying himself to-night, now 'e was going to command the Regiment.

Well, Mess-Sergeant Palsover would have to watch his step. But the man who had been clever enough to keep on the right side of Colonel Jason was clever enough to diddle half a dozen Colonel Carthews, provided he was careful. And if the worst came to the worst, Mess-Sergeant Palsover had made his pile, and when he got into civvies, would be Mr. Samuel Palsover, Esquire, with such a comfortable bank account that the interest from his investments would make his nice little pension look like chicken-feed.

Ar! And they'd be *some* investments too, when he got back to Blighty, and had nothing else to do but addle his brass.

Well! Here they came. Time to tip off the Band Master to pipe up *The Roast Beef of Old England.*

§ 2

" Splendid-looking chap, isn't he ? " said the Senior Subaltern's guest, Mr. Croombe of the 9th Bengal Lancers, eyeing Colonel Jason far away on the other side of the table. " You must be devilish sorry to lose him."

" Yes. Best Colonel the Regiment ever had. Best Colonel any Regiment ever had," replied the Senior Subaltern. " There's not a man in the Regiment that doesn't admire and respect him, and who isn't sorry he's going."

" Popular, eh ? "

" No. No, I wouldn't say that. Admired and respected is what I said. But not exactly beloved. Just a trifle on the inhuman side. The Kitchener touch. I've been in this Battalion now, man and boy, for ten years, and haven't had a kind word from him once, the whole time. Nor an unjust one. I've never seen him lose his temper nor heard him bawl a man out, but I'd sooner walk twenty miles in bare feet than walk on to the mat and get a telling-off from him, for all his quietness. Quiet, cool and—deadly."

" Not like our Old Man," smiled Mr. Croombe.

" Raging like a lion. Blow your head off, curse himself blue in the face, swear he'll have your scalp and your blood, and forget all about it by the evening. Never lets the sun go down upon his wrath."

The Senior Subaltern smiled.

" Same here. Sun never goes down upon his wrath because there isn't any. Don't go in for wrath here. Cold. But I'm not sure I don't prefer a hot hell to a cold one, especially a hot hell that is soon over. But don't you think for one moment that I'm crabbing him. Truly magnificent chap. Just what a Colonel ought to be."

" I think he's one of the handsomest men I ever saw," replied Mr. Croombe. " So austere. So superior, in the best sense of the word. Wonderfully dignified too."

" Yes, dignity incarnate, isn't he ? " agreed the Senior Subaltern. " Not exactly overflowing with the milk of human kindness ; but although you might call him hard . . . curt . . . clipped . . . and perhaps proud and haughty, he has got something to be proud about."

" Yes, the type of British Colonel that our know-ledgeable penny humorists caricature and laugh at, and whom the foreigner is apt to understand a bit better than some sections of the British Public do."

" Yes, rigidly correct, imperturbable. Why, do you know, I've heard fools wonder whether he had much brain, and whether he wasn't dead from the neck up. Rather amusing to anyone who knows he's as clever as a fox. He may look like a bronze bust, but the bronze is still molten hot in the middle. . . . And a more honourable and upright man never lived."

" Spot of hero-worship ? " smiled Mr. Croombe.

" Well, no. You can't get sufficiently fond of him

34

for that. Can't make any sort of human contact with him. There's always that sense of a thick glass wall in between. But that doesn't prevent one from appreciating his outstanding soldierly qualities, and admiring him unreservedly. Perhaps, if one could get to know him . . . But you feel that, after ten years, he doesn't remember either you or your name ; and that when you say ' Good-morning,' he might at any time reply ' Good-morning. And who the devil might you be ? ' "

" I see. Icy isolation, what ? " smiled Mr. Croombe.

" I should say there is only one man in the Regiment that really knows him ; and he was at school and Sandhurst with him, as well as in the Regiment all their service."

" What, Major Carthew ? "

" Yes. Now there you might talk about hero-worship. I should say that old Cart-horse believes in God, King and Jason. Don't know which he puts first. I'd say loves Jason, honours the King and fears God, in that order—and that he loves Jason more than anyone or anything on earth. Real case of hero-worship, if you like."

" What sort of a chap is Carthew ? "

" Oh, he's got his points. One of the best, really, but not in the same street with Jason. Kind-hearted a chap as you'd meet in a day's march. An incredible linguist too. Interpreter-rank in all the Latin languages from French to Portuguese, and takes the Higher Standard in a new Oriental language every year, out here . . . Persian . . . Arabic . . . and what not. Keen as mustard. And absolutely married to the Regiment, but he'll find it a difficult matter, stepping into Jason's shoes."

" Certainly a great contrast to him in appearance," observed Mr. Croombe, as he glanced at Major Carthew.

" Yes. No beauty, is he ?   I believe he has always been a sore trial to Jason.   Going on parade with his helmet backside foremost or his most important buttons undone.   Never looks right, somehow.   Still, he's a damn fine fighting soldier, though no great Mess ornament.   Wonderful gift for upsetting inspecting Generals.   Been a good thing for him, once or twice, that Jason is really fond of him.   About the only thing Jason is fond of.   Don't believe he has ever owned a dog in his life, and I've never seen him pat a horse, let alone a deserving human back.   Such as mine, for example. . . .   I shouldn't think that his Mrs. . . . H'm ! ''

The Senior Subaltern stopped abruptly, somewhat shocked to realize that he had been about to mention a lady's name, a thing which is not done in British Messes.

" Why, God sweeten my soul ! Hasn't young Bickersteth got a coloured handkerchief up his sleeve ? I'll have him undressed later on, and if he has, he shall eat it.   Foul little hound !   The sort of thing he would do !   Handkerchief up his sleeve, and a coloured one at that !   What's the Army coming to ? ''

§ 3

" Well, Reginald," said Major Carthew to Colonel Jason, " it doesn't seem *possible* that this is the last time you and I will sit at this table.   I simply cannot believe it.''

" No.   Hardly believe it myself.   Almost sorry, in a way,'' replied Colonel Jason.   " A great change.   Probably find being a General quite a lonely sort of job, at first.''

" Yes.   But you won't be as lonely as I shall.   I

can't tell you how much I shall miss you. Probably don't know myself yet. Don't realize it, quite. No one's more pleased than I am that you've got your Brigade, Reginald, but . . . I feel like sending in my papers. You and Antoinette gone! It doesn't bear thinking of."

" Oh, don't talk nonsense, Henry. . . . Make me cry in a minute. Twelve o'clock to-night you'll be our Colonel Carthew. Now you've got the Battalion you'll have something else to do than think of old times and old friends."

Did Reginald really think that he'd ever have anything better to do than think of old times and his old friend? Didn't *he* feel it at all? Probably not, and a good thing too. He wouldn't like to think that Reginald was hating it as much as he was. Really suffering. It was awful. And he hadn't quite realized it yet, himself. He'd do that to-morrow morning when he saw him and Antoinette off. It was like a bad dream. How he wished he could only wake from it.

Mess-Sergeant Palsover approached, bent over and whispered in Colonel Jason's ear, was answered with a curt nod, and departed.

" I shall positively miss that old scoundrel," smiled Colonel Jason.

" I should like to have the opportunity," replied Major Carthew.

" You do hate him, don't you, Henry? I don't know why. I'm rather fond of Palsover."

" Well, you gave him his right name just now."

" Scoundrel? A term of endearment," smiled Colonel Jason.

" Never endeared himself to *me*, although he has done his best. He is a scoundrel. A damned scoun-

37

drel. Biggest scoundrel unhung," growled Major Carthew.

" Oh, come, come ! He's not as bad as all that. It's not like you to talk like this, Henry. No doubt he has his little tricks. Possibly heard of watered beer and wonderfully-blended whiskey, and what are called ' illegal gratifications,' I believe. But . . ."

" Oh, I suppose most Mess-Sergeants have their little ways," interrupted Carthew, " but Palsover's an out-and-out wrong 'un. I don't mind telling you now "— he had been going to say " *now that you are going*," but found it difficult, painful, to put the plain and simple fact into so many words—" that I believe he was wholly and solely responsible for the death of young James."

" But Private James committed suicide. There was never the slightest shadow of doubt about that," objected Colonel Jason.

" Yes, he committed suicide. Shot himself with his own rifle ; but it's my firm conviction that part of the pressure on the trigger came from Palsover's finger."

" You don't mean literally ? "

" No. I don't mean that Palsover was there when it happened, or had the least idea that it was going to happen. He'd have prevented it if he had, for fear the wretched lad left a letter. But I am absolutely certain, in my own mind, that Palsover drove him to . . ."

" But how ? "

" Dunning him. Putting the screw on him persistently. He had kept on lending him small sums of money until the total was, from James's point of view, a very big one ; and then he not only put the screw on, and made the wretched lad's life a burden to him, but used his power over him in various ways, till James couldn't stand it any longer."

38

" But none of this ever came out at the time. There was no evidence that . . ."

" No, I know there wasn't, unfortunately. It was all hear-say. But everybody knew. And nobody knew—when it came to saying what they knew—in evidence at the inquest. I had it all from my man. Long afterwards, of course. Knowing my Palsover and his little ways, I made it my business to learn all I could. Of course, Jackson tied my hands by speaking in strictest confidence—whenever he would speak at all. But . . . well, there was no doubt about it, I knew he was the regimental bookie and that *sub rosa* he ran various games of chance—or no chance—and that he lent everybody money at about five hundred per cent per annum, though it was all very difficult to prove. And I know that—although it was the last thing he wanted to happen, if only because he lost his money—he was the cause of James's death."

" I wish I had known before," said Colonel Jason.

" You could have done nothing. No evidence whatever. Neither Jackson nor anyone else would have said a word—officially."

He emptied his glass.

" But I'll catch him out, if it's the last thing I ever do," he said. " And then . . . ! "

Mess-Sergeant Palsover, his hands looking fantastically colossal in their white gloves, placed a decanter of port and one of madeira before the Mess President at one end of the table, and a similar pair before the Vice-President at the other. These officers, each with his left hand, sent them on their way.

A few minutes later the Mess President at the head of the table rose to his feet.

" Mr. Vice, the King ! " he called.

The Vice-President at the other end of the table also rose.

" Gentlemen, the King Emperor ! " and chairs were pushed back as all present stood up, and raised their glasses.

Mess-Sergeant Palsover at the central door of the Mess waved a vast white hand to the Band Master without, the band struck up *God Save the King*, and the Officers of the Royal Wessex Fusiliers drank the loyal toast.

II

"WELL, good-bye, Henry," said Mrs. Jason, as it came to the new Colonel Carthew's turn to say the last farewell. "We shall be off in a minute or two now, I suppose. Hope so, anyway. One feels so extraordinarily silly, saying good-bye at a railway-station, doesn't one ? *'Good-bye, good-bye. Now we're off,'* and then we're not, for another half an hour."

Why couldn't the poor man utter, instead of holding her hand and gazing at her like a nice dumb animal that has got so much to say and cannot say it.

Poor dear Henry, she'd really miss him. She would only realize how useful he had been, now that he wouldn't be there to—be useful. Yes, she would really miss him. After all these years. What a pity he couldn't come too. Perhaps Reginald would be able to wangle it ? Surely Henry would rather have got a job on Reginald's staff and come with them, than stay here and command the Regiment ? Brigade-Major or something. She must talk to Reginald about it.

"Good-bye, Antoinette," said Colonel Carthew, making a kind of convulsive grab at her hand and raising it to his lips. "Good-bye. I . . ." and stood staring, still holding her hand in a grip that was beginning to hurt.

"I really don't know what I'm . . . It will be simply awful. . . . I don't know how . . . It doesn't bear thinking of."

41

" You must come and see us, Henry."

" Oh, *rather* ! Yes, *rather* ! " But how often would he be able to get over to the other side of India, especially now that he commanded the Regiment ?

It couldn't be possible that she was going ; that this train would start in a minute, take her out of this station, out of his sight, out of his life. . . . He hadn't felt quite like this since the day when, as a small boy, he had said good-bye to his mother, as she went off leaving him stranded to face his first term at school. A dreadful sense of loss, desertion, loneliness. He'd be glad when the parting was over. Had Antoinette the faintest idea as to what he was feeling, how her going affected him, what it meant to him ? She looked, as usual, perfectly calm and cool ; apparently absolutely untouched, unaffected, her magnificent beauty unruffled ; unflushed, not a hair out of place, not a sentence hurried, not a movement uncertain, much less a tear in her eye or voice. Perhaps she felt more than she showed ? She could hardly feel less.
Did he himself look as composed, as indifferent, as that—after sitting up all night wrestling with his misery, wretchedness and pain ? Certainly Reginald did. Dignified and aloof, of course, but if anything, a little more human than usual ; a pleasant smile for everybody, he who so rarely smiled. But as for grief or even regret, not the faintest sign of it. One would think he was going off for a month's shooting-leave instead of parting for ever from the Regiment with which, in which, and for which, he had lived for quarter of a century. If he felt nothing at leaving the friend who had been with him at school, at Sandhurst and in the Regiment, from the time they were small boys in their earliest teens, to this day when they were

42

grizzled veterans, surely he must feel something at leaving the Regiment? Well, perhaps he did. Of course he did. But no one would think so, for he showed devilish little sign of it.

What a magnificent General he would make, and what a picture of a magnificent General too. The most truly dignified man he had ever seen in his life. He'd be positively stately by the time he was a Field-Marshal and Commander-in-Chief, as he certainly would be. There was scarcely a King in the whole world who might not envy his bearing, his appearance, carriage and unassumed and unassuming—well—*dignity*. That was the word.

He had followed Reginald all these years ; followed him, admired him, slaved for him, loved him. Now he was going to lose him, and the flavour of life henceforth, though he had, at last, got the command, would be as dust and ashes in his mouth.

Well, he'd probably do as he said. Send in his papers. Damn the Regiment ! He'd clear out and go where he wouldn't be reminded every day of the friends he had lost, the man and the woman who were his greatest friends, his best friends, his *only* friends.

That was the worst of being such a one-man dog as he was. Splendid to have a man friend and a woman friend, to concentrate on them, to grapple them to your soul with hoops of steel and to dull not the palm with entertainment of each unfledged comrade, and all that. Wonderful—until they went and left you stranded high and dry ; and life was more dry than high ; dry as a damned desert.

" Well, good-bye, Henry," said General Jason cheerily. " Don't look so down in the mouth. The

43

best of friends must part, as the song says. Send us a line now and again. I shall never be able to hear enough about the Regiment. . . . All the gossip— and how you get on. . . . Don't break old Palsover ! . . . You're going to have the time of your young life. So's the Regiment ! . . . Good-bye ! . . . Good-bye, all. Good-bye, Mowbray. Good-bye, Weston. Good-bye, Fontwell. Good-bye, Carey. Good-bye, Wray. Good-bye, Blacker. Good-bye, Henry. Good-bye, everybody. Good-bye. . . . Don't forget to write. Specially if I can help you at any time. . . . And come and see us. . . . Good-bye, good-bye ! . . ."

Yes, Henry Carthew was just one of the crowd. Still, he was the only one whom Reginald had called by his Christian name, and Antoinette had looked at him last.

They'd soon forget him. . . .

Turning abruptly away as the train rounded the curve, Colonel Carthew walked quickly off in the direction of his bungalow, oblivious of the heat, the dust and everything else, save the fact that the Indian scene looked different, empty. Life looked empty, null and void.

Reginald had gone and Antoinette had gone, and there was nothing whatever left here—save a score or so of officers and about eight hundred men.

§ 2

" Well, that's that," observed the newly-promoted General Jason, as he turned from the carriage window and seated himself on the long leather-cushioned bed-settee opposite to that occupied by his wife.

44

" Phew ! . . .   Gad, how I hate these tearful ceremonies."

" I didn't notice you wiping your eyes—General ! " replied Mrs. Jason.

" Didn't you ?   No.   Your handkerchief's fairly dry too."

" Yes.   Though I could have wept with—not exactly boredom, but . . . the state of being bored."

" Yes, I know. Very trying. However . . ."

" Quite so, Reginald. Is Flagstaff House pretty good at Allahpur ? "

" From my point of view, yes. I think you'll find it all right. Nice change."

" Yes, and the climate is better than at Sitapur, isn't it ? "

" Much. ,Jolly good hill-station quite near too. You won't have a bad time up there in the hot weather, Tony. Quite a young Simla, in its way."

General Jason removed his helmet, placed it on the rack, sat down upon the broad seat, some seven feet in length, a couch by day and a bed by night, and leant back upon the rolled bedding and cushions arranged for that purpose by his servant.

Antoinette Jason regarded her husband, as she was wont to do, with coolly appraising speculative eye, a faintly mocking smile upon her lips. How like him to keep his coat on, hot as the morning was, and complete as was their privacy. Reginald must never relax, must never be caught unbuttoned—in mind, body or soul. If present, then correct. What a wonderful sight it would be to catch a glimpse of Reginald in an undignified posture or situation. It would be almost a pleasure, certainly a relief, to see or hear him being undignified. Not that there was any pose about it, or that he ever stood on his dignity.

45

He was born dignified, had lived dignified and would die with the utmost dignity, be the circumstances what they might. Had he never been drunk or excited in all his life? Of course he hadn't, any more than he had ever been called anything other than Reginald. . . . What would he say if, for once, she addressed him as Reggie, or, worse still, as Reg? He wouldn't say anything at all. He wouldn't hear. He wouldn't imagine that it was he who was being addressed by so familiar and foul a term. It would be like addressing a reigning monarch as Bert, Perce, Herb or Alf. No, it was just real natural dignity, as genuine as his imperturbable coolness and calmness, his inflexible honesty and untarnished honour, his flawless courage, and his perfect courtesy.

Damned old icicle!

Her eyes twinkled and her mouth smiled, faintly sardonic.

" Happy, Reginald ? "

" Why ? "

" Brigade, staff and flag-staff, galloper, sentries on the doorstep—and all that. Burra-sahib."

" Happy ? Well, if to be glad is to be happy, I'm glad I have got my Brigade."

" In a way, you'll enjoy life at Allahpur, won't you ? "

" Plenty of work. And I like work."

" Like work ! You love work, Reginald."

" I suppose I do."

" It's the only thing you do love, isn't it ? "

" Oh, I don't know. . . ."

" I do. Would you mind if I went to England ? "

" Why, no, my dear, certainly not. If you feel you'd like to go Home this hot weather instead of . . ."

46

" Think you'd get on better at Allahpur without a wife ? "

" Why, no, not at all. I didn't mean that. But if you'd like to go Home for the hot weather, or for a year or so, there's nothing on earth to . . ."

" No, I'm sure there isn't, my dear."

" Well, you asked, didn't you, Tony ? "

" I did. I'm a silly woman. A poor thing, but thine own. Not that anyone would notice it. I'm not really your wife, you know."

General Jason looked up from the paper on which, between the lurches of the carriage, he was endeavouring to jot memoranda.

" What *do* you mean ? Have I ever, in all our married life, done anything to suggest that you were not my wife ? "

" No, my dear, never. . . . Nor anything much that ever indicated that I was."

General Jason got on with his work.

§ 3

Mrs. Jason was awakened in the morning by the stopping of the train at a wayside station. She glanced at her watch, fastidiously dusted a light deposit of sand from her sheet and pillow, and glanced across at her husband.

Reginald. . . . Twenty-four hours a General. . . . Lying like a warrior taking his rest with his martial dignity around him. As dignified in sleep as when riding at the head of his Regiment. As dignified in pyjamas as in full war-paint, his hair as tidy, his lips as tightly closed. No man, and presumably no woman, had ever heard Reginald snore.

The perfect soldier, the perfect man, the perfect

47

husband. Yes, the model was perfect. Pity it wasn't a working model. Or did she mean a playing model?

Perfect model of a husband! But models are so apt to be hard, rigid, mechanical. Models have no emotions. If she had been blessed with a son or a daughter, she would have been inclined to advise neither of them to marry a model. Not a model of a husband or wife, that is to say. Of course, a model soldier was different. Kitchener was her idea, her ideal, of a model soldier, and Reginald was like unto him. Very. But in mercy to some fortunate woman Kitchener had remained a bachelor. A pity Reginald hadn't. From her point of view, that was.

She certainly hadn't done him and his career any harm, the career that was a beautiful blossoming tree which was just beginning to bear fruit. Brigadier to-day, Major-General to-morrow, Lieutenant-General and K.C.B. the next day, and then Field-Marshal and Commander-in-Chief in India next week, metaphorically speaking.

No, she had done him no harm. Always present and correct when required for social purposes. Never un-present or incorrect when put back in the box.

That damned box of a bungalow!

No, never incorrect. Never tempted to be, either. Cæsar's wife. Was Mrs. Cæsar also one of those unfortunate females who inspired terrific respect and nothing more—or less?

Poor dear old Henry. How she'd miss him. Dear old Henry! Literally everything that Reginald was not. Loving, warm-hearted, simple, clumsy, *gauche*, unkempt and untidy. Positively unsoldierly. Always present and never correct, except in his attitude to her.

Too correct for words, there! He thought himself

48

a perfect devil, kissing her hand in farewell, yesterday. Absolute Don Juan, going about kissing women's hands once every quarter of a century, without fail.

What would life have been like if he had done what he had wanted to do, any time in the said quarter of a century, and kissed her on the lips until it hurt ?

She'd have loved to have been hurt like that, just once or twice in her life.

Poor dear old Henry. Followed her about like a dog and worshipped the ground she trod on, all that time. Loved her desperately, passionately, for twenty years and—kissed her hand at the end of it !

Why couldn't Reginald have loved her like that ? What a time they could have had together ; and what a joy it would have been now that the grand steady river of his life, unsullied, unbroken, unhurried, was broadening out into an almost boundless sea of pride, ambition and reward.

But in point of fact, he didn't give a damn whether she went Home or not ; whether she went Home and stayed at Home.

And there, back in Sitapur, was Henry eating his heart out for her. Henry, almost literally broken-hearted.

Ah, well ! Life was like that, and it was time that Tulsiram brought tea. Not that he could do that until the train stopped at another station.

Well, so perfect a servant of so perfect a master should be able to produce a station.

Would Henry have been more on-coming if she had encouraged him ? An idle if interesting speculation, since she'd probably never see him again. Not for years, anyway. Two wasted and frustrated lives, hers and Henry's. Nonsense. She had never really

49

loved him. Not been in love with him, anyhow.
How could a woman of her type and temperament
ever be in love with a man whose back hair would
stand up in duck-tails, whose tie would wriggle round,
who never could look as though he had shaved that
morning, although of course he had. A man who
trod on your toes when he danced with you ; trod on
the train of your gown if he got a chance ; dropped
things if you spoke to him suddenly ; and always
blushed. No wicked sinner ever blushed as the
virtuous Henry did. . . . What little things have
colossal effects—influencing our whole lives. Things
like that. Why, if Henry's nose had not been a bit
of a blob, rather round and shiny and inclined to be
red, she might not be lying here gazing upon the really
rather beautiful face of her immaculate and impeccable
lord and master, General Reginald Jason, Field-
Marshal-in-the-sight-of-God Sir Reginald Jason, K.C.B.,
C.M.G., etc.

Well, he was a lovely creature and she'd certainly
be Lady Jason some day. She'd be Lady Jason in
Wildflower Hall, the Commander-in-Chief's house at
Simla.

Better than being Mrs. Henry Carthew in lodgings
at Exeter or somewhere.

Still . . . *Love !* Real mutual unquenchable love.
. . . Passion. . . .

The train slowed down again and General Jason sat
up. No, not a hair out of place. Perfect.

" Good morning, Antoinette," said he.

" And to you, my Reginald," she said, suppressing
behind her faintly mocking smile, " my passionate
lover."

" Do you know what day it is ? " she asked.

" Thursday."

" It is even more than Thursday."

" How ? "

" It is the bright anniversary of our wedding-day."

" Really ? How time flies. . . ."

" D'you think it does ? "

" Well. Look at us. . . . How old are you to-day, Tony ? "

" Thirty-five, my dear. Thirty-five years and seven days. I had a birthday last week."

" They do come round, don't they ? "

" Yes. Mine do. But no one notices the little things. So what matter they, my Reginald ? "

" Why should they matter ? Thank God I'm only forty-seven and . . ."

" In time to be the youngest Commander-in-Chief in India. Splendid, my dear. . . . How I wish I were only forty-seven in spirit—and that Tulsiram would bring tea in a brown pot. . . ."

PART III

M R. SAMUEL PALSOVER, better known on the little coasting cargo-passenger ship *St. Paul de Loanda* as Fritz Schultz, bedroom-and-table steward, knocked at the door of Senhor Pereira's cabin and entered simultaneously with the knock.

Mr. Palsover believed not so much in the knock-and-enter system as in the enter-while-you-knock ; and, even more firmly, in the watch-while-you-wait. Particularly in the case of this silly beggar of a Senior Pereira. He'd bear a lot of watching while Mr. Palsover waited on him.

That biggish flat steel box with a tray ! Like a cash-box. Mr. Palsover had caught a glimpse of it once when it was open and the Senior was putting papers into it. When a gent carries a little key on his watch-chain and uses it to open a box of that sort, there's generally more than moths in it.

" Good morning, Sir. Your coffee," he said, as he closed the door behind him, and observed that Senhor Pereira hastily pushed something under his pillow.

" And will you be getting up this morning, Sir ? "

Senhor Pereira regarded his cabin-steward thoughtfully. According to the name-card in the slot on the bulkhead, the man was named Schultz ; and he professed and called himself German. Fritz Schultz, a citizen of Hamburg. And yet he spoke what to Senhor Pereira seemed fluent, easy and fairly idiomatic English, but at the same time he stubbornly and unaccountably refused to understand German !

That this might, to some extent, be due to his own ignorance of the language and faulty pronunciation of the few words and sentences that he did know, Senhor Pereira was prepared to admit. Yet it was curious that the fellow never responded to, or even appeared to understand, such simple orders as

" *Kommen Sie hier !* " or " *Weggehen Sie !* " or " *Konnen Sie mir sagen, wieviel Uhr es ist ?* " or " *Geben Sie mir das Buch !* "

A citizen of Hamburg, possessed of a German name, and calling himself a German, who understood nothing of the German language, seemed to Senhor Pereira to be something of a curiosity ; and concerning all curiosities he was himself curious when approaching Santa Cruz. And apart from idle curiosity, he felt he really must get to the bottom of the mystery, for it intrigued him.

Could he actually have done this, he would have discovered it to have a very simple explanation, not unconnected with the sudden and probably quite painless death, in a queer house in one of the queer streets of La Boca, of an authentic German steward, and the annexation of his passport and papers by a cosmopolitan sort of gentleman who later sold them in Shanghai to Mr. Palsover, at that time interested in such curios.

" *Guten Morgen*, Herr Schultz," smiled Senhor Pereira playfully ; and then, in what he believed, to be German, observed that he was free from fever this morning and would be getting up for *Mittags-essen*.

Silly old cove ! Why couldn't he talk plain English, since he could talk plain English as good as anybody ? The ship was enough of a bloomin' floatin' Noah's

Ark and Tower of Babel already, without this old blighter—whose own lingo was Portuguese and who not only talked proper English but had been heard to jabber like a maniac to boatmen, in what must have been Arabic—wanting to talk German and make Mr. Palsover talk German as well !

He had told the silly geezer once that, personally, he had forgot all his German, having been kidnapped as a child and brought up as an orphan, speaking only English and Hindustani.

"You understood what I said then, didn't you ? " smiled Senhor Pereira.

"Ar ! That's right, Sir. Every word of it. What was it all about ? Your bath ? I'll go and turn it on for you immediate."

"Now, now, Schultz ! You know I didn't say anything about my bath. You know perfectly well what I said. I believe you are a bad man, Schultz," and Senhor Pereira shook his finger reprovingly.

Mr. Palsover smiled in a manner that might be described as the waggish non-committal, thereby increasing Senhor Pereira's doubt and suspicion the more.

Curiously enough, he, on his side, decided that Fritz Schultz would bear watching.

As soon as the door closed behind his steward, Senhor Manoel Pereira rose from his bed, went to his medicine-chest and busied himself about prophylactic measures against the return of the malarial fever to which he was something of a martyr, in spite of the fact that he was an amateur of medicine, who considered himself almost as good as a doctor, and who was deeply interested in the etiology, course and cure of tropical diseases. Intravenous injection of quinine. The Saints grant that he steered clear of black-water fever, and that he was not sickening for another bout of tropical jaundice.

Having doctored himself, he took from the shelf above his berth a well-worn copy of his beloved Camöens, and lay down again to read. After a while, having reached for note-book and pencil, he settled down to his current hobby and relaxation, the making of a metrical translation into English of the beautiful and sonorous lines of what he considered the poet's finest work. . . . Put it into Arabic verse later, perhaps.

But soon he tired, frowned, lay back and closed his eyes. He could not concentrate.

That confounded steward.

A most likeable man, a really perfect servant, capable, skilful, attentive ; positively fatherly. There was something benevolent about him, almost affectionate. One was tempted to regard him rather as a friend than as a servant—and the paid servant of someone else at that ; a servant of the Anglo-Portuguese Equatorial Steam Navigation and Trading Company.

Why, those terrible great hands of his were gentle as a woman's, though powerful as a giant's. The Senhor had been as a baby in his hands, when the good fellow had changed his wringing wet pyjamas after the breaking of the bouts of malaria when the life-saving sweat had streamed from every pore of his body. As good as a nurse. In fact, he was a first-rate male nurse. What an invaluable chap to have about one always, as a general factotum, handyman, valet and nurse when one was ill.

This damned fever. . . . It wasn't doing his heart any good either. He'd really give the matter a second thought, if it weren't for the fact of the fellow being so obviously a German, while pretending that he knew

58

no German. Why, the very first time the man had come into the cabin, he had shot the question at him, quite suddenly :

" Are you a German ? " and he had replied,

" Why, yes, Sir. Name of Fritz Schultz. I'm German all right. Got me papers to prove it."

And privately, Mr. Palsover had wondered what the silly old geezer was driving at. What did it matter to him, anyway ?

And now, as he went along to his glory-hole for dust-pan and brush, Mr. Palsover again wondered what was biting the Portuguese gent. Why couldn't he mind his own silly business ? He didn't look like one of those blasted Nosey Parkers that go out of their way to get an innocent man into trouble. He had got his papers proving he was Fritz Schultz all right, hadn't he ? And he had oiled the right palms to get his job, hadn't he, all good and proper ? And he was paying the Head Steward what he asked, wasn't he ? Well then, couldn't he be an English-speaking German on an old tub of a Portuguese black-beetle barge without being beggared about and badgered by every silly old geezer who wanted him to sling the German *bāt* because he had got a German name ? He'd have to get hold of a few German words.

Ja! Ja! Schnitzelheimer! Schlossenboschen poop! and Mr. Palsover broke into a soft and blithesome whistle.

Cor ! What a World it was. What a thing was Life. Fancy him, late Mess-Sergeant in the Royal Wessex, stewarding on a ship ! Nice and warm and cosy again—after the 'orrible English winter. More like good old India. And piling up the dollars, not to mention the francs, pounds, pesos, pesetas, rupees,

escudos, lire and what not. But wait till he was
Head Waiter or Chief Steward—Purser, even—on one
of these old cockroach-coffins. Be in the big money
then. Nice pickings as well as tips. Even better
than being a money-lending Mess-Sergeant in a British
Regiment. And no earthly reason why a downy bird
who had been a first-class Mess-Sergeant shouldn't rise
to any rank in the stewarding line of business, if he
kept his eyes open and squared the right people.
That's the way the money comes—and pop goes the
beetle, every time you put your hoof down in one of
these dark corners here.

Dirty foreigners. . . .

What had that funny old Portuguese got in the big
cash-box that he was always diving into ? One thing
he had got, and that was what looked uncommon
like a fine fat wad of nice clean new paper money.
Big denomination, probably. British one-pound notes
too. . . . And some foreign-looking ones, out-size,
with photos of Presidents and things on 'em.

The old boy seemed to have plenty of dough, and
to be free with it.

II

THERE was no doubt about it that the old Portuguese duck was getting pretty bad. Mr. Palsover had seen tropical illness and sudden death in India. Cholera camp, once. And any amount of nasty tummy troubles—dysentery and such—that the R.A.M.C. poultice-lancers said was microbes caused by eating bazaar melons and mangoes, not to mention drinking out of irrigation ditches on manœuvres, or out for a bit of sport. Malaria too. That could knock a strong man end-wise, as quick as anything. Yes, fever, bowels and sudden death ; here to-day and here again to-morrow, if you was lucky.

What the ole geezer wanted was a bit of barrack-room treatment-and-cure ; a quart of beer, boiling hot, with a tumbler of gin in it, a fistful of quinine tablets and then all the blankets, dhurries, horse-rugs and what not that could be piled on to the bed. Sweat it out of him. Still, since he thought he could do more by jabbing that little squirt in his arm, let him. It wasn't for Mr. Palsover to interfere uninvited, especially with that little key on the gold chain dangling from the watch hanging from the hook on the bulkhead beside the old boy's pillow.

Time Mr. Palsover shoved that little key into the lock of that very interesting-looking steel box. Always had an enquiring mind, he had, right from a boy. Full of curiosity. Made it worth while sitting up with

61

the old bird, even if it was all night. Nothing Mr. Palsover wouldn't do to oblige. Stooard? Reg'lar sick-bay stooard he was, nowadays. Well, well, perhaps the funny old bloke would leave him something in his Will. Might leave him something without any Will. Leave him something without knowing it, if he popped off, one night. Seemed to feel the heat even more than Mr. Palsover did himself, although he was some sort of a Dago and ought to be used to heat. This wasn't nothing much, not compared with a real hot night in Umbala, say, about the middle of June. Be hot enough when they coaled, though, and shut every port-hole and door in the whole ship. Then it would get nice and warm. Pop off then, as like as not. Heat apperplexy. Good job, from Mr. Palsover's point of view, that there wasn't any doctor on this old floating bug-walk.

Did the silly blighter know what he was saying, or was he just talking through his hat, delirious like, the way the lads with malaria and what-not used to do when they went one over the hundred and reached the winning-post on the thermometer.

Sounded as though he was talking barmy whenever he talked his own lingo—whatever that was. Portuguese presumably. But it sounded all right when he talked English. Just as though he wanted Mr. Palsover to get what he was saying. Wasn't likely though, because he wouldn't gabble such silly nonsense if he wanted to talk sense. Stood to reason, didn't it?

Uncommon fond of him the old boy was getting. What about hanging on to him for what he was worth? Pickings. Worth thinking about. Might take on the job as his nurse, valet, confidential man, and so on, and then leave his service all of a sudden, one day, in a great hurry, with something useful in his ditty-box. Something like that couple-of-inch-thick wad of pound notes—if that's what they was—that he'd caught a glimpse of in that box.

§ 2

Senhor Pereira raised his head, stared round and let it fall back again upon his sodden pillow. Stretching out a hot and shaking hand, he seized Mr. Palsover's wrist.

" It's *wrong*, really, you know ! It's *wrong* ! " he said in the quick, almost toneless, staccato accents of the delirious.

" Ar ! That's right," agreed Mr. Palsover.

" It should be used instead of lying there, benefiting nobody. Enough of it to bring the price down to that of—silver. To that of any common drug. Bring it within the reach of every hospital, every doctor. Why, in a year, cancer could be stamped out. Mankind could be for ever freed from that terrible scourge. For ever, throughout the whole world. It could be made a thing of the past, conquered more effectually than consumption has been. Other diseases too. All microbic diseases—typhoid, cholera, anthrax. . . . Think of the results of merely having radio-active water, for example, available in every centre of civilization, in every city, town and village in the world. Think of the radium-application discoveries that might be made, that certainly would be made, if every research-institute, every research worker, had unlimited radium with which to experiment. There are no bounds to the good that might be done."

" Ar ! That's right," agreed Mr. Palsover, as the clutch of the burning hand tightened on his arm.

63

" And They need not fear publicity . . . exploitation . . . invasion. Of course it would be worse than any Alaskan or South African gold-rush, worse than any diamond-rush, if the news leaked out, and it were known generally. The sort of secret that would spread like wild-fire. Encircle the globe in a day. Compared with that, the Klondyke rush would be child's play—two crippled men and a blind boy. Do you know that to-day the price of radium is twenty thousand São Thomé moidores a gram ! Fifteen thousand pounds a gram ! Do you realize that the man who owned a pound of it would be the richest multi-millionaire in the whole world ? "

" Ar ! That's right," agreed Mr. Palsover, yawning cavernously.

" Eh ? What ? " he said, suddenly sitting upright and turning toward Senhor Pereira. " What you talkin' about ? "

" Why, the other day a great philanthropist gave fifty thousand pounds' worth of it to a London hospital. A princely gift, and all in a little glass bottle in a little lead case that you could carry in your trousers-pocket without inconvenience."

There was nothing somnolent about Mr. Palsover now. Late as was the hour, there was no hint of weariness in his manner or expression.

" Have you got some with you, Senior ? " he asked in an urgent whisper, putting his large bland benevolent face down toward that of the sick man.

" And They've got what is probably the only example of free barium-radium in the world. Nature has done in São Thomé what Madame Curie did in her laboratory. . . . Great underground heat . . . alkalis . . . acids. . . . Crystallization under boiling water . . . terrific pressure. . . . I don't under-

64

stand it—but Norhona does. And They've got the biggest pure uranium deposit in the world. Certainly by far and away the biggest known one. Norhona says there's actually almost unlimited radium there just for the refining, as well as the uranium. And none of it's your one-gram-in-a-hundred-tons stuff. There's more uranium in that mountain in São Thomé than in all the Belgian Congo, Czechoslovakia, Colorado, Utah and Australia put together. Norhona says the richest ore in the world only contains one gram to five tons, and this ore is pure uranium. And They refuse to let a grain of radium go out of the island. It's wrong. It's the biggest crime against Humanity. I've told Them again and again. Mind, They are right, a thousand times right, in preferring Peace to Prosperity, the ' prosperity ' of wealth, commercialism, finance and the rest of the devilish damnable lures to destruction. A thousand times right. They have all They need. São Thomé is self-supporting, self-contained. Why should They deliberately introduce the filthy poison of what passes for Progress and is called Civilization ? Why should They turn that Garden of Eden, that Eden on the sea, into a Hell upon earth ? "

" Ar ! That's right ! " agreed Mr. Palsover, again nodding his sagacious head.

What was the old bird talking about ? Rayjum ? Rayjum ? Fifteen thousand quid a gram ? Off his onion. Clean off his poor old rocker.

" But there's not the slightest need to run the risk of anything of the sort. They don't suppose that I would ever disclose Their secret, do They ? They don't think *I*'d ever bring evil to São Thomé, do They ? I would rather die."

" 'S right," agreed Mr. Palsover. "So'd I, any day."

" They need not fear that I should be traced to São Thomé, and the Island become known as the source of my huge stocks of radium. I could take away a big supply in proper lead and glass containers, in a strong steel case, just nailed up in a crate marked . . ."

" Tinned salmon," suggested Mr. Palsover.

" I could distribute it from Stockholm, Vienna, San Francisco, New Zealand, anywhere. Why should it ever be supposed that I got my supplies from São Thomé ? But They wouldn't hear of it. They won't listen to me."

" Dirty dogs," yawned Mr. Palsover.

The old bird wasn't talking sense, and if he didn't soon wilt, pass out unconscious, or go to sleep, he'd give it up for to-night. And Mr. Palsover eyed the curious-looking key as he licked thirsty lips.

" They could trust me. They do trust me. What They fear is Chance, Fate. That some accident might let the secret out. Yes, They trust me absolutely—otherwise how should They let me come and go. Few come and still fewer go. Almost none. I ; because I am a son of São Thomé. The Hadji ; because he is trustworthy, though They only trust him because They must, since he is essential. I, the Hadji, the future Archbishop, the future Commander-in-Chief, and a few others of the Blood. Yes, They trust me, but They would destroy me as readily as They would trust me, if it were for the country's good. And if They suspected me of wrong-doing ? They would not kill me then. No. . . ."

And Senhor Pereira shuddered.

" I almost fear to ask again. What do They care about the good of Humanity ? And why should They ? The good of São Thomé is enough for Them. The only

66

humanity of which They know is São Thoméan. . . .
Narrow. . . . Hide-bound. . . . Insular. . . . But
how should it be otherwise ? "

The high metallic voice fell suddenly silent. Bend-
ing over again, Mr. Palsover studied the dark handsome face, lined, yellowish, the skin now drawn and
of a parchment-like quality.

Asleep ? Fainted ? Passed out ? Proper ill, he
looked. Better wait a while.

" And that amazing quicksand. God alone knows
what wealth that contains in rare metals and elements.
. . . Helium, Strontium, Cerium, Polonium, Cana-
dium, Barium, Pitchblende, Thorium, Carnotite, Autu-
nite, Inonium, Rutile, Uranium and compounds of
which as yet we know nothing. Priceless, invaluable.
And all They use it for is—as a grave. A bottomless
pit for the disposal of the bodies of those whose disappearance is considered desirable. And as a moat
and a defence. I tell you that quicksand at the
entrance to the Great Ravine is an eighth wonder of
the world. It is an inexhaustible mine. No, not a
mine, a store-house. Of the things that mankind
values most, and some of which are of the utmost
value to mankind, whether he knows it or not. . . .
Rarity value ; utility value ; curative value. . . .
And the radium with its highest of all values, a combination of all values. . . . Well, there it is, and
there it will remain, unknown to anyone outside São
Thomé, and to very few within. Properly understood,
in its true value, to only one within. To one, the
greatest of them all—and who is as rigid and hide-
bound a patriot, as narrow and fanatical a reactionary
as the worst of them. Yet the greatest brain in all
the world, in its own line ; greater than Freud ; greater
than Mesmer, Braid, Liebault, Bernheim, Janet, Charcot

—greater than Einstein. The greatest scientist; the greatest psychologist and neurologist in the world; one of the greatest physicians, and perhaps the greatest surgeon.

" And all he cares about is to be the greatest São Thoméan.

" It is incredible, even to me, the wandering São Thoméan, the ever-seeking dove of that ever sea-girt Ark. To think that he, doctor, surgeon, alienist, scientist to his finger-tips, the world's greatest hypnotist, who can play upon human heart-strings and do what he will with the human brain, should support Them and refuse me, refuse Humanity!

" Refuse to release one gram of those tons of radium for fear São Thomé should be opened to the world; be invaded. And that not even by troops, by greedy country-grabbing annexationists—but merely by an alien civilization; merely by strangers; by commercialists, industrialists; by the foreign flag that precedes the foreign trade. . . .

" How could he ? Such foolishness with such immeasurable cleverness; such ignorance with such stupendous knowledge; such foolish fear with such immeasurable courage; so little faith and trust in me who am so trustworthy; such terrifying narrowness in one whose mind is as broad as the Universe. For him to think that the secret should ever be betrayed through me !

" Why, without one soul in all the world dreaming that the supply came from São Thomé, I could reduce the price from fifteen thousand pounds a gram to . . . to . . . a shilling."

Mr. Palsover stretched, yawned and rose to his feet.

" And *that*'d be a damn silly thing to do, that would ! " he said.

Cor ! About enough for one night. . . .

III

NEXT morning, Senhor Pereira was undoubtedly better. Weak, but perfectly clear-headed. Clear-headed and light-hearted, until a word let fall by Mr. Palsover, as he tidied the cabin, reduced him to something more than his normal gravity, not to say depression or anything like a pessimistic condition of mind.

"Well, Governor, you don't look so much like the Wreck o' the 'Esperus this morning. Fair worried me, you did. Light-'eaded a bit, at times, you was," observed Mr. Palsover as he stood and beamed at the Senhor.

"What about a nice glass o' salts before your coffee?" he asked. "No?

"That was a rare ol' tale you told me last night, Senior," he remarked with friendly and benevolent geniality, as he placed shaving apparatus and hot water beside the basin which he had just cleaned.

"Tale? What about?" asked Senhor Pereira, sitting up with a sudden movement that almost spilled his coffee.

"St. Tommy. And some stuff called rayjum. Millions of pounds' worth of it," smiled Mr. Palsover.

"*São Thomé? Radium?*" whispered Senhor Pereira. "Did I . . .? Well, well! What extraordinary matters to talk about! And did I speak in English?"

"Ar! That's right," replied Mr. Palsover. "Some

of the time. And some of the time in that funny lingo you slings to your Portu-geese friends. Unless it was the Arab *bāt.*"

Senhor Pereira lay silent, staring at his steward in obvious perturbation, the expression of his face reminding Mr. Palsover of a well-known army phrase—" calculated to cause consternation and alarm." He was consterned and alarmed all right. Not 'alf he wasn't.

He had shut his eyes—like as if he had fainted clean off. What was biting the funny little blighter, now ?

Suddenly Senhor Pereira looked up and shot a cunning glance at him.

" And some German, I suppose ? " he asked quickly.

" Now, now, Senior ! " soothed Mr. Palsover. " 'Aven't I told you, time after time, I don't know any German. I don't understand it and I don't talk it."

" Yes, you certainly *told* me," was the reply. " And you say I talked to you about a place called . . . What did you say it was ? "

" St. Tommy. Fair old yarn about it."

" São Thomé. Strange. I never heard of the place."

" Well, I heard about it. Hower after hower."

" And what else, did you say ? "

" Rayjum, I said. So did you. A lot."

" And what did I say about radium ? "

" Any amount. . . . That it was worth fifteen thousand pounds a gram, and that St. Tommy was stiff with it, and that you could bring out enough in your trousers' pocket to make you as rich as Jesus."

" Rich as Crœsus ! " Senhor Pereira said something in his own language, something that even to Mr. Palsover sounded like a prayer to God, His Son, the

Virgin Mary and all the Saints, if that was what
'*Todos los Santos*' might mean, in the Dago's silly
lingo.

Didn't look so well now. Seemed to think he had
given himself away—bad. (Something *in* this.)

Yes, this undoubtedly was inter*est*ing. Very. The
Senior might have been barmy and talking through
his hat, but he had said something. And now he
wished he hadn't said it. Therefore there must have
been something in what he said. Stood to reason.

" Yerss. You got a lot off your chest last night,
Senior. All about millions of pounds' worth of rayjum,
and how there'd be a fair old rush that would make
the Klondyke scrimmage look like a kids' Punch and
Judy Show, and how you'd plant the stuff in 'Frisco
and Bombay and Chamschatker and Berlin and sell
it artful-like, in small packets—so as to keep the
price up."

" What else ? What else ? Tell me."

" Oh, lots. All about your pal in St. Tommy.
Him that's the greatest doctor in the world."

" What was his name ? "

" Same as the Goanese bloke that keeps a sort of
little dry canteen in the Sudder Bazaar at Sitapur.
What's his name—Machado ? Fernandez ? Gon-
salvez ? . . . No, Norhona ! That's it."

Senhor Pereira's eyes appeared to be starting from
his head in terror.

" Wonderful what nonsense people talk in delirium,
isn't it ? " he said, smiling mechanically with his lips.
" Amazing nonsense. And you know, they can actually talk of things of which they know nothing. Sometimes in a language which they have never heard."

" Ar ! That's right," agreed Mr. Palsover. " I do
meself. I've 'eard soldiers too. . . . 'Orrible, some-

71

times. Shocking. Language that you'd hope they'd never heard."

" There's the famous case of the servant-girl who, in an induced hypnotic trance, talked Greek," said Senhor Pereira.

" Just as well, perhaps," opined Mr. Palsover.

More and more interesting ! The silly old geezer— trying to put him off with this sort of stuff !

" Well, you talked good English and plenty of it, last night, Senior," he said.

" Yes. Talked in what is to me a foreign language, though I know it perfectly ; and talked of places of which I have never heard and of things of which I know nothing."

" Never heard of this St. Tommy, eh ? "

" Never. I know no place called São Thomé."

" And never heard of rayjum, eh ? "

" Of course I've heard of radium. But I know nothing whatever about it. Not any more than you do, that is to say."

" Not even its price, eh—fifteen thousand quid for a gram ? Well, well, now ! Will you be gettin' up for lunch to-day, Senior ? "

" Yes, yes. No. I don't know. I'll ring."

What had he done ? He who would give his right hand rather than give one word of information on matters that were *tabu*.

What had he said, he who had always been a model of discretion, silent as the grave on all subjects that should not be discussed ? Discreet, secretive, trusted by Them for those very qualities.

But who could control the subconscious mind ? Who curb its follies and babblings when itself was not controlled ? It was hard that he who had never in his life touched alcohol—because of its power to weaken inhibitions, to loosen the tongue, and to dethrone the conscious mind from its empire over the unconscious—should be defeated by a wretched microbe, should be turned, by this infernal fever, from a respected and proved repository of secrets into a babbling fool, a wretch that shouted aloud the things that he would willingly give his life to keep concealed.

He had talked of São Thomé! He had talked of the radium-producing deposits that would make the place a magnet for every gold-seeking ruffian, syndicate, mining company and financial corporation in the world. Their prospectors would come down upon the place by the ship-load. They would settle down upon it like a cloud of flies upon a carcase. Yes, and before long, São Thomé would be a carcase, stinking, rotten and corrupt. What had he done? Sooner would he have cut out his tongue.

He, Manoel Pereira of São Thomé, had talked? And to this man! Almost certainly one of the Nation-that-Breaks-Faith, one of the people whose Rulers' bond is as worthless as their word! Fritz Schultz, clumsily pretending that he knew no German, that he understood no German! They were the clumsiest people in the world in their international psychology, in their attempted diplomacy. But apart from his name, one would never have suspected him. Why didn't he take a French, Italian or Spanish name; or, since he spoke English quite well, why not an English name? Passport difficulty, presumably. Of course Fritz Schultz was a German. A Nazi German agent and spy.

But what if he were a German? There was no reason to suspect the worst of him. No reason to imagine that he was on this boat because it touched at Santa Cruz, the one and only place whence there was regular communication with São Thomé, and that only through the Hadji.

There was no doubt that They had rather got Germans on the brain. She, especially. Norhona too. It might have been the merest accident that the last intruder in São Thomé was a German. He might have known nothing whatever of the radium, nor of the quicksands. He knew all about them in the end, anyway, poor devil. But his coming might have been purest accident. Or he might, perhaps, somewhere, somehow, have heard something, and just come, not as a prospector, but in a purely exploratory spirit without any special knowledge and without any ulterior motive.

Well, as They say in the Citadel, ' Few come and fewer go.'

In point of fact, none at all ever went. Scarcely one, in the memory of living man.

What would be the best thing to do ? The fellow might be innocent enough, but—there it was. He had got what were to Senhor Pereira the two most important words in the whole world : São Thomé and Radium. And he had got them in juxtaposition. Or rather, had got them in union, in close connection ; had got them linked in his mind. São Thomé— Radium. São Thomé *for* radium. Radium at fifteen thousand pounds a gram.

Even if he were the most innocent and ignorant of Germans, even if he were not a Nazi German at all, the fact remained that he was a human being with human passions, almost the strongest of which would of course be greed of gain. And he was free now to go up and down the Coast talking of São Thomé and radium—at fifteen thousand pounds a gram ; free to sail the Seven

Seas talking of São Thomé and radium—at fifteen thousand pounds a gram ! In every port and every pot-house in which sailors congregate, he would talk of São Thomé and radium—at fifteen thousand pounds a gram. Free, too, to go home, to go to the great commercial and financial centre of his country, Berlin, London, New York, whichever it might be, and get in touch with one of those ruthless men whose life-work it was to discover and exploit to the utmost such secrets. Financiers they called themselves. Company promoters. In São Thomé it was by other names They called them—vultures . . . thieves . . . destroyers . . . *vermin* !

And what a secret for such a man. São Thomé and unlimited radium. Radium at fifteen thousand pounds—seventy-five thousand dollars, three hundred thousand marks—a gram.

What had he done ? And what would They do to him, if They knew ? Mercifully put him to death, in consideration of his past services to the State ? Or hand him over to Norhona with orders that he be hypnotized and . . .

Again Senhor Pereira shuddered.

Norhona ! A pity he was not here now. Whatever might be the ultimate fate of Pereira, there would be no question as to this steward fellow, Schultz, ever becoming a danger to São Thomé. Why, in ten minutes Norhona would . . .

It might have been a recrudescence of his fever that caused Senhor Pereira, at this point, to shiver slightly.

What to do ? How to undo ? Can mischief ever be undone ?

It can be arrested. It can be stopped. It can be prevented from going further.

This steward must be prevented from going further ; prevented from going where he could talk of São Thomé, radium and untold gold, all in one hideous relationship.

How could he be prevented from going further ?

What about endeavouring to attach the man to his own person ? Keeping him under his own eye ? Strange that he should already have dallied with the thought of making him his valet, body-servant, nurse. But even so, he could talk. . Where could he get him, place him, keep him, so that he could not talk ?

Senhor Pereira was well aware that dead men tell no tales, but although that may be a fine-sounding and, in certain circumstances, comforting proverb, it is not always either safe or easy to turn live men into dead men. No—apart from the fact that, to a sound Catholic in good standing and satisfactory state of conscience, there are objections to the turning of live men into dead ones. But better the death of ten thousand potential tale-bearers than that one of them should live to lift the veil that guarded the secret of São Thomé.

And without wasting any time in considering nine thousand nine hundred and ninety-nine potential spies, what about this one—the one who had actually cried aloud in this very cabin the words, " São Thomé. Radium. Fifteen thousand pounds a gram " ?

Might he not be already uttering them in the steward's pantry, telling the tale to a crony, whispering it in the ear of the Purser ?

No, he'd have more sense than that. Either he was too dull a clod to give the matter another thought, or he had just sufficient intelligence to consider his own interests, to keep the matter secret until he could divulge it to someone with whom he could do real business, either by selling his secret outright, or going shares in the fabulous profits of exploitation.

No, assuming that he were a man of intelligence, the real danger to São Thomé would arise when he got back to Europe.

Then he must not go back to Europe.

And since it would be almost as impossible as it was distasteful to kill him here and now, on this ship, he must be inveigled ashore, when Senhor Pereira landed.

Inveigled! A better idea. Far, far better. At first sight, anyhow. He must ' inveigle ' the fellow into São Thomé itself. Once he set foot ashore there, he'd be absolutely harmless, a serpent sterilized of poison. Perfectly harmless. He'd be at liberty to talk of radium and its value all day long, especially as he could only do so in German, English and Hindustani, none of which languages was of much value on an island where the aborigines spoke some strange Polynesian tongue ; the middle classes an impure and debased Arabic, somewhat akin to Malayan ; and the aristocracy a Latin-Arabic language which, though recognizable as Portuguese, was not that spoken in Lisbon.

That was a splendid idea. Offer him much better wages than he was getting on the ship, take him ashore at Santa Cruz, keep him there until the Hadji arrived, take him to São Thomé—and then leave it to Them to dispose of him.

Splendid. . . . Excellent. . . . Very good. . . . Good. . . . No ! . . .

No—not so good.

Senhor Pereira's ingenuous countenance fell. No. Not good at all. For what would They say, even to their privileged Senhor Manoel Pereira, when he confessed that he had uttered words that were completely *tabu*, words the pronunciation of one of which was a death sentence for the pronouncer.

How could he go to Them and say, " I have brought you a man who knows the secret of São Thomé, a secret that he learned from me. From me, who am myself a living secret. From me, who exist only to know that there is no such place as São Thomé whenever You let me leave her shores " ?

Of course he could plead that it was done in delirium. But the most lenient view that They could take would be that a man who indulges in the luxury of delirium is not the sort of person to be entrusted with even the least important of São Thoméan affairs. The most lenient punishment They could give him would be to prevent and prohibit his ever leaving São Thomé again ; and, much as he loved his native land, he loved this freedom even more, this precious privilege of being allowed to travel far and wide, to visit the capitals of Europe, to be the emissary, the agent, the eyes and ears, though never the mouth-piece, of the Council.

But more likely—almost certainly, in fact—They would say to Norhona, " Apparently a case for a little of your wonderful hypnotism, Doctor. Obviously our good Pereira needs mental treatment, a little suggestion. You will know what to suggest to him."

And They might order Permanency. They might . . . they might . . . they might even make him . . .

And Senhor Pereira raised thin yellowish hands to his face and placed them across his eyes, as though to shut out some vision too painful, indeed too terrible, to contemplate.

IV

SENHOR PEREIRA, lying awake that night, worried, anxious, very ill indeed, and giving much thought to the problem of what would be the best thing to do, long halted between two opinions.

It might be catastrophic to take Schultz to São Thomé and confess the truth ; and on the other hand, it might be extremely dangerous to leave him to go his way and do his worst, whether intentionally or unintentionally. That was to say, whether by organizing an attempt upon the fabulously valuable resources of São Thomé, or by merely talking about them until, inevitably, other persons made the attempt.

Senhor Pereira could not but feel that to let Schultz go whither he would, to talk as he pleased, was for himself almost as dangerous a course as taking Schultz to São Thomé. When it was known to Them that the secret had leaked out, it would be Senhor Pereira whom They would suspect either of carelessness or of treachery. The thought that They would scarcely be likely to accuse him of the latter, was of little comfort. A trusted emissary and agent who could be careless was just as dangerous as a traitor, and his suppression just as desirable. Nor, for suspected carelessness, would They punish him with death, torture or imprisonment, but They would completely end all possibility of his being careless again.

Alive, free, not halt nor lame nor blind, not deaf nor

dumb, not suffering in any way—but rendered quite incapable of further carelessness or treachery for as long as he lived, and that might be to a great age. . . . He must not think of it.

It did not bear thinking about.

He must do something. He must save himself.

He was not a cruel man. Of that he was certain. He was not violent. His hands were clean. He had never shed, or caused the shedding of, blood. But how excellent a thing it would be if this Schultz should die. In no spirit of cruelty, punishment, hate or vindictiveness would he think of Schultz—but how desirable it was that he should die.

Murder ? . . . No, no ! No ! But what They would do to him, Pereira, would be far, far worse than murder. And They would do it in no spirit of cruelty, punishment, hate or vindictiveness.

Kill Schultz ? No, he could not possibly kill the man in cold blood. And if he would, how could he ? The great powerful fellow, with his enormous hands, huge and strong as those of a gorilla. He could shoot him, of course, and especially if he had a pistol, and knew how to use it.

He had never shot anything in his life. Of course he could not kill him. Not on this ship.

He dare not take him to São Thomé.

He must not leave him to wander and to talk ; to go to some financier, some Company-promoter, with the words *São Thomé* and *Radium* on his lips. He might be what he appeared, a mere ignorant menial— which was extremely doubtful—but a shout can stir an avalanche, a whisper can start a legend which may go round the world, till everybody knows it and somebody looks into it.

Anyhow, one thing was certain, Fritz Schultz must

come ashore and stay with him at Santa Cruz, until he had made up his mind as to what was the best thing to do. He must not lose sight of the German. Perhaps at Santa Cruz he could . . .

No, he could not kill him. But he might get him killed.

Mr. Pereira's mind recoiled from the horrible thought and what he realized to be a strong and swiftly-growing temptation.

§ 2

Curiously enough, though for somewhat different reasons, a similar intention with regard to Santa Cruz and Senhor Pereira was forming in the mind of Mr. Palsover.

It would be easy enough to jump ship at Santa Cruz. He could get a couple of hours' shore leave and get left behind ; or, for fear of leave being refused, he could get the Senior to ask that the services of his steward be granted him, to help him get safely ashore and up to his hotel, he being ill and very weak.

The old geezer would jump at the chance ; and even if the two of them did not fix it up beforehand, he could go to him after the ship had sailed and suggest that, now that he was out of a job, no doubt the Senior would like to take him on as valet and what not.

Yes, he had a sort of a feeling, a hunch, that it would be a more paying proposition than this stewarding. Stewarding wasn't much, even with a view to something better later, a job with rake-off attachments and frills. The graft would be good when he had the catering contract and such, but it would take a long time to get to it, and it could cost a good part of what it was worth.

There might be something to this rayjum talk (fifteen

thousand quid a gram !) or there might not, but it was
the sort of thing that ought to be looked into, and
that was how millionaires made their piles.   All bunk
and bilge about millionaires getting rich by always
leading pious lives ; being virtuous apprentices ; stay-
ing in the office and working after the others had gone
home ; leading old ladies across the street ; getting
in good with Chaplains and the Y.M.C.A., and saving
your pence till you could take care of somebody else's
pounds.   Chicken feed !

Why, you c'd do it quicker on the race-course, with
a bit of luck.   Think of the bloke who had the stable-
tip and put his shirt—ar ! and his employer's shirt
too—on the hundred-to-one outsider belonging to the
Agger Kann, and sat back next day with a hundred
thousand quid in his pants pocket.   Get that out at
five per cent, and you'd got five thousand a year.
Take the virtuous apprentice a bit of a long while to
do that, working overtime after the clock-watchers
had cleared out of the office, and goin' to church on
Sundays.

The way to get into the big money was to get hold
of a good tip and have the sense to know it was a good
tip, whether it was a horse, stocks and shares, diamonds
kicking about round a native kraal, or nuggets of gold
up the Amazon.   Some of them savages didn't know
it from brass, if half the tales were true.   Why, gold
cooking-pots they 'ad.   Gold jerries too, like as not.
But you had to get the tip where to go.   And better
still, you had to know how to get away with a boat-
load of the boodle.

There was Buried Treasure too.   Those pirates all
round Jamaica way.   Lots of the lucky lads had had
tips about buried treasures, written on bits of old
parchment.   Maps.   Treasure Islands.

82

Ar! And what about old Kroojer! Buried all the sovereigns in the Johannesburg Bank before he hopped it. Stood to reason, there must have been others in it too. That'd be a tip worth getting.

And the whole lot put together didn't amount to much alongside of this rayjum at fifteen thousand quid a gram.

That was a tip, if you like. And that was the way tips came to the people who had the savvy to pick 'em up. Why, it was just like they wrote in books. Old geezer dying. Can't die with a secret on his chest. Tells his faithful servant or what-not all about it and how to get it. Like that yarn old Dinty O'Donnell was always reading at Sitapur. King Solomon's Gold Mines. Old Dinty reckoned he was going to go and have a dig in 'em some day. All rubbish, got up to make a book of! Only fit for kids or barmy Irishmen like Dinty O'Donnell.

But this was something different. What really opened his eyes to it was the way the old Senior tried to take it back next morning. No such place as St. Tommy, eh? And no rayjum on it neither? Tell that to the Marines! When he was talkin' through his hat owing to delirium trimmings, he kept on about St. Tommy, and he kept on about rayjum too. And he only said it because he didn't know he was sayin' it. Stands to reason that when a man keeps on talking about a place, there is such a place; and talkin' about stuff worth fifteen thousand quid an ounce, whatever it was, there must be such stuff. Anything couldn't come out of his mind that wasn't in it.

And then to deny it. He must listen in, good and plenty, next time the Senior's malaria came round.

Yes, just how it happened in real life. The dyin' man tellin' the faithful servant. Only the silly beggar

83

didn't die. Bobbed up again next morning and took it all back. That wasn't playing the game. Having said it all, he had ought to die. . . . Perhaps he would, next time. Would, if he had a little help. . . . Snuff out like a candle, the old Senior would. Mustn't do it till he'd told it all, though.

Suppose he told it all, and gave what they call clues. That'd be the time for him to die!

And if it turned out there was nothing in the story, there was something in that box! And he'd got a lot of stuff in the baggage-hold.

Mr. Palsover decided, then and there, that he would not desert the Senior sick and lonely, when the ship reached Santa Cruz.

V

THERE may be less desirable spots on the surface of the earth than Santa Cruz de Loango ; and it is, though with difficulty, conceivable that there are less hotel-like places, calling themselves hotels, than the *Casa Real*—though Senhor Pereira in his wide experience did not think so.

The town of Santa Cruz de Loango consists of a few streets, and these are not paved with gold but only with sand. Nor is the sand gold-bearing. It is, however, deep and dirty, with a top-dressing of fine flour-like dust. There are no pavements or boarded side-walks. Nothing but sand.

This makes Santa Cruz a curiously quiet town ; and, for some reason or other, the quiet is of a sinister quality. Almost the only sounds are those of human voices ; not as a rule pleasing voices, nor raised in laughter, good-fellowship and merriment.

Senhor Pereira had a theory that the inhabitants lived by taking in each other's washing and selling it, as new, when washed. Anything in Santa Cruz could look almost new, if washed. As rain but rarely fell upon this City of the Holy Cross of Loango, its cleanliness was about on a level with its godliness.

When he had once remarked to the Hadji that Santa Cruz was the last place God ever made, that widely-travelled man had demurred,

" No, Senhor, the first place.   A somewhat amateur-ish effort.   As for the people . . . ! "

And now to wait for him.   God send him soon, or he might be too late.   For what with malaria, jaundice and abdominal unhappiness that suggested typhoid, he was not feeling too well, especially as the repeated and increasing dose of quinine wherewith he endeavoured to combat the malaria, seemed to promise an addition to his little troubles in the shape of blackwater fever. And his heart was getting very troublesome.

Meanwhile . . . Camöens.

And lying on a very dreadful bed, in an oven-like filthy room of the adobe-and-corrugated-iron two-storeyed shed that called itself the *Casa Real* and leading hotel of the salubrious city of Santa Cruz, Senhor Pereira endeavoured to merge the present with the past, to raise the threshold of his consciousness, and rise superior to himself and his surroundings.

What a joy, what a triumph, if he could live to make Portugal's great epic writer, greatest lyric poet, Luis de Camões, better known to the English-speaking world ; worthily translate him and make an English metrical version that would be real poetry, great poetry, like that of the original.

It seemed impossible that it had not been done before ; that *Os Lusiads* was not as familiar to the educated British public as were the Greek *Odyssey* and the Latin *Aeneid*.   Were not both the story and the verse of the *Lusiads* as noble as the Greek and the Italian ?   Was not Camöens as true an epic poet as Homer or Virgil ?   In his mother tongue he was. He who denied it was unfit to hold an opinion.   The *Lusiads* was, to any cultured mind, as delightful as the *Odyssey*, as magnificent as the *Aeneid*. Oh, that he could render it into such English as would deserve an enlargement of the phrase " the glory that was Greece and the grandeur that was Rome," and include ' the wonder that was Portugal ' in the days of Vasco da Gama ! He would like to do that. And when he had done it, why should not he, Manöel Pereira, do for the founders of São Thomé what Camöens had done for Vasco da Gama and his super-men of the Golden Age when those heroes first rounded the Cape of Good Hope and made their way to India's mythical strand, whence they ventured and conquered far and wide till they held the golden East in fee.

That would be a worthy ambition.

And if he were an artist, what a picture he would paint of Luis de Camões swimming ashore when his ship was wrecked off the coast of Cambodia, by the mouth of the river Mekong ; swimming ashore, holding something above his head. His money-belt ? The jewels that represented his fortune ? His commission as *Provedor* at Macao ? No, his manuscript, the manuscript of the *Lusiads* ! Holding it high above the hungry water, holding it from the grasp of envious Neptune, as he swam, saving his life that he might save his manuscript, his gift to the ages to come. Why, oh why, had Fate not willed that Camöens himself should write the glorious history of the founding of São Thomé by just such men as those who built the Portuguese Empire, and made Portugal the fore-most nation of the world ? Had not Camöens himself landed at São Thomé, on his way from Goa to Mozam-bique, where he was stranded and lay sick and wretched, even as Senhor Pereira himself lay sick and wretched, stranded in this dreadful Santa Cruz ? Why could he not have remained in São Thomé and written one of the world's great epics about that semi-Eden set in the tropic sea ?

But no. Fate was wiser than Manöel Pereira. That would have meant the end of São Thomé—as a Garden of Eden. An unveiling. Inevitable exploitation. The curse and barbarity of Civilization. Strange to think in this present year of grace and dreadful twentieth century, that Camöens, nearly four hundred years ago, had written a fine ode " *To the Discontents of the World* " !

Well, well. Now first to make a good prose translation of the lovely *canzone* beginning " *Van as serenas arguas,*" and then to try his hand at some *redondilhas*, Portugal's native octosyllabic verse at which, if he might say so, he was not too bad ; or perhaps some *quintilhas*, the five-lined octosyllabic stanzas on which Norhona, no mean judge, had been good enough to congratulate him.

Well, he couldn't do everything at once ; and, so far, he had done nothing, for his head ached most terribly. But when he got better he really would translate the *Lusiads* worthily and write exactly seventy-three *quintilhas*, as Camöens had done.

But oh, what an inspiration it would be if only it were permissible for him to take São Thomé as his subject.

An inspiration ! He would be to São Thomé what Camöens had been to Portugal, Shakespeare to England, Molière to France, Cervantes to Spain, Homer to Greece, Tolstoi to Russia, Dante to Italy. . . .

Pereira . . . to São Thomé. . . .

Pereira . . . to sleep. . . .

VI

TREADING softly as a mouse, looming bulky as an elephant, Mr. Palsover slowly, gently, opened the door.

Gawd! What an 'ole. Worse than the native *chawls* and *gurs* in the slums of an Indian town. Ceiling-cloth sagging down a yard, dirty as the Duke of Hell's ducks; walls oozing bugs, and covered thick with the marks where they and bloated mosquitoes had been squashed; floor covered in plaited palm-leaf with a top-dressing of dust and dirt that came up in clouds if you dropped anything on it; furniture—a rusty iron bed, legs leaning all ways, with a stained straw-stuffed mattress that just stank; remaining junk —two chairs that anybody would be a fool to sit on, and a rickety table with a rusty jug and basin.

Poor old Senior! And him a perfect gent and used to the best.

And he had got it. The best room in the best hotel in Santa Cruz.

Well, well! . . . No doubt he'd be glad to leave it. . . . And he had better leave it, glad to or not, before this Arab bloke came. What a rum game it was, the Senior a real toff, with wads of money, hanging about in a God-forsaken Hell-blistered dog-hole like this, to meet a bloke who only turned up in these parts twice a year, according to the story. Poor old Senior. Not dead, was he? He did look bad.

89

Moving almost soundlessly across the room, Mr. Palsover bent over the apparently lifeless body of his patron and employer. Hardly breathing. Now where was that watch and chain with the key on it? Under the pillow?

Senhor Pereira opened his eyes.

Where was he? In Hell? The dark frightened eyes focused on the considerable target of Mr. Palsover's benevolent face. Ah! Thank God! The splendid fellow! The noble fellow! The mere sight of him made one feel better at once.

"You wouldn't leave me!" he gasped. "You'd never leave me here alone to die!"

"Naow, naow, Senior, don't talk silly. Of course I wouldn't. I'd never leave you, Senior," replied Mr. Palsover.

"Not while you got a shilling," he added in a pleasant aside.

"No news of the Hadji? You've watched? You've looked out for him? You've done your best? . . . You couldn't mistake him."

"No. He hasn't come yet."

"But of course he'd come here to the hotel, wouldn't he? The first thing that he would do, would be to come and enquire whether I was here. A man like the Hadji would be sure to do that."

"Ar! That's right," agreed Mr. Palsover.

Very annoying if the perisher walked in on them too soon, though. Might be a difficult bloke to talk to, and an expensive one to square. Might be too much of a Nosey Parker. Might be a bit of a nark too.

"Yes, yes," babbled Senhor Pereira, "he would. He'd never go on to São Thomé. I mean he'd never sail away without having made sure as to whether I was here or not. He only comes twice a year, and

90

he'd be expecting me last time, this time, or next, and he'd make sure . . . Schultz, it would be a terrible thing if we missed him. Think of waiting here for six months till he came again."

"Think of somethink better than that, Senior. Think of a number and double it."

And Mr. Palsover thought of the number of English pounds there might be in the steel box, and of how he could double it.

"No," he continued, "if he doesn't come within a month we'd take the next Anglo-Portuguese that put in here."

"What? To São Thomé? God in Heaven, no! You can't go to São Thomé by a ship of the Anglo-Portuguese Steam Navigation and Trading Company, my good Schultz. In the first place, they don't know where it is, and in the second . . . No, no, what nonsense! There's only one way to São Thomé from here, and no one but the Hadji has the chart, the sailing-directions. . . . Do you know, there is only one harbour in all that vast island; and that nothing bigger than a *dhow* can get into that harbour."

"Reely?" observed Mr. Palsover, suppressing a yawn. The old Senior was working himself up. He'd be talking barmy in a minute.

Senhor Pereira grasped his wrist.

Cripes! How hot the old bird's hand was! Fair burnt you.

"Don't leave me! Don't go! Stay here till I'm asleep. Get me the medicine-chest and then sit by me till I go off."

"Ah! That's better. This cursed fever again. I feel terrible. Thank God you came with me, Schultz. You are a tower of strength and comfort. Schultz, I

91

trust you absolutely. You must stay with me always. You must come with me to São Thomé. They will accept you for my sake ; accept you when I tell them how you stood by me and saved my life—and the reports for Norhona. . . . So you must watch for the Hadji.

" Swear you'll keep a constant look-out for the Hadji. Watch every *dhow* that comes in, and the men who come ashore from it.

" Swear you'll get me on to the Hadji's *dhow*, whatever happens, at any cost. Swear, Schultz, that. . . . But no, there is no need for you to swear. If you are a bad man, your oath is worth nothing ; if you are a good man, your word is worth everything. And you are a good man, Schultz. You shall have your reward. Get me on to the Hadji's *dhow*, and you will never regret it. You will bless the fate that made you my servant . . . that impelled you to help me.

" I believe in Fate, you know, for Fate is only another name for God. It was Fate that sent you and me on to that dreadful ship ; Fate made you my steward, and now my servant . . . and friend.

" All you have to do is to whisper *São Thomé* in the Hadji's ear.

" You can't mistake the Hadji. He stands head and shoulders above the rest of them, the tallest Arab that ever lived. A great broad-shouldered powerful man, such a man as I should have loved to be. And his face, like yours, Schultz, is good. Strong and firm. Hard, perhaps, but a good face, and his eyes steady and straight and true. Slow of speech and economical of gesture, he is a fine man. He is a man whom those, who know him, do not ask to take his oath upon the Koran, for his Yea and his Nay are reliable and are accepted. A model to all merchants, an ornament to his Race and his Religion. You cannot mistake him, Schultz. There is no such other man on all this coast. No, nor in the Red Sea or the Persian Gulf. Not such another in all Arabia or Africa.

" You'll know him by his stature. You'll know him by his face and by his bearing. And you'll know him by his green turban of a Hadji."

" In fact, I'll know him, eh ? " observed Mr. Palsover.

THREE o'clock in the morning. . . .

Yes, the poor old Senior was sleeping like an innocent child. And that was just about what he was too.

One of Mr. Palsover's great hands slowly, softly moving, scarce perceptibly, extended flat, explored beneath the pillow.

Ah, the chain. . . .

With the utmost gentleness, hardly seeming to move, the hand withdrew, drawing the watch, chain and key after it.

Now for the box, the box packed round with underclothing in the cabin-trunk.

Nice of the Senior to have given him charge of his keys—except this little one, of course. It showed a good trusting spirit, a right and proper spirit between a man and his confidential servant, valet and nurse.

From his pocket Mr. Palsover drew a bunch of keys, unlocked the trunk, very gently raised the lid which was apt to creak, removed a layer of silken underclothing and unlocked the box.

Yes, they were English one-pound notes, brand-new, and the packet a couple of inches thick. And the other wad ? That must be Portuguese money. Nice-looking stuff, but you could never tell with these foreigners.

Reis ? Escudos ? And what might they be ? Any-

94

way, it was money, and money's—money. Interesting, to think each of those might be worth a five-pound note. From time to time Mr. Palsover glanced toward the bed.

Sleeping like an 'og.

Well, there was a nice bit of stuff, if anything happened to the poor old Senior.

And these papers in the big envelope ? That was important-looking stuff and it would be too, locked up in such a box as this. Pity it was all in some silly foreign lingo. He'd hang on to it, nevertheless, when the time came. Might be all about this rayjum concession. Something of that sort.

Senhor Pereira opened his eyes and glanced across at Palsover. Quickly he closed them again.

Ah-h-h-h-h ! As he had thought. As he had feared. It had been too much to hope. Of course the fellow was a Nazi German. It had been foolish of him to hope, on the strength of his always talking English, that he might, after all, have been an Englishman calling himself a German. It was the other way about, of course. Not a Briton pretending to be a German for some reason, but actually a German, as indeed he professed to be, who always talked English—for some reason.

The British, ancient allies of Portugal, did not behave like this. Not for people of this man's kind had that honourable phrase been coined : " Word of an Englishman."

And this dog had given his word ; had solemnly sworn that he would serve him with the utmost fidelity and truth and honesty.

A liar, a thief, a snake. . . .

Well, well. Life was like that, unfortunately. Very disappointing. He had come quite to like the man, almost to regard him as an Englishman, as he spoke nothing but English, and had almost decided to let

95

him live, in spite of his having learnt too much. Almost decided to take him to São Thomé and—keep him there as his servant.

But now ! Now he should certainly go to São Thomé —but he should not live.

Or if he did live . . . he would scarcely . . .

No—it would not be as the big powerful Fritz Schultz that he would live, nor as any other kind of Schultz.

He looked again. Yes, he was not mistaken. The cur had got the box open and was rummaging in it.

Turning his head away, he closed his eyes and groaned aloud. In a few seconds, without a sound of closing of boxes or moving feet, Palsover was beside him.

" Not so good to-night, Senior ? Mustn't give way, now. Nice drop o' medicine, eh ? Have a taste of something good out of the medicine-chest, eh ? What would you like ? "

" What I really want," whispered Senhor Pereira, " is paper and pen. I'm a little worried, my friend ; a little anxious, in addition to not feeling too well. I am troubled in mind—as to your getting safely to São Thomé . . . if anything happened to me before the Hadji comes."

" Naow, naow, don't you worry about that, Senior. I'll get there all right. The Hadji'll take me when I tell him all about it."

" No, that's just what he won't do. No one is taken to São Thomé. But I'll write you a pass. I'll write the Hadji's name on an envelope, and a short letter that will explain matters to him. Then he'll take you. And the other letter which I will write you must give to Them."

" Who's ' Them ' ? " enquired Mr. Palsover.

" Well, show it to the Port Officer and the Officer

96

who stops you at the Ravine bridge. Show it to anyone who asks you who you are and where you are going ; and at the Capital you'll have to give it up. You will be taken to Doña Guiomar, or to de Braganza, or to my friend Perez de Norhona, or the Marquis Sebastien da Barettero or to Dom Xavier da Silva, or one of the other *cavaleiros fidalgos* of the Council. You know, there are two da Gamas among them to this day ; brothers, Simão and João. Yes, same family. Not direct descendants of Vasco but descendants of the great Estevão da Gama—Count of Vidigueira really, in Portugal.

" Yes, the letter will receive every attention—and so will *you*, my good Schultz.

" And what'll the letter say ? " enquired Mr. Palsover, the wary man.

" Why, that you have befriended me. That, as my fate overtook me here in Santa Cruz de Loango, I have sent on the information, notes, papers, documents, all that sort of thing, that my friend and patron, Dom Perez de Norhona, required. . . . That you have heard about the marvellous deposits of all the most valuable minerals in the world ; about the uranium wealth—and especially about the radio-active quicksands, and that you want to know more about those. (And you will, Schultz. You'll know more about them, all right.) And that you are fully deserving of reward. Don't doubt that They will reward you fully, my good Schultz.

" Now, a pen, a couple of stout envelopes, and some sheets of paper. You'll find everything in my attaché-case. I don't think the ink in the fountain-pen will be dry yet, even in this heat.

" Ah ! Good ! That's better. Now prop me up,

97

and give me something flat to rest the paper on. Yes, the attaché-case will do. Thank you."

And painfully Senhor Pereira wrote, in plain round hand, but in a curious language. The person who read it accurately would require a knowledge of medieval Portuguese ; of Arabic ; of a Polynesian tongue akin to that spoken by the natives of certain of the South Sea Islands, as well as of a number of code-words known only to the members of the Council that governed São Thomé during the minority of its hereditary ruler, and to the few who were their emissaries and messengers.

The gist of the letter was to the effect that the writer, at the point of death, was making the best arrangements he could for the despatch to São Thomé of—that for which he had been sent to Europe. The paragraph relevant to the bearer, Herr Fritz Schultz, stated that he was, as his name implied, a German, and that if he changed his name he would still be a German ; that he was obviously a commercial agent ; the prospecting representative either of a financial and commercial group, or of the Foreign Commerce Department or Board of Trade of the Nazi Government ; an investigator of mining and other concessional interests ; an exploiter spy, and one of the vanguard of the vultures of Civilization.

He was, moreover, apart from his commercial position and interests, a rogue, a liar, a thief and a swindler. And, worst of all—he knew something ; he knew too much. He knew about the radium-bearing deposits.

Senhor Pereira therefore commended and committed him to the especial notice and care of Dom Perez de Norhona who might, with clear conscience and easy mind, make good use of him—experimental use.

" There," said Senhor Pereira, as he folded the letter

98

and placed it in an envelope, " it may never be needed. I sincerely hope that it will not. But if it is, you may rest absolutely assured, my good Schultz, that, if only you get that safely to São Thomé, the result will surprise you. They won't be able to do enough for you. . . . But They'll try. They'll do their best. . . .

" And now to make sure that the Hadji will take you —in the melancholy event of his arriving too late to take us both."

Mr. Palsover spoke soothing and reassuring words while Senhor Pereira made curious hieroglyphics that ran from right to left across a sheet of paper, and then more on an envelope.

" There," said he, " that's Arabic—of a sort. Show it to any *dhow*-master, to any Arab, in fact, who looks as though he might be the Hadji, a huge great man, probably wearing a green turban. And when you feel sure that you have found the right man, whisper ' *São Thomé* ' in his ear. He'll know you are authorized when he hears that and reads this.

" Can't he talk English ? " enquired Mr. Palsover, with a faint note of contempt in his voice.

" I should think not. Why should he ? He trades north from here to the Persian Gulf—Bahrein way—for pearls, I believe. To Cairo, Alexandria, Haifa, the Holy Land and Turkey. And to Bombay, where I understand he meets other pearl-merchants from the South—Ceylon and the pearl-bearing lagoons of the Southern Islands. He might have learned a little English in Bombay."

" Hindustani, perhaps ? " hazarded Mr. Palsover.

" Quite possibly. I don't know."

" How do you talk to him then—you and the other Seniors of St. Tommy ? "

" Arabic. A kind of Arabic, anyway. More like

Malayan ; but we understand each other quite clearly Anyhow, his name is on this envelope, and this note says that if he finds that I have died here, he is to take you to São Thomé without fail, and to see that you get safely up to the Capital."

" He'll go there, then ? "

" To the Capital ? Oh, yes. He'll probably have a consignment of pearls for Doña Guiomar, the Regent, as well as crates and boxes of various articles of luxury that São Thomé does not produce. Quite a little cargo. Sacramental wine for Father Xavier ; his special cigars for Senhor João da Gama ; clothing and haberdashery from Cairo perhaps, for Dom Miguel de Braganza ; silks and finery for their ladies—that sort of thing. He executes all sorts of commissions, every round. And in fact, he's our chief—what d'you call it ? Pedlar ? Purveyor ? Yes. All sorts of little foreign luxuries.

" And he'll take the trunks and cases that came ashore with me from the ship. Give him the list and papers attached. There's a case of drugs and apparatus for Norhona and a box of books. Very special and important. And I'm afraid the cases marked ' Sewing-machines ' contain something even more impetuous. For the Chief of Police. So do those marked ' Type-writers.' For the Commandant. The list is all right, written out in Arabic, in the despatch-case here. This is it. You'll want that. . . .

" You'll help him in every way, won't you ? And when you get to São Thomé you will receive your worthy reward.

" But there ! I expect I shall be up and about before the Hadji comes, and be able to see to everything myself."

Mr. Palsover privately doubted this.

VIII

MR. PALSOVER doubted it very much indeed.
In fact, it would not do at all ; and he must
see that nothing of the sort occurred.

As he figured things out, it would be quite a mistake
for the Senior to see to everything himself, or to see the
Hadji either.

Mr. Palsover—who was fond of a quiet bit of fishing
off the end of a nice pier, with a nice pub handy, for
preference—thinking in piscatorial terms, decided that
there was certainly a sprat, probably a mackerel, and
possibly a whale, all to be fished up out of this queer
business, if he were skilful and lucky—as, of course, a
fisherman needs to be.

If this perishin' Arab turned up all of a sudden, Mr.
Palsover might lose the lot. Almost certainly he would
lose the lot, and all he would have left would be the
melancholy pleasure of telling himself—as he could
scarcely tell anybody else—of the size of the sprat, of
the bigness of the mackerel, and the thundering enor-
mousness of the whale, all of which had got away—just
the usual melancholy consolation of the unsuccessful
fisherman.

And he wasn't an unsuccessful fisherman, nor did he
intend to start being one now. Especially now ; now
when everything was cut and dried and all ready to his
hand, including the introduction to the Hadji, which
would be his ticket to St. Tommy in the *dhow*, and the

letter that would be his safe-conduct to this Capital place, and his introduction to the Nobs there.

Not that he intended to go that far with it, not by any manner of means. He hadn't the education nor the experience for that sort of game. Ask him to run a catering job, now, and he'd undertake anything, from a Sunday School Treat to a Buckingham Palace Ball. Anything. He'd cater for a Battleship Dance or a Brigade Dinner ; quantity or quality or both ; superintend everything himself, and give entire satisfaction to all concerned. Ar ! And pocket a pretty rake-off for Samuel Palsover.

And there were plenty of other nice things he could handle, outside his own line of business. But this, he realized, was altogether too big a do. Too strange, too difficult, too awkward for him.

This wanted not only the brains that he himself had got, and the experience that he hadn't, but special knowledge that wasn't so common. It would want financial experts and mining experts, both of 'em ; and working together. And it would want big Capital.

What was more, it would want somebody who could find all three, and play fair by the man who was behind it all, who started it, found it, and could lead 'em to it.

That was the worst of Big Business. You couldn't trust nobody, and if you could, they did you down.

The moment he had given the secret away, where would he be ? Mug Street.

What he wanted was a gent, somebody like a Bishop or a Judge or an Officer. Colonel of a British Regiment. That sort.

But what did they know about business ? Nothing or less. Mugs from Mug Street, when it came to that. Gave their money to somebody else to invest for 'em. (And he'd have a shot at that game himself by and by ;

investing other people's money.) If he went back to London and walked into one of those City Offices, whether it was the Bank of England or McIsaacstein's On-note-of-hand-alone, or any sort or kind of Financial Corporation, how could he sell them what he had got in his head? They wouldn't pay until they knew, and when they knew they wouldn't pay.

And perhaps it was all moonshine, after all?

No! Not it! The old Senior here was the goods. Straight as an arrow, honest as the day, and simple as an Army Chaplain. Half-witted, almost.

Of course it was all right. Otherwise why all these precautions? Nobody mustn't go to St. Tommy except in this Hadji's *dhow*. Nobody couldn't go ashore without a pass. Few as there were got into the island, still fewer got out. What about all that?

Anyway, he had a hunch he was on to a good thing. He'd got a grand nose for money, there was a strong smell of money about, and he was going to get to the bottom of this. Follow it up for all it was worth. But they weren't going to give Samuel Palsover the muddy end of the stick. He wasn't going to burn his own fingers, and he wasn't going to dive ack over tock, head foremost into this St. Tommy—like a fool who couldn't swim, walking up to his neck in a swift river and that full of muggers.[1]

No, he'd go about this in the right way.

Suddenly Mr. Palsover sat bolt upright, and though his eyes gazed upon the face of Senhor Pereira, he saw that of the man whom above all others he admired.

That proper gent; that fine figure of a man; that downiest of wise birds; that best of Commanding Officers, his old Colonel, now retired, General Sir Reginald Jason, K.C.B., C.M.G.!

[1] *Crocodiles (Hindustani).*

Raising a mighty hand, Mr. Palsover soundlessly smote his thigh. The very man! Honest and truthful as a perishin' Archangel; with the brains of a bookie, the guts of a prize-fighter, and the style and gentlemanliness of two kings and a dook. Retired, at a loose end and—unless he had come into money—about as hard up as any gentleman could wish to be. Young too.

Lord love us, thought Mr. Palsover, what a brain I got, and what a bit of luck. The very man. He'd know exactly how to go about it; how to form a Company, raise Capital, get hold of the right kind of mining-expert fellers and engineers, and start getting a Concession.

And if, for any reason, he wouldn't go into it himself, there'd be nothing lost, for he'd keep his head shut. General Jason was a gent, and not the sort who'd get the secret and then, if he didn't want to use it, sell it to somebody who did, and leave the rightful original owner, the Old Firm, out in the cold.

No, he'd take it or leave it, and say nothing to nobody.

Or better still, if he didn't want to come in on it himself, he'd tell his old friend and Mess-Sergeant how to go about it. Give him good advice, so that he shouldn't be cheated out of his lawful dues.

But he'd come into it. He would come into it all right, bald-headed. He was that sort. Just the very man to be Chairman of a big Company, a wealthy Corporation. Fine figure-head, too, for a prospectus.

The St. Tommy Radium and Precious Minerals Corporation. Capital One Million Pounds. Chairman, General Sir Reginald Jason, K.C.B., C.M.G.

That's the stuff to give the troops.

Fine. And all Samuel Palsover would have to do

would be to sit back and take his share of the money that the Company earned.

What would that be ? Halves ? Well, he'd talk it over with the General, and leave it to him. But he'd start with asking for halves. Halves for him because it was his own property, and without him they couldn't make a Company ; half for them because they'd find the capital and do the work.

Anyway, he'd leave it to the General.

Mr. Palsover sat staring with unseeing eyes at the sweat-bedewed pale yellow face of Senhor Pereira who lay with closed eyes, his quick and shallow breathing audible above the trumpeting of the justly-famous mosquitoes of Santa Cruz de Loango.

Yes, that was the way to do things, and there was the scheme cut and dried. He'd get the sprat, use it for the catching of the mackerel—for it would cost a bit to go home and do the thing properly—and then see what sort of whale-bait the mackerel might make.

Right !

And Mr. Palsover, a man of quick decision and prompt action, stood up. That perishin' Arab might walk in at any minute and queer the whole pitch !

Senhor Pereira opened his eyes and raised his hand to his left breast.

" My heart," he whispered, " . . . I have these heart attacks. . . . Medicine-chest."

" Yes, yes, in a minute, Senior. What you want first of all is your pyjammers changed. All of a muck sweat, you are. And a pair of nice clean sheets and a clean pillow-slip. All comfortable."

" Medicine-chest," whispered Senhor Pereira again.

" Half a mo', Senior, now. Don't you take on. You're goin' to be all right. Fair all right you'll look soon as I've fixed you decent an' proper."

Crossing the room noiselessly, Mr. Palsover went out and descended the rickety stairs to the floor below. Pushing open a door that led into the bar, he ignored the gigantic coloured bar-man who snored in a corner, lifted up his voice and called for the landlord.

" *Boy !* Diego ! Hi, you pink-eyed Dago. Where are you ? "

The tiny wizened Goanese who owned the *Casa Real* scuttled into the bar.

" Sah ? " he said. " You calling ? "

Mr. Palsover had had considerable experience of Goanese mess-boys, servants, and bazaar shop-keepers in India and, holding them in low regard, was toward them rarely kind. His benevolence ended at the line that marks off the lesser breeds without the Law and the Palsover pale.

" Calling ? No. I was whistling like a perishin' canary to show I didn't want you. Strike me pink if you and your seven-foot bar-keep don't look like the dwarf pimp and the giant pander. Fact. . . . No, I was 'ollering, not calling." Silly beggar.

" Sah ? " And Mr. Felice Diego automatically turned about for bottle and glass.

" Yes, that's all right, Boy. Quite a sound idea. But what I also wants is a couple of clean sheets and a pillow-case for the gent upstairs. And jump to it."

" Very good, Sah. But the sheets and pillow-case in Number One were clean only . . ."

" Yerss. Clean only once—and that was when they was made. Go and get me two clean sheets and a clean pillow-case, or I'll . . . *Jalditum !* " he bawled, bitterly insulting Mr. Felice Diego who, though bred and born in Goa, educated in Bombay, and widely experienced in domestic employment in every part of India, affected to understand no word of Hindustani.

Nowadays he was a Portuguese. Portuguese was his mother-tongue, though as a man of education and travel, he spoke serviceable English. Mr. Felice Diego was, however, accustomed not only to insults, but to loud-voiced Europeans and especially to Britons of the Sergeant-Major type, urgent and impetuous people who always got what they wanted—if they didn't always want what they got.

" Si, si, Senhor. All right, Sahib. I getting."

And a couple of minutes later Mr. Palsover ascended the creaking stairs with sheets and pillow-case that, by the standards of Santa Cruz, were practically clean.

Senhor Pereira still lay breathing quickly and audibly, and looking, to Mr. Palsover's experienced eye, definitely ' queer.'

From an unlocked cabin-trunk he took a clean pair of pyjamas and then, with the tenderness of a mother dealing with a month-old baby, removed Senhor Pereira's wet things. Placing the rusty water-jug and basin beside the bed, he took the Senhor in his arms, gently and skilfully sponged him from head to foot, and dried him with a towel and the top sheet. Folding these latter on the floor, he then carefully laid the sick man down, removed the other sheet from the mattress, changed the pillow-case and re-made the bed.

Again handling Senhor Pereira as though he were an infant, he clothed him in the clean pyjamas, laid him on the bed and covered him with the top sheet.

" There, Senior. All ship-shape and army-fashion. . . . Your 'air could do with a brush though. And for two pins I'd shave you. If I only knew how much longer that Wandering B . . . that Wandering Boy of an Arab, I mean . . . was going to be, I'd do it. . . . Lumme ! I'll take the risk. You've been a perfect gent to me and I'll do the same by you."

Again descending to the bar room and bawling " *Boy !* " Mr. Palsover demanded " *Gurrm pani* [1] *!* " and bade Mr. Diego to look slippy.

" Bring it up to Senior Pereira's room," he directed. " And in less than two shakes of a duck's fanny.

" Bring it yourself," he added. " I want you to cast an eye on how Senior Pereira looks this mornin', seeing there isn't so much as a horse-doctor in this Gawd-forsaken 'ole. Santy Crews ! Out of bounds for the Devil's Own troops in 'Ell I sh'd reckon," he grumbled.

When, a few minutes later, the proprietor of the *Casa Real* knocked and entered the best bedroom of his hotel, he was constrained to agree with Mr. Palsover that Senhor Pereira didn't look none too good.

" *Sahib bemar hai,* [2] " said Mr. Palsover.

" Without doubt," agreed Mr. Diego in good if queerly-accentuated English. " The poor gentlyman ! Looking not so good. No doubt he has perhaps got fever probably."

" Ar ! 'S right," agreed Mr. Palsover, " and you can lay to that. Fever ! Not 'arf. His chubes too. Hark at 'em. And his heart. Poor gent's heart don't hardly tick over. I took his temperature and his pulse just now. Bad. Very bad."

" How much fever ? " enquired Mr. Diego.

" Hundred and ten," Mr. Palsover assured him, " and still risin'."

Mr. Diego clacked a sympathetic tongue and shook a foreboding head.

" And his pulse beatings ? " he asked.

" Fifteen to the minute. Exactly nine hundred to the hower," admitted Mr. Palsover.

" Thatt nott so good ? " enquired the Goanese, who was a little vague on the subject.

[1] Hot water.   [2] The gentleman is ill.

" Bad as can be. Farenheit too. . . . ' Not so good ? ' It's absoberlutely rotten," sighed Mr. Palsover. " You haven't got a bottle of champagne wine, I suppose," he asked. " There's nothing I wouldn't do for him."

Mr. Diego smiled sadly.

" Whiskey. Brandy. Gin," he said. " Best Bombay Spirits."

" We don't drink even the best o' the methylated class of liquor," snubbed Mr. Palsover.

" Anyt'ing I can do ? " enquired the proprietor.

" Bung off," requested Mr. Palsover as he started to strop a razor.

With the care and skill of a first-class valet, Mr. Palsover lathered and shaved his apparently-unconscious employer, carefully unfastening the neck of the pyjamas, and so arranging the towel that they should not be soiled.

Having sponged the waxen face, he powdered it as he had seen Senhor Pereira do, brushed the silky moustache and combed and arranged the greying hair to his satisfaction.

" There ! Proper picture he looks, don't he ? " he murmured aloud, with a pardonable self-satisfaction.

Senhor Pereira opened his eyes.

" Schultz," he whispered, " don't leave me. You won't leave me, Schultz ? There's something I want to say to you. I want to apologize, Schultz. I'm sorry. So sorry I misjudged you. I know you were doing it for the best. You were anxious and concerned about me, and, naturally, about yourself and your future. . . . Our future. Now listen. I'm weak and confused—but listen carefully.

" If anything happens to me, *don't* fail to meet the Hadji, whisper ' *São Thomé* ' to him, and give him the letter, I implore you. The envelope with the Arabic writing on it. And whatever you do, *don't* fail to take the other letter with you to São Thomé. It's absolutely essential. For your own sake, I mean. I want to make you a rich man. It's the least I can do for you in return for your care and kindness. And see that Norhona gets the steel box that is in that trunk. It's full of manuscript. Notes, information, opinions, all sorts of writings—things that are not of the slightest value to anybody but him. He'll be *most* grateful to you and he will reward you well, apart from . . . apart from . . ."

The voice died away.

" Yes ? Apart from what, Senior ? Speak up ! Go on. Apart from that Rayjum Concession, was you going to say ? "

Senhor Pereira smiled weakly, deprecatingly.

" Well . . . well. . . . No good trying to deceive you, Schultz, is it ? "

" Not a bit," Mr. Palsover assured him. " Not a bit, Senior."

Senhor Pereira smiled again. God bless and help São Thomé. God forgive him for endangering her sacred privacy and peace. God guide this dangerous German reptile safely there—and the Council would draw his sting, once and for all.

Would the Hadji never come . . . ?

Painfully raising himself a few inches from the bed, " *God save São Thomé !* " he crowed feebly, and collapsed, gasping for breath.

IX

WELL, thought Mr. Palsover as he gazed mournfully at the sick man, he had probably said it all ; and if he hadn't said it all, he wasn't likely to say the remainder.

So the time seemed to have come. Nothing much to learn, nothing more to do, and the poor old Senior just about ripe for it.

No need for any unpleasantness.

Nothing of the sort of rough stuff the Police call "with a blunt instrument." Nothing of the kind of evidence that looks ugly in a Police Court . . . "Signs of a struggle " . . . "Pools of blood." Nasty expressions, those were. 'Orrible. Vulgar. Mr. Palsover didn't like them. Bad as "Disgraceful frackass." "Great force had been used." "Signs of terrific violence." "Clear evidence of manual strangulation."

Leave all that to criminals.

Not, of course, that the Police of Santa Cruz took much interest in that sort of thing. Too busy earning their livings, as they couldn't get their salaries. Get away with anything here, if you paid for—transport.

But these were morbid thoughts.

Looked quite nice, the poor old Senior did, now he had shaved him and done his hair. . . . Might as well have that watch and chain beforehand. Wouldn't want to go disturbing him afterwards. Disrespectful, for one thing.

Once again the great hand explored beneath the pillow.

Ar! Yes, there it was.

As Mr. Palsover drew out the watch and chain, with the key of the steel box attached, Senhor Pereira opened his eyes, almost automatically it seemed. It was as though his mind, his soul, his conscience watched even though he himself fainted or slept.

" Now is there anything more you want to tell me, Senior ? " enquired Mr. Palsover. " If so, now's your time. . . . Never mind about the watch. I'm only going to wind it up. . . . You're sure you've told me everything ? "

With his eyes on the watch that Palsover was winding, Senhor Pereira smiled, raised his eyes to those of his faithful servant and whispered,

" *Wait for the Hadji. Whisper the words ' São Thomé' to him. He'll take you to São Thomé. Give the letter to Norhona.*"

" Yerss, yerss ! *That's* all right, Senior. Don't you worry. What I meant was, anything *more*. Anything you kept back, like. Anything about getting the rayjum out of the country ? You know—Sufferin' Humanity. Getting out a hundredweight or so at Fifteen thousand pounds a gram, and bringing it within the reach of all, at a bob a time. Sell it in small packets in Timbuctoo and Strathpeffer, Singapore and Skibbareen, like you said. . . . Think of all them hospitals, doctors and Sufferin' Poor, and tell me how I can help."

" Norhona will tell you everything," whispered Senhor Pereira, and closed his eyes.

" Well, that's that, then," sighed Mr. Palsover, and softly crossing the room, locked the door.

Returning to the bed, he long and regretfully regarded Senhor Pereira with moist pale eye, and then gently, and with great care, seated himself on that gentleman's narrow chest, placed his right hand over his mouth and nose, and began to sing lustily and not untunefully. His mother had been quite musical and a confirmed admirer of the operas of Messrs. Gilbert and Sullivan. This may have been the sub-conscious reason for Mr. Palsover's selection.

" *The flowers that bloom in the Spring, tra la*," he trolled with all the strength of his lungs.

> " *The flowers that bloom in the Spring, tra la,*
> *Have nothing to do with the case.*
>
> *Not a damn thing,*"

he added, improvising relevant words when memory failed.

> " *Not a damn thing to do with the case.*"

Senhor Pereira died quietly, as a gentleman should, any feeble sounds which he may have emitted being completely drowned, like mewling kittens, beneath the uproarious rushing spate of Mr. Palsover's song.

After a while, Mr. Palsover rose to his feet as with that sudden burst of energy of one who has dallied and wasted time too long.

Again noiselessly crossing the room as he took a bunch of keys from his pocket, he opened the cabin-trunk, and with the key on the watch-chain unlocked the flat steel box.

Yes, by Cripes. As he had seen. All of them good old honest-to-God British 'Treasury one-pound notes. A good two inches thick. About four hundred of the best.

113

Well, well, well! What a lad he was. What a nose he had got for the money! Chucking a good job on the *St. Paul de Loanda* to follow that nice wad.

Slipping the elastic-banded packet into his capacious pocket, Mr. Palsover again considered the foreign paper-money. Rum-looking stuff, but it might be worth a lot. He'd take that home and pay it into his Bank and see what happened. Real bit of luck that the English money was in one-pound notes and not those nasty fivers that suspicious-minded people keep the numbers of.

Now what should he do with the scribble? Looked as though the Senior had been writing a young book.

And these papers put together looked as though he had been making a book. Been to the Derby, perhaps.

Might be as well to keep 'em. You never know. Might be helpful when it came to forming the Company and getting the Rayjum Concession. . . . And all these letters and these papers in big envelopes? Better scoop the lot, perhaps.

On the other hand, if old Diego did think he had better bring the Police in, to save trouble in the long run, it might be as well for there to be something in the box. Otherwise some evil-minded blackguard might start them thinking it had been looted.

But surely he could square Diego.

Might be risky again if this Arab perisher turned up in the middle of it all. According to the old Senior, he might come any minute or any month. No telling how much he knew, or how much of a dust he might kick up if all were not above-board. If he was the only one who knew where this St. Tommy was, and the way to get there, the one and only go-between, the only what you might call lines-of-communication, between Santa Cruz and this St. Tommy, and came here a-purpose to pick up the Senior, well, he'd want to know what had become of everything, and how about it.

And if he was the white-headed boy at St. Tommy and an important man here too, there might be lots of trouble if he arrived before Mr. Palsover had departed.

And that Mr. Palsover couldn't do until the next Anglo-British put in.

The Arab would soon find out that the Senior had come to Santa Cruz, and had come ashore with another European. Anybody'd tell him; the Customs people, Police, long-shore loafers, not to mention Felice Diego. No knowin' how much he and the Arab were hand-in-glove. No tellin' how many people, of his own, the Arab might not keep planted here, or that might roll up about the time of year he was expected.

No, Honesty is the best Policy. Keep the party pure, and your hands clean. Everything above board, ship-shape, and army fashion. And even if he got away on an Anglo-Portuguese before the Arab came, he might have endless difficulty in getting the Senior's stuff back on board ship and clearing out with it. Quite possibly the Police wouldn't let him take it on board when the ship came; not with Pereira's name painted all over it, him having come ashore as Pereira's servant, and Pereira dead on his hands, so to speak.

They'd want to hang on to it. They'd talk about next-of-kin—hoping to pinch it themselves in the end.

And he mustn't do anything that looked like a bolt. They'd be capable of saying he had done the old Senior in, for the sake of his dunnage and the coppers in his trousers' pockets!

And, besides, it might be unsaleable stuff or very difficult to dispose of. There wouldn't be much profit on the books, drugs and doctors' junk that the Senior was taking to this Norhona, for example; and Samuel

115

Palsover would be a damn sight better without the automatics and rifles that Pereira was taking for the Armed Police or Civil Guards or whatever it was he had called 'em. Get himself into trouble, with that sort of stuff in his baggage.

No, let it all alone. Be content with the four hundred quid and whatever the foreign money was worth, and call it a day—until he could get his share of the rayjum and the other what-d'you-call-it.

Very nice work when you could get it—at fifteen thousand jimmy-o'-goblins a pinch. . . .

Closing and re-locking the box and trunk, Mr. Pereira returned to the bed, placed the watch on the rickety bed-side table, and regarded the face of Senhor Pereira.

The poor gentleman certainly did look very queer indeed. Very nice and tidy though. What about crossing his hands on his breast ? No. Not yet. Wouldn't look quite natural, perhaps. Still, with the nice clean sheet smoothed out and drawn up to his neck, he looked a fair treat.

As nice a stiff as you could wish to see.

Well, he'd take a stroll down to the harbour for a bit, and see if there was any news of a big *dhow*. That Arab blighter could come any time he liked now.

Strolling round the derelict and almost deserted purlieus of the port of Santa Cruz, Mr. Palsover could see no signs of any new arrivals. *Dhows* could, of course, creep in and out, silently and unobtrusively as grey cats in the twilight ; and of those that came and went in the night no record would remain. But so few were the ships, even *dhows* and bunder-boats, tied up in the harbour, that the presence or absence of only one would be noted by the accustomed eye.

No, there was no change. He didn't know a Lamu

m'tepe from a Zanzibar *betela*, nor a Muscat *baggala* from a Bombay bunder-boat, but he knew that there was no new craft, and from what he had gathered from the Senior, the Arab's *dhow* was noticeable among the rest of the native ships, being bigger, smarter and better kept.

No, it wasn't there.

Well, he'd mooch round, have a chin with the ragged Port Officer and Customs men, in bazaar Hindustani, of which they understood not a word, listen to their foolish gabble in Portuguese, of which he understood not a word, and all laugh heartily together at the excellent jokes. Then perhaps a snifter at Sousa's American Bar, so called because there really was some American liquid in the place—the oil in the lamps.

And so back to the *Casa Real*.

Nothing had happened.

Senhor Pereira had not moved—and would never move again.

Descending the stairs in apparent haste, Mr. Palsover burst into the empty bar-room, the wind of his coming and the roar of his voice rousing from slumber the very large and dusky man who, dressed in a long night-shirt and embroidered skull-cap, was lying on the dirty floor behind the bar.

" *Boy!* Diego! Diego! " called Mr. Palsover. " Hi! Here, quick. *Ither ao! Jaldi*[1]! You boss-eyed bat-eared beggar. Hi! Come here, will you— and jump to it, you minnacher pimp."

" Sah ? " enquired little Mr. Felice Diego, hurrying from the back premises in which he lurked, and pulling on a pyjama coat over his naked torso as he did so.

Staring, somewhat alarmed, he perceived that Mr.

[1] Come here! Quick!

Palsover's usually bland and benevolent face was now dark, suffused and swollen. Obviously he was labouring under the influence of some violent emotion. Almost certainly this would be rage. These second-class Sahibs were men of wrath, and spoke loudly in their haste. Generally unkind things.

" Here ! You Snuff-and-Butter bastard ! " shouted Mr. Palsover. " What you been doing to Senior Pereira while I was out ? "

" I doing, Sah ? Nutting. I am not going up to his room. I have not seen."

" Well, up you go and see now ! *Chello*[1] *! Jaldi !* 'Op to it, you flat-footed sunnuvabitch. Go on."

Raising the flap of the bar, the proprietor emerged and, not without propulsion from behind, hurried to the stairs, bounded up them and entered the room of the late Senhor Pereira.

Going over to the bed, he peered, drew back, turned a rapidly yellowing face to the minatory and accusing countenance of Mr. Palsover, and whispered something in Hindustani.

" Yes, yes ! Mr. Schloots, he iss dead ! " he whispered. . . . "*Murgya*[2]."

" Mur*der*ed too, if you ask me," replied Mr. Palsover. " Done-in while I was out. He was all right when I left him. Merry as a cricket. Chirping like a bloomin' canary. And now look at him ! "

" But no one has been to the room. No one has entered in."

" And you mean to say he didn't let a shout ? "

" No, Sah. Nutting. He has died without mentioning."

" You tell that to the Marines," advised Mr. Palsover. " 'Ere I leave him singing like a dicky-bird, and comes

[1] Go on !   [2] He has died.

118

back and find 'im corpsed, and you pretend that no one has been up here ! And never a squeak out of him, you say. Who's going to believe that ? I *ask* you ? What are you going to do about it ? "

" Sah, he was very ill. Last night you are telling me. Very bad fever. Heart not working much."

" Well, yerss. That's true enough. I'll say that for you, Diego. I'll help you 's far's I can. No doubt you'll wish to make it worth my while. I don't want to make trouble for you. God knows you'll have trouble enough. . . . I better see what's missing."

" Well, *thatt* is nott missing, Mr. Schloots, Sah," observed Felice Diego, pointing to the valuable watch and chain lying on the aged bed-side table.

" No ? . . . No. That's there all right," agreed Mr. Palsover. " I better take charge of that, perhaps. . . . Well, what you going to do about it ? "

" Send for Police, Sah," replied Mr. Diego bravely, though with a gulp suggesting pain, fear and horror. A dreadful thing, God wot, and an expensive, to send for the Police.

" Well, perhaps you're right. So long as you've got a clear conscience. But I got to obey my own, you know, Diego. I got to say he was all present and correct, merry and bright, when I went out 'smorning."

" Yes, yes. Man, you must speak the truth. Then you cannot be caught in lies."

At this simple proposition an almost cynical smile appeared on the benevolent face of Mr. Palsover.

" Butt, Sah, you will say how ill he was ? " begged Diego. " You will say that he was at last gasps yesterday evening, and that you called me up into this veree room to see them ? "

" Ar ! But that was last night. He was right enough this morning. Yes, he was talking about going on a gin-crawl with me to-night. And, why, almost the last thing he said to me was, ' *What's the girls like here, Mr. Schultz?* ' he says, and I replied, ' *Like they are everywhere else, Senior. Snares and delusions ; and same value at any price you like.*' . . . That don't look as though he was thinking of his latter end and preparing to meet his Maker, do it ? "

" Sah, I t'ink he had a stroke," said Mr. Diego brightly, as one who has probably solved a difficult problem.

" Wasn't a stroke o' luck, anyway, was it ? " observed Mr. Palsover.

No, it was he who had had that, he told himself with an inward smile.

" Last night he was very ill, Senhor Schloots. Sir, he was veree sick. Sahib, you will give witness that he was dying man last night and therefore dead man this morning ? You will tell that to the Police ? Or, better still, saying nutting and helping me and Toto give gentlyman nice burial to-night ? " begged Mr. Felice Diego, as he stood with bowed head and hands placed together as in prayer—to Mr. Palsover.

" M-m-m-m ! What's it worth, Diego ? "

Rapidly the proprietor of the *Casa Real* made calculation and submitted an estimate.

Mr. Palsover acknowledged its adequacy.

And, soon after midnight, all that was corruptible of Senhor Pereira received reasonably Christian burial in the mangrove-swamp that stretched its oily blackness from the lagoon to Mr. Diego's back premises.

PART IV

I

GENERAL SIR REGINALD JASON, K.C.B., was suffering from the insidious and horrible, but not incurable, disease of boredom.

Like many another man of his type who has retired or been forced from a very active life, he bitterly regretted the step that had led him from the narrow path of work, activity, adventure, stress, strain and strife. He wanted to return to it and have them all before him again.

At the time, it had seemed the only thing to do, when his father, the oldest retired General on the Army list, had suddenly and most unexpectedly been cut off in the prime of his early nineties, leaving an extremely encumbered estate for his son to clear from debt, to save from the hammer and keep solvent, if he could. Apparently he could not. Taxation grew heavier, the times grew harder and harder, money became tighter and ever tighter. Things could hardly have been worse if he had remained in India, pursuing the straight course of his brilliant career. However, the dying wish of his revered father, expressed in what were almost his last words, and his own temporary but strong inclination for English country-life, had turned the balance. He had retired, come home, worked valiantly at straightening the desperately involved affairs of the estate, and had come to the conclusion that filial he must have been, bold he might have been, and a fool he had been.

To do the estate well, keep the house up properly, live as he and Antoinette liked to live, both in the country and in London, he needed about five thousand a year more than he had got.

And revolving these thoughts in his mind as he turned to enter his Club, he was aware of a bulky, upright and still soldierly figure, saluting him with vigour and the well-simulated guardsman-quiver of the raised right arm.

And who the devil was this ex-service-man in mufti standing before him with the back of the still quivering hand to the brim of a bowler hat ? One of the Royal Wessex Fusiliers ? God bless his soul, if it wasn't that old scoundrel Mess-Sergeant Palsover, whom he had always rather liked, and of whom Henry Carthew had taken so jaundiced a view. Called him the damnedest scoundrel unhung.

Lord ! Why, the fellow looked as though, labouring under almost uncontrollable emotion, he were going to burst into tears of affection and joy. Not the emotions that General Jason had usually inspired in " Other Ranks," or in any other ranks.

" Sir . . . Colonel . . . General Sir Reginald, I mean," stuttered the worthy fellow. " You don't remember me, Sir, I . . ."

" Oh, yes, I remember you, Palsover. How are you ? " replied General Jason, extending his hand, which Mr. Palsover wrung warmly.

" How are you ? " he asked again, kindly.

" All the better for seeing you, Sir," Mr. Palsover assured him, his large face shining with happiness, veneration and a respectful benevolence.

" All the better for seeing you, Sir," he repeated.
" And I been looking for you for a long time."

" Looking for me, Palsover ? "

" Ar, Sir ! And you can lay to that. I've walked up and down Pall Mall, and hung about this Club, Sir, since . . ."

" And what did you want to see me for ? Want me to help you into a job ? "

It would probably be something in the Club-servant line that he'd be looking out for ; and an excellent one he'd make. First-class head waiter. But jobs like that weren't easy to get.

" No, Sir. No, Sir. Almost the other way about, Sir, though you wouldn't believe it. Putting it respectful like, I mean."

" And what the devil *do* you mean ? "

" Could we have a talk somewhere, Sir, very private ? I'm on to a thing, Sir, in which there's hundreds of thousands of pounds. Millions. And I'm afraid of losin' the lot through going to the wrong parties. I haven't said a word to a living soul, Sir. I waited till I could see you. I want to tell you all about it, because you are a gentleman and would never do a man down. And I want to let you in on the ground floor, Sir. There's big money in it ; and if, when you've heard all about it, you don't want to come in, well, no harm done, and perhaps you'd be so good as to give me advice, Sir. It's *my* thing. I'm sole proprietor. And it's *the* chance of a life-time—a dozen life-times. The chance of a century. And I'll lose it, Sir. I'll lose the whole lot, if I get among sharks. If you'd go into it with me, Sir, there'd be more money for both of us than we could ever spend."

General Jason's cold and expressionless face almost thawed into a smile of amusement.

" Really, Palsover ? You always were a bit of a financier, I understand."

" Ar ! Financier is the word, Sir. What we want is a financier to help us to handle this—and it's ten thousand per cent per annum profit for us, if only things could be kept honest and straight and above-board. Fair play for the man that discovered it. But you see, Sir, the moment they know, they've *got* me ! And it's

' *Thank you, Mr. Palsover. And good morning to you.*'

" They get the secret, they find the money, and they —carry on. Make millions."

The man was obviously sincere, patently genuine and speaking with the deepest conviction. If General Jason knew anything of men at all, here was an honest man labouring under the stress of an unshakable faith and belief in something big, something far too big for him to handle, but of the truth of which he was absolutely certain.

" And what kind of thing is it, Palsover ? " he asked, half banteringly, in the style which Mr. Palsover knew only too well, the Orderly Room mockery that was apt to turn cold and savage before pronouncing a sharp sentence. " Infallible turf-system ? If so, I'll tell you a profound truth. You can win a bet—but you cannot win at betting. Or are you setting up as a bookie ? "

" No, Sir. No, Sir. Nothing of that sort."

" Don't say it's an infallible system for me to take to Monte Carlo to break the Bank. That's only done by arrangement with the Bank. . . . They are there to break *you*."

" No, no, Sir. No. This is honest-to-God real business. It is . . ."

" Not a gold mine, Palsover ? Don't say it's a gold mine. I had the prospectus of one this morning.

'The Summit Flat.' Thought I was a *con*summate flat, I suppose."

"No, Sir, no."

"Well, tell me in a word. I must be getting along," and the General glanced at his wrist-watch.

"In confidence, Sir?"

"Absolutely," replied General Jason, eyeing the large earnest face with its moist yearning eyes which watched his own so beseechingly.

"*Rayjum!*" whispered Mr. Palsover.

"Radium?"

"Yes, Sir. D'you know the market price of it?"

"No. Pretty expensive article, I believe."

"Fifteen thousand pounds a gram, Sir. Fifteen thousand golden sovereigns for as much as you could put in a thimble."

General Jason eyed Mr. Palsover speculatively.

Thimble? Wasn't there a game known as Thimble-rigging? . . . The pea and the thimble. . . . Like 'Find the Lady.' . . . Yet perhaps he was hardly the person to whom ex-Mess-Sergeant Palsover would come with three thimbles and a pea, hoping to turn an honest penny.

"Fifteen thousand, Sir, for as much as you could put in your hollow tooth."

"Shouldn't care to do that, Palsover. But assuming one did want to, well what about it?"

"I got it, Sir. I got it."

"What? . . . A hollow tooth?"

"No, Sir. No, Sir. The rayjum. Unlimited supply, Sir. I know where there's a rayjum mine. I know where you could get it like getting coal in sacks. And at fifteen thousand pounds a gram!"

"Well, it wouldn't stay at that price long if you produced it in sacks."

"No, Sir. But even suppose the price fell until it was only a thousandth part of what it was, how would you like to sell rayjum at fifteen pounds a gram? Why, Sir, if you brought the price down to a fifteen-thousandth part of what it is, just work out what a quid per gram would be. And I believe that even coal-owners are pretty rich men, aren't they?"

"Well, I'd change with the Duke of Northumberland —financially speaking," replied General Jason. "Look here, Palsover, we must have a talk about it, as you say. Very interesting. Now, when and where . . .?"

"Well, Sir, no time like the present, if you could spare it. And I know a nice little bar, near here, where we'd be quite to ourselves at this time of the morning, and I could give you a rough outline, if you wouldn't be too proud to . . ."

"Lead on, Palsover. I'm not too proud to make kind enquiries after a line of goods selling at fifteen thousand pounds a gram. Tell me some more about it as we go along."

§ 2

General Jason had a friend who knew quite well a man whose brother was In the City. Up to his neck in the City. A live wire; a company promoter; a man who had tremendous financial interests and dealings, the interests being his own, the dealings being with other people's money. And the friend, being a fellow-member of one of the General's Clubs, was delighted to give him a letter of introduction to the gentleman who was up to his neck in the City. A little telephoning led to an arrangement whereby General Jason should meet the financier at his office at eleven o'clock on a certain morning.

The office proved to be luxuriously comfortable, its occupant charmingly agreeable—at any rate, to such people as General Sir Reginald Jason who came to him with Sound Propositions.

" Radium ? " he said, after the pleasant preliminaries, as he leant back in the well-sprung deeply-padded swivelling arm-chair behind his vast and magnificently-appointed desk. " I suppose the man who could corner radium would be just about ten times as rich as the ten richest men who ever lived—all put together. But you'd want a United Multi-Millionaires' Trust Company to start cornering radium."

" Suppose one discovered a new and enormous source of supply—and got control of it ? " asked General Jason.

" Nearly as good," replied Mr. Scott-Marx, eyeing his visitor. What an extraordinarily handsome and distinguished-looking chap. What a figure-head Chairman for a Company. Nice useful-sounding name for a prospectus too.

" Very nearly as good," he continued. " I don't know much about radium, except that there are only seventy-five grammes of it in Britain, and that it is, I should say, by far the most valuable thing in the world. But I am under the impression that you don't dig it up quite in the same way·that you do diamonds. I believe there is a process. . . . But I can go into that. I rather fancy you've got to have a uranium mine or quarry or what not, and then set up some sort of chemical smelting-works and treat your uranium as ore."

" Like smelting gold, for example," said General Jason, who knew much less about radium than did even Mr. Scott-Marx.

" Yes. Perfectly simple matter. They are getting

various chemicals out of the waters of the Dead Sea at the present moment, for example. Well, this would be just as easy to do, and about exactly one million times as profitable. Where is this uranium deposit— if that's what it is ? "

" Well . . . that I'm not at liberty to say, at the moment," replied the General.

" Quite so, quite so," agreed Mr. Scott-Marx, tapping his blotter with his pencil. He had heard very similar words before. They were almost routine with regard to this sort of thing.

" Well, now," continued General Jason, " suppose you found out all about the process and went into figures, I expect you could put up a proposition that would, well . . . that, while being attractive to yourself, would be—what shall we say, entirely fair to myself and my—er—principal."

" You can take my word for that, General," smiled Mr. Scott-Marx.

By Gad, he could ! Supposing this chap really could deliver the goods. Suppose he, or rather his principal, some mining-engineer presumably, *had* discovered a real radium-bearing deposit. Made one's mouth water to think of it, in these hard times. He'd go into this to the uttermost farthing, but in point of fact he didn't believe that a very big capital would be required.

He flattered himself that he'd got a pretty cool brain. *But !* By the Seal of Solomon ; by all Golconda ; by the gold of Ophir and El Dorado—*and* a hatful of Koh-i-Noors ! . . .

It didn't bear thinking about. Not in cold blood. Nobody could think of such a thing coolly. He had got to behave as though he could, nevertheless.

And as Mr. Scott-Marx smiled, the General smiled in apparent sympathy. In point of fact, what rather tickled his fancy was the idea of ex-Mess-Sergeant Palsover as General Sir Reginald Jason's "principal."

"Of course I appreciate that, at this stage, you don't want to blurt out details, General, such as where this deposit is, but it would facilitate figuring if I knew within a few hundred thousand miles. I don't want you to give anything away at all, but I'd like you to provide me with some idea if you could, roughly, as to what Continent it is in and what part of it, so that one could do a little costing, so to speak. The amount of capital required would be tremendously influenced, of course, by such questions as supply of local labour, transport ; building, and other, materials ; probable attitude of the Government of the country ; accessibility ; proximity to ports and rail-roads, and all that sort of thing."

"Yes," replied General Jason non-committally, "yes. All those are important factors."

"Might I ask whether you yourself know exactly where it is ? "

"Well, I couldn't stick a pin in it, on a very large-scale map of the World, but I know within a little. I know the—er—jumping-off place for it, for example. My principal, at the present stage, prefers to be the only living person who knows the exact spot."

"Quite so, quite so. Naturally," agreed Mr. Scott-Marx. "Quite. Quite," he murmured, thoughtfully tapping his desk. "Oh, quite. Now, look here, Sir. You've come and put this proposition up to me. . . ."

"In theory," observed General Jason. "To ask your advice on a more or less supposititious case ; but with a sort of a kind of a proviso that if the thing became at all concrete, we'd consider taking you into

our confidence—very strictest confidence, of course—
on the subject of how to set to work ; how to go about
floating a Company to develop this property, this
deposit; and of how far you'd care to go into the matter
with us yourself . . . financially and—so on.

"But meanwhile," he added, "secrecy is of the
essence of the, at present, non-existent, contract.
Absolute secrecy. A gentlemen's agreement to do
something or nothing. And if nothing—to *say*
nothing."

"Quite ! Quite ! Quite ! " agreed Mr. Scott-Marx,
slowly nodding his head. "What you've told me . . .
not that it is much "—he laughed a little wryly—
"doesn't go outside this office, except in my head.
At the same time, we want to go a step further. I'm
taking it for granted that you know what you are
talking about, and are not wasting my time and your
own ; and I suggest two things.

"First of all, I find out all I can—and that will be
pretty well everything—about radium. How, when
and where you get it ; what the process is, and what
are the factors in production that make it cost—what
did you say—fifteen thousand pounds a gram ? And
there again there are two things to bear in mind : first,
that even if we can produce it no more cheaply than
the few other concerns that market it, there should
still be colossal profits ; secondly, that we must know
what sort of a proposition it is, from the point of view
of estimated productivity and costs of mining, production, and marketing and so forth. Does it go an
ounce to the ton of ore, or a hundredweight ? That
sort of thing.

"And the other thing is—what you yourself can
do. Well, now, the moment you send somebody to
look into the matter on the spot—there's somebody

else right into the very heart of the secret, isn't there ? "

" I'm going myself," said General Jason.

" Splendid ! *That's* what I was hoping. Then we've got those two steps to take. Mine short and yours long. I learn all I can about radium production and marketing. I work out, as near as is possible in the circumstances, the general figures, going on probables and averages as to every class of costs. You carry on with the practical part, visit the actual spot, and bring back all the details on which the right sort of expert, mining-engineering-actuary or what not, could work. You could tell him absolutely everything except the place. As I said before ; distance from railways and ports, conditions of local labour-market, if any ; attitude of Government or competent authority, if any.

" And then I could get to work. With your name and guarantee, there will be no difficulty about floating a Company. . . . Without giving away the essential secret—not that I could do that if I wanted to—I could get hold of Aaronson and let him know how much we wanted, and he and his bunch would find the money and come in with us. No need to go to the public at all, I should think."

" Won't do to talk about it too much," demurred the General.

Mr. Scott-Marx laughed.

" My dear Sir ! Talk about it ! No. I'm not a fool. Deaf, dumb, blind and silly I may be, perhaps, but *dumb* I am certainly. I say nothing, ' and the rest is silence.' But I'll find out everything at the market-end of the business, while you study the production part on the spot. . . . How long do you suppose you'll be away ? "

" Don't know, I'm sure. Take me about a fortnight to three weeks to get to the jumping-off point. Give me three months at the place itself. Back in six months, say."

" Splendid. Lunching anywhere this morning ? "

" Er—no."

" Come with me, and we'll talk over details afterwards."

" Thanks very much. But before we go a step further, I want to make it clear once again, at the risk of being tedious, that my principal must be absolutely on velvet. Up to now it is a one-man show, and he is the one man. He has got it in his pocket and all he needs is capital for its development."

" Quite ! Quite ! " agreed Mr. Scott-Marx once again. " Not but what there's a little more to it than that. ' Development ' covers a lot. There's raising the capital ; expert knowledge for production ; expert knowledge for marketing. Your principal's concession isn't worth twopence to him until all that is found. He has got a cast-iron concession, by the way, I suppose ? "

" There again I can't tell you at the moment, but . . ."

" Quite ! Quite ! Quite ! " agreed once again Mr. Scott-Marx, who had heard something like this also, many a time and oft. " What's his idea, roughly ? "

" Well, he talked about halves."

Mr. Scott-Marx smiled.

" What sort of a chap is he ? Any brains or experience ? Prospector ? Expert ? Mining engineer ? Could we buy him right out and out-right ? "

" I don't know. I don't think so. We must go into that. As I say, he talked about halves. I have guaranteed nothing at all except that he will not be swindled, and that I shall put his interests first—and protect them absolutely.''

And again Mr. Scott-Marx fired off a gentle burst of '' Quites ! ''

Very interesting indeed. *Very.* This innocent would require both gentle and careful handling. . . . *Interesting ?* Oh, God of Golden Opportunities and Great Crimson Clean-ups ! . . .

A gentlemen's agreement !

A radium-producing concession !

And a retired General straying with it into the City. Radium at fifteen thousand pounds a gram.

Be still, fond heart. . . .

Oh, *boy* ! . . .

II

ONE evening, General Jason casually broke to Lady Jason the news that he was going away for six months or so. Lady Jason bore the blow with exemplary fortitude.

" Going alone, Reginald ? " she asked, knowing quite well that, technically speaking, he was going " alone."

" Well, yes. Except for the man with whom I am going, and perhaps a score or two of porters and such."

" And who's the man ? "

" I don't think you've met him. A very tall thin Scot with sandy moustache, freckled face, piercing blue eyes . . ."

" And piercing pink eyelashes, no doubt," interrupted Lady Jason who knew when her lord was romancing.

" Haven't noticed them. He speaks with a very broad Glasgow Highland accent and answers to the name of McClochity Angus Maclan," and the unsmiling General almost smiled wintrily as he compared Mr. Palsover with this inaccurate description.

Lady Jason was never inquisitive and rarely curious, but always pleasantly interested.

" Porters," she mused. " Waterloo Station kind —or for African safari ? "

" Oh, both, my dear. Both, if I should ever get as far as Africa. I wonder what they'd call them in

Tierra del Fuego. Doubtless porters by any other name would smell as sweet."

" Where is Tierra del Fuego ? "

" Don't say you are as ignorant as all that, Tony. Have you never heard of Sinkiangkuankylung ? "

" No, Reginald."

" Well, it's the capital of that parish."

" And is it to be a voyage or a journey ? I mean, expedition or exploration ? "

" Yes, I think so, Tony," replied the General gravely.

" And the object ? Exploration ? Scientific ? Discovery ? Pleasure ? "

" Yes, like that. Largely. Have you ever heard of that queer animal that . . ."

" Yes, Reginald. Are you going to get one ? Will it be house-trained, or live in the park ? "

" The Zoo, I expect."

With apparent irrelevance Lady Jason began to sing quietly to herself. Had the General listened—and considered the foolish words of her song—he would not have been interested.

> " *Gaily bedight a gallant knight*
> *In sunshine and in shadow*
> *Journeyed along singing a song*
> *In search of Eldor-a-do*
> *Over the Mountains of the Moon*
> *Down the Valley of the Sha-a-a-dow. . . .* "

She stopped abruptly and shivered slightly. The evening was getting colder.

" The Valley of the Shadow . . ."

No, on the whole it could not be said that General Jason was communicative on the subject of where he was going and for what purpose he was going there.

There was not, in the whole country, a single person

who knew his destination, and only two who knew his purpose. He himself did not know his final destination, nor, for the matter of that, did Mr. Palsover.

This did not trouble General Jason in the least, and he counted it to the worthy fellow for righteousness, that he either could not or would not tell him more than that they changed for their terminus at Santa Cruz Junction, so to speak.

He might, of course, have hinted to Lady Jason that he had the highest hopes of making a truly enormous sum of money by this expedition, but for two reasons he judged it better not.

In the first place, it was *just* possible (so far along the primrose path of romantic hope had Mr. Palsover led him) that the expedition might fail to discover the source of fabulous wealth ; and in the second, it was just possible again that Antoinette might talk. Not likely but possible

For is it not well known that women are not only weaker vessels but leaky vessels ; and that they have, practically speaking, nothing else to do but talk ?

Nor, as General Jason was well aware, can they keep anything for long—their heads, their secrets, or their . . . No, no. Mustn't think like that about Antoinette. But still, what she didn't know she couldn't tell.

And Lady Jason was quite content.

Poor Reginald, within a year after retirement, had been first, worried to death ; secondly, chagrined and regretful to the point of desperation ; and thirdly, bored to tears.

And now he was perfectly happy again.

He had come down from Town one day, positively radiant—for him, that is to say. He didn't whistle or sing in his bath or give any such wild and unseemly demonstrations of light-heartedness as that, but he almost smiled once a day, and the austere and handsome countenance was not masked in inspissate gloom.

Yes, he was happy. She could tell. And she was very glad. Poor Reginald. It must be terrible to be so austere, so rigid, so statuesquely proper and correct. He was a dear, if he'd only let himself be one ; and one of the finest men who ever lived. She was quite unworthy of him. How she did wish he'd be unworthy of her, now and again, just for a change. So much more human. . . .

And one night, after a particularly busy day at his desk and at superintending his packing, he told her that he was going up to Town on the morrow and sailing the next day.

" Letters, Reginald ? "

" Bank."

" Positively no fixed abode ? "

" And no visible means of support, by the time I get there."

" Return ticket, of course."

" Oh, yes. Kept line of retreat open."

" And I'm to expect you in six months' time."

" Roughly."

" Drop in to tea, or shall I keep dinner back, or . . . ? "

" I'll send you a wire."

" And if anybody should make kind enquiries as to where you've gone ? "

" Patagonia. Between Polonia and Begonia."

" And Moronia," murmured Lady Jason. " It's beyond Ruritania, isn't it ? "

" That's the place, Tony. You've pinned me down,"

admitted General Jason. And Antoinette knew how riotously joyful he was feeling.

And herself? Well . . . six months. Of this. And that. She'd write to Henry Carthew and make him fix up something. She would like a glimpse of the Season . . . and the sea, somewhere in the direction of Cowes . . . and she'd like to walk across some moors again . . . and lie in a deck-chair on a yacht off a Scottish island. And generally come up to the surface to breathe for a while.

Two or three months out of the six, anyhow. And Henry to be useful—as only Henry could—and without thought of reward.

" Well, good-bye, my dear," said General Jason, the next morning, with a kindly kiss and a cordial handshake. " Take care of yourself."

" I'm going to, Reginald."

" Have a good time."

" I'm going to. I'm going to have a marvellous time. Pity Henry Carthew's not in England. I'll send him a cable and ask him to take a spot of privilege-leave."

" Splendid. My love to the old boy. I was going to write to him. Good-bye. I shall be seeing you again in about six months' time. Good hunting. . . . G'-bye. . . ."

III

IT is indicative of the fundamental adventurousness and romanticism of his sternly repressed nature, of the terrific boredom to which inactivity had reduced him, and of Mr. Palsover's amazing persuasiveness, that so essentially methodical, rational and disciplined a man as General Sir Reginald Jason should ever have entered the Fenchurch Street Offices of the British Southern and General Royal Mail Company and purchased, through them, a first-class and a second-class ticket that would enable him and Mr. Palsover to travel by one of their ships to Belamu, whence by changing to an Anglo-Portuguese Steam Navigation and Trading Company's boat, they could proceed to Santa Cruz de Loango.

But this he did, for Mr. Palsover had completely convinced him. General Jason knew when a man was speaking the truth, and he knew as well as he knew his own name, and better than he knew his own wife, that his former Mess-Sergeant whom he had known for twenty years, was speaking the truth, the whole truth and nothing but the truth, when he told him the story of the dying Portuguese and the radium concession. It was too like a " whole-cloth " tale ; too like a cheap film story ; too like the confidence man's trick ; too like the gold-brick swindle and the Spanish-prisoner ramp, to be anything but truth.

No man, especially Mess-Sergeant Palsover, could go

to General Jason with a yarn like that, unless it were true.

Some clever people would have laughed it to scorn, scouted it utterly, and have bidden Mr. Palsover to go while the going was good. But General Jason was a little cleverer than that. Palsover was the wrong man to invent such a tale, and General Jason was the wrong man to whom to take it. You couldn't have both men in it. Not two such men.

Given a Palsover who could think up such a *banao*,[1] he'd look for a mug, as he would call him, a flat, a fool, a Jubilee Juggins.

Given a General Jason who could accept such a yarn, the man who came to him with it would have to be something very different from a fat old ex-Mess-Sergeant of his own former Regiment. It would take something more like a plausible City shark, to come to General Jason with any hope of getting away with a thing like that.

That the real Mess-Sergeant Palsover could come and tell it to the real General Jason and be at once believed, showed what sort of story it was—one that bore the stamp of truth and carried the conviction of its own genuineness.

There were moments of course, such as those around four o'clock in the morning, when General Jason, with a sinking feeling in the pit of his stomach, asked himself if it were really possible that he was putting every spare penny that he could raise, into a wild-goose chase whereon he was led by the nose to an unknown destination by a silly old fool who had got hold of a Boys' Story-paper yarn about an inexhaustible mine of immeasurable wealth. A wonder it wasn't a tale of

[1] *Plot, swindle, frame-up (Hindustani).*

buried treasure, a story of hidden gold, or some such moonshine as that.

§ 2

As, on the voyage to Belamu, he sat in his deck-chair, going over the story again and again, General Jason's faith grew, his faith in Sergeant Palsover, in Mr. Pereira, who had so opportunely died, and in the account of the radio-active quick-sand and the uranium deposit—the uranium mines, indeed, as he began to think of them.

With a hint of the *credo quia incredibile* attitude of mind, he again and again worked through to the conclusion that the tale was too fantastic to be untrue, and Palsover too fantastic a tale-bearer to bring anything but the truth. . . .

The only weak spot in the story was provided by the unknown Arab. There imagination boggled, and cold practical common sense intervened. But whenever Realism conquered Romanticism and said,

' You are behaving like a boy. You are being silly, over-suggestible and gullible,' Hope came to the rescue and told a flattering tale. Why shouldn't there be a pearl-merchant, or any other kind of merchant, who called at Santa Cruz de Loango twice a year ? Nothing more probable, and few jobs more profitable in that line of business—for the man who could get it. The twice-a-year arrangement was probably decided by the two monsoons. They blew every six months almost to the day, first north-east and then south-west. The Arab would go up with one and down with the other. And why shouldn't he be met at this Santa Cruz place, on each journey ? Probably he had appointments with several different people at this last port that he touched on the mainland.

143

And not only did Hope come to the assistance of Romance and romantic imagination, but the somewhat comforting knowledge of the fact that this was a thing that was going to be put to the test. When they reached this Santa Cruz place, Palsover would, according to his story, take him straight to a Goanese feller who kept a ramshackle native hotel, at which this Arab was in the habit of calling every voyage to enquire whether there were any letters, messages, or a passenger for him. General Jason did not really doubt this part of the Palsover story any more than he doubted any other part—particularly as it was open to proof and shortly would be proved.

Well, if this Goanese told him that he expected the Arab pearl-merchant but that he had not yet arrived, it was pretty certain that he would come toward the end of the north-east monsoon. Palsover had worked out the feller's dates pretty carefully, from the information the Goanese had given him.

He'd only have to sit down and wait for him, sit down in that same hotel, and the Arab would roll up. Very interesting and very romantic, to think that he, General Sir Reginald Jason, recently of Simla, London and Hardingley Park, should be bearing down upon a tiny obscure spot on the map of the Southern Hemisphere, a place so insignificant and small as almost to answer to the definition of a point—that which has neither parts nor magnitude but only position—and that an Arab pearl-merchant from Basra, Abadan, Mohammera, Bahrein and Muscat would, in his *dhow* with its single sail and crew of three or four men, be also bearing down upon the same spot to meet him, though unconscious of that fact. . . .

Some part of each day General Jason spent in the

company of Mr. Palsover, talking over the endless subjects of interest connected with the expedition.

" What are we going to do if this Arab fellow doesn't turn up ? " he said one evening, as they walked the deck together after dinner.

" He'll turn up all right, Sir, sooner or later," Mr. Palsover reassured him. " He has never failed yet, according to the landlord of the *Caser Reel*. . . . Oh, yerss, he knows him all right. Knows him well. One of his regulars, you might say."

" And you've got the letter of introduction to him all safe ? "

" Ar ! That's right, Sir ; and you can lay to that. I'll hand that over to you as soon as we gets to Santa Cruz. I keeps it locked up in my trunk for fear of losing it."

" That's right. Trust you to keep it safe, Palsover. We should be in a bit of a fix if you hadn't got it."

" Ar ! That's right, Sir. Fair up a gum-tree. But don't you worry about that. And when I hand it to you, Sir, I'm going to ask you to take charge altogether —and carry on. Work it off on the Arab yourself, I mean. Just take charge and go ahead."

" Very trusting of you, Palsover. I appreciate it."

Mr. Palsover smiled, partly with pleasure at the General's kind words, and partly at the thought that he would thus stand from under.

Mr. Palsover had for many long years been an expert in the art of standing from under, and an unerring judge of the right moment at which to come in out of the rain.

Whatever danger there might attach to this St. Tommy business, began at the moment the Senior's letter was handed over to the Arab, and the bearer of

it set foot on the Arab's *dhow*.   The Arab had got him
then, and got him for keeps, good and proper.   Got
him right where he wanted him, if so be he did want
him.   And if he didn't, but was quite prepared to
take him to this St. Tommy place, the next danger-
point, if any, would be that at which the bearer of
the letter to this bloke Norhona, handed it over, and
Norhona read it.

For Norhona had got him then, good and proper,
and just where he wanted him, and no going back
about it.   Not if what the old Senior had said was true
—that there was no way of getting from Santa Cruz
into St. Tommy and out again except by the Arab's
dhow.

Of course, there might be no danger at all, but that
was not Mr. Palsover's impression.   The old Senior
had talked too much about ' *Them* ' and what They'd
do to yer if They felt like it.   And if all the truth was
known, the Senior himself was in a bit of a perishing
blue funk of doing anything that They did not like.
Not only this Norhona fellow—who seemed to be the
Big Noise there, or one of them—but this Regent or
whatever she was, Donah What's-her-name, and the
old Dook who had the same name as the greengrocer
in the very street in which Mr. Palsover had been
born, and that was a queer come-uppance if you like.
Braganza.   He'd been a very nice old Jew and kept
a greengrocer's shop.

And then this Council that the Senior used to babble
about, when he was off his rocker with malaria.   From
the way he had talked, the Senior wouldn't like to take
a running kick at the pants of any one of that lot.
No.   Not he ; not at any price.   Talked about them
like a rookie might talk about the Regimental Sergeant-Major ; or like Mr. Palsover himself might talk

about a set of Officers sitting on him in Court Martial, yes, or about the Commander-in-Chief and the whole Army Council put together.

No doubt about it, the old Senior had certainly got the wind up when he thought about that lot. And he somehow gave you the impression that anybody who got into St. Tommy uninvited would get on about as fast and far as a small fly in a big spider's web, and come to about the same sort of an end.

Well, far from wishing the General any harm, he wished him all the good luck in the world, but—better him than Mr. Palsover, wandering about St. Tommy. He was a British General and They had ought to have a proper respect for such. He'd know some silly foreign lingo in which they'd all be able to talk together, friendly and comfortable, and—well, he'd know the right knives and forks ; know better what to do. Probably one look and two words out of him would blast 'em out of his way.

Anyhow, Generals first, Sergeants afterwards. A long way afterwards—if at all. No. He'd keep out of St. Tommy.

" Thank you, Sir," he said. " I'm quite sure it will be best for all concerned if, as soon as we get to Santa Cruz, I hand over, stand aside, and leave the rest to you. Everything."

" Well, probably you are wise, Palsover. You can trust me to do my best and to look after your interests," replied the General.

" I can, Sir. I do. From the day we land at Santa Cruz, I'm an on-looker. I won't even come to the place, or, at any rate, I won't go ashore there. I'll just keep out of it, for fear I said or did the wrong thing. Queered your pitch like, Sir, and was a hindrance and a drag on you."

147

This rather touched General Jason, although he gave no sign of the fact.

" Then I'll simply give the Arabic letter to this pearl-merchant, if and when we meet him, and tell him I want him to give me passage to—Where-is-it. By the way, you've never yet told me the name of the place, Palsover."

" No, Sir. No, Sir. We can't be too careful ; and I thought if I didn't so much as whisper it, not even to you, Sir, until we had found this Arab, there couldn't be no possible chance of its leaking out."

" Quite a sound idea. But you don't suppose I should tell anybody, do you ? "

" No, Sir. No, Sir. Not for one moment. But as my old mother used to say, when more than one has got a secret, it isn't a secret any longer. Of course, you wouldn't tell anybody, Sir ; nobody at all, neither that shark—I mean that finnanceer gentleman—in London, nor anybody on the ship here. I didn't even think it would slip out in conversation when some gentleman said to you in the bar,
' *And how far are you going, General ?* ' or something like that. I didn't think such a thing, for one moment ; but I did think that if I just kept it to myself, the same couldn't happen to you as happened to that poor old Senior Pereira what died."

" How do you mean ? "

" Why, he told me in his sleep, Sir ! Well, not to say sleep. Delirium trimmins. Fever. Kept on babbling nonsense—and some damn good sound sense among it, Sir, though he didn't know what he was saying."

" Delirious ? Fever ? "

" Ar ! And you can lay to that, Sir. Delirious as you like. And through it he talked by the hower ;

and told me all about this Where-is-it place, and about the you-know-what mines and concessions, and how he had got to meet this Arab who would take him from Santa Cruz to the place. . . . And—well—gave the whole show away."

" Well, no doubt you are right, Palsover. Don't go and do it yourself, though."

" Do what, Sir ? "

" Get delirious and—talk."

" Me, Sir ? It's many a long year since I had malaria in India ; and I keeps my cabin door locked and bolted, and my coat hanging over the key-hole. No, Sir, anybody as wants to listen to me doin' deliriums has got to come down over the side on a rope and shove his head in the port-hole.

" And then he'd hear something to his disadvantage, Sir," added Mr. Palsover, and his benevolent face looked, for the moment, quite unkind.

IV

A ND in the fullness of time and exactly up to
that time, the British Southern and General Mail
Company's liner *Gibraltar* reached Belamu, and along
with one or two other unfortunates, General Jason and
Mr. Palsover exchanged its innumerable and admirable
amenities for the comparatively squalid discomfort of
the *St. José de Coimbra* of the Anglo-Portuguese Steam
Navigation and Trading Company.

Fate in sportive merry mood and in the guise of a
Portuguese gentleman, who probably hailed from Goa,
and performed the functions of Chief Steward, Head
Waiter and Purser of the *St. José de Coimbra*, allotted
to General Jason the cabin corresponding to that
occupied by the late Senhor Pereira on the sister ship
St. Paul de Loanda. This was not a very remarkable
coincidence, in view of the fact that each was the best
cabin on the ship, and that the best was what General
Jason demanded.

It afforded Mr. Palsover considerable private amusement and it tickled his fancy enormously, to knock on
the General's cabin door in the early morning, enter,
and regard him lying in what appeared to be the very
same cabin and on the very same berth that was for-
merly occupied by the late Senhor Pereira.

It seemed somehow to be a good omen.

Not that it would ever for one moment enter his
head to do anything so disrespectful as to sit on the

General's chest and place his hand over his mouth. But—well—there it was. Lying in that berth, the Senior had given him one of the most colossal tips ever given by one man to another. Lying in that very berth now was General Jason, the man who would turn that tip into the gold it promised.

And he absolutely insisted on being allowed to valet the General, to bring him his morning tea, to tidy his cabin and to shave him.

Quite like old times with the dear old Senior, God bless him.

§ 2

In spite of what Mr. Palsover had already told him, the *Casa Real* and its proprietor, Felice Diego, came as something of a shock to General Jason. He had not visualized anything quite so low in the scale of accommodation for man and beast, although he had travelled Home by the overland route from India, and was not unacquainted with *khans* and *caravanserais* that were never intended for the entertainment of Europeans.

However, it was a small matter, and his sojourn in the leading hotel of Santa Cruz might be brief. He earnestly hoped that it would.

Having introduced General Jason as an English Sahib of the highest and noblest class, and demanded for him all of the best that the *Casa Real* could supply in the way of dirty rice, skinny chickens, fried bananas, goats' milk and Best Bombay Spirits, and seen the General installed in not only the room but the very bed in which Senhor Pereira had died, he sought a private interview with the proprietor.

" Well, Boy, so the Police haven't got you yet, then ? "

" Police, Senhor Schloots ? Why Police getting me ? "

" Why not ? Over the murder of poor old Senior Pereira, I mean."

" *Sah !* Sh-h-h-h. Master must not talk like that ! Murder ! . . . Senhor Pereira died in his bed. Willingly. Freely."

" And you never heard any more from the Police at all ? "

" Not officially, Sah. No. When there was Police question about something of Senhor Pereira's at Customs House, I say he go off one night in *dhow* very sudden, very quiet, paying his bill and saying he not coming back for a long time."

" And then you paid the policeman's bill, eh ? And *he* didn't come back for a long time, eh ? "

Mr. Felice Diego put his head on one side, waggled his hands deprecatingly and smiled copiously.

" So you was lucky, eh ? Well out of a nasty mess. Now when that trouble crops up again . . ."

" Sah ? "

" Crops up. Turns up. Comes back. Trouble. When there's trouble for you again about Senior Pereira, I can help you. I can get you out of it. *Listen !* I *saw* him last month. Place called Belamu. See ? "

Mr. Felice Diego saw, thanked Mr. Schloots or Schultz (*né* Palsover) effusively, and poured him a drink of the Best Bombay Brandy, Volcano Brand. Guaranteed Pure. Manufactured by Messrs. Yusufali Alibhoy Rahimtoola.

" Yerss, I saw him all right. Had a long talk with him. And I'll tell the Police so, if they give you any more *dik.* . . . And now *I* want a talk with *you.* Look here. *Listen.* And get it straight, if you want to flourish like the green bay-rum tree."

" Sah ? "

" The Hadji hasn't been yet, has he ? "

" Not since last time, Sah."

" Strike me pink ! Not since the last time, eh ? You don't say ! Fancy that ! . . . You mean it's about six months since he come ? "

" Yes, Sah. I am expecting."

" You look like it. What you want is exercise. Well, when he does come, you be careful what you say. About Senior Pereira, I mean, and the General upstairs. . . . How long after the old Senior—er—left, did the Hadji come ? "

" Oh, some time, Sah. Some days. Some week. Some month."

" And he asked for the Senior, did he ? "

" Yes, Sah. He asked if Senhor come yet."

" And what did you say ? "

" I spoke truth, Sah. I say he gone."

" What did the Hadji say to that ? "

" Nutting, Sah. He say ' *So ?* ', and wait here for a few days to see if he come. Then he give me note for Senhor Pereira. And then he go."

" Well, now he'll come. . . . And you got to be careful—if you want me to look after you. Directly he comes, you let me know, if I haven't seen him first. And you tell him there's a gent here that's got a letter for him, *a letter that was given to the gent by Senior Pereira*. Savvy ? *Sumja*[1] ? "

" I understand, Sah."

" Right ! That's number one Great Thought for the Day. There's a gent here wants to see the Hadji *because he's got a letter for him from Senior Pereira*. . . . Now another Great Thought, if you can hold more than one at a time. Can you ? "

[1] Understand ?

153

Mr. Diego assured Mr. Schloots that he could.

" Well, then, here it is. *I never had any truck at all with Senior Pereira.*"

" Truck, Sah ? "

" Sure. You seen a railway-truck, haven't you ? Well, it's nothing to do with that. Listen. *I never knew Senior Pereira ; never spoke to him ; never came here with him ; never set eyes on him.* Never. . . . See ? "

" Yes, Sah."

" It was the Inglez gent upstairs. The General. The Burra Sahib. Got it ? "

" Yes, Sah."

" I don't suppose the Hadji will want any particular song-and-dance about it, out of you, but if he asks any questions, that's how it goes. Nothing to do with me, and I never been here before. But the gent upstairs is the very one as came here with Senior Pereira. And here he is, back again. Perhaps he's come on purpose to meet the Senior here, eh ? "

Mr. Diego smiled and waggled hands in a gesture that signified appreciation, amusement and doubt. Most expressive hands.

" Oh, and another thing. Get this. Don't you call me Schultz any more. It's a sort of a rank, a title, if you know what that is, Boy ; and now the General's here, *he*'s the Schultz. See ? And don't you forget it."

" Yes, Sah. You are not the Schloots Sahib any more, but the General Inglez is the Schloots Sahib."

" That's right. Now that's the three things, and I'll tell you them all over again to-morrow morning, because if you make a mistake over one of them, it might be awkward. For *you*, Boy. See ? Very awkward, it might be."

154

And Mr. Palsover ran the tip of his forefinger round his neck, jerked it upward and emitted a curious sound which might be expressed as *Tchkk !* It seemed to Mr. Diego to come from under his own right ear, where the knot of the rope would be.

" Well, now everything's straightforward, cut and dried, and clear as mud. If the Police or anybody bothers you about him, I can testify that Senior Pereira is alive and kicking ; and if the Arab questions you, you can testify that I have never been here before, but that *General Schultz came here six months ago with Senior Pereira.* Hang on to that, Son, and you won't have to hang on to nothing else. Not on to the end of a rope, anyway."

And when valeting the General next morning, Mr. Palsover explained that he was improving the shining hour by making straight the General's path, making things as easy as possible, and preparing the way for his reception by the Hadji without any sort of suspicion or doubt arising in that sea-farer's mind.

But one had to be, well—diplomatic. One had to be careful in the matter of giving information. One had not only to withhold as much as possible, but one had to, well—colour—the rest.

For example, it would be of no service to their undertaking if it were known to the Hadji that Mr. Palsover had visited Santa Cruz before. Still less that he had been in the place in the actual company of Senhor Pereira.

What the Arab would naturally suppose, on reading Mr. Pereira's letter, would be that the latter had given it direct to General Jason in person. Nor would there be any point in disabusing him of this very natural supposition. It was, as Mr. Palsover unnecessarily

155

pointed out, a matter of strategy and tattics. The great thing was to get to the Where-is-it place ; and Mr. Pereira's letter was the ticket that would authorize and direct the Arab to take its holder there.

"Quite so, quite so. I understand," said the General. "I'm not really an Arabic scholar, and unless this Hadji speaks English, which is extremely improbable, we shan't make speeches to each other, nor have heart-to-heart talks. I'll give him the letter, and if he is under the impression that this Pereira gave it to me direct, I shan't disillusion him."

"And the same with the other letter, Sir, if I might be so bold as to make the suggestion and give advice. When you get to the Where-is-it place, you produce Senior Pereira's letter of introduction ; and when they take it for granted that Senior Pereira gave it to you, there's no need to undeceive them."

"Quite so, quite so," agreed the General. "If I started trying to make explanations, they might get the idea that I was an impostor, mightn't they ? Bad for Business ! " The General smiled bleakly.

"Particularly if I were talking a language which they didn't understand," he added.

"Yes, Sir. And Them answering in a language which *you* didn't. Plenty of room for misunderstanding," agreed Mr. Palsover.

"I'll just present it to this—Dr. Norhona, did you say ? "

"Yes, Sir. If you just hand it to him, it will speak for itself, as the saying is. That's what Senior Pereira said to me.

' *My dear old friend,*' he says, ' *these letters speak for themselves. Give this one to the Hadji and he'll take you straight to Where-is-it. When you get there, show this other one to anybody who questions you, and*

156

and it over to Dr. Norhona, to whom it is addressed. It will prove that you come direct from me, and that he has to do everything he can for you. . . . And, by Gum, he will too. Just about everything.' "

General Jason was yet further interested, enheartened and intrigued.

V

RIGHTLY or wrongly, General Jason decided that there could not be, on the whole surface of the earth, a more miserable abiding-place for one who waited from hour to hour, from day to day, and from week to week, than Santa Cruz de Loango.

Although accustomed to hard living in tent, bivouac and trench, he found this accommodation the most distasteful he had ever known ; and increasingly he desired conditions under which he could, as he expressed it, either really rough it or not rough it at all. This was not rough, but disgusting. It was not hard, but it was definitely beastly.

Not only was there something curiously repulsive about the frowsy bed in which he slept so badly, but the bedroom itself had an unpleasant and disturbing atmosphere.

One of the least fanciful, sensitive or psychic of mankind, the General was nevertheless unable to ignore this minatory and charnel-house aura and suggestion. Although he well knew the room to be empty, and himself to be a fool if he imagined otherwise, he was aware, notwithstanding, of a curious sense of company —invisible and undesirable. Without being in the least degree perturbed or alarmed, he found himself constantly turning round, under the impression that there was someone behind him ; often someone or something that moved just on the edge of his vision.

This was very annoying, and it added more than a little to the foul frowsiness of the room, its air of damp decay and dissolution ; it made him wish that there were some spot of clean dry earth on which, beneath a decent tree, he could spread his ground-sheet and valise and sleep in the open air. But the compound of the hotel consisted of sand and filthy dust ; in front of it ran a road of similar consistency ; behind it lay a mangrove swamp that imperceptibly merged into an open lagoon which appeared to consist neither of land nor water, but of a black and oily-looking silt that was not quite liquid nor nearly solid. On the far side of this lagoon a sluggish river made its secret way into the sea.

The heat was terrific by day and scarcely less by night ; the exhalations from the swamp and lagoon making the atmosphere like that of a hot-house or a Turkish bath. The appearance of the inhabitants of the abominable place bore plain testimony to its extreme unhealthiness. Without exception they crawled feebly and listlessly about, and bore the stigmata of sufferers from malignant fever.

Once again the General was moved to wonder why people live where they live. In many parts of the world this question had presented itself to his mind. Passing through a remote and ugly village of England, Scotland or Wales, he had speculated on the probable reason why any particular person should live in that particular place. Similarly in various corners of Europe and in out-of-the-way places in India and elsewhere. When a man inherited land, a house, a business or what-not, the question was answered ; but as such people obviously formed but a very small minority of the inhabitants of any given place, it remained a problem.

And of all places on this earth, why should people select Santa Cruz de Loango as their residence or, having been born there, why should they remain ?

Inertia probably, he decided, and if inertia were excusable anywhere, it was in this place where everything was inert, the very air stagnant, the water thick and poisonous, the earth sad and unfertile.

And why to this skeleton—or rather decayng corpise —of a port should people come, people like this man Pereira and this Arab ? Well, for that matter, why should he, General Sir Reginald Jason, and ex-Mess-Sergeant Palsover have come ?

On business.

The business of meeting the Arab.

And that was the business on which Mr. Pereira had come—and might it not conceivably be that the place's utter lack of attraction was the attraction that had brought such people there ?

Well, he had put his hand to this queer affair. He had come all this way from Home. Here he was in Santa Cruz de Loango. And here he would stay, at any rate until the monsoon broke ; and if the Arab did not arrive before the south-west monsoon was unmistakably blowing, he would have to make up his mind whether he would try again some six months hence, or whether he would cut his losses, refrain from telling Palsover what he thought of him and his wild-goose chase, and go back.

After all, no one need know how much of a fool he had made of himself. He could inform Scott-Marx that he was going no further in the matter, and tell Antoinette that he had enjoyed his expedition very much and had some excellent sport. Deep-sea big-game fishing—for shrimps.

He must write to her, by the way ; let her know

that he was still alive. And inasmuch as he himself did not know where he was going from this infernal spot, there would be no harm in mentioning the name of the place. The post-mark would show it, anyway. It would be something to do ; and having done it, he would once more walk down the wide road of dirty sand, through the corrugated-iron-and-sacking Indian bazaar where the inevitable but amazing farthing-profit traders appeared to thrive by the keeping of shops the entire contents of any one of which would be dear at a shilling. One would think that if daily, between sunrise and sunset, each sold all that he had, the weekly profit on the turnover would be less than sixpence. And yet they found their way here from the Malabar Coast of India.

But once again, why, in Heaven's name *here*, of all places in the world ? If they could come here they could go to Jamaica, Mombasa, Trinidad, Colon, Cape Town, Aden, Nassau or Zanzibar. Why come here, to about the most malarious, moribund and horrible place in the world, to sit from morning till night behind a small pile of green mangoes which might be worth about three a penny in times of greatest demand ?

§ 2

General Jason wrote his letter to his wife, described Santa Cruz as his jumping-off place and as a really magnificent spot from which to jump, provided you jumped far enough ; and added that it was in no sense an address, inasmuch as he would have been gone, please God, for a long time before she got this letter, and was not likely to return there. He informed her that it possessed no sort or kind of British Consular Agent and very little else save one or two policemen

161

who were badly in need of safety-pins, a minor Government official who was badly in need of cash, and some ragged Customs sharks badly in need of victims ; and that he hoped she was, like himself, having a splendid time. Love to Henry Carthew when she saw him ; and he'd send her a line again from the next place.

A knock came at the door of the room and Mr. Palsover entered.

" Ah ! " said the General. " I was going to ask you about the postal arrangements, if any, in this charming spot. Does one take one's letters away with one or . . . ? "

" Oh, that'll be all right, Sir. If you'll give them to me, I'll see them properly stamped and posted. There's a boat goes . . . well . . ."

" Every so seldom," suggested the General. " Slow but not sure."

" Yes, Sir. But I'll see them into the right hands," Mr. Palsover asserted briskly.

" Well, I should think they will probably stay in those hands if they are already stamped. However— thank you very much. What did you want to speak to me about ? "

" Why, Sir," replied Mr. Palsover, lowering his voice almost to a whisper, " them letters of introduction. It struck me it might be a good thing if you had the Arabic one with you in your pocket, in case you see the Arab come ashore, or ran into him somewheres between here and the quay. It would look more natural-like if you had them with you, instead of having to come and get them from me."

" Certainly the Arabic one, at any rate," agreed the General. " I don't know whether the other envelope would convey anything to him."

" Just as well to have 'em both, Sir, perhaps. Sort of double proof that it was all right. I expect he'd know what the other was, even if he didn't take your word for it that it was a letter of introduction to the people where he's going."

" You may as well give me both, then."

And Mr. Palsover produced from his pocket, and proceeded to open, a flat package fastened with tape and sealing-wax. From this he produced a sealed envelope of stout paper, and from this again two letters, one of which was addressed in what the General recognized to be Arabic, and the other, in European writing, to

His Excellency Dom Perez de Norhona,
  c/o His Highness Dom Miguel de Guzman de Braganza,

                          Marquess de Estoril.

" And where's the place, Palsover ? " asked the General. " Or are you still going to keep that up your sleeve ? "

" Yes, Sir. Yes, Sir. No offence, I hope—until the Arab comes. Just business, you know, Sir."

" Quite so," agreed the General. " Can't be too careful. Though some people might think you can— and are."

" I hope this Arab will come soon," he added as Mr. Palsover turned to go, with the letter addressed to Lady Jason in his hand.

" Oh, well, Sir, Diego says he's bound to come any day now."

" I suppose ' any day ' is an earlier date than ' some day,' Palsover ? "

" Oo, *yes*, Sir. Much ! " agreed Mr. Palsover confidently as he departed to give quiet thought to Lady

163

Jason's letter, its handwriting, information, idioms, and particularly, its signature.

Also to the question of its posting or other disposal in the event of certain contingencies.

VI

THE General yawned, rose from the rickety table at which he had been writing, took his sun-helmet, and descended to the street of dust and sand.

Well, any day, some day—this year, next year, some time, never. What a queer thing life was, and what funny situations one found oneself in.

One more stroll down to that wretched tidal creek they called the harbour. Beginning to feel as though he had been born in the place. Even the pathetic pot-bellied children ceased to follow him about, and the half-Latin, half-Oriental-looking women to glance shyly through the doorways of their adobe pink-washed huts.

What did the men, other than the alien East Indians, do all day—beyond yawn, spit, scratch and adjourn to one of the numerous corrugated-iron bars to drink coloured wood-alcohol, weird vermouth, synthetic wines, syrups and near-absinthe?

And who might this be?

The General's pulse may have quickened a little, but no look of eagerness disturbed the serene cast of his austere countenance.

By gad! This was a Man.

It was *the* man. A very tall, broad-shouldered, fine-looking fellow in clean cotton robes; and an Arab undoubtedly.

Well, it would be a pleasure to have dealings with a

chap of this type. What a contrast between his open self-reliant face, frank, fearless, handsome, and those of the European, Indian and half-caste Santa Crucians. How a man's profession and way of life stamped him! Here were the eyes of a seaman, eyes accustomed to distance and to danger.

" *Salaam !* " said General Jason as he and the stranger met face to face. " *Salaam, Hadji Sahib.*"

" *Salaam, Sidi,*" replied the Arab, eyeing the General with some surprise and considerable interest. Saluting courteously, he enquired whether the Roumi gentleman spoke Arabic.

" I'm afraid I don't know what you are saying," replied General Jason. " I suppose you don't speak English—or perhaps French ? "

With a flash of white teeth the Arab smiled pleasantly and admitted that he knew some English and as it happened, a few words of French. He added as an afterthought that, as he traded to Bombay, he also knew enough Hindustani to make himself understood.

" Well, we shall get along splendidly then," said the General. " I used to know some Hindustani, and I speak French pretty well. Er—*Hamara nam Jason hai. Main General hoon. Hadji Sahib ka nam kya hai ? Ap kiwaste chithi hamara-pas hai.*[1] "

And from the breast pocket of his tussore silk coat, he produced a couple of letters, one of which he gave to the Hadji.

" *Mera nam Abdulla hai,*[2] " replied the Arab. " *Hadji Abdulla,*" and he read the superscription on the envelope.

" Ah, ha ! *Mera waste béshak,*[3] " he said.

[1] My name is Jason. I am a General. What is your name, Hadji Sahib ? I have a letter for you.
[2] My name is Abdulla.   [3] For me, without doubt.

166

Having studied the envelope for a few moments, the Arab read the letter with obvious interest and considerable surprise.

" *Ce Monsieur . . . le Senhor Pereira. Où est-il ?* " he asked.

" *Je ne sais pas,*" replied the General truthfully. " *Il n'a pas attendu. Il est parti.*"

The Arab seemed puzzled, and after a few more attempts at conversation in Hindustani and French, tried English. This was an improvement, for in this language the General was reasonably fluent and the Arab quite comprehensible.

" You wish then to go to São Thomé ? " said the Hadji Abdulla.

" Do I ? " replied General Jason, and was about to add, " I didn't know it. Never heard of the place," when he realized that this must be the Missing Word, the name that Palsover had so long and wisely concealed.

São Thomé ? . . . And where the devil might that be ?

" Yes," he said quickly. " I've been waiting for you here for this purpose. The letter, I believe, instructs you to take me to São Thomé."

" Without doubt," replied the Arab. " When do you wish to sail ? "

" The sooner the better."

" What is that ? Sooner ? Better ? Go soon ? " " Yes."

" I would wish to wait for Senhor Pereira if he will come."

" He will not come. I am here instead."

" Instead ? In place ? In place of Senhor Pereira ? " " Yes. Could we sail to-morrow ? "

" To-morrow. Perhaps. I must get some things for

167

my crew. Water, food, fruit. I need salt and oil too. And I have business."

" All right, Hadji Sahib. We'll go as soon as you can. I'll be ready to start at any moment. Get everything packed up."

" Packed . . . Up," murmured the Arab. " To-day is *aljuma*. . . ."

" Friday," said the General.

" We sail *alahad*. It is Sunday. I hope to."

" Good ! "

" Where has the Sidi pitched his tent ? "

" Beneath the roof of Felice Diego," smiled the General.

" Ah ! " nodded the Arab. " *Casa Real*. The Royal Palace," and his grave eyes twinkled. " I have business with that man also."

" Well, I'm going back there. Shall we go together ? "

" I am honoured. It is as the Sidi pleases," replied the Arab.

The General felt that, although the conversation had been in dubious Hindustani, French and English, interlarded with Arabic terms such as *ma, sukkar, samak, milh* (which he believed to be water, sugar, fish and salt) he and this admirable and attractive fellow understood each other completely. . . .

As they crossed the compound of the *Casa Real*, the enormous man who was bar-keeper and general factotum, and who was sitting listlessly on the doorstep, caught sight of the Arab, roared in obvious excitement that the Hadji Abdulla had arrived, and advanced salaaming humbly.

Quickly Felice Diego appeared, buttoning a coat over his naked body as usual, and welcomed the

168

Hadji with every sign of respect, a regard apparently not untinged with fear. Possibly he had an uneasy conscience.

From an uncurtained window behind the balustrade of an untrustworthy verandah, Mr. Palsover appeared. As he edged forward, wisely clutching the door-post of that upper chamber, it might almost be said that literally he hung in doubt.

VII

WELL, the Hadji had come at last, and, although to outward eye unchanged, the General felt a new man. It really began to look as though he was justified of his faith, and that what had, at times, appeared to be a wild-goose chase, was really the sober and sensible following of a star, the steady treading of a hazardous path leading to great undertakings and vast wealth.

Particularly was he pleased that this part of Palsover's story had proved to be true; for from the very first it had seemed to him to be the weak spot in it. Or to change the metaphor, the fact or fiction of a wandering Arab who would turn up at some obscure and distant place at some vague and unspecified time and act upon incomprehensible signs, tokens and hieroglyphics, scribbled by a mysterious Portuguese—had been the most difficult part to swallow. Even if one accepted the tale of a radium concession, of vast uranium deposits only waiting to be worked, of a delirious Portuguese, and all the rest of Palsover's story, as feasible, reasonable and probably true, one had boggled at the point where the Arab appeared. One felt that here improbability entered; that one had come to a weak link in the chain of the story.

And now—behold the Arab. Here he was in the flesh, behaving exactly as had been foretold and making every other part of the story seem not merely probable but almost completely proven.

And Palsover, now challenged on the subject, immediately and joyfully admitted that São Thomé was the place.

He, too, seemed enormously cheered by the Arab's arrival, and delighted at his spontaneous reference to São Thomé. Quite evidently there was such a place, and most certainly it must be the place of which Senhor Pereira had talked in delirium, and the existence of which he had admitted when sane and coherent. And who but a fool would now doubt that his reference to the radium—the radium that ought to be produced in vast quantities for the benefit of Suffering Humanity—was an allusion to something real and actual?

Suffering Humanity! Suffering Moses. . . . And what price Suffering Samuel now?

Samuel Palsover the multi-millionaire.

The conversation that morning between General Jason and Mr. Palsover was more than cheerful, and was marked by an optimism that bordered on certainty. With a light-hearted hopefulness that almost suggested gaiety, the General, ably assisted by Mr. Palsover, set about the work of selecting and re-packing the outfit that he proposed to take with him to São Thomé, a task not rendered easier, if more interesting, by the knowledge that he would either be in SãoThomé for a few days or some six months.

A matter that seemed greatly to exercise the mind of Mr. Palsover and which he discussed at length with the General, was the question of his own sojourn on the island. Anxiously he reflected once again. Should he go ashore at all? Hadn't he better remain on board the *dhow*? Trusting to the prestige of the General's name and his power to protect him, should he go up to this Capital place that the Senior had talked about, and then clear out again when the Hadji did ? Should he stay there the whole six months and keep his eye on things ? Against that he had already practically decided, but the fact remained that if you wanted a thing done well, you must do it yourself. If you have to trust somebody moreover, there's only one person you can really trust and that is yourself. Look after Number One for nobody else will. Very good proverbs, and guiding stars on Mr. Palsover's mental horizon.

On the other hand, why burn your own fingers if someone else will get your chestnuts out of the fire ? Silly to let the General in on this business, and then not trust him. Of course the General was straight. He was a white man, and wouldn't double-cross anybody, let alone the man who had put him on to a thing like this. And as for ability in handling the matter, Mr. Palsover fully and freely admitted that the General was worth a hundred of himself. No good going up to the Capital with any idea of being useful, and no need to go with any idea of preventing the General from cheating him.

Better not go at all. From what the Senior had said, both sane and barmy, St. Tommy wasn't a healthy spot for visitors ; and although the old Senior had been all right and had given him the chit as a sort of Free Pass to the Show, the others, whom he called Them, didn't know Samuel Palsover and might not give themselves time to get to like him and appreciate him properly.

No, there was something very queer about that place. Something wrong about it ; and he wasn't going to run any foolish and unnecessary risks. He'd go and have a look at it and he might perhaps go ashore, but he wouldn't go up-country. No inland journeys for Samuel. If he didn't stay on board the *dhow* the whole time, he'd keep pretty near it.

A rum start. Puzzling. . . .

§ 2

The long-awaited sea-farer, known to some as The Arab, and to others as the Hadji Abdulla, was also puzzled.

Six months ago he had come to Santa Cruz expecting to pick up Senhor Manöel Pereira and take him to São Thomé. Apparently Pereira had arrived according to arrangement, but had not waited. According to Felice Diego, he had disembarked from one of the Anglo-Portuguese coasting tramps with this other European, and, after waiting a few days, both had gone again.

Nor had there been any message save a verbal one from Pereira to the effect that he could wait no longer as he had to go elsewhere. Quite possible, but in the circumstances, rather strange ; and there had been nothing to do but take delivery of the boxes left with Felice Diego and consigned to himself for delivery elsewhere. The boxes and packages had, as usual, borne the name of Manöel Pereira in roman capitals, and the Hadji Abdulla's, as consignee, in Arabic.

And now again, on this occasion, Pereira had failed to meet him, but a stranger had presented him with an incontestably genuine letter from Pereira directing him to give the bearer passage to São Thomé. Curious. Very curious indeed. And, what made it more so, was the fact that the bearer of the letter should be an obvious Englishman, and apparently an English Army Officer of high rank. Queer.

Still, there it was. Definite instructions in black and white, in Pereira's handwriting, and attested by what he could not doubt to be Pereira's signature. He had seen it too often to be deceived. And had he had the slightest suspicion about this document, there was the other letter, or rather envelope, of unknown contents. No one but an authorized official from São Thomé could have written what was on that envelope ; and again, no one who knew it could doubt that the handwriting was Pereira's.

Well, São Thomé was a somewhat mysterious country and its Government had its own rather mysterious ways.

Most certainly he must, and would, give a passage to this stranger, as Pereira's letter directed, and he would also take his servant. That wasn't in the bond, nor was any mention made of a second person, but presumably one might accept the guarantee of the person guaranteed. Since Pereira could vouch for this General, presumably the General could vouch for his servant, especially as the man, far from being inquisitive and anxious to explore, appeared to have no particular wish to go ashore. Nor was it as though the fellow was a seaman. He might have been suspicious had the second man been an obvious sailor and navigator whose object might have been to learn the whereabouts of São Thomé. He was quite an obvious land-lubber and what he purported to be, the General's valet and servant.

Besides, Pereira would hardly have instructed him to give a passage to anybody who was either a spy or likely to bring a spy with him.

Yes, an interesting business, but no concern of the Hadji's. Perhaps Doña Guiomar was going to marry again? The Hadji smiled at the thought.

Perhaps the Council wanted expert opinion and advice on some important technical matter or other. Hardly anything naval or military though. And in any case, it was definitely queer that Pereira, or one of the other official Messengers of the Council, should not be personally escorting the General.

The mere notion of anything of the sort was rather fanciful, but had they actually been bringing someone from Europe, they surely wouldn't have wished him to find his way to Santa Cruz by himself, nor left him provided with no better credentials than a note to the Hadji Abdulla?

However, there it was. On his instructions he must act.

And on Senhor Pereira's instructions he acted, setting sail again in his *dhow* toward midnight, on the third day after his arrival, and taking with him General Sir Reginald Jason, Mr. Palsover, and their respective and not inconsiderable impedimenta.

It was not his habit to be inquisitive, but there was an enormous number of questions which he would have liked to have put to his eminent passenger.

What on earth could a man of this type be doing in the Hadji's particular and peculiar galley? For what possible reason could he be proceeding to São Thomé? Who could have invited him to do so, and what could have been that person's object? It must have been a Member of the Council, which in a way meant that the invitation must have come with the knowledge and consent of the Government, the Council as a body. Surely no one, unless perhaps it were Norhona, who seemed to be something of a law unto himself, would have instructed Pereira to bring such a man as this General to São Thomé. It all seemed contrary to the centuries-old policy and custom of the rulers of that shy and exclusive country, so remote, both historically and geographically, from the thronged highways of land and sea and the busy marts of men.

It would have been puzzling enough had the General been some obscure person, a skilled mechanic of some particular kind, an artificer or engineer, somebody of such insignificance that his comings and goings would be entirely unchronicled and his failure to return home quite unnoticed, save, of course, by the members of his family, if he had one.

Had it been the other man, his servant, it would have been more understandable, as a person of that type, with some special technical skill or knowledge, might have been brought by Pereira on promise of a dazzling wage and a long-term contract, an agreement which would doubtless have been fully honoured by the Council of São Thomé, if never terminated. But even so, it would be a new departure, and one perhaps not unfraught with danger to São Thomé, in the case of an Englishman. But no, that was absurd, inasmuch as the man would know nothing beyond the fact that his engagement began at Santa Cruz ; and inasmuch as he himself would not know his real destination, he would be unable to name it to anyone interested in his future movements.

Well, to mind one's own business was an excellent plan—and had Koranic support, moreover.

As the days passed, the Hadji came to like the General more and more. His manners were accordant with his appearance. He was as pleasant, courteous and agreeable as he was handsome and dignified, qualities which particularly appealed to the Hadji, himself notably courteous, handsome and dignified.

It was matter for regret that he could not give the General more information concerning São Thomé, but in the course of their long and numerous conversations on the subject, he did his best to enlighten him and at the same time to warn him against—he knew not what. That São Thomé was a place of danger to strangers and uninvited visitors, he told him repeatedly; but inasmuch as the General bore not only Pereira's *laisser passer* but actually a letter to a Member of the Council, this danger did not seem to threaten him. But the fact remained that it was no secret that more people entered São Thomé than left it, and that so far as the Hadji knew, only those left it who were its accredited representatives, messengers, emissaries ; some of them something between agents and ambassadors, others corresponding to King's Messengers.

From the Hadji's answers to his questions and the items of information which occasionally he volunteered, the General, himself necessarily uncommunicative, being not only ignorant but a gate-crashing intruder, gathered that São Thomé was a considerable island and an independent self-governing State, the rulers of which fanatically worshipped the ideal of independence. To them, what is elsewhere known as Progress was anathema, and the standards of modern " civilization " an abomination. What they feared and hated most of all conceivable things was the poisoning of the blood of their body politic with the destructive, degenerative and fatal disease-germs that had brought most of the world to its present pass ; that had turned *homo sapiens* into a murderous and suicidal savage whose highest scientific attainments, whose greatest national effort, whose knowledge, resources and wealth, were devoted to—*destruction* !

As the Hadji, in slow and careful English, explained to the General, the rulers of São Thomé wished to avoid pestilence, commercialism, industrialism, wealth, impoverishment, anxiety, slaughter, conquest and enslavement. In other words, they feared their fellow men, dreaded contact with the Christian nations of the earth ; viewed, with horror and hatred, Civilization Uplift, Improvement and Progress. Let them stay as they were, peaceful, self-sufficing, self-supporting and happy. Let other peoples strive for wealth, for markets and for trade ; let them avoid commerce abroad and industrialization at home, for so long as a merciful God would hear their prayers. And, God helping them, they'd help themselves with every atom of their strength and ingenuity. Peace—and São Thomé for the São Thoméans. . . .

Who were they ? What were they ? And where did they get those quaint ideas ? enquired General Jason.

Well, so far as the Hadji could make out, São Thomé had originally been populated by a mild and peaceful Polynesian people, much like the Hawaiians and the Tahitians, a simple and delightful race who were naturally gentle, amiable and unwarlike. They still formed the bulk of the lowland population. But at some far-distant time, there had been an Arab invasion, probably quite accidental, and the more virile Arabs had either conquered the island or assumed proprietorship. These had inter-married with the Polynesians, but their descendants were to this day quite distinguishable from the aborigines, being bigger, stronger, more active and enterprising. Then, some three or four centuries ago, two or three ships of the

178

great " silk and silver " fleet of Portugal, returning from the Far East, and bringing with it the retiring Viceroy of the Indies, had been wrecked on São Thomé. Apparently, the whole fleet had been driven far from its course, scattered and sunk, and the few ships that had been driven ashore at São Thomé had been the only survivors. As it happened, the Viceroy and his family and suite had been on one of these ships, and all of them had been saved.

As a matter of fact, according to what one heard at São Thomé, everybody and everything had been saved, the storm abating just after the ships had gone ashore in what, at low tide and quiet weather, were very shallow waters shelving to a sandy beach.

Nobles and ladies of high rank ; officers and officials ; soldiers and sailors ; merchants ; artisans ; men of the long robe as well as those of the long sword ; priests, doctors, artists, architects, lawyers ; all had been saved ; and, before the ships broke up or were swallowed in the soft and shifting sands, their entire contents had been salvaged in the ships' boats, with the help of the friendly and welcoming natives.

They named the island São Thomé, the day of their reaching it being that of St. Thomas, the Viceroy's patron saint.

It was as though a completely equipped expedition had set forth to found a Colony, as was later attempted and achieved in the Americas and elsewhere, by England, France, Holland, Spain and Portugal.

But there were two great differences between this new foundation in the Southern tropic seas and those systematically-established Colonies.

The first of these differences lay in the fact that these people knew not where they were, having been driven many hundreds and perhaps some thousands of miles from their course, by that terrible storm of phenomenally long duration, which had sunk the greater part of the fleet and cast up the survivors to live or die in this unknown strange uncharted land. Whatever theories their captains and navigators might have were incapable of proof without ships wherewith to put them to the test, and the one or two tiny bands of heroic stalwarts who had set forth in small boats had been heard of no more.

The second of these differences lay in the fact that His Serene Excellency the Viceroy, a sick and ageing man, weary to death of the pomps and vanities of this world, of the cares of high places and the responsibilities of rule, desired nothing but peace, rest and surcease from trouble and tribulation.

To him the island was as one of the Islands of the Blest, another Eden ; and all he asked was to be allowed to end his days in the green shade of its lovely dells and beneath the cool shadow of its mighty trees.

Listening to the Arab's slow, careful and sonorous English, the General was reminded of a Poet who might have been a contemporary of this world-renouncing Viceroy, and who wrote of another disillusioned courtier, the melancholy Jacques who, to his " co-mates and brothers in exile," said : " *Are not these woods more free from peril than the envious Court ?* "

Quite in the spirit of the melancholy Jacques must have been the address made to his compatriots and followers by this disillusioned Governor who may have known Albuquerque and indeed St. Francis Xavier himself.

General Jason had visited Goa, had seen the shrine

of St. Francis and what remained of the works of those mighty men of old who preceded the British in India, as they had done in so many other parts of the world, and could visualize this curious group of Portuguese *cavaleiros fidalgos* starting, undismayed, to build a new life in a new home, at the bidding of their leaders.

A most interesting and truly romantic story.

And there they had remained, the Hadji continued, marrying, first of all, among themselves, for several of the high officers and officials were accompanied by their wives and families; later inter-marrying with the daughters of the leading Arab land-owners who were the aristocracy of the country.

Doubtless, at first, there were rebellious spirits, hearts filled with a deep sense of exile and bereavement, brave spirits almost crushed beneath this weight of woe, and broken by this sense of loss of all that had hitherto made life worth living—this knowledge of ruined ambitions, wrecked careers, lost homes, estates and loved ones. But as the years passed and the second and third generation took the place of the original fathers of the new community, the beautiful and productive island became Home.

Within a very few more generations it was not only a home in which to live and move and dwell, but one to guard, protect and keep private, to keep hidden and secret; a garden enclosed, set in a protecting sea.

Naturally the new-comers had quickly become the aristocracy of the island, the Viceroy its supreme ruler, his nobles its government, and the remainder his trustworthy representatives throughout the island, administrators, executives, judges, soldiers and police. And, as naturally as they breathed the air, the priests who, proselytizing from Goa, had been converting Indians by whole villages at a time, set about the work of Christian-izing, teaching and disciplining the aboriginal inhabit-ants of São Thomé.

Apparently for many years, for several generations, for more than a century probably, it was, in Europe, assumed that the entire fleet had been lost and that the Viceroy had perished with the rest. It had hap-pened before and would happen again, while caravels of a hundred tons set out to circumnavigate the world.

Had the Viceroy and his entourage been normally anxious to communicate with the mother country, make known their fate and appeal for help, it was improbable that any such communication would, in their own life-times, have been feasible. Circumstances were in any case against it. But in view of the earnest desire and careful precautions of The Viceroy, His Excellency Dom Sebastian Gonçalo de Braganza (who now took the title of Marquess de São Thomé) that—in order to ensure their being left in peace to found a newer, higher and nobler state of their own—nothing should be known of their fate, it is not remarkable that the remote island remained unheard of and unknown unto the third and fourth and probably the fifth and sixth generations of the descendants of these argonauts, these founders and architects of a New Model and a real Utopia.

It was not at one session, or in one day, that General Jason learned thus much of the history of the island State of São Thomé ; and as he listened and the story was unfolded, a doubt grew in the General's mind as to whether the tale or the teller were the more remark-able. With practice, the Hadji's English had grown more fluent, his vocabulary more copious. Nor did his explanation that he had been sent to an English-speaking school in childhood and had actually served and sailed on an English ship, seem to account for his fluency.

A most attractive and intriguing man, and his *dhow* an uncommonly fine specimen of the craft that have sailed the Southern seas and traded from Basra to Bombay, from Mombasa to Ceylon for a thousand years, and, in the past, had not only frequently but regularly made their way east of Ceylon and west of the Cape of Good Hope.

This particular *dhow* was a much bigger vessel than most of its kind, better built, and far better kept and equipped. In its high-built poop, with its flat broad stern, glass-windowed and beautifully carved, there was evidence of the history of its descent. From the waist aft, a Portuguese galleon ; from the waist forward, a native Oriental galley, its low pointed stem rising with a long slope from the water, its strong thick mast raking forward and supporting the enormous yard, far longer than itself, which carried the one great sail.

Even to the eye of the General, a landsman, it was clearly apparent that the *dhow* was extremely well-handled, and that its crew, Arabs of dark complexion and mixed blood, were fine seamen. Moreover, to his surprise, one of them was also an admirable cook in his own line, chiefly that of rice, fish and chupatties. As he told the Hadji, he had eaten worse curries in India and in places where the cook had everything he required for success.

In fact, he thoroughly enjoyed the novel voyage, and not the less because he had his suspicions about it. He was sure that the Hadji left Santa Cruz with some suddenness and secrecy that night ; that he had been somewhat insistent that his passengers should retire at once to the berths allotted to them aft ; and that the *dhow's* course for its destination was a curiously indirect and circuitous one.

Although he saw neither chart nor compass, he knew from the position of the sun by day and of certain of the stars by night, that there was something as queer and unusual about the sailing-directions as about so many other details of the whole fantastic business.

What was the Hadji thinking as he eyed him with those long speculating looks ? What made him so meditative, and why did he thus ponder and ruminate upon the matter of his passenger's position and business ? Plainly he was greatly interested. Was he also doubtful, possibly a little anxious as to whether the General quite understood what he was doing ?

The latter decided that, while fully accepting the genuineness of Pereira's letters, the Hadji was extremely puzzled by them and by the whole situation. Without actually asking the questions,

" Do you really know exactly what you are doing, and are you provided with adequate guarantees and credentials ? " he gave the General clearly to understand that this was something entirely new in his experience, and that the General and his servant were the first passengers whom he had ever carried to São Thomé unaccompanied by a São Thoméan official.

" We shall reach São Thomé to-morrow," he told him one evening as they sat cross-legged on the poop-deck and ate rice and curried fish which reminded the General of Bombay ' duck.'

" Oh, good ! " he replied. " Though I shall be quite sorry to leave the *dhow*. When shall we get our first sight of the coast ? "

"We shan't," smiled the Hadji. "We shall approach after sunset and drop anchor before dawn."

"Quite so," thought the General. "All very secretive—and interesting."

He felt himself to be on the threshold of a great adventure. It was almost like going to the Front again, on the outbreak of a war.

VIII

FROM the first minute of catching a glimpse of
São Thomé, the General was in a state of thrilled
excitement, though no one would have imagined it.
On waking in the morning and coming out on to the
deck, he found the *dhow* was at anchor in what appeared
to be a land-locked creek, the shores of which were
fringed with mangrove, behind which rose a profusion
of palms and other trees, tall, green and magnificent ;
obviously a place of great fertility and enjoying a very
adequate rainfall.

In the distance rose a great forbidding ramp, a solid
wall of mountains.

So far as he had visualized anything at all, he
had imagined and expected a harbour and town of
the Santa Cruz sort. Here, there appeared to be
neither harbour nor town ; merely an anchorage for
the smallest type of sea-going boat, such as that on
which he stood ; and what appeared to be a fort, a
barracks, a look-out station and a few other official-
looking buildings, trim, neat and well-kept.

As he gazed, a boat smartly rowed by dark-skinned
sailors in white uniform, put out from a small wooden
jetty and approached the *dhow*. As it drew nearer, he
noticed that the man who sat in the stern appeared
to be a European, the type of official who might
have sat in the stern-sheets of such a boat in any
Mediterranean harbour.

" With much apology," said the voice of the Hadji behind him, " will you please go aft into the cabin, while I speak with the Port Officer ? "

As the General reluctantly turned away to comply with his request, the Hadji added,

" He is also the Doctor, the Customs Authority, the Senior Naval Officer, the Chief of Police, the Officer Commanding Troops, and several other things."

When later he was asked to join the Hadji and the Port Officer, it was to gain the impression that the Port Official was as surprised and as puzzled concerning him as the Hadji had been. What was said between the two he did not understand, but from time to time the Hadji enlightened him as to the drift of the Port Officer's observations, enquiries and objections ; but in the end the position seemed to be summed up in the official's statement that he had received no instructions, had no authority, and did not intend to take any responsibility.

After reading Senhor Pereira's letter at least a dozen times, he had decided that it did not concern him. It was addressed to the Hadji, and doubtless the Hadji had acted correctly in obeying its instructions. It bade him take the bearer to São Thomé—and he had done so.

And did the Senhor imagine that Senhor Pereira had been so anxious that the bearer of the letter should be safely conducted to São Thomé in order that he might be immediately taken away again ?

The official intimated that he was not privileged to know the contents of Senhor Pereira's mind or to understand its workings. He repeated that he had no instructions.

And the letter addressed by Senhor Pereira to Dom Perez de Norhona ?

That was another matter. No one had any objection to that being delivered. On the contrary.

And having said all that he had to say, and demonstrated his power to obstruct, the Port Officer informed the Hadji that he would communicate with the Capital and obtain instructions. Meantime, the bearer of the letters was not to leave the *dhow*, and a soldier would be left on board with very definite instructions to see that he did not do so. Also the Hadji would be held strictly responsible for his passenger's " safety." And the letter addressed to Dom Perez de Norhona had better be handed over to the Port Officer who would see that it reached him safely.

But to this General Jason flatly refused to agree. He quite understood that there might be some difficulty about his admission to São Thomé ; but this was his passport, his credentials, his letter of introduction, and he intended to deliver it in person. Would the Hadji kindly inform this Officer that he was not a stowaway, a tripper, a beachcomber or a casual wanderer looking for a job, but a retired British Officer of high rank, a General in fact, and that he had not the slightest doubt that the official's superiors would greatly deplore any discourtesy that might be shown him. Meantime the Port Officer need have no anxiety about his leaving the *dhow*, for he had neither wish nor intention to do so. Whenever, hitherto, he had visited civilized parts of the world, he had met with a different kind of reception from this.

Which, being interpreted, caused the Port Officer to smile and request the Hadji to inform the General that it was the particular boast of São Thomé that it was not a civilized part of the world—as civilization was understood to-day. However, he would communicate with the Capital, and when he received instructions would inform the General immediately.

Meanwhile, he hoped he would enjoy excellent health and walk with God.

§ 2

Mr. Palsover was neither depressed nor despondent. On the other hand, he was fully confirmed in the opinion which he had already formed, that St. Tommy was no place for him. He had rather gathered from his conversation with the Senior, and especially from what the poor gentleman had said during his bouts of delirium, that St. Tommy was going to turn out to be something like this.

No, that Capital sounded to him like a very good place to keep away from. For Mr. Palsover to keep away from, that is; but a very good place for the General to visit.

All this secrecy showed there was a secret.

All this defensiveness showed there was something to defend.

Why such a lot of fuss and bother over letting the General even go ashore, if they hadn't got something to hide?

Yes, so far so good. What price Samuel now? Here he was, right on the spot, right on the doorstep. What a nose he had for money! He had followed the scent straight from that cabin on the *St. Paul de Loanda*, where the poor old Senior started babbling about stuff at fifteen thousand pounds a gramme; followed it to where the Senior had gone to ground (or mud, rather); back to London where he could find the right man for the job; back again to

189

Santa Cruz where they had found the Arab; and now to St. Tommy itself. What a nose he had for money, and *what* a smell of it there was here! Afraid to let you set foot on their golden island. . . .

He'd much sooner have gone up-country with the General and kept his eye on things. Not on the General, of course, but on things *in* general. It would have been interesting, and he might have learned a lot. And he'd have liked to have talked things over with the General, day by day, as they arose—and put his oar in, when there was any occasion. It might give him a bigger claim, too, when the sharing-out was done—the shares allotted, as they called it—and they were making out who was who and who got what. After all, it was his show, wasn't it? It was he who had discovered the stuff. But he didn't like the sound of ' Them ' at all. There was what the Senior had said about Them.

Ar! And there was what he knew for himself about a poor chap who went ashore in a place once, and was never heard of again. Gun-running, he was—and the wrong lot got the guns and him too. Nothing of that sort for Samuel P.

> " *I'll stick to the ship, lads,*
> *You've children and wives,*"

he hummed, and smiled humorously as he sorted the General's kit again.

IX

ALTHOUGH General Jason had in his time travelled in most parts of the world and used most forms of transport, varying from the yak, elephant, mule and camel to the aeroplane, he considered his journey from the *dhow* to São Ildefonso, the capital of São Thomé, as the most interesting that he had ever made.

It fell into two widely differing parts, that across an intensively cultivated plain, from the harbour to the bridge across the quick-sand ; and that up a hair-raising zigzag track that literally climbed the mountain-wall to the plateau on which the Capital with its citadel was built.

The first part of the journey was made by bullock-carts which reminded him of those used for regimental transport in India, but differed from them in that the bullocks trotted at a speed hitherto unimagined, while the wheels of the lightly-built carts were well-greased and silent. To his mind, the word bullock-cart had hitherto connoted a speed of two to three miles an hour ; a vehicle clumsy as those that crossed the steppes of Europe behind the armies of Ghengiz Khan ; and a creaking, groaning, shrieking and screaming noise of never-oiled wheels revolving on their crudely-rounded axle.

The country and its crops also reminded him of the more fertile plains of India ; swamps of rice ;

fields of sugar-cane ; vast areas of corn and millet which he called *bajri* and *jowri* ; large patches of intensive cultivation of vegetables, such as might have been the work of Chinese market-gardeners. The villages were less suggestive of India, with their pink, pale-blue, yellow and cream adobe huts and houses, neat and well-built, some of them thatched with palm-leaf, others tiled with what appeared to be slabs of wood.

Obviously a country of great fertility, agricultural industry, peace and plenty.

The natives reminded him more of those of Malaya, Samoa and Tahiti than of those of India, a bright, cheerful and happy people whose demeanour was in marked contrast to that of the sad, over-serious, poverty-stricken and malaria-ridden people of the plains of India. He was also reminded of a verse of Gray's *Elegy* which he had learned by heart at Prep. School and, God forgive him, had recited at the last prize-distribution. How did it go ? He had a splendidly tenacious memory. . . .

> " . . . *The threats of pain and ruin to despise,*
> *To scatter plenty o'er a smiling land*
> *And read their history in a nation's eyes.*"

The rulers of this country could read in this people's eyes, a very laudable and creditable history of their governing. A smiling land indeed, and endowed with plenty.

At the end of the first day's journey, part of which he made in the Arab's bullock-cart, part on foot, marching with him, the General was in no-wise surprised to find, in a big clearing, what might well have been a superior *dâk*-bungalow on the Grand Trunk Road that runs from Calcutta to Peshawar. In a very large and well-kept compound stood a good-sized one-storeyed bungalow, in which was a big central dining-room on either side of which were three very adequate bedrooms, all opening, back and front, on to wide verandahs. This rest-house for travelling officials was clean and quite well-furnished, with plain strong chairs, tables, and beds of a dark and heavy wood.

In one corner of the compound were stables for the oxen.

What did surprise him was the fact that the excellent servants did not understand his Hindustani. So like were they to the Goanese "boys" of his Indian experience, that it seemed unnatural that they should understand neither English nor Hindustani. In their plain white suits buttoning up to the neck, they might almost have been Officers' Mess servants, ship's stewards, or the domestic butlers to whom he had been accustomed for a quarter of a century, whose mother-tongue was Hindustani, and who understood and spoke English almost equally well.

After an evening meal of excellent soup, of fish unknown to him, of rather tough chicken, and a choice of papaia, melon, bananas and admirable yellow-and-red mangoes, he sat for an hour in the verandah talking with the Hadji Abdulla, who had dined, presumably, in his own room.

After conversation concerning the Island and its Government, about which the Arab appeared to be either ill-informed or uncommunicative, the latter uttered once again what General Jason could only regard as a warning.

" You will not think me inquisitive," he said, " a rash, foolish and impudent person who would pry into your affairs, if I ask you whether you are quite certain that the letter you carry for His Excellency

Dom Perez de Norhona, guarantees you—what shall I say—safe conduct . . . safety . . . freedom to come and go ? And by that I mean not only to come and go as you please about the Island. I mean more than that. You have come here. Are you sure you will be able to go away again, when you wish to do so ? "

" Oh, but surely . . . damn it all. . . . There's no danger of my being arrested, is there ? " growled the General.

" That depends on the contents of the letter you have for His Excellency Dom Perez de Norhona," replied the Arab gravely. " Are you sure that Senhor Pereira gave you full and ample guarantee ? "

" Well . . . suppose he didn't ? " replied the General, beginning to wish that he knew more about the contents of the unopened letter.

" Then I would most strongly advise you to go no farther. Once you cross the bridge to-morrow, there will be no turning back ; but, although it will cause awkward inquiries—and difficult explanations on my part—I will take you back to the *dhow* and leave you on board while I conclude my business at the Capital."

" Thank you very much. That's very decent of you. But I haven't the faintest intention of turning back. Why should I do such a thing ? I have a letter of introduction to this Member of Council, or whatever he is, from his own representative and agent, Senhor Pereira, and I am going to present it. What should I have to fear ? What is there dangerous about it ? "

The Arab gravely shook his head, as though pondering his reply and choosing carefully his words.

" Come, come, Hadji Sahib ! You can't arrest a British General for presenting a letter of introduction !

Why, bless my soul, I come here in good faith with a view to doing mutually profitable business with this Government, and if they don't like it they can leave it. It would be wholly advantageous to them, but they are quite free to turn it down; and surely I should then be quite free to go? How could they detain me? I expect they've heard of British Consuls, not to mention the British Navy?"

The Arab smiled.

"To how many people is it known that you were to meet Senhor Pereira at Santa Cruz with the intention of going on to some place called São Thomé?" he asked.

"Well—er—nobody, I suppose. No, nobody."

"Ah!" observed the Arab non-committally.

"What exactly do you mean by that?"

"Nothing. Nothing, Sidi," replied Hadji Abdulla in a tone and manner that contradicted the statement.

"Well, then?"

"I was just wondering how these British Consuls and the British Navy are going to know anything about it, should you be—er—detained here."

"Has Britain no representative whatsoever in the capital of this São Thomé?"

"No country has any representative in the Island State of São Thomé," was the reply.

"But why should they wish to detain me?"

"By reason of their distrust, their hatred, indeed their fear and loathing—of visitors. They consider that the State of São Thomé has the Government that suits it best, the civilization that suits it best, and that peace which is of all things the best—and the greatest of all blessings bestowed upon ungrateful mankind by the wisdom and mercy of Allah."

" But damn it all, Hadji, don't they want to improve their trade, to enrich and widen their industry and commerce, to enlighten and develop the lives of the people by getting from every part of the world the things they cannot get here ? Don't they want to raise the standard of living ? To add luxuries to their necessities ? Don't they want to march in the front rank of Civilization ? Have they never heard of Progress ? Don't they want Wealth ? "

" No," replied the Arab. " They don't. Nor do they want any trade or commerce whatsoever. They don't want to change the wants and ways of living of a perfectly contented and entirely prosperous people. And not only do they not wish to march in the front rank of Civilization, or in any other rank of what the world calls Civilization to-day, but they want to avoid it entirely. And as for desiring what is called Progress, it is their greatest object to escape it. To them Progress is another name for the Devil himself, and modern Civilization the Hell in which he works against mankind. . . . That is why they hate and fear visitors who come as emissaries, agents, scouts and forerunners of that Civilization."

" Good Lord ! A pretty stick-in-the-mud lot, aren't they ? " snorted the General. " Don't they want rail-ways, telegraphs, telephone, electricity, motor-cars, aeroplanes, wireless and all that ? "

" They don't. There is not one yard of railway in this island. There is not a motor-car. No aeroplane has ever risen from its soil or landed on it. Electricity and wireless are as unwanted as they are unknown."

" So they prefer these bullock-carts to motor-cars, eh ? "

" Infinitely."

" And why don't they want aeroplanes ? "

" Because they think they have brought little but evil to mankind."

" On what grounds ? "

" Well, they have an idea that the inhabitants of the great capitals of the mightiest nations turn pale and quiver with fright as they look up into the air, because the aeroplane has brought war to their very doors, and made their lives as hazardous as those of soldiers engaged in the most terrible battles. The Government of São Thomé has no wish to see their people digging holes in the earth and living like moles, rats and rabbits rather than as men—by reason of the blessings that aviation has brought to mankind."

" H'm. And wireless ? What is their objection to that ? "

" Its disturbance of the lives of peaceful simple and unspoilt people. Should you spend a day or two in one of the villages, watching the lives of these well-fed, well-clothed, well-housed happy agriculturists, you too will wonder as to what might be gained by providing them with jazz music, the voice of the crooner, the raucous cries of the advertiser, the vitiation of their simple tastes, and the provision for them of a thousand new and undesirable wants, needs, habits and vulgar luxuries. These people have their own music and their own legends and literature. They know nothing of alcohol, tobacco, patent medicines and the rest of the poisonous injurious trash that makes up quite a considerable part of this wonderful trade and commerce."

" You don't mean to tell me . . ." began the General.

" Pardon me, Sidi. I don't wish to tell you anything, except the views of the rulers of this country on the subject of what is good and what is bad for their people. And strange as it may seem, foolish

197

and wrong as it may appear, they include among the things that are necessarily and wholly bad, visitors from the outside world.''

Ah ! smiled the General to himself, they'd have rather a different attitude toward a visitor who brought them a proposition like this. Why, was there any Government in the world that could or would refuse to have its revenues doubled, quadrupled ? Good Lord, in a place like this, the royalties from a radium-concession would probably multiply the Government's annual income by ten. Talk about Balancing the Budget !

And apart from that, what about the individual members of the Government ? Was there a single man, in any more-or-less coloured Government in the world, who'd vote against a scheme that was going to give him a noble personal and private rake-off, as would inevitably be the case here—quite apart from what accrued to the State Treasury by their action as a Governing Council ? Each single member would naturally sit-in on it as a private individual.

If—and it was a colossal *if*—they were above flagrant bribery and corruption, would not each one of them expect to have a seat on the Board, a block of shares, and fine guinea-pig fees ?

The Hadji was talking nonsense.

§ 2

Next day the bullock-carts were left behind at the rest-house. The General, the Hadji and a number of porters carrying boxes, crates and personal luggage, crossed the bridge on foot, and found riding-horses, pack-horses and mules awaiting them at a sort of rural livery-stables on the other side.

To the General, the crossing of the bridge was the most interesting part of the whole journey. This bridge spanned no river or other water, but what resembled the narrow sandy bed of an almost dried-up stream, for the sand looked wet, and, here and there, was a small pool of unattractive water.

" River ever flow here ? " he asked the Hadji, as they crossed the bridge.

" Never. It is a quick-sand, and whatever goes into it disappears almost immediately, and is seen no more. It is the haunt and abode of *djinns*, *afrits*, devils— and their breath is poisonous. As you see, nothing green lives within a hundred yards of the banks of this unmoving ' river ' of wet and quaking sand. Farther up, on either side, it opens out into a bog of sand which nothing can cross, neither man nor beast. In my country we have lakes of sand covered in salt— they are called *shotts*—but they can be crossed. Here there is no possibility of crossing, save at this spot by this bridge which, in the almost impossible event of invasion, could be destroyed in a few minutes."

The military aspect of the situation immediately interested the General.

" But an enemy force could march round, of course," he mused.

" Yes, and come face to face with a perpendicular cliff from two thousand to three thousand feet in height, which only lizards can climb."

" And suppose they marched all along the base of this cliff ? " asked the General.

" They would, in time, come to the sea. In either direction."

" And if they re-embarked and sailed on ? "

" In time they'd come back to the only harbour,

such as it is ; the spot where they had originally landed, and whence they had originally marched."

" They could make a landing somewhere else, surely ? "

" Only into mangrove swamps through which one or two of the hardiest and luckiest *might* eventually penetrate, exhausted ; though I doubt it."

" So no one could get up on to the main part of the Island, except across this quick-sand ? "

" That is so. Possibly an individual here and there might contrive it, with the help of Allah. But not across the quick-sand."

" And does the breath of the *djinns* and *afrits* and devils destroy all vegetation round the other parts of the quick-sand too, as well as by this narrow crossing ? "

" Everywhere. Not only is it death, by engulfing, to attempt to cross ; but it is death for man and beast and vegetation to remain within a furlong of it."

" And nobody knows why this should be ? "

" No."

Whereas I do, smiled General Jason to himself. It is radio-active. This quick-sand is just a few million tons of highly radio-active minerals blended with earth and sand. And probably worth nearly its weight in gold. Pitchblende. Helium. Uranium. Tungsten. Manganese. Zircon. Rutile. Phosphorus. And rare valuable chemicals and minerals used in bulb-filament-making and the hardening of special steel for armour-plating, guns and such. He didn't know much about these minerals, but he knew that this tremendously radio-active stuff must be enormously valuable, any-way. And it only needed carting away and shipping.

" When I say that nobody knows, I mean the

simple people are ignorant as to why devils should occupy this place," observed the Arab.

And thinking the matter over the General decided that the phenomenon of radio-activity was caviar for the general of this island State, and probably understood only by the more enlightened members of its Government, such men as this Dr. Norhona. Anyway, Pereira had known. And he himself was going to know before he set foot on that *dhow*, or any other boat.

"This Dr. Norhona," he said, "he's a Member of Council, I understand. Pretty important man, eh?"

"His Excellency Dom Perez de Norhona is an extremely influential and important member of the Government," replied the Arab. "Also Secretary to the Cabinet."

And what sort of a Government would it be, wondered the General. Presumably a Dictatorship, either that of an individual or a clique.

"Who's the ruler of the country?" he asked.

"Doña Guiomar is the Regent during the childhood of the hereditary Governor."

"And can she do as she likes? A kind of Begum of Bhopal? A sort of female King Feisal, Ibn Saud, Sultan of Muscat or Zanzibar? Like a female Sheikh of an Arab tribe, if there were such a thing as a woman-Sheikh."

"Well, no. Not quite. She could do nothing against the will of the Council. On the other hand, no order or act that the Council passes becomes law unless she signs it."

"And who elects this Council?"

"They are not elected. They are hereditary, and elect the Cabinet. The Council consists of the heads of the families of the descendants of those who occupied the Island and named it São Thomé, hundreds of years ago."

" I see. Sort of House of Lords without the Commons," observed the General.

" Yes. But just as the Sheikh of a tribe discusses all measures with a *mejliss* of elders, so the Government every year calls a meeting of the heads of the big land-owning families. They can thus ventilate their grievances, if any ; and put forward suggestions—generally agricultural. They are men of mixed Arab descent."

" Big men, eh ? Wealthy ? "

" Wealthy in everything but money. They have vast estates, flocks and herds."

" And the people who cultivate the estates—are they what one might call slaves ? "

" Slaves ! No. They are free men. In some cases they own their own land. In others, share with their employers."

" And it works well, eh ? "

" For centuries there has been peace and plenty. There is no poverty. Crime is almost unknown, and there has never, since the Island became São Thomé, been anything in the nature of a revolt of the peasants."

" And they have no share in the Government ? "

" No, nor do they want one. They ask only to be governed and lightly taxed, and they are governed and taxed with justice and wisdom."

" Huh ! The wisdom of excluding Civilization and Progress, eh ? " grunted General Jason.

" By exactly that wisdom, Sidi," replied the Arab, as he led the way to the gates of the horse-corral which surrounded the thatched house of its overseer, and by which stood two good hacks and a collection of pack-horses, ponies, mules and donkeys. " Will you choose which of these horses you would like to ride ? "

§ 3

And after three days of easy riding and two nights in *dâk*-bungalows (rest-houses) the wayfarers reached São Ildefonso, the capital of São Thomé. To General Jason, who had travelled in Portugal and Spain, following, for his interest and instruction, the course of Wellington's Peninsular Campaign, Ildefonso was reminiscent of a smaller and walled Lisbon, if it were crowned and overshadowed by the citadel of Cintra. Faintly, too, it suggested Goa, by reason of the dark complexion of the general populace. A clean attractive town ; its better-class houses, each in its own be-flowered compound, of colours pleasing to the eye and suggestive of cool repose, in the green setting of the great trees that shadowed and protected them. The bazaars again reminded him of those of India and somewhat of the villages of Cyprus.

But the castle was a little grim, a little awe-inspiring, and as he and the Hadji rode into the great outer court-yard, and ere the sound of the horses' hooves ceased to clatter upon the old grey stones, the clang of closing gates struck an ominous note. He shivered slightly, and wondered whether it presaged an attack of malaria.

Soldiers, neither particularly smart nor noticeably slovenly, had emerged from a guard-house on the shout of a sentry with whom the Hadji Abdulla had held brief colloquy at the outer gate.

Scarcely had the new-comers dismounted than two of the soldiers came to lead their horses away, and

203

an official dressed in white European tropical kit descended the flight of steps and approached them.

With him the Hadji conversed a while, and then, turning to the General, asked for the letter of introduction to His Excellency Dom Perez de Norhona.

But the General was still obstinate on the point.

" No," said he, " I'll give it to de Norhona himself."

" How do you know that this gentleman is not His Excellency ? " smiled the Arab.

" Well, is he ? "

" No."

" Then if he will be good enough to take me to Dr. Norhona, as quickly as possible, I will present my credentials and talk business with him as soon as he likes."

" I'm afraid it won't be quite as easy as all that," replied Hadji Abdulla. " And listen, Sidi. You have come to São Thomé of your own free will. You have insisted on going with me to the Capital. Now, I would most strongly and earnestly advise you to remember that you *are* in the Capital of an independent State. Also that His Excellency Dom Perez de Norhona is a powerful member of its Government. So far as you are concerned, he is the Government ; and there is no appeal from him. You have placed yourself in his hands and you are absolutely in his power."

" Well ? "

" Don't anger him, Sidi. Approach him rather as the English nobleman, Sir Thomas Roe, approached the Emperor Akbar."

The General smiled somewhat bleakly.

But the Arab shook his head.

" I am speaking words of wisdom to a wise man, Sidi," he said. " Do heed them. And another thing.

Have you any idea as to when your business may be concluded ? Because I shall be sailing again soon. Probably in a few days. It would give me the greatest pleasure to carry you back to Santa Cruz.

" *Safely*," he added.

The official coughed to draw attention to the fact that he was present and extremely correct. Also, waiting.

" One minute," said the Hadji in Arabic. " I am taking farewell of the Sidi and receiving his instructions."

The official smiled meaningly.

" And look, Sidi," the Hadji said, turning to the General. " Suppose you don't sail with me, and suppose I hear nothing of you for a long time, and possibly don't find you here when I return, half a year hence ? Is there anyone with whom you would like me to communicate, if I can, and tell them where I last saw you ? "

" Good Heavens, no ! " ejaculated the General. " Absolutely not. I do most particularly beg of you not to tell a living soul that I came to São Thomé. It is the last thing in the world that I want anyone to know. Is that clear ? "

" Perfectly, Sidi. No one knows you have come here, and you want no one to know that you are here, should you unfortunately be detained longer than you now expect."

" That's it. Not a word to a soul."

" And your servant, Sidi ? "

" Oh, he won't tell anybody."

" And is he to return with me to Santa Cruz ? "

" He can please himself about that. If you'd be good enough to take him, I expect he'd be very much obliged to you. What about his passage-money ? "

205

" Nothing, Sidi. It is the affair of the Government of São Thomé. I now ask your permission to leave you. May Allah protect you, Sidi."

" Good-bye, Hadji Sahib, and thank you very much indeed. You have been most helpful and obliging. Best of good luck. Good-bye. Hope to see you again soon."

" *Wallahi!* I hope it too, Sidi. Farewell. Allah guard you."

And with a long look into the General's eyes, he bowed, turned and strode back in the direction of a door in the thick grey wall at the far side of the vast courtyard, the expression of his face grave and sad.

The official, saying something of which the General understood not a word, pointed toward the flight of steps and bowing, indicated that he should proceed in that direction.

At the top of the stairs the man opened a small but massive door and led the way along a dark corridor. This debouched into a great hall, medieval, raftered and stone-flagged. Crossing this, he led the way to another flight of stairs which climbed to a gallery. This they ascended, walked along the gallery to the entrance of another gloomy passage, and, at a door therein, halted.

The official unlocked the door, stepped back and bowed General Jason into a fair-sized lofty room lighted by a large but heavily-barred window. Glancing round the apartment, the General got the impression of the sort of room one sees in a very old English house or castle, furnished in what is known as " period " fashion.

Again, saying something of which the General understood nothing, the man turned to depart.

" Oh, by the way, will you have my kit sent up here when the pack-horses arrive ? " said the General.

Probably the fellow understood English, though he couldn't speak it.

The man stared uncomprehendingly. How like an Indian Eurasian head clerk or hotel-manager or police official or lawyer he was. Surely he must understand Hindustani ?

The General repeated his request in that language. And again in French.

No gleam of comprehension lighted the sallow face of the São Thoméan.

Well, one more shot—in German ; though there wasn't much hope of his knowing that, if he didn't know French. Like many other keen and ambitious British Officers, the General had learned German, and had spent a year of his leave in that country studying on the spot, and as far as possible, the theory and practice of its military methods.

He repeated his request in German, but without result. Again with expressionless face, the man bowed politely, turned and departed.

Not only did he close the door behind him but, to the General's slight consternation, most audibly locked it.

Well, he was an old campaigner. He'd make himself comfortable. Very good bed. Very good chairs and table. What he would have liked would have been an arm-chair such as that in his study at home. Be rather nice to be back there for a while, relaxed in that deep comfortable chair, with one of his cigars alight and the morning paper in front of his face.

But he'd be doing that, before long ; and without any of the old financial anxiety gnawing at the back of his mind like a rat at a wainscot.

Well, he had had far worse accommodation than this. Many and many a worse room, during the War.

But he had never been locked in one. Never in his life, so far as he could remember. And it wasn't a pleasant sensation. Not exactly a " bed-sit. with running h. & c. bath "—but really very decent quarters. He'd have to explain that he washed occasionally, and that this was one of the occasions. Doubtless he could explain in pantomime what he wanted. Somebody would be bringing him some food before long, of course.

He sat down on the brown blanket folded at the foot of the heavy wooden bed and, with equal mind, pondered the situation.

Anyway, here he was, and—by good luck, good judgment, the fortune of Fate or the will of God—right in the very middle of things.

§ 4

The door opened and, preceded by the same official, who bowed low and retired, a short swarthy man with big head, extraordinarily brilliant eyes and the general air, appearance and manner of an important Portuguese gentleman, advanced toward him.

As he rose to his feet and extended his hand in greeting, the General was reminded of someone whom he had met and liked in India. Who was it and where ? Yes, at the Bombay Yacht Club. The Portuguese Consul-General, a cultured, charming and aristocratic individual, taller than this man, his handsome face less remarkably interesting.

What was it about this face ? The eyes, of course. Almost luminous. Uncanny.

" Good evening, Senhor. How do you do ? I . . ."

began General Jason, apparently even more than usually reserved, reticent and uncordial. "I wonder if you—er—speak English or understand it?"

"Yes," replied the visitor, to the General's great relief, "I understand English perfectly and speak it as well as . . . you hear. Will you kindly introduce yourself?"

From the breast pocket of his khaki shooting-jacket the General produced the letter with which Senhor Pereira had provided Mr. Palsover.

"My name is—er—Reginaldo—er . . ." he said. He hated boggling and equivocating but—he must be careful. There might perhaps be good reason, later, to be glad he hadn't blurted out his surname, at once. And Palsover's own name might be in the letter. But no—he said this Pereira feller never knew his real name, "General . . . British Army. Retired. I have a letter here for Dr. de Norhona. A letter of introduction from Senhor Pereira."

"I am de Norhona," replied the other. "Thank you. Won't you be seated?"

And as the General sat down again upon the bed, the man walked across to the window, opened the letter and read it.

Having done so, he turned and favoured the General with a long appraising stare.

"Ah!" said he. "You are an Englishman? A British Officer? A General? Reginaldo, did you say? And this letter was given to you by my friend Pereira? Interesting. *Very* interesting."

Again he studied the letter thoughtfully, his brows drawn together in a heavy frown.

The General felt a little uncomfortable, and devoutly wished he knew the precise contents of the letter of introduction. Possibly this feller Pereira hadn't admired the worthy Palsover as much as the latter thought he did?

Anyway, the letter had got him here. Got him to the one spot on earth where he wanted to be. And that was the great thing.

Dom Perez de Norhona folded the letter and returned it to the envelope.

"And where is Pereira himself at the present moment?" he asked. "I have rather been expecting him. Did so six months ago, in fact."

"I'm afraid I cannot tell you, Senhor. My information is that he left Santa Cruz . . . in a hurry. Rather suddenly."

"I don't doubt it, ' *General*,' " was the reply. "I feel pretty certain that Pereira left Santa Cruz quite suddenly. And before he went, he certainly wrote this letter. Unquestionably it is a perfectly genuine letter of—er—introduction."

"Oh, yes, quite so," agreed General Jason. "Shall we talk business now, or would you rather postpone that until to-morrow or till—after dinner, say."

Dr. Perez de Norhona smiled pleasantly—or perhaps unpleasantly.

"I think we will postpone business until, as you say, after dinner, or perhaps till to-morrow. Unless, of course, you'd like to tell me, in a few words, to what São Thomé owes the honour of your visit. What is your *real* object?"

"Well, to put it bluntly and briefly, a radium concession."

"*Ah? So?*" smiled the doctor.

"I want to make an extremely advantageous proposal to the Government of São Thomé. We want to pay them a lump sum and a handsome royalty in return for permission to—er—mine for uranium and produce radium. And also to purchase a few hundred or a few thousand tons of that queer quick-sand of yours."

" *Ah!* So ? " was again de Norhona's only comment, but he showed most of his gleaming teeth in a pleasant or unpleasant smile. " I shall give myself the pleasure of coming to see you later to-night or to-morrow, when we will talk of . . . many things. Meanwhile, is there anything that you require ? "

" Well, I've been riding all day and I don't deny that I should enjoy a bath, and after that, a spot of something to eat and drink."

" *Cela va sans dire.* You speak French—er— ' General ' ? "

" Oh, yes. Pretty well. No one would mistake me for a Frenchman, but I read and speak it pretty well."

" And German ? "

" Yes, yes. Rather better than French."

And suddenly the surprising Dr. Norhona inquired in fluent if faulty German as to whether Senhor Pereira had given him any particular verbal message ; as to whether it was he who had introduced the General to Hadji Abdulla ; and as to how long he had sojourned at Santa Cruz.

And to humour this excellent linguist, the General replied to the best of his ability and in his best German, which was indeed very good.

Whereafter the accomplished doctor, bidding the General a courteous good night, bowed, and, still smiling his peculiar and enigmatic smile, withdrew, locking the door behind him.

That was a queer cove, mused General Jason. He hadn't spent his life in São Thomé—to speak English,

French and German like that. Naturally he'd have to go abroad to qualify as a doctor, and he might, of course, have studied medicine in London, Paris and Vienna.

Well, an interesting little adventure. Quite amusing, being locked in his bedroom like a naughty boy.

Anyhow he had got hold of the right man, straight away, the man who could start things going as soon as he had been sufficiently interested and had seen, not only his personal profit, but how enormous it would be.

So far, so good, and, after a most refreshing bath which involved getting into a large jar—as did those whom he humorously thought of as " the other Forty Thieves "—and quite a good dinner, the General retired to rest in a fairly happy and hopeful frame of mind.

§ 5

That night there was a meeting of the Cabinet of the Grand Council of São Thomé. At the head of a long table in the centre of the great hall sat Doña Guiomar, in a kind of chair-throne, Dom Miguel de Braganza being on her right hand and His Excellency Dom Perez de Norhona on her left. Among the other members present were the soldier somewhat grandiloquently known as the Commander-in-Chief of the Armed Forces of São Thomé ; the Minister of Justice ; the Chancellor of the Exchequer ; the Secretary of State for Agriculture, Fisheries and Health ; the Minister of Transport, Roads, Bridges and Public Works ; the Minister for Education ; and other Members of the Cabinet who, with the consent of the Council, governed, under the Regent, the State of São Thomé.

Each of them was a gentleman of aristocratic and almost pure, Portuguese, descent.

His Excellency Dom Perez de Norhona, other business concluded, addressed the Council. One passage in his speech would have been of painful interest to General Jason, could he have heard it.

" . . . I'm afraid that it sheds no light on the fate of our excellent servant and friend, our agent and representative, Manöel Pereira, of whom I have, alas, already begun to think in the past tense, so to speak. But this letter is, without the faintest shadow of doubt, from him, written in his own hand, on our own paper, and in our own private and particular official language, and using certain words and phrases which no one else could have used. He describes this man, who pretends to be a British General, as being not only a German, an emissary and agent of the German Government's Department of Commerce, but also as a scoundrel, a thief and assassin. Also he is desperately disturbed—and indeed it is a most disturbing thought—by the fact that this fellow has, in some unaccountable and incredible way, learned of the mineral resources of this country. As I discovered long ago, and duly informed this Council, we are blessed, or cursed, with the possession of certain substances which in Europe are regarded as being of enormous value. This Nazi German, whose name is Fritz Schultz, has come here to open negotiations with us for the exploitation and commercialization of these mineral deposits ! He, of course, wants concessions and mining-rights. He desires—and to-morrow will propose—the industrial invasion of São Thomé. . . . Why he should pretend to be English I don't know. It may be because the English are the ancient allies

213

and friends of Portugal, or because there is English financial backing to the Company which he doubtless proposes to form."

" It is certain that he is a German ? " asked Doña Guiomar, Regent of São Thomé.

" Pereira so describes him, here, and as I said, gives his name as Fritz Schultz, which is most definitely a German name. Also the man himself speaks German perfectly."

" And he actually referred to these minerals and the granting of a concession to mine them ? " asked the Regent.

" He did. Briefly and in outline, of course ; but he proposes to lay the whole matter before me at length and in detail to-morrow."

" Then I venture to suggest," said His Excellency the Marquess Dom Miguel de Braganza, " that we welcome our visitor, bid him stay here just as long as he likes and perhaps a little longer, and start him to work personally at the quick-sand to-morrow."

" Quick-sand and slow death," he added, and smiled pensively.

There was a general movement and word of assent from each member of the Cabinet.

" He certainly must not leave São Thomé," observed the Regent.

" No. He certainly must not," agreed de Norhona. " But I would ask that the Marquess should reconsider the question of his being invited to fill his buckets from our remarkable quick-sand. It would be in the nature of waste."

" Oh, but we have plenty of sand. We can spare a little," smiled the Marquess de Braganza.

" Waste of a good visitor, I meant," replied de Norhona, flashing his gleaming teeth toward the speaker. "If the Council would kindly place him in my charge, I could make far better use of him."

"And not waste him, eh?" said Doña Guiomar, her extremely beautiful face, strong and very intelligent, lighting up as she smiled quizzically at her favourite Member of the Council.

"Definitely not. Far from it. He would be extremely useful to me, and I beg your Serene Highness to—er—allot him to me, so to speak."

"Why, certainly. Certainly. I see no objection whatsoever. You'd take care, of course, that he never left the Island."

"I can most certainly assure Your Highness that he will never leave the Island," replied de Norhona.

And after the Council had given its unanimous consent to Dr. de Norhona's dealing with this German business and with the German himself, the Council passed on to matters of graver import.

PART V

I

FOR Colonel Henry Carthew life was never again quite the same after the departure from Sitapur of his life-long friends, Reginald and Antoinette Jason. To gain command of the Regiment that he also loved was small compensation for the loss of the only two people whom in the whole wide world he loved.

At first, he was utterly wretched, lost, lonely and depolarized. Nor was he ever quite clear in his mind as to whether he missed Reginald or Antoinette the more. He loved his friend Reginald with the amazing, abiding and selfless love with which a man may love another man, with a love passing the love of woman : the love of David for Jonathan.

Antoinette he loved as the best sort of man does love a woman, with adoration and something of apotheosis, the love and dazzled yearning of the moth for the star. Had she not married Reginald, he would have done his utmost to be worthy to marry her, and would have dared to lay his life and career at her feet, while overwhelmed by a sense of his utter unworthiness. As it was, he loved her with a gentle and unselfish devotion which is not too common. She was the only woman in his life, the only woman whom he had ever loved.

And these two were gone, leaving him desolate, lonely and miserable. Almost daily he wrote to one

or other of his two friends, and occasionally he received
a reply.

Realizing that he might be boring them, he then
wrote weekly ; and finding that this produced a reply
from Reginald or Antoinette about once a month,
wrote to each in alternate weeks, so that each had a
fortnight of peace from his pestering.

When at length these letters remained almost
unanswered, he began to write long and intimate
letters, such as a man may write to his wife, a woman
to her beloved husband—and then destroyed them.

Finding this destruction distasteful and indeed painful, he changed the letter-writing to diary-keeping, and
to this diary he confided his inmost thoughts.

While fond of Henry, both Reginald and Antoinette
Jason had always, and quite rightly, considered him a
queer chap.

When the day came that General Jason retired,
Colonel Carthew decided that, after giving them a few
months or perhaps a year in which to settle down at
Home, he would send in his papers, retire to England,
and try to find a small house as near Jason's place as
possible. Of course, it would be nothing like his
friends' fine old house and timbered estate, but he'd
be able to afford a nice little cottage *de luxe*. Perhaps in a tiny orchard with an acre of garden. Keep
a dog or two and possibly a horse. Then he'd be able
to ride over and drop in just whenever he felt like it,
or rather, as often as he thought they could stand it.
If he didn't over-do it, he would always be welcome.
Reginald would be delighted to see him and to talk
over old times far into the night, and Antoinette would
be glad to have him about the place, making himself

useful. He'd potter in the garden with her. She loved gardening and he knew a bit about it himself. He'd get some books and learn some more.

§ 2

One day toward the end of the time that Carthew had allotted himself as his final period in India, he received a rare and tremendously welcome letter from his beloved Antoinette. For a time he forbore to open it, gloating upon her handwriting on the envelope. He would keep it till the evening, and after his return from Mess, would settle down in perfect peace and comfort to read and re-read her words, which always delighted him with their playful, kindly, friendly badinage and jests at the expense of the crusty old bachelor and misogynist.

Misogynist ! If she only knew. Indeed it was surprising that she didn't. It was wonderful that he had never given himself away in all those years when he was seeing her daily. Rather clever of him, really.

But actually he did not read the letter in great mental peace or any degree of comfort. Antoinette was troubled, worried and anxious. And no wonder, by Gad ! Reginald was what she called " more or less missing." He had never returned from that trip ! Carthew knew that Reginald had suddenly been moved to rush off on some mysterious expedition to some unknown place, leaving her with no more information than that he would be back in six months' time.

And now, not only had the six months expired but another six months as well. And in all that while she had had no communication from him whatsoever, save a brief and flippant note from a place called Santa

Cruz, saying that this was the *starting-point* of the expedition.

Had he written to his old friend Henry within the last twelve months and given him any idea of where he was and what he was up to, she asked.

No, indeed, he hadn't, mused Henry Carthew. The old beggar hadn't written him a line for well over a twelve-month. Getting damned lazy, that was the fact of it. Not that he had ever been a brilliant correspondent—from the point of regularity and punctuality, anyway. Really too bad of him, to push off into the blue like this, and leave Antoinette to worry. Too bad to go even for six months without her knowing where he was. And then to make it twelve. What on earth could be the game ? Some Government job ? Surely not. Not with all that secrecy. He would have told Antoinette something about it. And if he couldn't take her with him, he would write to her.

Queer ! What could it mean ? Could there be a woman in it ?

No. Utter rubbish. Reginald had always been a model husband. Never dream of doing a thing like that.

Greatly puzzled and somewhat perturbed, Henry Carthew thought of little else than this strange disappearance of General Jason. And, after chewing the matter over by night and day, revolving it in his mind until his mind almost ceased to revolve, he answered Lady Jason's letter, and told her that he hadn't had a word from her husband, alas, for quite eighteen months. And that he hadn't the faintest idea as to what he was doing, nor where he could be. But would she please bear this in mind—that there was nothing, literally nothing, he would not do to help her. As she knew, Reginald was his oldest and best, indeed his only friend, except herself, and if she thought Reginald was in danger or trouble, if she thought he was really lost, she had only to say the word, and he would throw up everything and come home by the next boat.

But of course, the first thing to do was to find out where, approximately, he was, or was last heard of. And if she could learn nothing from the British Consul or appropriate authority in that part, he himself would go to this Santa Cruz place, or any other from which she had received later information.

It was almost a year before Colonel Carthew received another letter from Lady Jason. In this she told him that she was reduced to a state of hopelessness and despair. Such was her anxiety, and so difficult was her position, that she was now being selfish enough to accept her dear friend Henry's offer of a year ago, and to ask him to come and help her.

Freely she admitted that she had been unable to discover anything at all, and knew nothing whatsoever as to Reginald's whereabouts, save that he had reached this place, Santa Cruz, from which he had last written.

By appeal to the War Office, the Foreign Office and Scotland Yard; by advertising far and wide; by writing to the offices of the Shipping Companies, she had discovered nothing at all, save that Reginald had sailed by the S.S. *Gibraltar* of the British Southern and General Mail Company, and had left the ship at Belamu where he had transferred to the S.S. *São José de Coimba* of the Anglo-Portuguese Steam Navigation and Trading Company. This ship had stopped to land him at Santa Cruz, an almost harbourless place which was not one of their ports of call, inasmuch as it was not worth calling a port.

Letters to such people as the Governor, the Mayor,

the Chief of Police, the principal hotel (under that name) had all remained unanswered. And in any case, she was afraid, if any representative of General Jason made his way to this Santa Cruz place, it was unlikely that he would learn anything as to the General's destination. Since he had kept that information from her, he would hardly impart it to casual acquaintances, if he made any, at Santa Cruz.

Having done everything of which she could think, moved Heaven and earth to get news of him, she now appealed to her oldest and best friend, her dear Henry, to do anything that he could and would.

Colonel Carthew replied by cable that he was sending in his papers at once, and would come to England immediately his affairs were wound up. He then wrote a letter telling Antoinette that he would henceforth devote his life and all his worldly goods to the search for his friend, her husband.

§ 3

Henry Carthew found Lady Jason in better case than he had expected. He had feared to find a haggard and broken woman, half-dead with anxiety, fear and worry. He found a lady in excellent health, good spirits and a state of glowing resentment, annoyance and, indeed, anger toward her husband—not because he was lost, of course, but because he had gone and got himself lost in such an exceedingly silly way. Why on earth couldn't he have told her where he was going and why he was going there?

Sneaking off with all that secrecy and mystery!

Going off without making proper arrangements for the future, should he by any chance be away for more than his anticipated six months.

Going off and leaving her stranded, neither wife nor widow, nor—what was more to the point—his accredited financial agent. Things were getting terribly difficult from that point of view. Extremely so.

No, it was not so much a case of " my poor lost darling with his romantic ideas " as " the silly old fool with his idiotic tricks."

It was of course all to the good that Antoinette should bear up so bravely and incline rather toward indignation than to sentimentalism and premature grief. Or so Henry Carthew told himself, as he stoutly denied and rejected the idea that he was just a little shocked at Antoinette's hardness. No doubt this apparent hardness covered real grief, a sense of terrible bereavement, great anxiety and immeasurable tenderness. It was a good thing that she should show so brave a front to the world, and talk rather of the idiotic way in which Reginald had let her down and given her all this worry, financial bother and general annoyance, than bemoan the fate of her beloved lost darling. Better a warmly indignant woman than a miserable weeping Niobe.

But of course she must be desperately unhappy and must go in perpetual fear. How could it be otherwise ? She must love Reginald completely. What woman would not ? Especially one who had lived with him so long and really knew his wonderful virtues. Why, he himself felt sick with anxiety when he realized that Reginald Jason, his hero, his beloved friend who had been the star of his boyish admiration and the object of his whole-hearted and single-hearted love, had been lost for a couple of years ; Reginald whom he had always followed with a fidelity which was but just this side of blindness ; Reginald whom he had literally reverenced, and who, from his childish Prep. School days, had been his guide, philosopher and friend.

Friend. That noble word.

And now it was the turn and the time for Henry Carthew to be a friend indeed to his friend in need, and to show what a friend could do.

§ 4

And thus it came to pass that, upon a day of sullen heat when the white incandescent sky brooded low over a waveless oily sea, Henry Carthew was rowed ashore from the old *S.S. St. Paul de Loanda* and landed at the rotting quay of the rotting, sun-smitten, swamp-encircled, disease-infested town of Santa Cruz, made his way to the *Casa Real*, and received what was undoubtedly the very greatest surprise, not to say shock, of all his life.

For, entering that dismal and all-but-derelict hostelry, he came face to face with the man who had once, and for years, been his best *bête-noir*—Mess-Sergeant Samuel Palsover !

" *Good Lord above us !* " ejaculated Henry Carthew, blinking his eyes, almost rubbing them in his incredulous amazement.

" *Blimey !* " responded Mr. Palsover.

And the two men stared at each other in utter wonder.

Well ! thought Henry Carthew, of all the amazing coincidences ! It is a world's record. Last time I saw this beggar was in Sitapur, and *now*—to find him here in this hole at the back of beyond, the last place God made !

226

Ah, but is it exactly coincidence ? Reginald Jason
came here. Is this fellow Palsover in any way connected with that ? Of course he is.

Lumme ! thought Mr. Palsover. Well, well, well !
Who'd have thought it ? What's the old devil doing
here ? Cor ! You'd have thought you was safe in
Santa Cruz, wouldn't you ? And here of all people
on God's earth, the old Colonel rolls up and walks in as
large as life. That's a rum go, if ever. But was it
so much of a rum go, after all ? He must be on the
track of the General.

Yerss. . . . That letter the General wrote to his
wife. Perhaps he himself had been a fool to post it,
after all. But there, it gave nothing away, except
the name of this Santa Cruz place. And that was what
had brought the Colonel here. Depend on it ! He was
doing the blooming hero salvation act. And here was
as far as he would get.

He couldn't know anything about St. Tommy now,
could he ? A million to one against the General ever
having said a word to him about it. Why no, damn it
all, what was he thinking about ? He himself had
never told the General, even ; not until they got here
and met the Arab. Could the General have written
from St. Tommy ? Not according to the Arab. Could
the General himself have escaped ? Not according to
the Arab. And he himself had never seen hide nor
hair of him, nor heard a word of him, for nigh on a
couple of years. No, that was it. The old Colonel
was on the noble salvation stunt. " Dr.-Livingstone-I-
presume " stuff. Well, he'd soon get it out of the little
Stanley. Stanley the Explorer lost in Santa Cruz, and
finding his old pal Palsover behind the bar of the *Caser
Reel*. Laugh ! . . . Enough to make a cat laugh !

227

But half a mo' ! What if the General had gone and told his wife all about the rayjum business—and she had gone and told Carthew ! . . . He'd shoot him as soon as look at him, the old fool, if there was going to be any hankey-pankey, any double-crossing. Nobody in this world wasn't going to do S. Palsover, Esquire, out of his rights, and get away with it. No, by Cripes ! . . .

On the other hand—suppose the General was really scuppered, as it began to look like. Couldn't sit here waiting for him much longer. The Colonel was an old swine—but he was straight. He'd play the blooming game, fair and square, if he was let in on it. Perhaps the best thing, after all, would be to . . .?

" And what the devil are you doing here, Palsover ? " asked Henry Carthew, none too cordially.

" Me, Sir ? Keeping this little pub. Been here the last, oh, couple of years, nearly. Always thought I'd keep a pub when I left the Army, but I never thought it would be in this God-forsaken country."

" Well, how does it come to be in this country ? Did you, by any chance, come out here with General Jason ? "

" That's right, Sir. That's right. Met the General in England. And almost as soon as he claps eyes on me he says,

' *Coming with me, Palsover ? I'm going out on a expedition.*' And ' *What do you think, General ? Not 'arf,*' says I. And here I am."

" And where's General Jason ? "

" Ar ! Where, Sir ? "

" But you know where he went from here, don't you ? "

" That's right, Sir."

228

" Well, presumably he is there."

" You're telling me. *I* can't find out that he's there."

" Haven't you been there ? Haven't you tried to find out for yourself ? "

" Ar ! And you can lay to that."

" But he can't have absolutely disappeared."

" You're telling me again. It's just percisely what he has done."

" Why did he go there ? "

" Now you're asking me, for a change. I expect you know as well as I do, don't you, Sir, what he went there for ? "

" I do not. I haven't the very faintest idea as to why he went there."

" Cross your heart ? Cut your throat if you tell a lie ? Strike you blind ? " Mr. Palsover had evidently had a morning eye-opener. Or possibly an eye-closer.

" When I say I don't know why General Jason went to this place, you may take it for granted that I *don't* know," replied Henry Carthew coldly.

" Well," replied Mr. Palsover, politely raising his hand to excuse, if not conceal, a gentle hiccup, " he went to this place with the idea of making a bit of money—or so he told me. Brought me as far as here and left me stranded. And here I am to this day."

" Faithful hever," he added pensively as he reached for a bottle.

" I wonder you didn't go home, Palsover."

" No, Sir. No. ' *Wait here,*' said the General. And here I waits. That's me, Samuel Palsover."

And even Colonel Henry Carthew was almost moved to sympathy and admiration as he gazed on the yearning, trustful, faithful-hound-like countenance of

Mr. Samuel Palsover, now regarding him with those large, moist, and alas, somewhat yellowing eyes.

" And you positively have no information as to where General Jason is, what became of him, or whether he ever left this other place ? . . . Where is it, by the way ? "

" Well, Sir, in a manner of speaking, I don't know."

" But you've been there, you say."

" Regular. Once every six months for the last couple of years or so."

" Well then, what do you mean by saying you don't know where it is ? "

" Well, Sir, you goes by sea in a bloomin' bunder-boat, and how are you to know whether you're going north, east, south or west ? Boat clears out of here at night, and lands you at this place at night too. How are you to know which way you come ? Bloomin' boat may keep on tacking all night, or sail round in a bloody great circle, just to confuse you. That's my belief what it does."

" How long does it take ? "

." Oh, best part of a fortnight. Time slips away like, when you got nothing to do but eat, drink and sleep."

" Well, could we get a boat and set off at once, to-morrow ? "

Mr. Palsover laughed long and loud, to the great annoyance of Henry Carthew, who found something in his laughter that he disliked intensely. Cynicism ? Contempt ? Patronage ?

" What the devil are you laughing at ? " he asked sharply.

" You, Sir, in a manner o' speaking. Also the idea of taking a bunder-boat and pushing off to-morrow. Why, nobody here don't know where the place is.

Never even heard of it, let alone the way there. You only get the chance to go twice in the year."

" How's that ? "

" Because every six months a native feller comes in a big bunder-boat, what they call a *dhow*, on his way there. Puts in for water and grub and perhaps to pick up a feller or drop him on his way back. Letters perhaps, or messages or somethink. *I* don't know."

" And he took General Jason to this place ? "

" Ar, that's right. Me too."

" When is he due again ? "

" Oh, in a month or two. Any old time between now and the change of the monsoon."

" I'll wait for him," announced Carthew.

" The devil you will, Sir ? " replied Palsover. " How do you know he'll take you ? "

" Why shouldn't he ? "

" Visitors not invited. *Not at Home*, if they call. ' *Keep away with both feet. This means you* ' sort of hospitality."

" How could they stop my going ? "

" Because you couldn't get anybody to take you there. And if you could, it would not be a case of stopping you from going, but from coming. Coming back. Damned difficult place to get to and a damned sight more difficult to get away from. That's what General Jason found out."

" You think he's still there then ? "

" Yerss. That's right, Sir. Unless he grew bloomin' wings, he's still there. Course he might have grown 'em.

" *Angel's* wings," added Mr. Palsover mournfully.

" Look here. You say that this mysterious fellow in his mysterious boat takes you. Couldn't you get him to take me ? "

" I could try, Sir. I could try. We might square him. But it would require considerable dough. . . . Perhaps if you could put up enough, I might be able to work it."

Yes, that'd be the thing, pondered Mr. Palsover. Next time the Arab came, tell him this gent, another British Officer, wanted to find out what had become of his old pal General Jason. Find out for himself. And they could tell the Arab that if he wanted to save the St. Tommy people trouble, he had better take Carthew, otherwise he'd go back home and raise hell, and the first thing they'd know would be that there was a British warship banging off at 'em.

Perhaps the Arab would grin and say how was the British warship going to find the Island, for a start ; and, *if* they found it, how was they to know that General Jason hadn't pushed off long ago ?

Anyway, it was worth trying. For, to tell the truth, he was getting sick, sorry and tired of being Felice Diego's partner in this blasted pot-house, and living in this God-forsaken one-eyed hole. Trading up-country wasn't too bad, but it was mouldy chicken-feed compared with what he had come out here for. And many a time he had been tempted to " cut his lucky "—his unlucky, rather. Cut his losses and clear out. But he couldn't bring himself to do it, not with all those millions waiting to be picked up on that island, and the General there himself.

He had never thought much of old Carthew. He had hated his guts. But he was a gentleman. He wouldn't double-cross anybody, and no harm could come from getting him on to the Island. And a damn lot of good might come of it if he found out all about the General. And if the poor old chap had got one of these nasty diseases, or died of malaria, then the thing

to do would be to let Carthew in on the rayjum business, and let him take the General's place. He'd
sooner work with the General ; but Carthew was just
as straight. He wouldn't double-cross anybody. And
that was the real danger, when you were up against
big concessions that were worth millions.

Yes, he'd get Carthew over to St. Tommy, next time
the Arab rolled up.

II

FOR five weary weeks, each as long as an ordinary
month, Henry Carthew endured the society of
Samuel Palsover, the appalling climate of Santa Cruz,
and the amenities of the *Casa Real*—in that order.
And it was a pleasure to him to do so, for increasingly
he felt sure that he was on the track of his dearly-
loved friend.

Little by little, Mr. Palsover, whom he could not
bring himself to like but forced himself to tolerate,
raised his hopes and increased his tiny stock of knowledge as to the probable whereabouts of General Jason
and his reason for going—wherever he had gone. But
until the arrival of the Hadji Abdulla, the words *São
Thomé* were never uttered by the garrulous master of
the *Casa Real*. Half proprietor Mr. Palsover might
be ; but wholly in charge, command and possession he
was ; Senhor Felice Diego being occasionally seen but
seldom heard. Henry Carthew gained the impression
that Palsover had some hold over the little man, and
the certainty that the latter went in fear and trembling
of the burly and overbearing Palsover.

'All done by kindness,' as Mr. Palsover would say,
but done very effectively.

By the time that Henry Carthew had begun to
wonder whether Palsover had been telling him a pack
of lies, and was keeping him kicking his heels at Santa
Cruz in the interests of the profits of the *Casa Real*,

the auspicious day dawned when Mr. Palsover, bringing him his morning tea, announced with great solemnity and evident joy, that He had come. Mr. Palsover spoke with the *empressement* and solemnity of one who announced the Second Coming.

After a hasty shave and sketchy breakfast, Henry Carthew, dripping with perspiration, hurried down to the quay of the almost silted-up harbour, and there beheld, among the coasting bunder-boats and *dhows*, a remarkably fine *baggala*.

Seating himself on a bollard, he watched and waited until a large *tony* was paddled ashore from the big *dhow*. In its stern sat a big bearded man whose face, size, white robes and green turban marked him as the individual so often described by Palsover as " the Arab," the Hadji Abdulla.

Carthew, long a student of Arabic, and holder of the Indian Government's Honours standard certificate for proficiency in that language, correctly greeted the man who ascended the rickety ladder and stepped on to the quay. He announced himself as an Englishman, a soldier, retired Colonel of a British Regiment and the friend of one General Jason, who was now definitely regarded as missing, and whom, as he was informed, the Hadji Sahib had given passage in his *dhow* from Santa Cruz.

While studying the speaker gravely and with deep interest, the Arab replied that his information concerning the British General was correct, and that on one of his visits to Santa Cruz he had taken that Sidi to São Thomé.

"São Thomé!" repeated Carthew. "Where's that?"

" Well," replied the Arab, " it's a long way from here. Quite a little voyage."

" You are going there from here, are you ? "

235

" I'm going to many places from here, Sidi."

" São Thomé among them ? "

" I shouldn't be surprised."

" Look here. I want you to take me, and I am prepared to make it worth your while."

" To take you to São Thomé, Sidi ? I couldn't do that. I never take strangers to São Thomé."

" But you took my friend, General Jason."

" Oh, but that was different. He had a letter of introduction—a letter which proved to be perfectly genuine—given him by a Government official, and addressed to a member of the São Thomé Government."

" But you took another man with him ? "

" Yes, his servant, Sidi. I took him too, because the Sidi who had the letter guaranteed him."

" Well, now let him in turn guarantee me."

" That's hardly the same thing, is it ? " replied the Arab. " The British Officer had a letter for me as well as the other letter, and said,

' *This is my passport to São Thomé and I wish to take my servant.*' You have no letter of introduction, have you ? No ? Well, I don't think I can take anyone to São Thomé because this servant guarantees him."

" Why, what harm could I do to the State of São Thomé ? "

" I don't know, Sidi. But there's another question' What harm could the State of São Thome do to you ? '

" Well, I am ready to risk that."

" So was General Jason. And he has not been heard of since he reached the Capital. I am the last person outside São Thomé who saw him, and that was two years ago ; and I have been entirely unable to learn anything whatever about him on my subsequent visits."

" That's why I want to come."

" Do you think, Sidi, that you could find out what is entirely hidden from me who am accepted and recognized by the São Thoméan Government, and who visit the Island twice a year, not only with their knowledge and consent, but at their request ? I take goods, letters, messages and so forth, up to the Capital. I sojourn there for days at a time. I go about the *suqs* and bazaars, talking with all manner of men. In the cafés and bazaars I hear all the rumours and the gossip of the town. Could you, an uninvited stranger, do more, even if you had the opportunity—which you would not have ? The Sidi General interested me. I liked him, and each time that I have returned, I have tried to find out where he is or what has happened to him. If I took you with me, without credentials, safe conduct, or letter of introduction, you'd be arrested instantly, and I should be summoned before the Council for examination—as to whether I had gone mad or whether I could give any other reason for having brought a stranger to São Thomé."

" Well, suppose you said that I told you that I had most important business with the Government of São Thomé ? And suppose I paid you a considerable sum of money to take me there ? And suppose you decided that you had no right to use your own discretion as to the importance of the matter ? It might be something of the most vital urgency, something on which the very safety of the State depended. Who are you to decide whether . . ."

The Hadji smiled and shook his head.

" Sidi," said he, " suppose that, when you were commanding a Regiment, you gave a certain subordinate the very strictest orders that never, under any circumstances whatsoever, should he do a certain thing. And suppose he did it, and for no reason except that he

237

thought he would ? . . .   No, it is probably more than my life is worth, certainly more than my trade is worth, for me to break the first and greatest of all the commands laid upon me by the Government of São Thomé. Let us come along to the *Casa Real*, and there give me the pleasure and the honour of hearing anything more that you would like to say.   The Roumi named Palsover can join in our conversation, should you wish. But let me repeat, once and for all, that I have no authority to take you to São Thomé, and cannot possibly take the heavy and dangerous responsibility."

" Oh, come, Hadji Sahib.   Dangerous ?   A man like you to use such a word ? " smiled Carthew.

" I have no hesitation in using the word ' dangerous ' in connection with São Thomé," was the grave reply. " Danger ?   It would be certain death for you, probably death for me ;   certain loss of my valuable trade, and probably confiscation of my *dhow*."

Henry Carthew's heart sank, but his courage remained high and his determination unshaken.

Where there's a will there's a way, and God knew he had the will.   There are other methods of killing a cat than by choking it with melted butter.   (How was it that Reginald used to paraphrase that ?   " There are other ways of making an elephant laugh than by tickling it with a feather.")   And he'd find some way of persuading this Hadji chap.   But damn it all—it began to look a bit grim for Reginald.   God grant that they hadn't done more than detain him there.   If they had, it would be up to him to help him to escape.   A prisoner's chances are quadrupled by having a friend outside, and surely, between them, they could put up enough to bribe the Hadji to take a risk.

What a nice fellow he seemed.   Sort of man one took to, at once.

As, talking amiably, the Hadji and Colonel Carthew entered the gate of the sand-covered compound of the *Casa Real* they heard a shrill scream and saw a young girl, almost a child, run headlong from the front door of the hotel.

As they looked in her direction, the huge negro, whom Mr. Palsover had whimsically gazetted as Giant Pander of Santa Cruz, appeared in the doorway, his ugly face convulsed with rage, a bottle in his right hand.

In a language which the Hadji understood, he roared filthy abuse at the child and, with all his might, flung the bottle as she fled a few yards in advance of him. The big heavy bottle struck her squarely on the back of the head and was shattered in pieces by the violence of the blow which sent the girl sprawling, face downward, on the ground, where she lay still and apparently dead.

It had all been so sudden and swift that the child was down and the negro seizing her by the hair, before Carthew and the Hadji had time to intervene.

With a shout, Henry Carthew sprang forward and rushed toward the negro. But quickly as he moved, the Hadji, though bigger and heavier, moved more quickly.

With a shout of " *Hi !* " he rushed at the negro, and drove a crashing straight-left at his face, knocking him down. Springing up, the powerful brute in turn leapt at the Hadji with extended hands, attacking him as might a gorilla. Closing in, the Hadji most scientifically hooked with his left, upper-cut with his right, and, as the man staggered back, drove a terrific left at the point of his jaw.

Tottering backward, the negro collapsed and fell,

239

and the subsequent proceedings ceased to interest him for several minutes.

Tenderly lifting the child from the ground, the Hadji carried her into the house, shouted for Diego, handed her to him, and bade him fetch Almeida who, at any rate, called himself a doctor, and see that the women-folk looked after the child properly.

" And you had better keep that brute of a *hubshi* out of my way, for a time. For if I set eyes on him I'll beat him insensible."

" What about handing him over to the Police ? " suggested Henry Carthew.

" Oh, a lot of trouble for nothing. Merely stirring up bribery and corruption and blackmail for both of us. I can deal with him better than the Police would."

" Right. Now may I ask you a question, or rather, make a statement ? "

" Certainly," replied the Arab with raised eyebrows.

" Well, look here. You're an Englishman and a remarkably fine boxer."

" An Englishman ? " replied the Hadji.

" Yes, of course you are. Do you mean to say that an Arab cries ' *Hi !* ' in an emergency, and drives the straightest left I ever saw, and hooks, upper-cuts, and goes for the point like a champion heavy-weight ? "

" Wonderful are the works of Allah," replied the Hadji somewhat evasively, as he regarded a skinned knuckle.

" Oh, quite," laughed Henry Carthew, " and I rise to remark that you are one of them. You really must forgive me for butting in, but I spoke hastily in my excitement at my own cleverness. In point of fact, it was a bit obvious, wasn't it ? "

" We'll have a talk later on," replied the Hadji in the ordinary words and accent of an educated Briton.

240

" I've got to fix up one or two things with the—er—management here, and then I must go down to my ship again. I'll give myself the pleasure of calling on you after dinner to-night."

" Oh, but won't you dine with me ? " smiled Henry Carthew.

" Thanks, very much. I'd love to, but it would be unwise. I don't want to cause comment. A Hadji I am, and a Hadji I must remain ; so I don't want any scandal concerning my holy name. If you'll excuse me, I won't eat and drink with Unbelievers, infidel consumers of alcohol, and those who smoke the Forbidden."

" I say, are you really a Hadji ? " asked Carthew as the Arab turned away.

" Just now it was ' *Are you an Englishman ?* ' " smiled the Hadji. " Yes, I am a Hadji. If I am not, there isn't one in this world, and never was. Yes, I've made the Pilgrimage all right. May I look you up at about eight this evening ? "

" Splendid."

And that evening, as Henry Carthew sat in his bedroom at the french-window that opened on to the untrustworthy verandah, he received the promised visit from the man known as the Hadji Abdulla.

" Come along. What about a whiskey-and-soda and a cigarette ? " suggested Carthew hospitably.

" I'd love to," replied the Hadji in English. " But I don't think I will. I expect Palsover will be coming up presently, and I don't want him to get suspicious. . . . Do you know, this is only about the second or third time I have given myself away, in half a lifetime."

" Well, I'm awfully sorry if I have . . ." began Carthew.

" Not at all, for I'm quite sure I can trust you never to say a single word to a living soul, that . . ."

" Good Lord, no ! Sooner cut my tongue out," Carthew assured him. " And look here, I won't ask you any questions at all with regard to yourself, but I'm awfully glad to find that you are English, and that I can really talk to you as man to man, about my friend's disappearance."

" Right. We will. I'll introduce myself first," replied the Hadji. " Name's Dysart. Brodie Dysart. My father was Rear-Admiral Sir Sinclair Brodie Dysart. I've been both a sailor and a soldier, and served my five years in the French Foreign Legion—in the Indo-China campaign. Lived in Moroccan Africa for years, and in Arabia. Did the Pilgrimage to Mecca. Got to like Arab life nearly as much as I do sea life, so went Arab again and combined the two. Bought a *dhow* and learnt the business, and then had that *baggala* built under my own eye. Finest craft of its kind afloat. And I live the finest life on earth—only it's on water. All the joys of a Cowes yachtsman and a deep-sea sailor as well. And those of a keen trader too—and they are many."

" Sounds simply wonderful," said Henry Carthew as the Hadji paused.

" Pearls, coffee, hides, silk and what not, up North, and a special cargo twice a year for São Thomé. Handle anything that's good value in small bulk, except hasheesh, guns and slaves. No trouble with the Police in any port, or with the British Navy in any sea."

" Gad, how interesting. Marvellous," murmured Carthew. " I said I wouldn't ask any questions, but I really must ask one or two. Only please don't answer me, if you'd rather not. I shan't be in the least offended, of course. No earthly reason why I should

242

be. I've no right to cross-question you. But I have come down here to find out what has happened to my oldest and dearest friend, General Sir Reginald Jason. I'm going to track him down, find him and rescue him, if he is alive ; and I want you to help me."

"Wish I could," murmured the Hadji. "Not only for the sake of helping you, but because I myself liked him very much indeed. Very fine specimen of a very fine type. I warned him. I begged him not to go to São Thomé, although he had a letter of introduction."

"Well now—the question that I am going to ask you and that you are going to answer or not, as you think fit. This mysterious São Thomé place. How is it that *you* can come and go safely ? "

"Oh, it's a long story. To cut it short—a good many years ago I was able to save a man who was in bad trouble in a certain port that has a very bad and very well-deserved reputation. He was up against the local Governor and in the hands of a pretty bad police-gang, and was undoubtedly for it. I thought he was a Portuguese and a fellow-European. Anyway, I got him away on my *dhow*, and he was more than grateful, because apparently something very much more important than his life was at stake.

"Well, in short, he paid me very handsomely to take him home—having made me swear on the Koran, the Beard of the Prophet, the head and the life of my first-born and all else that I might hold sacred, that I would not publish anything I might learn about his destination.

"We got very friendly on the voyage, and, having aroused my curiosity and horrible cupidity, he did, after long and deep cogitation and terrific mental struggle, make up his mind to take me ashore at São

Thomé, and actually to the capital of the State. His intention and object was to bring me before the Regent and Council and, more particularly, the Secretary to the Cabinet, with the view to my being appointed official business-agent, special messenger, bearer of a sort of private and confidential secret post-bag and what-not. There's no harm in my telling you all this, because you haven't the faintest notion as to where São Thomé is, and are not likely to visit the place.

" To them I am a trusted, and I think I may say, honoured and respected, servant, agent, employee ; an Arab *dhow*-master, to whose interest it is to keep a closed mouth, and who neither knows nor cares anything about São Thomé save its position on his secret chart. If they don't trust wholly to my integrity, they most certainly do so to my cupidity—to behave with the strictest honesty and discretion, inasmuch as I have nothing to gain and everything to lose by treachery."

" Now you know the position pretty clearly," he concluded.

" Thank you very much indeed," replied Henry Carthew. " I am honoured by your confidence and you can be perfectly sure that nothing on earth would tempt me to abuse it. Now some more questions, if I may ? Do you know why General Jason went to São Thomé ? "

" I haven't the faintest idea."

" Do you know how he came to hear of so unknown and remote a place ? "

" I have not the slightest idea."

" Do you believe he is still at São Thomé ? "

" I have every reason to do so, and none to believe otherwise. I don't want to depress you unnecessarily, but I am bound to say that, although I have heard of

244

people contriving to get there, I have never heard of any unauthorized intruder getting away again."

"But even if it is as lonely as Pitcairn Island, St. Helena or Ascension, surely ships must sight it sometimes."

"Well, it's hundreds of miles from any steamer-route, and there is no reason why any sailing-ship should be in its vicinity."

"Suppose one were blown off its course and driven there by a storm?"

"Well, that would be a case in point, I should say— of those who come but don't go."

"What—massacred?"

"Good Lord, no. Nothing of the sort. They are a most enlightened peaceful and friendly people. If sailors and travellers were driven ashore there—genuine castaways—they'd receive every kindness."

"And continue to receive it, eh, until they died?"

"Exactly. Until they died of old age. But that would hardly apply to people who deliberately and intentionally made their way there. It is conceivable that they would not die of old age."

"And if General Jason is still on the Island, do you think he's . . . well-treated . . . and unlikely to die any but a natural death . . . disease . . . old age?"

"Depends on his object in going there; on the opinion they formed of him and his intentions. The Government has a short way with undesirable intruders, and I am bound to confess that I am quite certain he is not at large, if he is still there. As I told you, I liked him very much, was interested in him and tried to prevent his going; and for those reasons I have always done my best to find out what happened to him. I have failed entirely. I have ventured to ask a member of the Government who is by way of being a friend of mine, and have been reminded that those who ask no questions will be told no stories. One or two people whom I trust and who have no reason for telling me any lies, have assured me that there is not now, and there never has been, an English General on the Island. Inasmuch as I took him there, I can hardly accept their statement—though from their point of view they may be speaking the truth . . . because they have never heard of any such person. Which seems to indicate that he wasn't at liberty, even for a short time, and probably never went outside the Citadel—to which I took him."

" He might be alive inside the Citadel, though."

" Oh, yes. Quite possibly he is."

" An honoured guest, eh ? "

" Yes. Honoured and beloved. So beloved that they couldn't possibly part with him."

" Well now, look here, Mr. Brodie Dysart. . . ."

" Hadji Abdulla while in fancy dress, if you don't mind."

" Right. What I was going to say was, doubtless you've heard of Richard I and his faithful Blondel."

" Yes. Richard was caught on his way home from Palestine, wasn't he, by his enemy the Duke of Austria and imprisoned in his castle of Durenstein ? And Blondel having some sort of a rough idea as to where he was, went round calling at all the castles."

" Or singing rather than calling, perhaps," contributed Henry Carthew. " Sang the Old Home Tunes under likely windows. Well, sounds a bit old-fashioned, but suppose you took me to São Thomé and I tried to get a look round this castle. Not that I'm anything of a singer."

The Hadji laughed.

" I could take you there, and if I did, you'd certainly

be invited up to the Capital, and you'd see the inside of the Citadel all right. Whether you'd ever see the outside again is another matter."

" I'll risk that."

" I won't, though," replied the Hadji. " If you've got no valid pass, letter, safe-guard or guarantee, it would be unfortunate for both of us, especially for you. I don't think they'd detain me because they trust me and I'm pretty useful, but I might lose what is at present almost my only visible means of support."

" Why should you ? "

" Simply for breaking the first and most important rule of my contract with the Government of São Thomé. I don't think you quite realize the extent to which they don't want visitors."

" Well, I should hate to be the cause of any trouble or anything unpleasant happening to you—but I'm going to get to São Thomé."

" How ? "

" I don't know, but I expect I'm going there with you. You see, my friend General Jason undoubtedly came here with this fellow Palsover. He undoubtedly went with you to São Thomé. That's where he was last heard of. And that is where I am going."

" To certain death, or imprisonment in São Thomé for life ? That won't help your friend, will it ? "

" I don't know, but I'm going to spend the rest of my life and the rest of my money in finding him ; or I'll ' perish in the attempt,' as the noble stories say."

" Well, you'll perish, if only of old age, if you go to São Thomé, and I'm not going to have any hand in your death."

" Now look here, Dysart—I mean Hadji Sahib—you are an Englishman."

" I'm not. I'm a Scot."

" All right. Better still, no doubt. And you're an honest man ; by which I mean to say you are not to be bought and sold, and your word is as good as your bond and all that."

" How do you know ? "

" I don't know how I know it, but I do ; and I realize that you are not going to betray—I mean, let down—your friends or principals in São Thomé. I'm not going to ask you to do them the slightest harm whatever. That clears the ground so far."

" Aye ? Well ? "

" On the other hand, there's a fellow-countryman of ours, a fellow Briton, who, if he is alive, is imprisoned in São Thomé."

" You don't know that."

" You believe it though. You think it, don't you ? "

" Aye. Well ? "

" Suppose you could save him, rescue him, get him away, without doing the slightest harm to São Thomé, wouldn't you do it ? "

" I advised him, I warned him, I begged him—not to go. And he wouldn't listen to me."

" Yes, so you see what comes of not listening to people. Now you listen to me, Dysart. Supposing I guaranteed you against any financial loss—if the Government of São Thomé, in effect, cancelled their contract with you and forbade you to return there any more."

" It would cost you a good deal, and I should be very sorry indeed. It is a most interesting business, and I have the greatest admiration for the São Thoméans, from the Council to the peasants. It is a unique place, and they've evolved an almost ideal way of life. It would be a damned shame to . . ."

" I know, I know ; and I'm not going to ask you to,"

interrupted Henry Carthew. "Don't forget that one proviso was that not the slightest harm of any sort or kind should come to São Thomé. Well now, suppose I guaranteed you against financial loss and took no step whatsoever of which you did not approve. Wouldn't you—to save a fellow-countryman, one of the finest men who ever stepped—take the risk of their being annoyed with you and telling you not to come there again ?"

"Suppose I would take the risk of upsetting a way and a habit of life to which I am very much attached. Suppose I took your word for it that you could and would reimburse me for the loss of my lucrative business as agent, *entrepreneur* and merchant. How would you propose to set about finding out whether General Jason is at the Capital or elsewhere, on São Thomé ; and, secondly, if you discovered him, alive and fit to travel, how would you propose to get him away ?"

"I haven't thought it all out in detail. Obviously impossible until I get there. Have to improvise. But the first step in finding out whether he is at São Thomé, is to go there."

"Well, I am the only person who can take you there," asserted the Hadji. "And suppose I did so, what would you propose to do ? If I, who am well known, trusted and respected, have been entirely unable to find any trace of him, what could you do, a stranger inevitably under suspicion ? Besides, you'd be more than under suspicion—you'd be under arrest," added the Hadji with a smile.

"I don't know. But I do know this. That I am going to spend the rest of my life in trying to get to São Thomé. Now look here, Dysart. General Jason is most happily married. Think of the appalling position of his wife, the constant terrible anxiety, hope and fear ; hope deferred. Look here, I hate to talk like this," continued Henry Carthew shamefacedly. " I don't know whether you have a wife yourself, Dysart, but surely you've loved a woman, and a woman has loved you. Well, think how she'd be feeling if you disappeared. . . . Lost. . . . Not a word from you for years and . . ."

The Hadji sighed involuntarily and thought of a woman whom he had loved indeed and who had loved him as dearly. Lost.

He broke the silence.

" I'll think it over," he said. " But bear in mind that if I did take you to São Thomé, you'd probably never be seen again. I might or might not share your fate, and if I were lucky, should only be ruined. . . ." Excuse me now. I must go to the *dhow*."

Henry Carthew rose.

" You'll do it, Dysart. You'll do it. As your father would have done."

" My father ? Did you know him ? "

" No. But you told me he was an officer in the King's Navy. A British Admiral."

A little ashamed and alarmed at such a flight of eloquence, he changed the subject abruptly.

" By the way, what do you make of this chap Palsover ? "

" Haven't seen much of him, but speaking with purely unwarrantable prejudice and unwarranted bias, I feel he's much too good to be true. In point of fact, I detest him."

" Good. So do I. And not wholly intuitively. I've known the gentleman for many a long year. Longer than I care to think about. What I cannot understand is Jason bringing him on an expedition like this. And I cannot help feeling that he knows a lot more than he says. Knows a deal more than he tells us. And what on earth has kept him here for a couple of years? In a hole like this!"

"Fidelity. Deep love for his master. Anxiety as to his master's fate. 'Ever faithful ever true'—I don't think."

"No, nor do I," agreed Henry Carthew. "The man is the most pernicious money-grubber I have ever met; and as for interest in General Jason's fate—the only interest Palsover ever took in anything was the interest on his capital. I wish we could make the brute talk. He knows why the General came here, and whatever it was that brought Jason here, is what keeps Palsover here."

"I'll see what I can do with him," replied the Hadji. "If we were Wicked Men, I have some lads on my *dhow* who'd make the dumb talk."

He sighed whimsically.

"Does he drink? We must consider the problem. . . . As to taking you to São Thomé. I'll think the matter over, and come round and tell you my decision in the morning. And do please understand that whatever my decision may be, it will be unalterable. It would be absolutely useless for you to try to change it."

"I'm going to São Thomé, Hadji Sahib," smiled Henry Carthew.

"Ah, we may meet there then—though I doubt it," replied the Hadji as he closed the door. "Good night."

HENRY CARTHEW did not sleep that night. Hope, fear, doubt and excitement kept his mind too active.

What he could do if this amazing Hadji Abdulla or Brodie Dysart flatly and finally refused to take him, he did not know. But in the simple faith of his simple mind, he felt that Fate had not intended him to come all this way ; and to find here, in Santa Cruz, Palsover, who had travelled with the General ; and then the Hadji Abdulla, who had actually taken him to São Thomé—unless it were intended that something more should come of it. And when Henry Carthew said Fate he meant God ; for in a personal and merciful and loving God, Henry Carthew, queer fellow, most firmly believed.

As he sat at his breakfast of curried eggs ; tea, with buffalo milk ; soggy toast and buffalo butter, papaia and mangoes, served in his horrible bedroom because it was less horrible than the one public eating-room below, he heard the sound of feet upon the bare wooden stairs.

With a perfunctory knock at the door, Mr. Samuel Palsover entered and stood aside to make way for the Hadji Abdulla.

" Morning, Sir. Finished breakfast ? Hope you found everything all correct ? Here's the Hadji wants a word with you. Any objections if I join you ? Just stand by, like, in case I could be of help, me having come here with the General and having gone with him to—where he went."

" I've no objection," said the Hadji to Carthew, in Arabic. " The man might be of some use ; and it's just possible he might say something of interest, something which would give us an idea of what General Jason was after."

" Yes," agreed Carthew in the same language. " He's a cunning brute, but he's not clever ; astute and artful, without being particularly intelligent ; and we might lead him to say something. For I am absolutely certain that he came here, and has also stayed here, for some very good reason—and it's the same reason that induced Jason to come here."

" Excusing me, gents," interrupted Mr. Palsover at this juncture, " but if I don't know a word of what you are saying, I can't very well give you my opinion on it. May be sense all right, but it don't make sense to me, yer see."

" No. I beg your pardon," replied the Arab. " I'll speak in your language to the best of my ability."

" Right. Let's all sit down then," was the sensible reply.

" Well, I've thought the matter over, back and forth, most of the night," said the Hadji Abdulla, " and I have decided . . ."

He paused, watching Carthew. How desperately anxious this poor chap was. How tightly clenched his fists and eager his gaze.

" Get on, man ! Go on ! Quick ! " implored Carthew.

" . . . that I will give you a passage on my *dhow*, provided you most clearly understand that the responsibility is yours, and that . . ."

Henry Carthew sprang to his feet, seized the Hadji's hand and wrung it.

"And I was about to add," smiled the latter, " you agree to follow the plan which I have evolved. . . . It is that or nothing."

"It's *that*, then, and God bless you," breathed Henry Carthew.

"Ah, but you haven't heard it yet. . . . I had a very bright thought and if you like to take the risk, I'll play my part."

"I'll take any risk," Carthew assured him.

"Well—provided you will agree to do nothing to injure the State of São Thomé, to give any publicity to its existence, or be the cause of anyone else going there, I will take you with me—in disguise."

"In *disguise* ! Disguised as what ? "

"As an Arab. My fellow pearl-merchant. They won't like my bringing you, even so, but they'll forgive me this once, because you've brought with you a pearl of great price, from which you refuse to be parted, and which you hope to sell to Doña Guiomar. I have a parcel of pearls for her, and I shall make it known that, while collecting them as she requested, I came across one of the most magnificent pearls that I have ever seen (which is true), and that I had not sufficient ready cash with which to purchase it. But I felt that I ought not to let it go. And as its owner wouldn't part with it, the only way to bring it was to bring the owner with it ! "

"By Gad ! " whispered Henry Carthew.

"That's the stuff to give the troops," guffawed Mr. Palsover.

"It is risky but it is feasible," continued the Hadji. " You speak Arabic extremely well, a good deal better than the Arabic-speaking people there do, and I have

254

got plenty of the right kit. I don't, for one moment, fear that you'll give yourself away, because the people with whom we shall be dealing speak Portuguese with a mixture of Arabic, and you'd not run the sort of risk that you would if I were to take you to Jiddah or any other such Red Sea or Persian Gulf port, in the guise of an Arab. The only risk is that the Council should take the view that, while not unappeasably angry with me for bringing you, they think that perhaps, on the whole, I had better not take you away again."

" Hardly do that with your fellow pearl-merchant, would they ? " protested Carthew.

" Probably not. We'll hope not. We'll have to hope for the best, in fact. . . . Now—are you willing to run the risk of being permanently detained ? " he asked, his eyes searching Carthew's face.

" That or anything else," was the reply. " Not that it looks to me as though it is much of a risk."

" Well, there I know better than you do, Colonel, and I assure you that there *is* a danger of the Secretary to the Cabinet or the Foreign Minister or the Commissioner of Police or some Member of the Council taking the view that it was very nice of you to come with the pearl—and that it would be even nicer for you to stay."

" But wouldn't the Regent, Doña Guiomar, protect me ? If I am going to take her one of the finest pearls in the world, wouldn't she rather I went off again to look for a better one ? "

" Probably. And if she expressed herself strongly on the subject, the Council might give way. On the other hand, they might take the view that after all, since it was I who had brought this pearl and its owner, I could bring more."

" But if you most strongly objected to my detention,

and pointed out that you had acted in the Regent's interest and all that, wouldn't they listen to you? Especially if you insisted on the fact that you have given me safe-conduct. It would look as though you had deliberately led me into a trap. And wouldn't it look uncommonly like theft, if they ' bought ' the pearl from me and then chucked me into prison? "

" Who said they'd do that? You'd have the freedom of São Thomé, no doubt. You'd be quite at liberty to build yourself a nice house and enjoy all the amenities of Utopia."

" Well, it's to get my friend out of Utopia that I'm going there, and I should certainly like to come away with him. Anyhow, more thanks than I can express. . . . I'm quite sure that I can say for General Jason as well as for myself, that if it cost us our last penny, we'd see that you lost nothing by your . . ."

" Well, we won't bother about that now," interrupted the Hadji. " Do you know anything about pearls? "

" Nothing whatever. Never bought one in my life."

" Well, I must tell you all about them. Teach you the selling-patter. By the way, what languages do you know beside Arabic? "

" The Latin ones. French, Spanish, Portuguese and Italian."

" *Wallahi!* Know them well? "

" Yes. I hold the army rank of Interpreter in all four."

" By Allah! That's good! And you understand Portuguese thoroughly, and can speak it well? "

" Yes."

" Well, the great thing at São Thomé will be the speaking. Don't speak it well. Not a word of it. Don't let anyone get the faintest idea that you know a single word of Portuguese, and that might be very use-

256

ful. Stick to Arabic, as I do—and listen hard when they talk Portuguese to each other."

" And they'll understand my Arabic all right ? "

" Yes. Though when it is a matter of doing business, or their giving me any instructions, they always have the Government Interpreter there, a chap who knows the three languages of the Island and a few from outside. I repeat it all to him in Arabic to show that I have understood.

" By the way, there's one man, a Dr. de Norhona, Secretary to the Cabinet and a Member of the Council, who speaks and understands English perfectly. Studied medicine in London and Edinburgh, not to mention Paris and Vienna. Quite a linguist. He's the man of whom we've got to be careful. Finest brain I've ever come across ; and one of the most scholarly and widely-read men I know. He's a great genius in his own line. Tell you more about him later. . . . Well then, you think all that over and . . ."

" My dear chap, I've nothing to think over ! I have only got to thank you, and I have no words with which to do it. I'll start growing a beard at once, and practise squatting cross-legged and so on. You'll have to put me through some of the drill when you teach me the pearl patter."

" And what about me ? " enquired Mr. Palsover who with closed eyes had sat nodding silent approval as the scheme had been propounded. " Reckon I'll go along too, if it's all the same to you, Mister ? " he added, turning to the Hadji.

" Well, if the Colonel Sahib agrees, and if you can give us a little more information about why General Jason came here in the first place, how he ever heard of São Thomé, and why he went there."

257

" Well now, it's like this, gents," said Mr. Palsover in his most confidential manner. " You see it's this way. I want to do anything that lies in my power to help you, but what I don't want to do is to betray the General's trust in me, or say anything that I ought not to say."

" And do you suppose it could do any harm to tell me anything, Palsover ? " asked Carthew.

" Why, no, Sir. No, Sir. Course not. But, in a manner of speaking, well—two's company and three's none."

The Hadji rose, glanced meaningly at Carthew, and again turned his sober regard upon the speaker.

" If that's the difficulty, I'll go away," he said. " Then you can tell the Colonel Sahib all you know, eh ? "

And forthwith Mr. Palsover told Henry Carthew not exactly all he knew, but all that he thought was good for him. Practically all that he had told Colonel Jason. And when he had set forth the facts and the fictions and completed his golden story, it was with difficulty that he believed his own ears when Henry Carthew observed,

" Well, *I don't give a damn for your radium mines* or anything else. What I want to do is to find General Jason and get him safely out of the beastly place."

Mr. Palsover was so hurt, so offended, so utterly disgusted with this—*fool*, that he arose and departed without another word, lest it be a word too much.

Right ! If the flaming B.F. didn't want a fortune, let him go without. Let him scratch along on his tuppenny pension, while Mr. Samuel Palsover, J.P., rolled along the highway of life in the biggest and finest motor-car that money could buy. Sir Samuel Palsover . . . Lord Palsover of Plaistow . . . Samuel, Earl of Palsover. . . .

Not care a damn about a concession worth a million, the pudding-headed, pie-faced . . . *Pah!* There were no words.

There was one thing, though. Carthew would keep his head shut, as he had given his promise; and he'd never play any tricks or do any double-crossing. Hadn't the sense, for one thing.

Yes, the best plan would be for Samuel Palsover to go over to São Thomé again, and once more try to get the low-down on what the General was up to. That's where Carthew would be some good, anyway. If the General was still on that perishin' island, Carthew'd find him. And if the old bird was shut up in the *calaboso*, or had passed out and passed over, then Mr. Samuel Palsover had better go Home and start afresh. Find somebody else, like the General, who'd be as straight as he was, and have more sense than to muck things up like this. Somebody who could have that São Thomé lot on a string. Josh 'em along. Fool 'em. Give and take, or promise and take—anyway. Promise a lot, so that they'd jump at it.

Still it might be all right, even yet. No doubt it takes a long time to fix up these concessions and things, and the General might have been doing a whole lot of spade-work these last two years. He'd ask Carthew and this Hadji chap to get the General to come down to the port place, and meet his old pal and business partner, Palsover, on the *dhow*, and tell him how things were going.

And if there was no news at all this time, he'd go home. Might not be half a bad plan to go and look Lady Jason up. She'd be glad to hear some news of her old man and what he was up to.   Pay for it too, handsomely, if he put the screw on properly.

Nothing for nothing in this world and damn little for sixpence, if you were dealing with Mr. Samuel Palsover, Esquire.

IV

A FEW nights later the Hadji Abdulla's big *dhow* again set sail for an unknown or, rather, unadvertized, destination.

During the voyage, the Hadji came to like Colonel Henry Carthew more and more, and by the time the *dhow* reached its devious journey's end, he felt as though he had known him for years, and that he had grown fonder of him than of any man he had ever known, save perhaps Dacre Blount and the man whom he had known both as Chandos and el Sidna el Sultan Mahommed el Kebir. He wrote him down as a gentleman, in that he was courteous, kindly and truthful ; simple, unselfish and honourable ; a man who thought of and for others before himself ; one who, to his friend, would be a friend faithful unto death. A man perhaps difficult really to know, to understand and to appreciate, but worth any trouble taken to those ends.

At times his heart sank as he thought of Carthew pitting his brains against those of the rulers of São Thomé, if ever it came to that. What he hoped and expected was that Carthew would pass muster as a somewhat stupid and inarticulate Arab, who had come all that way to get the best price possible for his wonderful pearl ; the type of man who would go round the world with it, rather than let it out of his possession, save to a satisfactory purchaser.

It might work. It ought to work. There was no

real reason why anything should go wrong. He himself would do nine-tenths of the talking ; and, inasmuch as it was really he himself who was selling the pearl, it would be easy enough to act as though he were the other pearl-merchant's representative and go-between, trying to effect a sale in which he himself would have, at any rate, a small financial interest.

Of course it ought to be all right ; and this sense of anxiety and foreboding was foolish and unwarranted.

But at times, as he sat on the poop of his fine *baggala*, watching the helmsman, the great sail, the moonlit water and the stars, he thought of the last passenger whom he had carried to São Thomé. What had happened to him ? He had vanished without sound or sign. He had last seen him in the outer court-yard of Ildefonso Castle, the citadel of the Capital, when he had said farewell.

Looking back at the gate he had cried " *Ma-es-Salaam.*" That had been the last word he had said to him, the last sight he had had of him, and the rest was silence.

When he returned six months later and ventured to ask His Excellency Dom Perez de Norhona if he, Hadji Abdulla, would be taking the General Inglez back with him this time, Norhona had stared at him coldly and uncomprehendingly.

" General Inglez ? What do you mean ? We have no foreign General here, English or otherwise, that I have heard of. What do you mean ? "

" The man I brought with me on my last voyage, Your Excellency."

" Oh, that rascal ! A scoundrelly Nazi German. No, he won't be going back with you this time, Hadji."

" German ! " said the Hadji, " but I thought . . ."

" Well, suppose we cease to think, shall we ? **And**

begin to remember. Let us also practise the great art of forgetting, eh ? "

Queer—and sinister.

One day, six months later, finding de Norhona in high good humour and delighted with his share of the cargo and the way in which the Hadji had executed his personal commissions, he had again plucked up courage to ask about the man who had, at any rate, called himself a British General.

At first de Norhona had either failed, or pretended to fail, to remember the man. But on the Hadji's endeavouring to refresh his memory, he had said,

" Oh, I remember the chap ; the German whom poor Pereira sent me. Yes, he masqueraded as a British Colonel or General or something. Dead ? No. Not so far as I know. He wasn't the other day. Saw him myself last week."

" I expect he'll be wanting to take a return-ticket soon, won't he, Your Excellency ? " the Hadji had said politely, with a smile that showed he was merely talking for the sake of conversation.

" No, I don't think so. I don't fancy he has the slightest wish to leave São Thomé."

" Doesn't want to go back to his home, even yet ? "

" Apparently not. But if he should ask you to give him a lift back to Santa Cruz, do so by all means."

" Without referring to you again, Your Excellency ? Without the written permit ? "

" Yes, yes. Certainly, certainly. Pereira asked you to bring him, and I give you full permission to take him back, if he asks to go."

But the Hadji knew his Norhona, as he knew all the members of the Government of São Thomé, and was not deceived. His Excellency Dom Perez de Norhona was an honourable man. So were they all, all hon-

263

ourable men. But the great doctor liked his little joke. They were apt to be grim little jokes, and the Hadji felt in his bones that this was one of them.

It was a favourite jest of de Norhona's to speak perfect truth when telling an absolute lie. Inasmuch as he said that the General was alive, he probably was alive.

Since de Norhona said that he had probably no wish to leave São Thomé, no doubt that was, for some reason or other, the case.

But—when he said that, should the General ask him to take him back, he was quite at liberty to do so—there the snag showed its ugly head. If the General were quite at liberty to make the request, then for some reason or other, he was not in a position to do so. He concluded that doubtless he was in gaol.

But when, on his last visit, he had casually inquired of de Norhona whether he wanted him to give anyone passage to Santa Cruz, and de Norhona had said ' No. No one this time,' he had (apparently jokingly) asked,

"Not the wicked German? Isn't he ready to go yet?"

"Apparently not," de Norhona had replied. " He has said nothing about it to me."

And when the Hadji had laughed again and said,

" Perhaps he hasn't had the chance, Senhor? " de Norhona quizzically, and with simulated indignation, had replied,

" Every chance! Every opportunity! Comes and goes as free as air. I see him almost every day of my life, and I assure you he has never broached the subject of his departure."

True again, no doubt. Absolutely true as far as the words went, but covering something false as hell.

Had he done rightly in bringing this Colonel Carthew to face the same dangers?

264

Well, he was a soldier and danger-facing was his trade. Moreover, had he left him at Santa Cruz, he'd have been there for the rest of his life, rotting in that foul hole, living in that appalling hotel, eating his heart out that he could find no one who knew where São Thomé was, or who would take him there if he did.

That would have been a bigger tragedy. If he read the man aright, as he felt sure he did, nothing would turn him aside from his purpose of finding and rescuing his friend. And this would be the better fate, even if it meant brief action and sudden death ; and if it meant detention on São Thomé, a thousand times better that than self-imposed detention in Santa Cruz.

He would have found his friend and that alone would make him happy.

At other times the Hadji realized that this last was the sheerest optimism. São Thomé was medieval, its Government four hundred years behind the times ; and the Middle Ages which still prevailed in São Thomé was a cruel time, an age when people were burnt alive ; when devilish torture, for the extortion of evidence or confession, was an integral part of the judicial system ; when inconvenient or offending people—such as the Prisoner of Chillon—were cast into underground dungeons and left there for a lifetime.

The São Thoméans were a happy, kindly and peaceful people, ruled by men of good-will, good heart and very considerable wisdom ; but undoubtedly they were centuries behind in the march of progress, and knew nothing of such refinements and improvements upon the medieval system as free, open and impartial Courts of Law, where the strictest justice was administered ; Parliamentary government by the elected representatives of the people ; vote by secret ballot ; equality

265

of all men before the Law ; compulsory free education ; wireless ; or aerial navigation. They knew nothing of such improvements and advantages as bombs that in a few minutes could lay towns in smoking ruins and reduce such places as Westminster Abbey, Canterbury Cathedral and York Minster to dust ; or of magnificently up-to-date engines of war that can slaughter the maximum number of human beings in the minimum period of time.

So São Thomé, being as backward as all that, it was quite possible that something very unpleasant had happened to the intruder, that charming gentleman who, according to his own account, was a British General but to that of His Excellency Dom Perez de Norhona, was a Nazi German, an assassin, a fraud—and a menace.

Occasionally, after long long thoughts on these lines, the Hadji Abdulla would make another attempt to dissuade Carthew from going ashore when the *dhow* reached São Thomé.

Let the Hadji, he begged, go up to the Capital alone and see how the land lay, do his utmost in the *suqs*, bazaars, arcades and cafés, to discover any news of General Jason ; do his best to find out, by the right, proper and judicious treatment of soldiers and policemen, as to whether there were any foreigners in the Ildefonso Gaol at which, from time to time, they did duty ; ask de Norhona once again, as though in idle and uninterested curiosity, whether his former passenger were returning this time, and try to learn from him something about the mysterious Anglo-German.   And if he could learn nothing whatever about the missing ' General,' let him then make formal request to bring up to the Capital a pearl-dealing colleague whom, bemused, bewildered and practically blindfolded, he had brought with him, in order that he might offer for sale to Her Highness the Regent a very marvellous great pearl.

But against this scheme Carthew protested, raising the undeniably valid objection that, in the event of de Norhona's replying with a flat and final refusal, it would make things a hundred times more difficult than they were already. No, the Hadji must let him accompany him to the Capital in the hope that de Norhona would accept the *fait accompli* and raise no objection to his remaining there.

And when the Hadji had to set sail again?

Why, then Carthew would decide and act according to circumstances. If he had discovered General Jason, and it were at all possible to do so, he'd somehow get him down to the coast and on board the *dhow*, with the Hadji's permission, and help—for which they could never be sufficiently grateful or offer adequate reward.

If, on the other hand, they completely failed to learn anything concerning the General, why then Carthew would of course stay behind.

" And what do you propose to do? " asked the Hadji.

Well, go into hiding at first, and act as seems wisest. Remain in disguise of course. Probably as a São Thoméan. Do his best to get himself up like one of the middle-class Arab-Portuguese agriculturists of whom the Hadji had told him; or perhaps as one of the aboriginal islanders, and keep to the uninhabited jungle country, the smallest villages, fishing communities; go into market with the others, bearing baskets of fruit or fish, like a coolie—and sit about in the market-place.

The Hadji smiled as he wondered equally at the man's courage, fidelity and ignorance.

V

AS General Jason had done, Henry Carthew gazed about him in amazement while he journeyed from the landing-stage in the creek up to São Ildefonso, the Capital of the Island. As the General had been reminded of the Gray's *Elegy* of his school days and its reference to that obvious peace, contentment and prosperity which were written on the faces of the people, making them an open book on which the observer could read the virtues of their rulers, so Henry Carthew, in his turn, was reminded of his favourite poem *King Robert of Sicily*, and could not forbear to quote aloud,

> " *Days came and went ;*
> *And now returned again to Sicily the old*
> *Saturnian reign ;*
> *Under the Angel's governance benign*
> *The happy island danced with corn and wine.*"

Happy indeed for the islanders, although the Government did not appear to consist entirely of angels. Happy islanders—but what of his friend ?

He thanked God literally and actually, night and morning, that he had reached this place ; and although, at times, depressed by the Hadji's complete lack of optimism, he kept a stout heart and a hopeful mind by telling himself that God had brought him on yet another stage of his journey so that he might be the instrument of His Will and fulfil His purpose. And what else could that purpose be but the salvation of his friend and his restoration to his wife and home and country?

As for this nonsense of Palsover's about radium concessions, money was the only thing the fellow thought about; but if Reginald Jason had come here with a view to opening commercial negotiations with the Government of São Thomé, surely there was no harm in that? And if these queer people did see harm in it, and were detaining him, surely there wasn't the slightest doubt but that Reginald would be perfectly willing to give the matter up and come home with him at once? Of course it would be all right.

" By the way," he said to the Hadji one night, as they sat on the verandah of a rest-house, " just supposing, for the sake of argument, that a foreign war-ship did by some strange chance happen to come this way, did sight São Thomé, dropped anchor, and sent a boat ashore, what would happen?"

" Well, they'd find the flag of Portugal flying, down at that landing-place."

" Does the Island belong to Portugal, then?"

" Oh, no! It is absolutely independent. It is Portugal's pet protégé, and they are very proud of its history. But it is absolutely an article of faith with the Portuguese Government that they should never in any way interfere here or allow anybody else to do so. If any wandering war-ship, if there were such a thing in these waters, came along, and thought of annexing it, they'd find they had caused an international incident of grave importance, and that the sooner they cleared out and apologized, the less likely would they be to find themselves at war with Portugal, backed by Great Britain, her oldest ally and guarantor."

" I suppose, though, that if such a war-ship came and

paid a perfectly friendly visit, without any sort of *arrière pensée*, the São Thoméans would be friendly and hospitable ? "

" Oh, yes, absolutely. No doubt about that. But it is extremely unlikely to happen. Coal costs money, and what would a war-ship be doing in this part of the world ? "

" There has never been any kind of British war-ship here, I suppose ? "

" No, never. Nor likely to be."

" Don't the Portuguese ever send one ? "

" No. Why should they ? They know that the constant prayer of São Thomé is ' Leave us alone, for we are perfectly happy and wish to remain so.' "

" But is there no communication whatsoever between São Thomé and the outside world ? "

" Oh, yes. Certain hand-picked Thoméans of the original Portuguese families go to Europe when young, to specialize in something useful to the State, as de Norhona did, for his medical training. Then at least one of the Members of the Council goes over every year to Portugal and other European countries—the Commander-in-Chief, the Foreign Minister, the Chief of Police, and other specialists. De Norhona went over about three years ago to see Freud, Jung, Adler and the other great neurologists and psychologists, as well as the Vienna surgeons and physicians. By all accounts, he's a wizard at medicine, surgery and this latest stuff—psycho-therapy, don't they call it ? Hypnotism is his special line, if you can mention any one thing that is more special than the rest, with him."

" Fancy a man like that being content to live in a place like this."

" Well, why not ? It's his home, his country, and to him the most desirable spot on earth, apart from its actual physical attractions. Even by the time a São Thoméan is seven years old, he knows, better than he knows anything else, that São Thomé is the Garden of Eden, the finest spot on earth, and the only place in which a sensible man can possibly live. They go on the Jesuit principle—' Give us a boy for seven years and you can do what you like with him afterwards.' No São Thoméan has ever left the Island and intentionally failed to return. Nothing but death would prevent him ; and if ever a messenger fails to return, as a São Thoméan named Pereira did, a couple of years ago, they know that he's either in his grave or a prison."

" No wonder so little is known of the place," mused Henry Carthew. " Personally I had never heard of it."

" No, in view of the facts, it would be a queer thing if you had," replied the Hadji. " To the outside world it is merely a Portuguese island of neither interest nor importance, which is self-supporting and has no productions and therefore no commerce. Not that the rest of the world, outside a Government office in Lisbon, has ever heard of it, anyway. . . ."

§ 2

At first glimpse, São Ildefonso, the capital of São Thomé, reminded Henry Carthew of Funchal and Madeira. Having passed the police guard and entered the gates, he likened the tree-embowered town to a miniature Adelaide, to a castellated Indian hill-station, to a town in Crete, and to Carcassonne.

Nevertheless, he realized that it was unique, and like his friend a couple of years earlier, thought of the combination of the castled crag of Cintra and an

271

extremely clean green and colourful Mediterranean town upon which it looked down, as mightily it dominated it.

In point of fact, he was too excited and anxious, to take very careful note of his surroundings, as he and the Hadji rode through the town in the direction of the Citadel.

At any moment he might come face to face with his friend !

Within the hour he might hear news of him ; might learn that he was dead and buried ; that he had lain in gaol all this while, perhaps in some noisome dungeon ; and he might hear that he was alive and well and free.

What a wonderful thing if he could promptly return to Santa Cruz and send a cable to Antoinette,

" *Reginald safe and well. Returning immediately.*"

If he could do that, he'd really feel that he hadn't altogether lived in vain. He'd be able to feel that he had done something in return for all their kindness to him ; something to make himself worthy to be Antoinette's friend, Reginald's friend.

Lord, how he hoped they'd let him share Dysart's quarters when they got to the end of this amazing journey. He'd be comparatively safe for his search-work, then ; could go everywhere with him, and use his eyes and brain to the utmost. What a mercy of Providence that he knew Portuguese so well ! But then, everything was an act of Providence and, in the long run, a mercy. More and more he felt that he had not been brought all this way to fail in the end.

Once again, the Hadji was permitted to cross the

272

drawbridge and enter the great outer court-yard of the Castle. A perfunctory glance at him was sufficient for the Sergeant of the Guard, who took it for granted that the other Arab, in white robe and turban, being in the Hadji's company, must be guaranteed by him, have a permit, and be allowed to enter.

In the centre of the court-yard, the Hadji dismounted, and Carthew followed his example.

As usual, soldiers came and led away the horses, and within a few minutes, a sallow man in a sort of civilian uniform, approached and conversed in fluent and faulty Arabic with the Hadji.

" Salaam, Hadji Abdulla the Merchant," said he. " And whom might this be ? And by whose permission have you brought a stranger into the Citadel of São Ildefonso ? "

" Oh, that's all right. No permission and none needed," laughed the Hadji. " Wait till Her Excellency Doña Guiomar hears about him, and why I brought him."

" Wait till His Excellency Dom Perez de Norhona hears," sneered the secretary-clerk or flunkey, his unpleasant tallowy face assuming a threatening look not untinged with contempt.

" Any need to wait ? " growled the Hadji. " I didn't really come here for the purpose of a long conversation with you. Tell His Excellency that I have come and await his pleasure."

As the man, with an ugly clearing of the throat, as though about to spit, turned away, the Hadji remarked to Carthew,

" I'm no Sir Richard Burton, but I know exactly how he felt when an English subaltern gave him a sharp kick in the rear, called him a black beast, and bade him get out of the way.

" *Cave !* " he added. " That's Norhona."

And looking up to where a man stood at the head of the flight of stairs which, as he knew, led up to the Great Hall of the Castle, the Hadji saluted by raising both hands to his forehead, touching his heart and bowing respectfully.

As he nudged him, Carthew did the same.

" Salaam, Senhor Hadji Abdulla," called the man. " Come up.

" Both of you," he added, staring hard at Carthew who, with his month-old beard, was not looking his best, and was indeed far from prepossessing.

Entering a room of noble proportions, on the walls of which were pictures that had been painted by masters in Portugal, taken to Goa and brought by the survivors of the ill-fated silk-and-silver fleet to São Thomé, de Norhona seated himself behind a great desk, and with a wave of his hand, indicated a rug upon which his visitors might sit in their favourite cross-legged attitude.

" Well, what's the meaning of this ? " he asked with a cold glance at Carthew, as soon as polite salutations and mutual inquiries as to health and prosperity had been exchanged.

" Oh, that ! " smiled the Hadji, glancing at his companion. " That's what Your Excellency might call a parcel or a package."

Norhona raised his heavy eyebrows.

" It contains the very finest pearl I have ever seen, and I couldn't get it out of the parcel or package, so I brought the whole bundle along. Doubtless Her Excellency Doña Guiomar will find a way to open it."

" Full of parables to-day, Hadji. I'll open him fast enough, if . . ."

" No, no, Your Excellency. It really is an amazing and incredible pearl. The Biblical Pearl of Great Price. But as I hadn't the cash to pay for it, and the fool wouldn't trust me, I was on the horns of a dilemma, and for long I halted between two opinions. Should I let it go, lose the chance of a lifetime, a chance of giving Her Excellency great happiness and of marvellously enriching the jewel-hoard in the State treasure-house—or should I do as the fellow asked ? "

" And what did ' the fellow ' ask ? "

" ' *If you have a market, take me to it, though it be a thousand miles away,'* says he.

" ' *It's all that,'* says I, and made up my mind to encourage such an enterprising merchant."

" You know the Law," replied de Norhona. " You know the very first order and charge that was laid upon you when . . ."

" Ah, but look, Your Excellency ! The man has not the faintest idea as to where he is, and hasn't the least notion as to how he got here. I shall take him back to his home at Bahrein, and if he sits and *faddhls* [1] with his cronies for the rest of his life, he can only say he went to a far country and . . ."

" Is he a *dhow*-master himself ? "

" Hardly ever been on a *dhow* in his life, Your Excellency. He's just a pearl-broker. He bought this pearl within a few hours of its being taken out of the oyster ; and I saw it, and was dickering with him about it the next day. We can get it from him at a price that will make him quite happy, and that will be about half what it would be worth—in Paris, say. Not that it will ever go out of São Thomé, of course, but the bargain will be as wonderful as the pearl."

[1] Gossips. *Arabic.*

" Let me have a look at it," ordered de Norhona.

The Hadji bade Carthew produce the pearl, and from some place of concealment beneath his voluminous sash, the latter brought out a little leather bag, tied at the mouth with a thong.

Opening the bag, he produced a pearl of almost the size of a pigeon's egg, a breath-taking marvel of beauty.

" *Madre de Dios !* " whispered de Norhona, " I don't wonder you brought the man. Her Excellency the Regent will certainly approve ! But listen, Hadji. Are your ears wide open ? Then hear my words and do not, on your life, forget what I say now, or disobey the order. Never again, under any conceivable circumstances whatsoever, bring anyone from your *dhow* up to Ildefonso. We trust to your discretion as to whom you take on board your *dhow* at Santa Cruz, but don't you ever again assume you've got any discretion as to whom you bring ashore at São Thomé. Do you hear ? "

" I hear, Your Excellency. And to hear is to obey."

" Well, we'll overlook it this time, in consideration of this pearl and the pleasure it will give Her Highness. But never again, my good Hadji. Never again. Meantime, you'll be responsible for your friend, and when you sail, you will take him with you, unless anything happens to give me the impression that it might be more desirable for him to remain here. And if he goes with you this time, you'll take him back to Bahrein yourself. And don't let him go ashore at Santa Cruz."

" While he's here, I had better have him with me in my quarters, Your Excellency," suggested the Hadji.

" Yes. And you had better keep him under your

own eye, the whole time. . . . You have my permission to go. But not to leave the Castle precincts until I have had another talk with you."

The two rose from the rug, and Carthew, cool as steel, acted his part well.

"And the pearl?" he grunted uncouthly, looking from de Norhona to the Hadji. "I want my pearl."

"May Mohammed bin Yussuf take his pearl, Your Excellency? I'm afraid he'll get no sleep otherwise."

"Let him remain awake then," was the cold reply. "I will take care of the pearl. Mohammed bin Yussuf has given hostages to Fortune! Worth a King's ransom and a little more than a pearl-broker's ransom, eh? . . . As I mentioned before, you have my permission to go."

"Come on, you fool," urged the Hadji in a loud stage-whisper, and took Carthew's arm.

"I wouldn't have left it in the hands of the Sheik of Mohammara," growled Carthew.

"*Imshi, ibn kelb* [1] *!*" growled the Hadji, and hustled the foolish fellow from the Presence.

[1] Get out, you son of a dog.

VI

FOR the next two or three days the two Britons enjoyed each other's company, talking all day and far into the night, Brodie Dysart telling of his experiences on the ship called *Valkyrie* which made one of the most tragically amazing voyages in the checkered history of the Merchant Service, a voyage on which murder and mutiny disposed of so many of the personnel that the ship, that started out with a Captain and full complement of officers, was brought home by the Apprentices.[1]

At another time, he told Carthew of his later experiences as a slave in Southern Morocco ; as an instructor to the native troops of a Sultan ; and of his experiences as a Pilgrim to Mecca [2]; at another, of his life as a member of the French Foreign Legion on active service on the Indo-Chinese frontier [3]; and again of further experiences in different parts of the world, ashore and afloat, experiences which led to his decision to buy a *dhow* and see life.

In return, Henry Carthew told him tales of soldiering and sport in India, of adventuring on the Pamirs when, by way of spending a year's furlough, he journeyed to Kabul and thence to Bokhara, Khiva and Samarcand and back by way of Kashmir to India.

And the more that Brodie Dysart saw and heard of Henry Carthew, the more he liked and admired him.

[1] *Action and Passion.*   [2] *Sinbad the Soldier.*   [3] *Fort in the Jungle.*

But no news could either get concerning the fate of General Jason. Time after time, Carthew was tempted to forget that he was a Gulf Arab, and to question soldiers and the minor personnel of the Citadel, in Portuguese. To talk to any but the bucolic and less educated people in pure Arabic was to be uncertain as to whether he was completely understood. The use of pure or diluted Portuguese would, he felt, have been much more helpful in the town.

One day a messenger arrived at the ground floor room which opened off the outer court-yard—and which was allotted to the Hadji's use when he was visiting Ildefonso—and bade the two Arabs follow him.

This man led them up to the main floor of the Castle, across the Great Hall, up a flight of stairs, along a gallery, down a corridor into another corridor, and so to a room in which sat the Doña Guiomar, the Regent of São Thomé.

Carthew, forgetting to salaam in the correct manner until nudged by the Hadji, stared in admiration at the extremely beautiful and intellectual face of the woman who, with the help of the Council of Notabilities, ruled the country in which, as he hoped and believed, his friend still lived.

She looked curiously attractive—but attractively curious also. Why was that ? . . . Because she was in a sort of Fancy Dress—as though going to a party, or as though this were an act in a film play.

Of course—she was dressed much as the women one saw in Spanish pictures of the seventeenth century. Old-fashioned. And with a high comb and mantilla. The men, too, looked old-fashioned in their " tropical " silk suits—like the pictures of wealthy American planters of the slave-owning period, in their Old Colonial style houses.

With a gracious wave of the hand, Doña Guiomar indicated that the two Arabs might seat themselves on the floor before her.

"Well, Hadji," she smiled, " I trust that your health and the health of your house is good."

" By the favour of Your Majesty," murmured the Hadji, bowing low.

" And what is this I hear about you bringing a man all the way from the Persian Gulf to show me a pearl ? "

" This is the man, Your Majesty," replied the Hadji. " A poor thick-headed nit-wit of Bazra—(the home town of Sinbad the Sailor, Your Majesty may remember)—who refused to be parted from his Pearl of Great Price. But as I was determined at all costs that Your Majesty should have the pearl, I got over the non-separation difficulty by bringing the pearl with the worthy half-wit attached to it. He was actually babbling of taking it up to Bagdad and showing it in the pearl-market there ; and, if he did not get his price, of taking it to show such people as the Sheikh of Mohammara and the Sultan of Muscat."

" However, I told him we could do better than that," he added.

" At a price, doubtless, Hadji. A nice little commission for you, eh ? "

" *Wallahi !* Your Highness. Is it not written in your Book that the labourer is worthy of his hire ? "

" Easy labour, Hadji, if a little dangerous—for you —in view of the Law. However, we'll say no more of that, as the pearl is indeed wonderful. Let me see it again."

Dom Perez de Norhona, from no more secret place than the trousers pocket of his light silk suit, produced the bag and the pearl.

"Yes. Wonderful. Truly wonderful. I must have it," said the Regent as she fondled the lovely thing.

"If we can come to terms with the merchant," observed de Norhona. "How much is the fellow asking for it?"

And with a strange cry of eagerness and of anguish the alleged pearl-merchant of Bahrein and Bazra broke into a torrent of impassioned Arabic. . . . *The pearl was to all other pearls as the Moon to the stars. It was perfect in shape and colour, incredible in size. Behold its flawless skin. Behold . . .*

"Yes, we are beholding, thank you," interrupted de Norhona. "It is a good-enough pearl. What have you the effrontery to ask for it?"

And the haggling began, the hot combat of wits and words in which the Hadji joined and quickly took the lead. Thankfully Carthew dropped out and gazed about him at the furniture, hangings and pictures which must be of priceless value and great age.

Some distance behind the Regent's chair a magnificent bird of the parrot or macaw family sat and, with a look of cynical wisdom, eyed the proceedings, from time to time contributing a cryptic remark.

At the base of the stand on which it perched, a beautiful little monkey sat and ate of the crumbs of fruit and sweet-meats that fell from the rich bird's table. From time to time each cursed the other with vindictive if perfunctory virulence. They appeared to understand each other perfectly.

Behind them, in the dark corner, lay what Carthew took to be a huge ape, and he wondered that so big a creature—something between a chimpanzee and a gorilla—should be found in those latitudes. And idly regarding it as it slept, with the top of its shaggy head toward him, he felt a little surprise that such an animal

281

should find a place in a lady's boudoir. He decided that it was quite possible that the creature was in the nature of a bodyguard, more powerful and intelligent than a dog.

Rather a bright idea, having a great ape of enormous strength, as a watch-dog, guard and companion. Not that he'd care about it much himself. He remembered the occasion on which he had visited a friend, a planter in Sumatra, and a huge brute of an orang-oútan had come in, toward the end of dinner, and been given a chair at table and a plate of fruit.

His friend had bidden him shake hands with the ' Man of the Forest,' and he had done so. But he had never forgotten the inexpressibly unpleasant feeling of having his hand in a steel trap, a vice, and his realization of what would be the feeble worthlessness of his strength, had he to pit it against that of the orang-oútan. The great brute had held him for a couple of minutes, and he had never forgotten it or quite forgiven his friend for the humiliation. And ever since, he had loathed meeting the gaze of any kind of ape or monkey and looking into its shallow soulless eyes.

What was that they were saying ?

" You have my permission to go."

That was good news.

" I'll think it over and give you my answer in a day or two, Hadji Abdulla."

And rising and bowing low, the two pearl-merchants departed from the Presence.

Later in the day, an orderly brought the Arabs written permission to leave the precincts of the Castle and go where they pleased within the bounds of the town of São Ildefonso.

Meanwhile, Mr. Palsover . . .

Existence upon a small ship, without employment, recreation or society, is apt to be boring, especially to one not blessed with particularly extensive mental resources.

Certainly Mr. Palsover found it so.

At first, it was well enough, this sitting and thinking, and then just sitting, but even to the most contemplative of Europeans, the attractions of mere sitting must, in time, begin to pall. And Mr. Palsover was no *faquir*, endowed and fortified with the blessings of an understanding of Yoga.

Within a few days of the departure of the Hadji and Colonel Carthew he got bored, got fever, and got drunk.

It must be said in his defence and indeed in mere justice, that only in such unusual and untoward circumstances could he have been defeated by those tropical enemies of white mankind, boredom and alcohol. Mr. Palsover was no drinker, but when he did drink he undoubtedly drank.

It is probably to this and this alone that his moral downfall and his abandonment of his own high standards of discretion, if not of loyalty, can be ascribed.

Thus, when young Ensign Fernandez Machado, who also had nothing to do, was rowed out to visit the *dhow*, Mr. Palsover was not himself. He was depressed to the lowest depths of mind, body and soul ; he was maudlin ; he was genuinely and unwontedly friendly and affectionate, nay, loving ; he was the soul of hospitality ; he was filled with joy and gladness, and merry, merry laughter alternated with lugubrious tears and fits of abandonment to despair ; he was forth-coming and communicative.

But he was not Mr. Samuel Palsover.

The mere fact that he was communicative proves it ; for, when sober—and for every hour of every day of at least fifty-one weeks of the year he was sober—there was no man alive less communicative than Mr. Palsover.

It was bad luck, bad luck for Henry Carthew especially, that Ensign Fernandez Machado should have found Mr. Palsover in one of his rarest hours, his defences down, his inhibitions relaxed, his noble mind o'erthrown, his benevolent and ultra-respectable self defeated ; should have found Mr. Palsover, in short, noisy, garrulous and—very drunk.

It was again unfortunate, for all save himself, that the Ensign was a boy of some intelligence, great ambition, and considerable education, his ' special ' foreign language being English. Marked out for promotion by his friend and patron the Commander-in-Chief, he was likely to be one of those meticulously-selected few who were sent occasionally to Europe ; and, besides studying, in Lisbon, Paris and London, the Arts of Love and War, would further study the English language. Were not the English the *chèrs alliés* of Portugal the Mother ; and was it not a passport to the very valuable favour of His Excellency Dom Perez de Norhona that one should be able to talk to him in English, his favourite foreign tongue ?

And so having cast a seemingly idle and casual eye over the *dhow*, its crew—big black tough-looking men who fished, disported themselves in the water, or did nothing with all their might—Ensign Machado mounted the poop and with punctilious courtesy answered Mr. Palsover's greeting.

284

Hullo, this was interesting. Who was this quaint bird in khaki shirt and shorts ? Spoke English, did he ? Most certainly he had said, among other things, ' *Good evening*.' But perhaps that was all the English he knew. Anyway, he'd soon find out.

But this there was no need for him to do, as Mr. Palsover, apologetically suppressing a noble if deplorable hiccup, asked him if he had seen anything of the Hadji—and that other silly old bastard who didn't know a good thing when it was shoved under his fat nose. . . . Hadn't the sense to go out in the rain when it was snowing five-pound notes. He was a fool, that's what he was. And the Hadji was a fool to have any truck with him. Carthew was his name, and he'd always had a down on Mr. Palsover. Was always picking on him, from the time he was a rookie and Carthew a one-pip wart.

Still, one thing he'd say for him. He was straight. He wouldn't double-cross anybody. And Mr. Palsover didn't regret having let him in on the ground floor. Not that he'd be any good, mark you, for N.B.G. was his initials. But he might find out something about the General. Had the gentleman come across him, by the way ? And wouldn't he have a drink ?

The gentleman would certainly sit down and have a talk with the Şenhor.

" Thass right ! Come and sit down and have a drink."

And Mr. Palsover hospitably wiped the neck of the bottle on his shirt.

Ensign Machado, as fanatical a teetotaller as a Wahabi mullah, courteously declined, and in fairly good English, begged Mr. Palsover to continue his most interesting remarks.

He was an Englishman, wasn't he?

Course he was! What a silly question! Couldn't any benighted foreigner see he was an Englishman? What else would he be?

Yes, yes. True indeed. Of course. And the man who had gone up to Ildefonso with the Hadji? What was his name, by the way? Kar . . . Kar . . .

" Wha' ? Colonel Carthew? Course he's an Englishman. Wha' cher think? Think he was Dutch? " jeered Mr. Palsover. No doubt about him being English all right. Never said he wasn't. All he said was that he was a B.F. and too fond of picking on people. And that Mr. Palsover had always hated his guts, right from the very first. Awful old swine, he was, when he was commanding the Regiment. And he didn't know enough to pick up a packet of fivers when he saw them lying at his feet.

Fivers? Yes? Well, it wasn't very likely he'd see any lying at his feet in Ildefonso, was it? No? opined the Ensign.

Now that's just where the young gentleman was wrong. In a manner of speaking. If old Carthew had had his wits about him, he could have picked up a sackful of fivers. A cart-load of fivers. More than he could bloomin' well spend with both hands and all his pals helping him. And who had shown him how? Why, Mr. Palsover. It was awful. 'Orrible.

And Mr. Palsover wept.

Now the General—*there* was a man. He was on to it in half once. But the trouble was—where was he? And what was he up to? Perhaps the young gentleman had run across him, had he, up at that Capital place? General Sir Reginald Jason. Used to be Carthew's Commanding Officer. Mr. Palsover's too.

No, the Ensign hadn't had the pleasure of meeting

the General.   He hoped to have the honour of meeting several famous Generals in Europe, but he had not met the one Mr. Palsover mentioned.   What was his name again ?   Ah, yes.   And what was the name of the other one—the one who had just gone to Ildefonso with the Hadji Abdulla ?

Carthew.   Colonel Carthew.

Ah, yes ?   And it was his humour to go about in the dress of an Arab at times, was it ?   Yes ?   No ?

Ar !   Silly trick.   Didn't catch General Jason acting the goat like that.   Where was the sense in it ?

True.   And did the Hadji Abdulla know all about this man . . . this British Officer . . . Colonel Kardieu, was it ?   And that he was an Englishman in disguise ?

Hiccuping with an explosive violence that made the welkin ring, Mr. Palsover apologized as one who knew his manners, took a drink for his stomach's sake, and, returning to the matter in hand, affirmed that the Hadji Abdulla did not know anything of the business at all.   He was just a blooming old boatman, a bargee-bumboat-woman, long skirts and all.   A bloomin' native, and little better than a nigger.   The gentleman —Mr. Palsover hadn't the pleasure of knowing his name.   Oh, Machado ?   Ensign Fernandez Machado. He'd heard a name like that before.   Place called Sitapur.   Bloke kept a nice little soldiers' canteen. Miggy Machado.   Done a lot o' good business with him.   But what was he saying.   The Hadji ?   No, the Hadji Abdulla wasn't in on the business at all. Didn't know anything about rayjum nor the concessions nor nothing.

No.   No, exactly.   The Hadji Abdulla was a very ignorant man of course.   A what was it ?   A bum-barge-boatman ?   Exactly.   But the man with him was Colonel Kardieu of the British Army. No? Yes?

" Late retired," murmured Mr. Palsover and settled himself to sleep.

Wouldn't Mr.—what was his name? He didn't think he'd had the pleasure of hearing his name—have another drink, suggested Ensign Machado.

Well, perhaps he would. For was it not written—and an accepted fact—that another little drink wouldn't do us any harm? Bloth-frower. Yes. Broth-flower. Wot? Yes. Floth-browers. Of course he'd have another. Here's to Down with old Carthew and up with the General. . . . And God bless ole Senior Pereira.

The eyes of Ensign Machado narrowed, and his brows drew together in a frown of concentration.

Yes. Yes-s-s. Senhor Pereira! We must not forget him. Where was he now, by the way?

The ole Senior? Where was he? . . . Well . . . *One* place or the other! And Mr. Palsover chuckled at some amusing memory.

Through the gathering clouds of alcoholism Mr. Palsover suddenly saw a light. Momentarily brilliant, shining its warning from the blessed light-house of sober sense and sanity.

Mustn't say too much. Had he said too much? No, he'd only said old Carthew was a fool. So he was.

" Senior Pereira? " he murmured. " He's . . . he's . . . where the birds won't bite him. Good old Senior."

" I suppose it was he who told you and this General and this Senhor Colonel Kardieu all about São Thomé and the—what did you say—radium? "

" Thass right. Thass right. Poor ole Senior."

And Mr. Palsover burst into a flood of bitter tears.
" Here's to 'um," he said, took a long drink at the
bottle and went to sleep. Nor could any amount of
the application of the toe cf Ensign Fernandez
Machado's boot awaken him.

Within the hour, one of the State's swift messengers
set forth from the port, bearing a cipher message which
informed His Excellency Dom Perez de Norhona that
the Hadji Abdulla's companion was an Englishman
in disguise, a Colonel Kardieu.

There is a providence that watches over drunks and
other good men, as well as over babes and sucklings.
The young Ensign could not refrain from being self-
important, mysterious and portentous, nor from acting
omniscience. He failed to describe the nature of the
accident that had provided him with such important
news, and entirely omitted mention of the humble
loquacious individual, lurking on the *dhow*.

Alone he had done it ! Ever watchful, ever brilliant,
he had performed this fine peace of Intelligence-work,
single-handed. (Why admit that he had merely
happened to hear a drunkard babbling ?)

Thus for a time was Mr. Palsover spared the con-
sequences of his indiscretion.

§ 3

And the Hadji Abdulla with the merchant Mohammed bin Yussuf, wandering about the town, entered
into converse with all sorts and conditions of men ;
in cafés ; in music halls (where Henry Carthew was
enchanted by the reed bands that discoursed marvellous music) ; in the market-places ; in the public
gardens ; and wherever São Thoméans were wont to
congregate. Persistently they sought information as

to a General Inglez who was said to have visited the country some two years previously ; but never a word of information could they glean.

Evidently General Jason had come, seen, and disappeared.

" I'm afraid it means that if he's in São Thomé he's in the Citadel—or under it," said the Hadji one night, as the two sat upon the floor of their room, on either side of a vast platter of rice and mutton flavoured and enriched with onions, chillies, pimento and strange, appetizing herbs.

" What's to be done ? " sighed Henry Carthew. " I suppose you'll be sailing soon ? Personally, I'm not going until I have found out what has happened to him. . . .

" If I learn nothing, and nothing else happens, sooner or later I shall tackle de Norhona," he added.

But in the event, it was de Norhona who tackled him—and much sooner.

VII

NEXT morning, early, there came a heavy knock at the door and, followed by a couple of soldiers, a Corporal entered and peremptorily bade the man calling himself Mohammed bin Yussuf to follow him at once.

As he rose slowly to his feet, Henry Carthew whispered to the Hadji, in English,

" You know nothing about my being a European—if there's trouble. I have deceived you. Stick to that. We must tell the same story."

And turning to the Corporal he bade him lead on, for he was ready. He also thanked him courteously for having so kindly waited until he had broken his fast.

" Good morning, Colonel Kardieu," smiled His Excellency Dom Perez de Norhona. " Won't you take a chair ? Cigarette ? I hope I am not being troublesome and intrusive, but I did so want a little chat with you."

Henry Carthew thought quickly. Obviously the game was up. His disguise was penetrated, and not only did this man know that he was a European, but he actually knew his rank and name. Treachery somewhere. Was it possible that the Hadji . . . ? No. He thrust the thought from his mind. Quite impossible. If the Hadji were a treacherous liar, there was not an honest and decent man on the face of the earth. That Brodie Dysart had betrayed him was out of the question, unthinkable.

Jason! Jason? Could Reginald have seen him here, and told this feller . . . that . . . ?

No, that was just plain silly. Why should Reginald do anything but rush up to him and shake his hand if he caught sight of him?

Because Reginald was under restraint? Saw him from a window? But surely the last thing in the world that Reginald would do would be to give him away?

But it might have been unintentional. He might have called his name. Nonsense. He'd have called out " Henry " if, in his amazement, he had called out anything at all. He certainly would not have shouted out " Colonel Carthew."

It was utterly amazing, astonishing.

But the question of the " how " of it could wait. The immediate problem was that of what line he himself should take. He must say something and say it quickly.

Well, the truth, the whole truth and nothing but the truth had, all his life, been his general policy, and it had been a good one. What about telling the plain and simple truth now? If you tell the truth you cannot be caught out in a lie ; and wasn't it an undeniable fact that the most subtle diplomacy, the line best calculated to puzzle and confuse an artful opponent, was that of the plain and simple truth?

" Charmed, Your Excellency," he said. " Thank you," and taking a cigarette from the big silver box upon the desk, looked round for a match.

" Allow me," said de Norhona, and lit the cigarette for him.

" Well, so you do talk English, and no doubt will admit that you are Colonel Kardieu, late of the British Army."

" Certainly," was the cool reply. " ' *But yesterday the word of Cæsar might have stood against the world* ' and so forth. . . ."

" But yesterday you were a thick-headed bazaar-Arab from Bazra, anxious to sell us what I must really admit is a most beautiful pearl. Well, well ! ' *All the world's a stage* ' and—er—*some men in their time play many parts*. Arab to-day ; Englishman to-morrow. *Here* to-day, but . . ." and his suave voice changed from light and pleasant banter, ". . . I doubt it you will be *gone* to-morrow, Colonel."

Suddenly with a deep and angry frown, he dropped his voice to a menacing growl.

" What do you want in São Thomé ? Why have you come here, eh ? Answer me ! *Instantly !* "

" Certainly, Your Excellency. I came to São Thomé for the sole and simple reason that I want to find my friend General Sir Reginald Jason, who undoubtedly came here from Santa Cruz. If you will be so exceedingly kind as to tell me what has become of him, I shall be infinitely grateful. I mean—what really *has* become of him ? . . . I had no other object whatsoever in coming here, and all I want to do is to depart, when I have either found him or got authentic news of him. I have come at the request of his wife. Or widow—perhaps ? "

" Really ! And who the devil might General Sir Reginald Basin be ? I've never heard of him in my life."

" No, nor I," replied Henry Carthew coldly. " I said Jason. A distinguished British General. Sir Reginald Jason."

" Well, I'm afraid you've come to the wrong place. This isn't Colchis, you know."

" General Jason came here about two years ago."

" I venture to doubt it, Colonel. I don't think many people come to São Thomé without my knowledge, or land here without my consent."

" Look here, Your Excellency. Whatever may be the ultimate upshot of this affair . . . to put it plainly —whatever you may do to me . . . would you kindly tell me just this, plainly and truthfully, as a gentleman and a ' man of honour ' as you'd call it. Have you ever seen or heard anything concerning General Sir Reginald Jason ? "

" I have never, to my knowledge, set eyes on any such person, and I most certainly have never heard any such name," was the reply. " But it was rather to talk about yourself that I asked for the pleasure of your company, Colonel. If, as you say, you came here in search of what I'm afraid I must view as a mythical Mason or Basin or Jason, or what you please —why exactly did you come in fancy dress, as an Arab pearl-merchant ? "

" Simply and solely as a means of gaining admission here," replied Henry Carthew, looking his inquisitor squarely in the eyes.

" Now, just supposing for one moment that that were the truth, how did you ever come to hear of São Thomé, and what gave you the idea that your friend, this famous British General, had also heard of São Thomé and had, in fact, come here ? "

" Well, he wrote home to England from this place Santa Cruz, and said that that was his starting-point or jumping-off place for his ultimate destination."

" And did he name that destination as being São Thomé ? "

" No, he didn't. He simply said he was at Santa Cruz, and was going somewhere else from there."

" And did you discover from our friend the Hadji Abdulla the name of the place to which this General went ? "

" No, Your Excellency. That I most certainly did not. And that is the plain and simple truth."

" Ah ! I don't want to sound medieval or melodramatic or just funny, but, among the other ways in which we São Thoméans are a little behind the times— or rather, perhaps, ahead of them, like the Nazi Germans—we have our own ways of making people speak the truth. If we don't think they are doing so, that is."

" Torture ? It doesn't sound very civilized ; but believe me or not, I am telling you the truth, and no amount of torture would enable me to improve on it. It was not the Hadji Abdulla who told me about São Thomé."

" Then who was it ? "

" It was the man who told General Jason."

" General Jason, General Mason, General Basin ! I'm getting a little tired of this figment of your imagination. *Suppose we talk about one—Schultz. Fritz Schultz !* Are you sure that *he* wasn't the man who told you about São Thomé ? Are you quite certain that you haven't followed him up, in the hope of getting what he failed to get ? "

" Quite certain, Your Excellency. I never, to my knowledge, heard the name Fritz Schultz in my life. It conveys nothing to me whatsoever."

" Do you speak German yourself, as you do Portuguese and English and Arabic ? " growled de Norhona.

" No. Not to say speak it. I could just make myself understood in a German hotel, or roughly make out the sense of a simple advertisement in a

295

German newspaper, but I certainly couldn't say that I know German."

" Ah ! Did you ever meet a man named Pereira ? "

" Pereira ? . . . Pereira ? . . . It isn't an uncommon name in India. The Indian Goanese all took Portuguese names, as no doubt you know, when they were converted. I have known da Silvas, da Costas, da Sousas, and no doubt Pereiras, but I cannot call one to mind at the moment."

" Not a São Thoméan gentleman, cultured, travelled, middle-aged, English-speaking ? . . . Manöel Pereira ? "

" No. No, I cannot remember ever meeting a Mr. Manöel Pereira. Would it be in India ? "

" No, it wouldn't. It would be in Santa Cruz, and it would be a little over two years ago when our friend, Rasin, Mason, Basin or Jason—or shall we call him Fritz Schultz—honoured us with a visit and certain fantastic get-rich-quick proposals. It was he and his gang who were to get rich—and São Thomé was to be turned from a Garden of Eden to a Ruhr Basin, Donetz ; a British ' Black Country.' São Ildefonso another Newcastle or Pittsburg ! "

" No, I certainly haven't met a Mr. Manöel Pereira within the last three years or so," replied Henry Carthew patiently. " In point of fact, I don't think I ever, in India or anywhere else, met a Manöel Pereira, and I'm quite certain I never knew a Fritz Schultz. Might have had a German prisoner of that name through my hands during the Great War, but . . ."

" But you didn't know he came here, eh ? "

" No, I certainly didn't."

" Well, as you weren't told anything about São Thomé by anyone named Pereira or anyone named Schultz, who is the mystery man who *did* tell you, since it was not the Hadji Abdulla ? "

"In point of fact, it was General Jason's servant who told me."

"Really, Colonel Kardieu, or whoever you are! Don't you think you are being a little unnecessarily aggravating? And do you think it is entirely wise in the circumstances?"

"I am extremely sorry if you find me aggravating," replied Carthew. "I haven't the slightest wish to be anything of the sort. I am merely trying to tell you the truth, and also to find out what has become of my friend."

"Well, look here. Let's make a bargain. You admit that your friend was named Fritz Schultz, and I will tell you what became of him, fast enough."

"I'm afraid I cannot admit it, Your Excellency. I doubt if I have ever heard of a Fritz Schultz in my life."

"Ah, well; that's that, then! We'll have a talk later on, when you may have thought better of it. I believe one's memory improves when the mind has no distractions."

De Norhona rang a heavy bell that stood beside his chair.

The door opened and a secretary entered.

"Take this man along to the room that Schultz occupied," he said, "and tell the Officer of the Day to put a sentry over the door, and that I shall hold the Officer personally responsible for the prisoner's safety.

"Sorry, Colonel," he added, turning to Carthew with a somewhat sneering smile and a slightly sarcastic note in his voice, "I'll come and see you this evening. Meantime, it would be a good plan if you'd try to stimulate your memory."

"Especially good for yourself," he added coldly.

" And send me Fonseca," he said, as the secretary turned to go.

A few minutes later a small insignificant man, yellow, rat-faced and unprepossessing, glided into the room.

" Anything fresh ? " asked de Norhona.

" Nothing important, Your Excellency. They still talk together and to the people they meet—shop-keepers in the bazaar, policemen off duty, soldiers, men sitting idle on the seats in the gardens."

" Ever any reference to the German, Schultz ? "

" No. I haven't been able to trace that."

" Puzzling. Very puzzling," mused de Norhona. " Very interesting too. I wonder whether Schultz— who certainly got the better of Pereira in some way— actually passed himself off on the Hadji and this man as an English Officer . . . ' General Jason.' It's possible. But then Kardieu really seems to be looking for an actual General Jason. *Corpo de Dios !* That's an idea. There may actually be a British General of the name of Jason who is really missing. And Schultz may have impersonated him to Kardieu. I wonder. Possible, but not very probable. Really puzzling, but I somehow think that our Colonel Kardieu will have to stay with us. Since he has followed Schultz so far, we might see that he follows him a little farther ; follows him to the end. Schultz's end. . . ."

" Go and tell the Hadji Abdulla I want to see him," he ordered, turning to his spy.

§ 2

" *Salaam aleikum*, Hadji Abdulla bin Ibrahim," smiled de Norhona, as the Hadji, escorted by the spy and an orderly, entered the room. " Sit down. I want to talk with you."

The Hadji, salaaming profoundly and calling the

298

blessing of Allah upon his kind patron's head, seated himself cross-legged beside the desk.

De Norhona regarded him long and thoughtfully, the Hadji returning his searching stare with a look of meek humility and simple innocence.

" Where did you pick up this Colonel Kardieu ? "

" Your Excellency ?   Colonel Kah-duh ? "

" Yes.   You introduced him as the merchant Mohammed bin Yussuf."

" Pick him up, Sidi ? "

" Yes, come on.   Who is he ?   What's the game ? "

" He's a fool, Sidi, but stubborn.   And I think his price is a fair one.   We shall have to pay it.   But even so . . ."

"That's enough! . . .   Where did you first see him ? "

" At Basra, Sidi.   He had just come from Bahrein, where he buys pearls."

" Sure you didn't meet him first in Santa Cruz ? "

" What would a pearl-merchant be doing there and with such a pearl as that ?   It would more probably be in Cairo."

" Do you mean that you met him in Cairo ? "

" No, no, Sidi.   I meant that that is the sort of place where one might meet a man with a big pearl to sell.   But I don't think he'd been farther than Baghdad in his life."

" How did he ever come to hear about São Thomé ? "

" He didn't.   How should he, Sidi ?   I simply told him that I knew where he could get the best and biggest price, and that I would take him there and help him to sell it ; the commission to include his passage money."

" Well, if you are speaking the truth, Hadji, you've been a fool, and somehow I have never taken you for a fool."

" The pearl is not real, Sidi ? "

" It's the man who isn't real. Does he know any language but Arabic ? "

" How should he, Sidi ? "

" Has he ever spoken to you of the man you brought here about two years ago ? Let's see, what was his name ? Jason, wasn't it ? "

" The name, Sidi ? Was it Yasoon ? Yes, that must have been it ; Yasoon. No, this man has never uttered the name Yasoon. Why should he ? "

" Did he ever speak of a man named Schultz ? "

" Schools ? No, Sidi, he is an ignorant man."

De Norhona studied the Hadji's face long and thoughtfully. Was he as simple as he looked, and as truthful as he sounded ? He hoped so. Almost passionately he hoped so, for the Hadji was invaluable. It would be really a shock to find that he had been bought. It would be one of the most painful things he had ever had to do, if he were compelled to . . . to detain him. To deal with him.

" Well, looks to me as though you have been fooled —as I nearly was. I'll talk to you again later, Hadji. But let me say once more now what I have said before. Bring *no one* to Sao Thomé unless actually accompanied by an authorized person whom you know. A São Thoméan like Senhor Pereira.

" Where is he, by the way ? " he added sharply.

" Sidi, who am I that I should know all things ? The last I ever saw of the Senhor Pereira was his handwriting—on the letters he had given to the General Inglez—Yasoon, who is—' Schools,' did you say ? "

The following day was a busy one for the Hadji. Almost every member of the Council sent for him and gave him commissions of a private and personal nature.

In the evening he was bidden to appear before the Council in session, to receive instructions, to be reprimanded for bringing an unauthorized stranger to São Ildefonso. Also to be informed that, while the parcel of pearls that he had brought was acceptable at the price he asked, and would now be paid for, the big pearl would be retained until more was known about the man who had apparently deceived him.

This last piece of information seemed to be something in the nature of a severe blow to the Hadji, who humbly and respectfully protested.

Had he not acted in good faith ? Was he not responsible for Mohammed bin Yussuf ? Would not the name and the face of the Hadji Abdulla be blackened among pearl-dealers from Basra to Bombay, from Zanzibar to Ceylon ?

No member of the Council appeared to worry excessively over this contingency, and the Regent, Doña Guiomar, bade him hold his peace even as she would hold the pearl, until more was known as to its ownership.

" If, as I am inclined to suspect, it is your own pearl, Hadji," observed de Norhona, " it is, as you know, in good hands and safe keeping. If it belongs to the man whom you brought here, why the anxiety ?

" Should we retain it, you shall have your commission," he added with a cynical smile.

The business of the Hadji being concluded, he was bidden by the Regent and Council of the State of São Thomé to start on the morrow for the coast, to sail forthwith to Santa Cruz, again make the fullest enquiries as to the fate of Senhor Manöel Pereira, and to return as usual six months later.

Arrived at the *dhow* he found Mr. Palsover in good

health and spirits and particularly interested in the fact that Colonel Carthew was, for the time being, remaining at the Capital.

And had the Hadji seen anything of General Jason ? He had not.

Mr. Palsover, after considerable cogitation, decided that he would continue his hotel-keeping and trading pursuits for another six months, and if, on the Hadji's next visit to Santa Cruz and São Thomé, there was still no news of General Jason, he would write him off.

He would return to England and find such another —unless of course, Colonel B. F. Carthew learned sense during the next six months and saw no fatal objection to picking up a bloody great fortune. Otherwise, he'd go home, start afresh, and incidentally find out how much the news about the General was worth—to his sorrowing widow.

VIII

HIS EXCELLENCY DOM PEREZ DE NOR-
HONA, Secretary to the Cabinet, and considerable power behind the throne, found himself more
and more inclined to like his ' honoured guest,' and to
enjoy his conversation.

It was becoming a real and great pleasure to have
long talks with this man of great experience, high
intelligence and admirable character. Really a most
likeable fellow and a gifted listener. The only thing
he regretted was that this Colonel Kardieu was not a
scientist. But one can't have everything, and he was
undoubtedly a widely-read and an extremely thought-
ful man ; and, if unable to argue and dispute on the
higher psychology, he could at any rate understand
one's discourse and grasp what was said to him, provided one's language was not too technical and erudite.
It clarified one's mind to put one's ideas before a man
of this type and to listen to oneself as one expounded
and expanded one's theories.

He hoped that, later on, the good fellow would lend
him his mind for experiment. Nothing injurious.
Nothing lasting, of course. He had thought, at one
time, of using him for another permanent-hypnosis
experiment, but he had come to believe in him—
almost ; to accept him at his face-value, and to feel
that whatever he said was the simple truth.

That was what he was—simple and truthful.

And these were traits that were not too common with the educated, the "upper" class, the sophisticated, especially the European of that type. And if he were, as really seemed to be the case, quite truthful and honest, he could not be a Nazi German follower of this Fritz Schultz ; for he still stoutly and solemnly swore that he was not a German and had never heard of Fritz Schultz.

And yet it was an amazing business, really puzzling ; and whatever puzzled Perez de Norhona was something pretty deep and intricate.

Not a German. Never heard of Schultz. He was looking for a Jason. And who was Jason but the leader of the Argonauts ? And of what were the Argonauts in pursuit but the Golden Fleece ? The Golden Fleece of Colchis.

Could it be that he, Perez de Norhona, was the simple one, and that this Kardieu was the second of the Argonauts in pursuit of the golden treasure, nay, the far more than golden, treasure of São Thomé ? It was possible. . . .

Corpo de Dios ! If he were German and he could catch him out ! He'd *use* him. He'd teach him to try to fool Perez de Norhona. He'd make such an example of him that if ever word of it got abroad, there would not be another of these Argonauts visiting this particular Colchis, for a century.

As Henry Carthew sat in his room, drinking his excellent coffee after dinner that night, there came a punctilious knock at the door and de Norhona entered.

" Not finished yet ? I'm sorry. I'll come in later, and . . ."

" No, no," replied Henry Carthew, rising. " Please do sit down, Senhor. Will you take coffee ? "

" No, thanks," replied de Norhona, seating himself. " I want to make you a proposal."

Henry Carthrew smiled pleasantly, perhaps a little sceptically.

" I wonder whether you'd accept my given word, my solemn word of honour ? " asked de Norhona.

Carthrew stared at his pleasant gaoler.

A difficult question. On the whole he would—with some reservations, some uncertainty. Undoubtedly he was—well—a trifle medieval in outlook, and perhaps a little cruel, but one really had no reason to think him treacherous.

" Yes, Your Excellency," he said, and then, with a rush of truth to the head, qualified the statement. " Up to a point."

" Ah ! And to what point ? "

" Well, in the first place, the point of probability. Naturally I couldn't take your word for it if you told me you were going to do something that I didn't believe possible. And of course I know that a man in your position has to use the language of diplomacy which is not always that of plain unvarnished truth . . . and all that."

" Well now, see whether you consider this improbable, or the language of diplomacy. . . . On one condition, I will let you do anything you like about this mythical, or at any rate, mysterious, General Jason. I will do my utmost to help you in your search for him, and when you have at last decided—what you will discover to be the obvious fact—that he is not in São Thomé, the Hadji shall take you back to Santa Cruz next time he comes. Or anywhere else —provided you give me your word of honour that you will supply no information to anybody concerning São Thomé, or endeavour to find your way back here.

305

. . . You see, I trust you, even if you don't trust me."

" And what is the condition, Senhor ? "

" That you write me, in German, a brief and simple account of yourself and your friend, and of your tracing him here to Ildefonso."

Henry Carthew laughed a little bitterly.

" I thought there was a snag somewhere," he said. " I tell you I don't know any German. I don't know a word of German. Well, that's an exaggeration. But I could tell you all the German I know, now, in one minute, and any educated European knows as much. *Hier Man sprecht Deutsch*, and *Schlafen Sie wohl*, and *Guten Tag, gnadige Fraulein*, and *Kommen Sie hier*. That's just about all the German I know, and I picked those scraps up accidentally and unintentionally. I don't even know whether *bitte* means *please* or *thank you*. I just don't know German any more than you know Chinese. Possibly less," he smiled.

" Well, the offer remains open, should you remember a little more German than that. Enough to write me a letter for my archives."

Henry Carthew sighed and shook his head. Wasn't this chap honest enough to know when he met an honest man ? Truthful enough to know when he was up against the truth ?

" By the way," said de Norhona, rising as though about to go, " didn't you say that your elusive friend had a loving wife now weeping and forlorn, heart-broken and distraught ? "

" Lady Jason naturally is in the lowest depths of grief and anxiety," replied Carthew coldly.

" And you'd like to—I won't say ' put her out of her misery,' for I keep that phrase for more unpleasant contingencies—you'd like to set her mind at rest ? "

" I'd give anything to do so."

" Well now, you write a letter to her, telling her that all's well, a letter that will relieve her mind and make her happy."

" Why ! Senhor de Norhona . . ." cried Carthew, taking a step toward him, " if it were only true, and I could write to her and . . ."

" Very well, you write it to her—in German—and we'll send an exact translation—and what you say in it shall come true."

Henry Carthew's hands clenched.

" I tell you I cannot write a letter in German. I tell you I know no German."

" H'm ! I wonder ! You know, Schultz wasn't so anxious to disguise the fact that he spoke German."

" *Damn* Schultz ! I know nothing of any Schultz, I tell you—and I am not concerned with what he did or did not do."

" No ? Well, I'm sorry we've got at cross purposes to-night, Colonel. I had hoped we were going to have a talk. A nice long chat. I am in a talkative mood this evening and I wanted to ask you to help me, if you would. The fact of your being a foreigner and a stranger—and an Englishman, if that's what you are . . . but never mind. Ah, well . . . a pity."

As he reached the door, de Norhona turned.

" Look, Kardieu," he said, " I'll make you an offer that will test your sincerity and give you a chance to test mine. You want to find your friend more than anything on earth."

" Yes, literally."

" More than a signed radium-concession, eh ? "

" I neither know nor care anything about radium or radium-concessions, and I would rather find my friend than a million tons of radium—all my own."

307

" Well, then. You shall see the man *to-night*. To-night you shall see the very man who came here with the Hadji two years ago; Fritz Schultz, the man who talked to me in English, and who said he was a British General. *Now then?* "

Henry Carthew stared at the speaker incredulous, bemused, as in a dream, a stupor of hopeless hope. Was the man still mocking him? Was he as devilishly cruel as all that?

" You *could*? " he whispered.

" I could. I can. I will. If you'll ask me now, in German, I'll do it—and I'll not demand it in German writing. Just ask me in your own tongue to bring you face to face with that man and I will do it *now*."

" Your Excellency, I am doing so. If you have any mercy, decency, honesty, believe me that I am now asking you, in my own tongue, to bring me face to face with my friend."

" And that is your last word, is it? "

" No, my last word is ' *Go* '—before I . . ."

De Norhona eyed his prisoner, sighed and went, locking the door behind him.

An hour later he returned.

" Now don't scowl at me like that, my dear chap. I have come to say that I believe you, that I am prepared to take your word that you are not a German, and to offer you an opportunity of finally removing the last vestiges of doubt from my mind. You'd like to prove that you are telling the truth, wouldn't you? "

" Of course."

" Right. You shall. And when you've proved it, I shall offer you your absolute freedom and put you on parole to undertake no sort or kind of investigations of a commercial or industrial nature. I mean that

308

you will promise not to use your freedom to look into possibilities of future exploitation of any of this island's resources. What do you say ? "

" Well, I don't wish to sound ungrateful, but what I say on the spur of the moment is—Snags ! There has been one in each of your offers to-night. Excuse me if I sound ungrateful or discourteous, but what is the snag in this ? "

" Oh, I don't think it is to be regarded as a snag. I want you to let me hypnotize you. I'll attempt to find out whether you know German or not. There you are, my friend, there's the final test—and your opportunity. If you accept, I will undertake to believe you innocent if I cannot prove you guilty—of being a Nazi German, and therefore a liar and a public danger to the free and independent State of São Thomé. On the other hand, refuse, and I shall know what to think."

" Why should I refuse ? I have nothing to hide," replied Carthew. " If you wanted to injure me, you could do so without hypnotism, I suppose. All right, I agree."

" Good. Sit down in that arm-chair, lean back and relax. Now then, look me straight in the eyes. Relax. Relax. No resistance now. Relax. . . ."

" Ah ! . . ."

And Dr. de Norhona got to· work.

§ 2

" He is not German, Your Highness," said Perez de Norhona that night when interviewing the Regent as usual, before she retired to her own suite in the " Royal " wing of the Castle.

" You are certain ? " replied Doña Guiomar. " How do you know ? "

" I'm as certain of it as one can be of anything in this world. If I don't read that man aright, as a simple and straight-forward Englishman of a common British Army type, then I'm no psychologist. First, I offered him all he wants and the only thing he wants, in return for a few words of German. He knows none. To make assurance doubly sure, I hypnotized him, talked to him in German, told him he was a German and dug up all the German he knows. You could write it on a postage stamp. He's no German. He's English all right."

" I'm glad, very glad, for several reasons. It was rather a dreadful thought that the new Germany had learned about us and our mineral possibilities, or rather certainties, at last. . . . If this had been another German looking for the first one, I should have felt that your Argonaut theory was right. It has been a nightmare. I've been expecting every day to hear that a German warship had anchored off the creek, and that a large and heavily armed deputation had landed to ' protect ' us—and turn us into a submarine base, a naval and military base, an airport, and one vast coal-field, mineral-workings, and industrial mining and smelting area. Three hundred years of peace shattered, our independence gone, and our civilization reverted to modern barbarism. . . . I am glad, too, for his own sake, for I have grown to like him."

" Yes, he's a lovable sort of chap, isn't he ? " agreed de Norhona.

" Yes, that's exactly what he is," mused the Regent.

" What's the position with regard to him now ? " she continued. " You haven't done him any harm, of course. Not one of your terrible experiments ? "

" No, no. Not the slightest harm. He found it

310

'very interesting'! As to his position, I think we will give him the Freedom of São Thomé, on a platter."

"And eventually?"

"Well. . . . See how he shapes. See if he drops this Jason obsession. If we came to trust him completely, he could be extremely useful to us."

"Yes, he could."

"Both here and abroad," he added.

"You'd trust him to that extent, would you?" asked Doña Guiomar.

"Not in a hurry. Not till I had satisfied myself as to what is in his mind. But, sooner or later—if he continues willing to submit to hypnosis—the day will come when I can say, with absolute certainty and finality, whether it would or would not be wise to use him abroad. I think he's going to turn out to be one of those perfectly simple characters with one-way one-track minds whose word literally is their bond, and who are absolutely trustworthy."

"Yes, a man whose word is worth a thousand stamped and witnessed contracts," agreed Doña Guiomar. "That's what I think you will find him to be," and she sighed deeply—perhaps over the rarity of such phenomena.

"Suppose he simply wants to go. Just say good-bye and . . . leave us," she continued.

"Well, I don't know. I pretended to offer him that freedom in return for the confession that he was a German—but I don't think we'll take any unnecessary risks. He knows too much. I don't for one moment suppose he could ever find his way here again, or direct anyone else, but if one takes no risks, one does nothing—risky."

"Quite so," agreed Doña Guiomar. "We'll keep him on the Island."

311

And she fixed the smouldering gaze of her heavy-lidded lustrous eyes upon those of de Norhona.

Faintly she smiled, and there was an answering smile on de Norhona's face, as he bowed deeply, took her hand and touched it with his lips. Between these two people who understood each other perfectly, enough had been said.

Next day, Colonel Henry Carthew was given the freedom of the City of São Ildefonso and of the State of São Thomé.

§ 3

As the days passed by, Henry Carthew discovered to his great surprise, if not pleasure, that he was not only a free man but a genuinely honoured guest, and although he realized that that phrase is apt to bear a sinister connotation, there was apparently nothing of the sort in this instance. Not only was he treated kindly, but his society was actually sought and culti-vated by certain of the Members of Council.

True, these were at first the Commissioner of Police, the Commander-in-Chief and the Secretary for Foreign Affairs ; their conversations were tendentious, their questions sudden and artful, as though he were still an object of suspicion. But after a while he began to feel that he was accepted for what he professed to be, and both regarded and treated as a very interesting English traveller of rank and position, whose inten-tions were completely innocent and harmless. It was realized that he really was looking for a missing friend, and that he had cleverly deceived the Hadji in pursuit of that object, and whether he ever left São Thomé again or not, was an acquisition and an ornament to the society of the Capital in general and the Citadel in particular.

And among the high Government officials and leading members of society, Henry Carthew was quickly accepted as an English aristocrat and representative of Portugal's oldest ally, and a personage who could give them all sorts of useful information about great and admired England and the rest of the outside world.

What surprised and puzzled Carthew more than anything was the attitude of Doña Guiomar, who seemed quickly—almost too quickly—to change, from a cold and offended attitude of hostility, to one of approval and friendliness that rapidly warmed. In point of fact, she too accepted him as precisely what he was, an English army-officer who, in some utterly incomprehensible manner, had heard that the lost friend for whom he was searching had made his way here to São Thomé. How this had come about was a complete mystery—one which could only be solved by Manöel Pereira.

Quite possibly, as de Norhona surmised, the evil Fritz Schultz was at the bottom of it.

All very puzzling indeed. But of one thing she was certain. This Senhor Kardieu was a *fildalgo*, an aristocrat and an Englishman, and had not the faintest interest in any commercial or industrial concerns whatsoever. . . .

Thus, at a series of strangely medieval social functions, formal, mannered, and of rigid Court etiquette, Henry Carthew found himself treated with signal favour by Doña Guiomar, seated on her right hand at State dinners, and occasionally given the somewhat embarrassing privilege of being promoted to partner-

313

ship with her in a Court dance of formal state-
liness.

Yes, not only was Colonel Henry Carthew a free
man, but one who, were he anything of a careerist,
might well think he saw a strange and brilliant future
opening before him.

But Carthew was not a careerist.   He was a simple-
minded man of single purpose.   Enough that he was
free to pursue that purpose.

IX

IT was almost too good to be true, and he scarcely believed it, even yet. To think that that damned door was really unlocked for good, and that he could, at any hour of the day or night, open it and walk out.

After dinner, one evening, Henry Carthew rose from his straight-backed uncomfortable chair of high old-fashioned shape, went to the door, opened it, looked out into the dim stone passage, and closed it again.

Yes, it was still true. He was still free.

Well now, what should he do—this evening and for the rest of his life ? As to the former, he'd just wander about for an hour or two for the sheer joy of the feeling that he still could do so ; could come and go as he liked. As to the latter, he would continue his search for Reginald, with the utmost of his energy and ability and resources, for as long as he lived.

He would now stroll about this floor of the Castle, for the ever-fresh pleasure of sampling his freedom, and in the hope of learning something from somebody —anybody.

Wandering along corridors, through galleries, across great empty stone-flagged rooms, seeing no one but an occasional belated servant, secretary or other func-tionary—for this non-residential part of the Castle was almost untenanted at night—he at length came out on to the broad inner balcony or gallery which

315

looked down into the Great Hall. The light of the full moon streaming through the high windows that gave on to the court-yard, lent the huge audience-chamber a somewhat ghostly and unearthly appearance, very attractive to the artistic eye.

To Henry Carthew it was like looking from this world into another, from this point of time into an earlier one, especially when a door opened and a woman of quite medieval appearance crossed a corner of the hall, passing as she did so, through a pool of moonlight, and looking, in her somewhat old-fashioned, somewhat Spanish dress, like a visitant from that earlier time.

Doña Guiomar.

A further note of eeriness and fantasy was added by the silent and shadow-like appearance of the great animal that followed her. A beast which, but for its somewhat clumsy movements, heavy and awkward gait, might have been a bear or a great ape ; except for its lack of grace and of ease of movement, a huge dog.

As the woman paused to produce a key and unlock the door through which she was about to pass, the great ungainly creature squatted down, raised its head, and gazed upward toward the window through which the moonlight shone.

As Henry Carthew, conscious of a queer discomfort and distaste, not to say fear, gazed at the animal, it threw back its head and bayed deeply.

So it *was* a dog ! A huge bloodhound, baying the moon.

Well, it was the strangest dog that he had ever seen. But São Thomé was a strange place, and might well contain animals that he had never heard of. How the kangaroo must have astounded the first Europeans who landed in Australia! Well, if the world could still produce animals, till recently unknown—creatures like the okapi in Western Africa and the giant panda in Mongolia, there was no reason why São Thomé should not produce a new breed of dog. As far as one could tell in this dim light and at that distance, it was the biggest dog that ever barked, and the least dog-like in shape.

But a dog apparently it was.

" *Quiet! Lie down!* " cried the woman sharply as she opened the door, and the animal instantly fell silent, crouching low with its head upon its paws. As she opened the door and the dog rose to follow, she spoke to it again.

" *No! Stay there! Wait!* " and she cracked the whip she carried.

Withdrawing the key from the door, she passed through, closed it behind her, and ascended a secret flight of stairs.

Carthew's enquiring mind was filled with curiosity.

What kind of beast could it be?

Neither bears nor apes bark. On the other hand, dogs do not walk as this animal did ; nor is the slope of a dog's back downward from tail to head.

A dog of the size and shape of a large bear!

Why shouldn't he go down and have a look at it? He had been told he could go where he liked, and that he was as free as de Norhona himself. Naturally, he wasn't going to construe this complete relaxation of all bonds into a licence to peep and pry, but there could surely be no harm in his going down into the hall and satisfying a normal and healthy curiosity as to what kind of a dog this was.

Evidently it was Doña Guiomar's body-guard and watch-dog, whatever else it was.

Of course ! It was the creature that he had imagined to be a great ape when he saw it lying asleep in the corner, behind her chair, on the occasion when he had been brought before her in the guise of Mohammed bin Yussuf the pearl-merchant. The top of its shaggy head had been toward him then, and he had noticed that it had a hairy or furry body, or else wore some sort of covering or clothing of fur or hairy skins.

He'd go and have a closer look at it.

Suppose it attacked him. It might be an enormously powerful beast ; and, even if he had been armed, it would be a poor way of celebrating his release and acknowledging his gratitude, to kill what was evidently the Regent's pet and body-guard.

But come ! This wouldn't do. He must have been getting soft in his easy captivity. Getting nervy and cautious. He'd go down and have a look at the beast. Why should it attack him ? Being a real dog-lover, he had always got on splendidly with dogs. The thing had been quiet enough when he had seen it before, that day in Doña Guiomar's room. He'd take a risk. What was life without them ?

As he went along the gallery toward the stairs that led down into the hall, he kept an eye on the dog. Hearing him move, it looked up, and he saw that it was evidently watching him through the shaggy hair that hung down over its face, as does that of an old-fashioned English sheep-dog. Pausing, he called to it, as he would have done to an ordinary English dog in like circumstances.

" Hullo, old chap ! " he shouted, and then whistled.

The dog instantly sprang up, alert, propping its body on its fore-legs, but without raising its heavy hindquarters from the ground.

"Hi! Here! Come here, boy! Come on. Here!" he called again, as he descended the stairs.

Suddenly the dog raised its head and uttered a curious cry; to Carthew a strangely moving sound, heart-rending almost, a sound between a banshee howl and a whimpering wail, as though the creature were in agony. It was somewhat like the noise his own dog made when, welcoming his return, its emotion was too powerful for any utterance but a whimpering—as though it wept aloud for joy.

But there was no joy in this dreadful sound. He found himself using a banal but useful cliché—'the despairing cry of a lost soul, a soul in agony.'

"Come on, old chap," cried Carthew. "Come on. What's up?"

And the great heavy animal, rising to its feet, lumbered toward him.

Was this its mode of attack? There had been no baring of teeth, no sign of snarl or growl.

"There, there, there! Well, well, well!" he said, and leaned forward confidently to pat its head as the dog reached him.

Sitting back on its haunches it rose, shook its head with an awkward toss, that threw back the overhanging hair, and gazed into Carthew's face.

Absolutely friendly!

But what an amazing creature!

What was it?

It wasn't a dog.

A barking ape?

No. No ape had square shoulders, a pale face, a moustache and beard, a high-bridged nose. . . .

Damn this dim light.

It was . . . it was . . . *human.*

It was a man.

319

" Here ! Turn your head this way ! " and he wrenched the head toward the moonlight as he swept the face clear of overhanging hair.

It was a man ! . . . It was . . . *Oh God !* *No ! No ! Oh, God—no !*

For a moment he closed his eyes and leant back against the great newel-post of the stairs.

It was not until he again opened his eyes and stared, sick, shaken and horrified to the depths of his soul, that his mind accepted the truth.

His search was ended.

§ 2

As he sat at the bottom of the stairs, trembling from head to foot, he looked into Reginald Jason's eyes and, recoiling, shuddered.

As the creature, the-man-that-thought-he-was-a-dog, his friend, raised its paw, its hand, and laid it on his knee, Henry Carthew's strong self-control broke down entirely, and burying his face in his hands, he actually wept, cried like a child, cried as he had not done since boyhood, his body shaken by hard, rending sobs. . . .

From an agony of grief, pain and dreadful despair, his mind turned to blind and terrible rage ; and then again to grief and pity inexpressible.

This had been Reginald Jason, his friend, this man-that-behaved-as-a-dog, that thought itself to be a dog, that, but for its skeletal form and structure *was* a dog, with the mind of a dog.

For how long he wrestled with it mentally he knew not. He did his utmost, using every device of which he could think, to strike a spark of human response.

320

But completely without success.

This, that was a man, was mentally a dog, a friendly good-natured dog that was devoid of anything but canine understanding and power of response.

Did it understand English better than Portuguese? No—not so far as he could tell.

Did it respond, in the slightest degree, to his attempts to awaken memories? Memories of the days when it knew it was a human being?

Not in the slightest.

At times, he found himself patting and stroking the long-haired shaggy head, and talking to it as to a dog.

At others, he would seize the creature's hand and beg, implore, *pray* that he would recognize him as Henry, Henry Carthew, his friend; remember Antoinette, Toinette, Tony, his wife.

Mastering himself with a great effort, he contrived to whistle the Regimental march of the Wessex Fusiliers, which Reginald Jason had heard ten thousand times. The effect was neither more nor less than it would have been if he had whistled it to his own dog in England.

This must be a nightmare. This was something happening in Hell, in the most horrible of all conceivable hells.

He was 'mad.

This dog was a *man*! . . . This man was a *dog*! This *dog* was General Sir Reginald Jason, one of the most dignified and distinguished-looking men that ever lived.

They must make him, Henry Carthew, a dog too. The good Dr. de Norhona would do it with pleasure. Then she would have two dogs. And Reginald Jason and Henry Carthew would keep each other company

321

as her bodyguard. They could be her double body-guard, pad about behind her, come to heel, and lie one each side of her chair. And he could live with Reginald in whatever cell was his kennel. Did he eat from a trough or use his hands ? No. He would think he was a dog, and dogs don't have hands.

And would they not one day spring upon her and kill her ? Would they not tear Norhona in pieces ?

No. Both would have first been hypnotized into thinking themselves good obedient dogs, faithful and devoted to their masters. And his brain would be maimed and injured as Reginald's had been, and he would remain a dog for ever. *Her* dog. . . .

And she might come back here now, at any moment ; and in his present state of mind, he would certainly kill her.

He, Henry Carthew, was thinking about killing a woman. Then he must be mad.

She would not have left it, him, the dog, lying there, having told it to wait, had she not intended to return. He must go before she came.

Would the dog follow him ?

He released the hand, the paw, that he was holding and patted the creature's head.

" Come," he said, and began to ascend the stairs.

The dog followed him.

That was curious. Was it something in his voice ? Was some elusive chord of memory touched by the voice of Henry Carthew in what had been the mind of Reginald Jason ?

Along passage and corridor, across gallery and room, the human being that thought himself a dog followed him to his door.

" Come in, old chap," he said, as he opened it,

scarcely knowing whether he spoke as to a man or as to a dog.

Having locked the door he flung himself down upon his bed, and was again shaken by uncontrollable grief.

Deeply ashamed of his surrender to emotion, he at length, by a great effort of will, contrived to conquer it, or, rather, to curb its expression.

When sufficiently calm and self-controlled, he again set to work to establish communication, if not communion, with the human soul of the creature who had been a man and his friend, and was now a dog and a living horror, the thought of which would haunt him to the last day of his life.

Can a human soul be killed ? Had this dog the soul of a man ? Had this man the soul of a dog ? Do dogs have souls ? . . .

He must not think, he must work.

And throughout the night he worked to awaken a memory, a response, a sign of humanity in what had been Reginald Jason.

Several times during the night, the man-who-thought-himself-a-dog lay down upon the floor to sleep, lying not as a man does, but at times unnaturally curled, at others, on its side, with arms and legs stretched out at right angles to the body. He could not induce it to take his bed.

And in its sleep it whimpered piteously.

For hours Henry Carthew endeavoured to establish contact with the dormant mind, quietly speaking the name Reginald ! . . . Reginald ! . . . Reginald ! . . . into the apparently unreceptive ear. He would then repeat Lady Jason's christian name ; then his own ; and, in a desperate hope of penetrating to the inner consciousness, the name of any mutual acquaintance of whom he could think. He talked of places and events known to them both, all with the vague idea and faint hope that some sort of connection might be established with the sleeping creature's subconscious mind, since he had been unable to reach its conscious mind when it was awake.

Occasionally the dog stirred in its slumber, opened its eyes, raised the upper part of its body and shook its head, yawned and lay down to sleep again. When this happened Henry Carthew would cry aloud " *Reginald !* . . . *Reginald !* " in the hope that, in the act of waking, the subconscious mind might be receptive.

By morning he had come to the conclusion that what lay sleeping at his feet was a human being with the mind of a dog, a creature with no human soul and with only such soul as a dog may have.

The man-who-thought-himself-a-dog. . . .

In the morning, the usual servant, looking so like a Goanese " boy," brought breakfast, glanced with some surprise at the dog lying in the corner, but made no comment.

With a sick feeling of utter horror and heart-aching grief, Carthew went to the corner where lay what had been his friend Reginald Jason, and put food and drink on the floor. The dog, propped on rigid fore-legs, looked up through its shaggy hair, a gleam of interest and pleasure in its eyes.

With a shudder of pain, Carthew turned away as the dog put its head down and drank from the bowl of milk, sucking and lapping until the bowl was empty.

At the egg dish it smelt dubiously, ignored the fruit, and hungrily devoured a fillet of fish, eating as a dog does. When the servant returned to remove the breakfast tray, the dog, rising to its feet, looked at him, looked at Carthew, and approaching, rubbed its head affectionately against his leg.

" Oh, God ! " he cried, stepping back. " Oh, *don't* ! Oh, *please* . . . ! "

Feeling blindly for his chair, he sat down before his trembling limbs failed him, and covered his face with his hands. The man-who-thought-himself-a-dog went out with the servant.

It is probable that had there been eye-witnesses present, from his first realization of this tragic horror, Carthew would have maintained for himself the reputation of being a cold phlegmatic Englishman, unemotional and imperturbable. Alone, he had not the strength of will and purpose, nor the incentive of fearing to show emotion ; and, within limits, he gave way to it. Had the great and famous man who once cried,

" *These English ! Bah ! A nation that knows not how to weep !* " been present, he would have seen one weeping, seen a usually calm reticent and inscrutable-faced Englishman sitting at a table with his head upon his arms ; abandoned to grief, horror and despair, a picture of a broken and broken-hearted man.

When at length, worn out, he threw himself down upon his bed, it was to try to think, to make a plan, to decide what would be the best thing to do.

In the first place, matters that were beyond doubt must be accepted and set aside.

To begin with, this creature, in its present state, could not be taken back to England, even if there were no obstacle to such a course. Judging by its effect upon himself, the sight would drive Antoinette stark staring mad. She must never see him . . . it. . . . She must never *know*, even. The very thought of

325

such almost unimaginable tragedy would be enough to cloud her mind for the rest of her life.

That was the first decision—and quite final.

Secondly, this animal must either die, as a dog, or live—as Reginald Jason. And what could be done must be done quickly. It was an offence in the sight of God, an offence against Nature, and against the profoundest feelings of the human mind.

Yes, that was the second indisputable fact. This Thing must cease to exist.

Thirdly, he must find out, in such a way as to leave no shadow of doubt in his own mind, as to whether de Norhona could undo what de Norhona had done. That he must somehow discover. And if he felt certain that de Norhona's sentence of living death was irrevocable, the lost soul of Reginald Jason irretrievable, and this dreadful act final and complete for ever—then the dog must die.

On the other hand, should there be the faintest glimmer of hope, then de Norhona must, in some way, be compelled to do his utmost to undo what he had done.

He must think of some way of compelling or inducing de Norhona to achieve this.

How could he compel him ? How could he induce him ?

He was in no position to utter threats. He was in no position to make offers. Could he play on de Norhona's vanity as a scientist ? Could he hide his own feelings sufficiently to be able to talk to de Norhona naturally and quietly ? Could he pretend to be filled with wonder and admiration of what de Norhona had done in this hellish triumph of Permanent Hypnosis, and then say to him,

" Ah ! But you are not clever enough to render

326

permanence impermanent. You are neither sufficiently great a neurologist nor surgeon to restore this brain to its natural condition, to make it function normally as it did before your experiment ! "

Yes, with Reginald's life at stake, he could dissemble sufficiently to pretend that he had not recognized this creature as his friend Reginald Jason, and was merely interested in the scientific aspect of this experiment in mind fixation, destruction, metamorphosis, or whatever it was.

He rose from his bed, and for hours walked to and fro, to and fro, thinking, scheming, deciding. Action of mind and body kept grief at bay, that horrific beast of grief and horror which, sooner or later, would spring upon him, and overwhelm him.

When the servant brought his mid-day meal, he told the man that he wanted nothing, but would be glad if he would inform Dom Perez de Norhona's private secretary that Colonel Henry Carthew would be grateful if he might have a few words with His Excellency, at some time that day.

The man returned later with the information that His Excellency Dom Perez de Norhona would give himself the pleasure of visiting Colonel Henry Kardieu that evening, after dinner. Until then, he would be very busy.

Throughout the long afternoon and evening, Henry Carthew fought like the soldier he was ; fought to retain sanity, normality ; fought against the devils of fear and despair ; tried to conquer grief and horror to the extent of keeping his mind sufficiently clear to be able to think. From time to time, nevertheless, grief, rage and horror had their way, and he was seized with a rigor of sheer agony. He was suffering unbearably, and utterly unable to think . . . to believe . . . to pray.

When evening came and a servant brought dinner, he had so far won his battle as to be able to force himself to eat and drink, that his strength might be maintained ; to force himself to appear calm and normal ; to speak naturally : and when, after dinner, de Norhona knocked and entered, his hands scarcely trembled as he placed a chair for him.

Now to be strong, to be wise, to be calm and cool, and to fight warily, to fight for the life, the mind, the soul of the man who, all his days, had been his admired and beloved friend, his more than friend, his brother— Jonathan : the man whom he had loved more than any other human being. And he was able to talk idly, as it were, with de Norhona until the latter said,

" Now what was it you wanted to see me about ? "

" Why," he said, gripping the arms of his chair and holding taut every muscle of his body, " I've been examining that extraordinary animal . . . creature . . . man-dog or whatever it is, that I caught a glimpse of some time ago in Doña Guiomar's room. . . ."

" Yes ? My prize exhibit. The most wonderful piece of psychology and surgery ever yet done in this world—though I say it who shouldn't. There you have a human being with the mind and attributes of a dog. I think I once told you how deeply interested I have been, for many years, in the phenomenon of Hypnotism. We are only on the threshold of it. As an applied science, Hypnosis is in its infancy. Personally, I think it's going to take the place of medicine altogether. . . . And when I had come to the end of my studies of what you might call normal hypnosis, talked with all the big men and read all the big books, I began to dally with the idea of inducing a condition of Permanent Hypnosis ; in other words, to hypnotize a person into a certain state of mind, and then make that state of mind unchangeable, fixed, permanent, and unalterable. I realized, of course, that it involved interference with the grey matter, damage to the cortex of the brain, and I determined to experiment. I thought about it so much that at length it became an obsession."

His Excellency paused to light another cigarette.

" I fail to see the scientific value of the experiment," observed Henry Carthew coolly, his mind a cold hell of inexpressible and almost uncontrollable hatred of this inhuman devil who talked so lightly of the minds, souls and bodies of other men.

" Well. Art for Art's sake. Art should not be prostituted to base commercial ends, nor used for propaganda. Science for Science's sake. Doubtless some other scientist would find some very valuable use and practical application for the scientific triumph of Permanent Hypnosis. I cannot say I have gone very deeply into the subject, but at first glance one can see uses, such as—operation on the criminal mind, say. Take a murderous thug of the gunman type, hypnotize him into the belief that he's a saintly clergyman, and then—nail him there."

De Norhona laughed loudly.

" I'd love to have one or two gentlemen who are troubling Europe at the present time, and see what I could do for them and the unfortunate nations who suffer from the workings of their minds. Supposing that by Permanent Hypnosis I could turn them into modest, retiring and peace-loving philanthropists ! *And* mind you, I could do it. If anyone submitted himself to me, I could hypnotize him into thinking himself to be whatever I wanted him to think himself to be. And I could then submit him to a somewhat difficult piece of brain-surgery, including trepanning, and then perform a delicate operation on the cortex of the brain. *And* I can guarantee that, on recovery from the operation, his mind would be permanently in the state in which it was when I operated.

" Would you consider that a useful piece of scientific work, Colonel Kardieu ? "

" It opens terrific vistas," replied Carthew, and drank a little water to moisten his leathern-seeming tongue and lips.

How long, oh Lord, how long ? . . . God give him strength and self-control.

" Well now, here's the point that interests me and what I really want to ask you," Carthew said. " To leave the hypothetical Dictator or what-not, and to return to the actual case in point—could you undo the marvellous work that you have done ? Could you restore this dog to manhood ? Operate again, hypnotize him again, and make him think he is what he used to be, *make* him what he used to be, a human being, a man of the highest type ? "

" No," replied de Norhona without hesitation. " Utterly impossible. No ! That would be a real miracle ! It would be a miracle as great as Christ's raising Lazarus from the dead . . . Jairus's daughter . . . or the widow's son of Nain. No, I have done what no man has ever done yet, but I cannot undo it. God alone could do that."

" If you could hypnotize him so that he thought he was a dog, why cannot you de-hypnotize him, so to speak ? " asked Carthew.

" I've told you. Because of the little surgical operation on the cortex of the brain. I cannot restore what I have removed from his brain, any more than I

330

could restore your appendix if I removed it. The hypnosis is nothing. Any fool with the gift and knowledge could hypnotize anybody who is willing to be hypnotized. But the whole point of my discovery, my successful experiment, is the cerebral operation, the actual elision of a tiny portion of the brain. As a well-educated man, although not a scientist, you must realize that a portion of the brain, once removed, cannot be replaced a couple of years later—or a couple of seconds later, surely."

" So the case is completely and utterly hopeless ? What you have done cannot possibly be undone, and that man will always be a dog ? "

" Yes, because he will always *think* he's a dog. The first example of Permanent Hypnosis and the last— until I, Perez de Norhona, choose to perform the experiment again. Not even Harvey Williams Cushing could do it, I believe."

" And *do* you propose to perform the experiment again ? " asked Carthew.

" I should like to. Yes, if I ever give an account of my successful attempt at establishing the possibility of Permanent Hypnosis, those fellows in Vienna and Paris will say that, if I really did it, it was an accident. Not that that matters much ; but for my own satisfaction I'd like to be quite certain that it wasn't a fluke, that I actually did what I set out to do— induced a state of mind and rendered that state of mind unalterable."

" You don't regard it as a form of murder ? The most terrible form of all—*soul*-murder."

" No. Why should I ? Where's the murder ? The whole point is that I did not kill the patient in attempting to perform the experiment. You cannot have a murder without a corpse, can you ? And as to murdering souls, I am not scientifically interested in souls. I'm only concerned with minds and bodies."

" I see. And this dog-man or man-dog is merely an object of interest to you."

" Of the deepest interest, as I said before. My prize exhibit. What else should it be but an object of the most intense interest ? "

" Not one of regret or remorse ? Not an object of pity ? "

" My dear Colonel, you've fought in many battles, no doubt. You've led your Regiment and sustained heavy losses. Are you filled with remorse, regret and pity ? Or is the battle a matter of the deepest professional interest to you ? "

" I pity the wounded and the dead."

" And lead the rest to fight again another day, eh ? "

" I've no doubt you will get the better of me in argument, every time, Your Excellency, so I won't pursue that particular train of thought, though I might remark that there is not the slightest similarity between the cases. I am not responsible for the death or mutilation of the men I command."

De Norhona smiled tolerantly, and, with an airy wave of the hand in which he held his cigarette, dismissed that aspect of the subject.

" Yes, I should like to do the experiment three times, given two more suitable subjects," he said, breaking the heavy silence of the room.

With a great effort, Henry Carthew contrived to ask, in his ordinary voice,

" What do you call suitable subjects ? "

" Oh, in the first place, criminals who ought to be executed, enemies of the State ; and in the second place, people of a certain standard of intelligence, high or low, according to my hypnotic intentions and object. I have, psychologically speaking, turned a man into a dog, faithful to its master, affectionate, responsive to kindness, absolutely reliable as a guardian and protector. Putting it crudely, I had, for my dog-experiment, a man with the best of the dog-attributes that are possessed by a human being, if you understand. One wouldn't expect to make a really admirable house-dog, watch-dog, out of some base, cowardly sneaking criminal. It would, on the other hand, be interesting to hypnotize such a human reptile into the belief that he was a high-minded virtuous man with a noble mission in life ; and, while he was filled with that belief, render the hypnosis permanent.

" But that wouldn't be quite as interesting. Critics would say afterwards,

' He was a man and he is still a man. You say he was a criminal and now you say he is a reformer. Nothing much in that. There have been plenty of such conversions, without any talk of hypnosis or cerebral operation.'

" No, I think if I had a man of that type for a subject, I'd hypnotize him into the belief that he was a snake and I'd say to him, ' On thy belly shalt thou go all the days of thy life,' and he'd damn well do it, after I had performed the De Norhona Cerebral Operation on him."

Words . . . words . . . words. . . .

How the man talked. . . . What a joy it would be to take an automatic out of one's pocket and shoot him dead, the smug cold-hearted devil.

But not yet.

No, nor ever. Colonel Henry Carthew, late of the Wessex Fusiliers, was not a murderer.

What was the fellow saying ?

Damn what he was saying ! He himself had something to say, when he got a chance to speak.

" Who was this man upon whom you so successfully operated ? I mean, how did he come to be a ' suitable subject ' for experiment ? " he asked, in a pause of the monologue that was in fact an infinitely erudite and interesting scientific exposition.

" Well, I'll tell you, Colonel. He's a German. One Fritz Schultz, who came here with the most evil intentions. . . . An Enemy of the State, if ever there was one, a secret and deadly dangerous Public Enemy Number One."

" How do you know ? "

" Because the clever fellow brought a letter of introduction from my own friend, one of the very best of our emissaries whom, almost certainly, he had murdered. And the letter introduced him as a Nazi German, a treacherous scoundrel, one of those loathsome villains who are sent into a country to foment trouble and cause unrest, the first of the vanguard of invasion. In this case, it may have been commercial and industrial invasion *which we will never allow*. But if it were, what is *that* but the preliminary to military invasion, of annexation, absorption and—destruction ? "

The hitherto cold and unemotional scientist began to warm, to glow with the heat of anger, and rapidly to turn from the detached man of science into the hot-blooded patriot and statesman.

" The indisputably genuine letter that he gave me was his death-warrant. Self-condemned he stood, lies in his mouth, the truth in his hand. The truth that he could not read.

" ' *You dog !* ' said I to myself, as I smiled at him. ' *You damnable dog. You shall go on all fours. A*

*dog you are and as a dog you shall live henceforth.
On all fours you shall crawl and your food you shall
eat from the ground.'*

"That's why he became the subject of my first
experiment. He had been a faithful dog to his
employer, even to the extent of risking his life.
His master's trusted hound. . . . Blood-hound. . . .
And I turned him into . . ."

But Henry Carthew ceased to hear what de Norhona
was saying.

What could have happened? What could be the
truth behind this horrible tragedy? Reginald calling
himself Fritz Schultz, and bringing a letter that
described him as a German *agent provocateur*? Impossible. What was the real truth? For de Norhona
was obviously telling the truth as he saw it. He had
done a terrible thing in the pursuit of scientific knowledge, but he had done it to a man whom he honestly
regarded as an appalling danger to his country. A
living danger—to be destroyed.

Why could not de Norhona be quiet for a moment—
hold his tongue and give him a chance to think . . . to
think. . . ?

Words . . . words . . . words. . . .

If the man wouldn't be silent, he'd lose control . . .
and seize him by the throat . . . and . . .

Henry Carthew buried his face in his hands. Covered
his eyes with his hands.

Reginald could never come back. Reginald must
live his life out—like this.

De Norhona had not done this thing to Reginald,
but to some German named Fritz Schultz. How could
Reginald have been Fritz Schultz?

How? . . . How? . . . How?

Why ? . . . Why ? . . . Why ?

What must he do ?

Suddenly he rose to his feet. He must make one final effort, cost what it might.

" Your Excellency," he said.

" *Corpo de Dios !* But you look ill ! What's the matter ? " exclaimed de Norhona.

" Nothing, Your Excellency ! I would ask you a favour. Might my friend . . . Might it . . . the dog . . . be brought here now ? "

" Certainly. Why not ? Do you want to see the scar, or . . . put him through his tricks, or what ? "

Rising and going to the open window, de Norhona whistled high and shrill.

" If he's loose, he'll come," he said.

Sick, faint and trembling, Henry Carthew leant against the stone mullion. A door was opened in a corner of the courtyard. A man appeared and stood aside as a great grotesque form bounded forth and crossed the court-yard in a clumsy gallop.

" There you are ! . . . I'll send someone down to open the door at the head of the steps below, there. See how he keeps to his hands and feet. Never stood upright since the operation. I suppose one could train him to do it as one trains a dog to sit up and beg. Extraordinarily interesting. He does as a dog all those things that his human structure permits—such as eating from the floor without use of hands. Other things that he must do, but cannot do in dog-fashion, he does as a man. Very interesting. Reflex muscular action—or purely subconscious memory ? He'll provide me with interesting study for years, apart from being my . . ."

Henry Carthew went from the room—in haste, before he committed murder.

A minute or two later, the man-who-thought-he-was-a-dog came panting toward him, sniffed at him in a friendly way, licked his hand and went into the room where de Norhona stood.

Henry Carthew followed, closing the door, locking it and putting the key in his pocket.

" Well, old chap," said de Norhona kindly, and patted the shaggy head.

The dog peered up through the overhanging mat of hair.

" Here ! . . . We are going to do some tricks. . . ."

" We are," said a quiet voice behind him.

And turning he saw Carthew about to attack him— holding, high above his right shoulder, a heavy chair.

" De Norhona," he said, " I'm going to kill you unless you restore this creature to manhood. I feel I should kill you, in any case. For that thing lying there was General Sir Reginald Jason, my friend ! You've done worse than kill him. . . . Why should I not kill you ? "

His voice broke on a kind of scream, a cry of cruel pain.

De Norhona did not flinch. Coolly he replied,

" Don't talk nonsense, man. That "—and he pointed contemptuously with his foot—" came here with . . . But why should I go all over it again ? He was Fritz Schultz and he murdered Pereira. You've talked a lot about your friend. What about *my* friend whom this dog killed ? "

Carthew moistened his lips.

" You talk too much, de Norhona," he said. " This is . . . this was . . . Sir Reginald Jason. Now—before I kill you—can you save him ? If not, save yourself from me, if you can. Quick, or I'll brain you ! "

And Carthew swung the heavy chair back

337

Dr Norhona smiled and shook his head.

" I can't. Can't be done, Kardieu. Sorry. Nothing on earth can . . ."

" *Then I'll* . . ."

There was a sudden low growl and a heavy body flung itself against Carthew, sending him staggering sideways, and knocking him down.

The dog had saved its master.

It stood growling, its weight pressing heavily on Carthew's chest.

Carthew lay still.

Dr Norhona laughed quietly.

" My experiment was quite successful, Colonel, wasn't it ? *Good* dog ! "

X

HENRY CARTHEW never knew how long the next period of his life lasted—the period between his attempted attack upon de Norhona and the day when he was arrested and told of the fate to which he had been sentenced.

What he did know was that, during that time, he was barely sane ; that certain things happened to him ; that he himself committed certain acts and deeds ; and that his reason or excuse for having done them was that he was really of unsound mind.

The only person to whom he afterwards spoke of those days or weeks or months was his friend Brodie Dysart, and to him he tried, later, to give a coherent account.

At the beginning of that utterly dreadful period, his memory of which was, to some extent, mercifully obliterated, two things surprised him.

One was that the incalculable and unpredictable de Norhona apparently bore him not the slightest ill-will for what he might well have regarded as a murderous attack upon himself.

The other was that it was a perceptible addition of sorrow to his almost unbearable burden of grief, that the dog should have turned against him ; should have defended against Henry Carthew, his best and oldest friend, the man de Norhona, who had done him this appalling wrong. But realizing how foolish, nay

339

childish, it was in the circumstances to feel like this, he told himself that it was, alas, only one more proof of the completeness of the success of de Norhona's experiment. Had there been one trace left of the original mind and soul of Reginald Jason, it could not have happened.

Night and day, eating little and sleeping scarcely at all, he wrestled with the problem of what he must do ; now deciding that he must wait and hope, now that he must accept facts and, abandoning childish optimism and wholly unwarranted optimism, accept realities and act accordingly.

He must not act precipitately.

But, on the other hand, how much longer could he bear it ? How much longer could he continue to see Reginald like this, knowing in his heart that the state was permanent. It would be a terrible thing if he himself were to die, to go mad, to be imprisoned, to be deported, before he had done what he knew he must do.

He must cease to ask himself how long he could bear it. He *must* bear it. He must bear it until the hour came that he felt was the appointed one, the hour of his destiny.

Another addition to his misery was the fact that de Norhona seemed increasingly to like him and to seek his company. He spent his life upon a rack of pain and grief, but an extra turn was given to the instrument of torture whenever de Norhona entered his room and talked ; bade him come out and walk, for his health's sake ; insisted on his riding abroad with him into the lovely semi-tropical country of the plateau ; or demanded his attendance at a State dinner or other function.

It seemed to Carthew that de Norhona was a living

intelligence, an intelligence almost freed from the hampering restriction and misguidance of emotion; a man whose mind was neither cruel nor kind, but almost purely scientific.

And yet he was human enough in his fanatical patriotism.

Carthew entertained for him curious and contradictory feelings of murderous hatred, fear, considerable respect and a most unwilling liking. So inevitably fair and just himself, Carthew had to admit that de Norhona had done nothing to Jason as Jason, an honest and honourable gentleman who had come to make certain right and proper proposals and suggestions of a commercial nature. Quite obviously de Norhona had used for his great experiment a man whom he believed to be a deadly enemy of his country, inasmuch as he was the first of an invading army, insupportable, detestable and loathsome in the eyes of people to whom independence was the very breath of life and the very religion of their soul.

And he fully admitted that de Norhona was as puzzled as himself at the inexplicable chain of events whereby Carthew's Jason had become de Norhona's Schultz.

And so, exercising great constraint and self-control, he talked with de Norhona as and when de Norhona wished, and restrained himself from precipitate action.

§ 2

Was it on that same dreadful day upon which the dog had attacked him, or on the next, that he had begged de Norhona to let him see as much of the dog as possible ?

De Norhona had had no objection. It was loose at

night. Doña Guiomar liked to have it about her in the daytime.

How could she ? How could she bear it ? One would have thought it would have made her ill . . . driven her mad.

Oh, nonsense. Carthew must remember that, here in São Thomé, they were still in the age when the Court had its jesters, dwarfs, freaks, monsters and such. Of course the Regent wasn't a cruel woman. She was deeply interested in de Norhona's amazing experiment, and there was no doubt that she derived a certain feminine and real satisfaction from seeing, crouching at her feet, one who had been the enemy of her people, seeing him reduced literally to the level of a dumb animal.

Was he for ever dumb ?

For ever. Absolutely. Inevitably. To the extent that a dog was dumb. He could growl and bark, of course. . . .

Was it that same night, after the dog had attacked him, that he saw it in the court-yard and whistled to it as de Norhona had done, had attracted its attention, found it friendly, and induced it to follow him up to his room ?

That night or the next, no doubt. And he had been curiously thankful to find that the dog was perfectly friendly again. But though he again spent the night in trying to effect more of a *rapprochement* between himself and the dog than is possible between a human being and any ordinary animal, he had failed entirely. It was just as friendly and responsive as a dog, in that it liked to have its head stroked, liked to be patted and talked to—but it would, on the whole, rather go to sleep.

Henry Carthew, all his life until now, a man of very sane and well-balanced mind, calm, undemonstrative, the tenor of whose way was even, knew that he was approaching the end of his tether, that he was losing grip, that such nights were dangerous.

He was in despair.

A man in despair is like a drowning swimmer who frenziedly clutches at straws.

Carthew could think of nothing but Reginald Jason, wherever he might be or whatever he might be doing. even if seated, incredulous and amazed, beside Her Highness Doña Guiomar at a dinner-party.

One day a thought suddenly came to him.

Might it not be possible that the power of suggestion could have some effect upon what was left of the mind of the creature that had been Reginald Jason ? He did not know much about psychology, though he had learned a lot from listening to de Norhona's eternal monologues on the subject. But like any other educated person who keeps abreast of current ideas, he knew that suggestion was now known to be a powerful weapon in the armoury of the mental physician.

Was it conceivable that some possible good might accrue from the dog being treated as though it were a human being ?

Suppose he could induce de Norhona to try the experiment of having it treated as decent and kindly people would treat a wild-man-of-the-woods whom they had captured and wished to reclaim ? Suppose the hair of its head were cut and the moustache and beard removed. Suppose the dress of shaggy skins, like that worn by a pantomime " animal " on the stage, were removed.

Suppose what had been Reginald were dressed as though it were Reginald ?

Might not that awaken a memory, strike a chord ?

Surely if he were bathed ; if his nails were cut and cleaned ; if he were shaved, valeted and treated exactly as though he were a man, he might respond ? Surely if an attractive meal were properly served at a table, he could be induced to sit on a chair and use a knife and fork ?

It was an idea. It was—one could hardly say a hope—but . . . he'd try it, if de Norhona would consent, and help by giving the necessary orders. . . .

De Norhona had not the slightest objection—nor the slightest expectation of any result.

" My dear chap," he said, " when I can amputate a man's leg and replace it so that he can walk perfectly, *then* what I have done to that man's brain can be undone."

And of course he was right.

The only result of the complete and careful carrying out of de Norhona's orders was to make things even worse for Carthew ; and, if such a thing were possible, to increase the pain that he suffered.

To see Reginald Jason, the most dignified man whom he had ever beheld, acting like a dog—or like a king playing at being a dog—was worse, far worse.

It had been as a knife in his heart to see Reginald Jason dirty and degraded, dressed in a suit of skins, his face hidden with matted tangled hair. It was as though the knife turned in his heart, cutting it to pieces, to see General Sir Reginald Jason, dressed, as he should be, in the tropical kit of an Englishman, behaving like the dog he now thought himself to be.

The very next night, Henry Carthew, with hands that trembled slightly, poured his after-dinner coffee into a bowl, added milk and sugar, and placed it in the dark old heavy cupboard which was used as a kind of side-board. This *café au lait* the dog was known particularly to like, de Norhona having discovered the fact by giving it small quantities in his saucer after dinner, his reason being that he was interested in the question of how far the dog retained any human tastes and likings.

And in Carthew's inner pocket was a little phial which he had almost constantly carried, ever since he first went on active service on the North West Frontier, where " the women come out to cut up what remains " . . . When going to the front or on what might be a dangerous journey, he always took it with him. No lingering death for Henry Carthew.

XI

HENRY CARTHEW spent in prayer the greater part of what he intended to be Reginald Jason's last night on earth.

Properly valeted and dressed in his own clothes, the tragic creature now looked like Reginald Jason. He *was* Reginald Jason—physically. Had Carthew come upon him suddenly, as he lay there now, he would have had no feelings in his heart save those of greatest joy and thankfulness, and a little wonder as to why Reginald should be lying on the ground.

Before dawn, he made the longest and greatest endeavour that he had yet made to find a mind, a soul, in the body of this his friend, and to communicate with it.

At dawn, the living effigy of Reginald Jason sat up, yawned as a dog does, shook itself and looked at Henry Carthew.

The time had .come.

Going to the cupboard Carthew took out the bowl of sweetened *café au lait* and put it on the table. The creature looked pleased and expectant.

Then, kneeling before it, he implored it to speak to him, almost prayed to it to do so.

Foolishly, childishly, he thanked God that it was friendly and responsive, much more responsive than usual.

What he had to do, he must do quickly or he could

346

never do it. . . . Never. . . . If he failed Reginald now . . . Never.

Rising, he took the bowl from the table, put it on the ground, and dropped the contents of his phial of cyanide tablets into it. Turning away, he sat upon his bed, his face almost touching his knees, his hands clamped hard upon his ears.

Thus he sat and prayed.

A few minutes later he looked up.

His friend was dead.

Putting forth all his strength, he placed his arms about him, raised him from the floor and laid him upon the bed, straightening the limbs and crossing the hands upon the breast.

His friend Reginald Jason lay there exactly as in life.

But, thank God, there was no longer any life in him.

XII

HE sat by the body of his friend, in a stupor of grief and of horror at himself and what he had done. The arguments of the night seemed treacherously feeble, inadequate and weak in the light of day.

He had killed his friend. He had murdered his friend.

He had done it for the best.

It was the only thing to do.

Who was he to say it was the only thing to do? How did he know that de Northona was right, and that the experiment was absolutely final and complete, a *fait accompli* which nothing could ever change?

But his sturdy common-sense, his singleness of purpose and the discipline of mind and body to which he had submitted all his life, stood him in good stead. Before the sun shone into the room he had attained a calmer and serener frame of mind. Whether de Norhona's act were final and irrevocable or not, his own was. He had done what he had done, and he would be a fool and a weakling if he now regretted it and permitted the intrusion of remorse.

Repressing emotion, thrusting it, for the moment, to the back of his mind, he sent a letter to de Norhona telling him of what he had done.

De Norhona came immediately, incredulous. His reaction to the realization of what had happened was anger almost uncontrollable. He seethed with a cold but furious rage, and uttered abominable threats, one of the least of which was that Carthew should become himself something lower in the scale of animal creation than any dog.

His savage contempt almost equalled his consuming wrath.

The fool! The lout! The wretched, interfering, clod-hopping half-wit! To dare to wreck and ruin and spoil and destroy and end the greatest and most successful experiment ever made by a psychologist-surgeon.

It was always the way! A sluttish serving-wench could burn a manuscript worth ten thousand times its weight in gold—or her own weight either. The lowest gutter-scum of the filthiest slum could set fire to a building housing pictures that were the world's master-pieces. And as for this accursed *louse*—he'd . . .

Colonel Kardieu! Let his infamous name be known as that of a man who destroyed an experiment that would have taught the greatest scientists facts that would have revolutionized their ideas on . . .

God grant him patience—to think out a fitting punishment. . . .

When again would he get such a subject for experiment as this Fritz Schultz? A man highly intelligent, but deserving of death and worse ; a man willing, in his ignorance, to submit to hypnotism.

When de Norhona's tirade was ended, it seemed but to anger him the more that, with a quiet dignity and no sign of being in the least intimidated, Henry Car-thew replied,

" He was my friend, a noble and upright man—no *agent provocateur* of Germany and no more German than yourself. It is only because I believe you to have been honestly mistaken, that I have not killed you, that I don't kill you now, de Norhona."

His Excellency Dom Perez de Norhona spat. His savage anger and contempt were rising fast again. As he turned to go, he eyed Carthew malevolently.

"And if you are thinking that you will resist hypnotism and prevent me from using *you* as a subject for experiment—don't build on it. . . . Believe me, I will deal with you . . . adequately."

As he flung open the door, Henry Carthew spoke.

"Your Excellency," he said, "look," and he pointed toward the bed. "Is that the face of a swindler and a rogue and a murderer? You know that there has been some amazing mistake. He has done you no wrong. You did him the most terrible wrong that one human being ever did to another. Admit it, and give him proper Christian burial."

"I'll give you burial—*alive*," snarled de Morhona, ere he slammed the door behind him—and locked it.

§ 2

When de Norhona returned, toward evening, he was again the philosopher-scientist. His wrath had evaporated, leaving a cold and bitter sediment.

"You've bothered and pestered me intolerably for weeks past about your accursed friend. You say this is your friend and you beg that he may be given Christian burial. Well, of course he will. He was a man. Whether he was a Christian or not, I do not know. But he served a far more useful purpose than you ever will. If he was your friend and an Englishman, I am sorry that it was he who was fated to be the subject of my experiment. If he was what I think he was, I am glad. But whoever he was, the

350

operation had been performed, and you had no right to interfere . . . to kill him . . . to cut short my experiment from which I still had so much to learn. . . . A lifetime's study. You have done me and Science a greater injury than any man ever did before, and I will punish you for it.

" Oh, I'll punish you. A case for the quick-sand, I think—if it's not too good a death for you . . . too easy."

§ 3

The body of General Sir Reginald Jason was removed with reverent care and gentleness, and his funeral obsequies, by direction of His Excellency Dom Pedro de Norhona, were like those of a São Thoméan gentleman of position.

Henry Carthew formally thanked de Norhona, who coldly replied to the effect that he had given the man the benefit of what doubt there was as to his identity ; that he had no quarrel with the dead.

It was against the living that his anger again burned.

XIII

" I DON'T care," stormed Doña Guiomar. " You and your scientific rubbish ! . . . And suppose it was the greatest successful experiment ever made in the history of surgery and psychology, as you're so fond of telling us ! . . . Can't you repeat it ? If it were not a mere accident, you can do it again. Do it a hundred times. There are plenty of subjects for experiments, aren't there ? "

" Your Highness, I . . ." began de Norhona.

" Don't talk to me. Don't interrupt. This man is of more importance to me than a thousand of your silly experiments. Suppose that poor sickly boy dies. No one knows better than you what a weakling he is, in-bred and in-bred for ten generations. Twenty generations. I am the last of the family, the last of the line, and if my nephew dies, who is to follow me ? "

" Your Highness, you . . ."

" Be quiet. I will not marry a São Thoméan."

Her hard proud face melted into a charming and delightful smile.

" Or I'd have married you, Perez, long ago—for the sake of your brain. Not your beauty, so don't strut. I had thought to remain content to be the Regent and the real ruler, even when the boy was a man, and if he died, to be Ruler myself, and appoint my successor. You perhaps, Perez. But now I won't. I have

352

changed my mind. Say I've fallen in love if you like. I am going to marry this English nobleman."

"Your Highness, he's not a nobleman. He is only . . ."

"Have I told you not to interrupt? Will you be quiet? . . . Not a nobleman? You will not be Perez de Norhona much longer, if you thwart me. Now then. You can just go back to Colonel Kardieu, and in spite of what you may have said to him about your beastly Schultz, you can eat humble pie, apologize, and tell him the gist of what I have just said to you."

"That Your Highness is graciously pleased to ask him to make you an offer of marriage?"

Doña Guiomar rose to her feet.

"Listen, Perez," she said quietly. "A truly clever man is never too clever. May I offer you, in spite of your wonderful cleverness, a word of advice? Don't go too far. We are old friends, but if you presume upon my friendship . . ."

"Your Highness, I was only doing my poor best to see that I have your message correctly, and that you wished . . ."

"Silence! Don't talk to me. Do as I tell you. And if you're as clever as you think you are, you'll do your utmost to obtain the forgiveness and the favour of the future co-Regent. . . . What? Of course he will be co-Regent. And should my poor little nephew die—in spite of your marvellous skill—my son will be the next ruler of São Thomé. And he'll be strong and vigorous, hardy, brave, not a puny hot-house plant of no stamina."

"But Your Highness, we know nothing of this man except . . ."

"You will interrupt me, will you? Suppose now I

353

interrupt you, and venture to contradict you. We know one thing about him. And that is that he is going to be my husband.

" You may go," she added coldly.

Dom Perez de Norhona went.

So she would kick over the traces, would she ? She would fight the most powerful man in the State. Defy and abuse and threaten Perez de Norhona. Amusing creatures, women. And His Excellency laughed aloud. She'd do this and that. Not only without consulting her best, ablest and most faithful counsellor, but in absolute defiance of his wishes and advice.

She would, would she ?

She'd marry this wandering mystery-monger who had destroyed the proof of the success of the most marvellous example of applied psychology and surgery that the whole history of medical science had ever known.

She would, would she ?

Well, she wouldn't. She'd marry Perez de Norhona. And she'd do it in his own good time. And if she produced a son, the child would be the heir to the throne. He'd succeed too.

Guiomar ! Guiomar ! Foolish woman. Haven't you yet learnt that Perez de Norhona has his way ? Has always had it, and will always have it ?

Colonel Kardieu ! Huh ! *Colonel Kardieu !*

§ 2

A few hours later, His Excellency Dom Perez de Norhona paid a visit to his prisoner, in spite of the fact that the mere sight of that abominable man disturbed his scientific calm, caused his blood to boil, and made

354

him a mere human creature of like passions with other men.

It was by no means an amiable side of his character that he now displayed to the unhappy Carthew. And after telling him that he would have submitted him to a remarkable surgical operation, save for the fact that it would render him ignorant of how grotesque and despicable a creature he would be. . . .

On the other hand, no. He would not say that. He would wait a year or two perhaps, and at the end of that time would inflict some such punishment—and during that period the good Kardieu could spend his time in visualizing himself in his metamorphosis. Perhaps. Perhaps.

Or again, there was that Bridge of Sighs that spanned the Quick-sand of Death. That could be either a reasonably quick or an unreasonably slow business. Just engulfment, or a slow rotting of the flesh from the bones.

And when de Norhona had finished his monologue on crime and punishment, Henry Carthew replied briefly,

" Really, de Norhona ! I thought this was a more or less civilized State, and you one of its enlightened Rulers. If you are as upset as all that by what I did, and are out for my blood, why not shoot me and have done with it ? I assure you I shall raise no objection."

De Norhona laughed unpleasantly.

" I thought I'd made it pretty clear that, whatever else we are in São Thomé, we are not civilized by your standards, and with the help and favour of our Eternal Father, we never will be. But don't make the mistake of thinking that because we loathe and abhor and despise your Civilization we are in the slightest degree barbarous, savage, or . . . cruel. No, no. But we believe in punishment for wrong-doing and in making the punishment fit the crime."

" Well, I killed my friend, your victim. Kill me—as humanely, and don't be barbarous, savage and cruel."

" Oh, come now. You're hardly putting it fairly," replied de Norhona, as one who expostulates in a just and reasonable manner. " That's not making the punishment fit the crime. You did not merely kill my victim. You spoilt my experiment. Wouldn't it be much more fitting if you offered to take his place ? Agreed to submit to hypnosis, and left me to do the rest. But not a dog. Not a dog this time, Kardieu. Not a dog."

Carthew repressed a shudder.

" Or there is another idea. How would you like, while retaining such wits as you have, to take the place of your alleged friend ? Remain a man and become the body-guard and pet of Her Highness the Regent ?"

Carthew stared at de Norhona in silence. What was the fellow driving at ?

" I don't suppose she'd thrash you, Kardieu, like she did Schultz. She trained him with the whip, you know. It was only after many a flogging that . . ."

Henry Carthew rose to his feet, his fists clenched, his eyes blazing.

" You damned Dago cur ! " he cried, " I'll . . ."

" Sit down ! " ordered de Norhona. " If you're going to behave like a wild beast, I'll chain you up like a wild beast. How would it suit you to wait in the late Schultz's kennel—until I have decided what I'll do with you ? . . . That's better. . . . Now then, listen to me, for I have something amusing to say to you. It's this.

" Her Serene Highness, the Regent, Doña Guiomar,

356

offers you a fair, free and full opportunity of escape. No—*not* from São Thomé, but from your present unpleasant position. She proposes to raise you up. High up—out of the rather awkward hole into which you have fallen ; or foolishly leapt head-long. She proposes—to propose, Kardieu. Thinks she'd like an English husband. I am not joking, Kardieu. She has always refused to marry in her circle of relations here. How would you like to be Vice-Regent, Viceroy-Consort, Doña Giuomar's tame . . .? "

" I'd sooner be shot. Much sooner," replied Henry Carthew without waiting for de Norhona's sneer to finish.

" Sooner be shot than marry Guiomar, eh ? And why ? "

" For several reasons. Chiefly because she kept my friend as . . . But why should I answer such a question ? And why should I take you seriously ? "

" She'll take you seriously—if I tell her that, with reference to her kind suggestion, you say you'd sooner be shot."

" If Doña Guiomar said anything of the kind, which I don't for one moment believe, my answer is that I do not wish to marry."

" Ah ! And you'll repeat that to Her Highness if she refuses to believe my report, and sends for you ? "

" Certainly," replied Henry Carthew.

" Ah ! . . ." smiled Perez de Norhona.

§ 3

When de Norhona went as usual, that night, for the final report-making and instruction-receiving interview with the Regent, he appeared worried, anxious and diffident.

When his mistress enquired as to how His Excellency the Colonel Henri Kardieu had received the news that she proposed to offer him a seat beside her in the Regent's place of power and honour, de Norhona appeared to be too confused to reply.

" Do not ask me," he said at length. " The man is mad."

" I suppose it turned his head, rather," smiled Doña Guiomar. " At first he would think it was a joke of yours. He would not realize that no one may propose marriage to the Regent, and that it is for her to choose. . . . What exactly did he say ? "

" That he would far sooner be shot than be married to Your Highness," replied de Norhona in a painful whisper, his eyes lowered, his expressive hands outspread, his whole body registering pain, horror, apology, shocked grief.

Blood tells, and Doña Guiomar's genuine dignity and breeding stood her in good stead.

With a shrug of her beautiful shoulders and a thin pale smile,

" His own choice," she said.

After a full minute's silence.

" I leave him to you, Perez," she added.

XIV

THE waiting, the uncertainty, the suspense were bad, very bad indeed, for, from time to time, de Norhona visited him and made unpleasant suggestions, dropped very disturbing hints, or made contradictory promises—sometimes that his case would be dealt with that night, sometimes that ten years rigorous detention would precede a painful and remarkable punishment.

Definitely, decided Carthew, the man in whose hands his fate lay, was a person of vindictive and cruel nature when his enmity and vengeful feelings were aroused.

Suppose this half-caste Portuguese-Arab, or Goanese or whatever he was, kept up this cat-and-mouse game for the rest of his life?

Well—he could shorten it himself, by his own act, when he had had enough. He hoped that he would never be driven to suicide though, for he had a duty to perform. Antoinette was still waiting, and he must not fail her if it were humanly possible to avoid it. He must live and hope—hope to escape and in some way communicate with her. While there is life there is hope, and he was still alive. So was the Hadji Abdulla—Brodie Dysart. It was quite possible that somehow, some day, he might have speech with him, tell him of Reginald's fate, and ask him to let Antoinette know that her husband was really and indubitably dead. No need to give her any of the dreadful details. . . .

Meanwhile existence was only just bearable.

§ 2

But Henry Carthew's patience and fortitude were not tried for long.

One night he was aroused from sleep by a Sergeant of Police, bidden to dress quickly, to prepare for a journey. . . .

" The Bridge of Death, as they call it," thought Carthew, and was filled with regret, grief and impotent anger that he should be killed thus without opportunity of sending a word to Antoinette—waiting, watching, fearing, heart-sick with hope deferred.

Of de Norhona or anyone else in authority he saw nothing. In silence, his cavalcade of the Sergeant and six men rode out of the Citadel and through the sleeping town. . . . As they halted while the city gates were opened at the Sergeant's order, the latter reminded Carthew that, inasmuch as escape was entirely impossible, he would not be shot if he attempted it, but would make the rest of the journey on foot, at the end of a cord, and with his hands bound behind his back. . . .

As the day wore on and he recognized various landmarks, Carthew could not forbear comparison of this miserable descent with the free and relatively happy journey up from the coast, in the company of the Hadji Abdulla.

At night, in the rest-house, a soldier with a loaded carbine kept watch, while others were posted as sentries at the window and door of his room. The Sergeant, in spite of his statement that escape from São Thomé was impossible, was evidently taking no risks. At dusk of a rather dreadful day, the little troop came in sight of the Bridge of Death, and Carthew's mind became painfully active with plans, fears and speculations as to the manner of his swiftly approaching end.

Would the seven men close suddenly in upon him, tear him from his horse, and fling him over the parapet? Should he put up a fight ? Of course he would. It would be entirely useless, naturally, one unarmed man against seven, with carbines, revolvers and ugly machete-like swords. Nor could he put spurs to his horse and make a dash for it, inasmuch as he had no spurs, a stout leather rein buckled the bridoon of his horse's bit to that of a trooper's horse, and on one side of the road rose a cliff, while on the other, a precipice fell away to the plains below. Still, fight he would, in the hope of dying fighting. Far better that than a hideous death by slow engulfment in the quick-sand— or a long-drawn lingering agony if, as de Norhona had hinted, he was so suspended from the Bridge that he would not completely sink.

What should he do ?

He decided to wait on circumstance, and fight like a tiger when seized by the escort.

Nearer and nearer to the Bridge.

Now it was but a few hundred yards to where the descending road levelled out toward the horse-corral and the Bridge head. A few more minutes. Past the *hacienda*. . . .

On . . . On . . . On to the Bridge of Death. . . .
On . . .
On to the centre.

He thanked God that his hands were free, as the escort closed in. The Sergeant and two men in front of him. Two men knee to knee with him. Two men close at his back.

Perhaps they would shoot him before throwing him over. The Sergeant seemed a decent fellow and had been quite correct in his attitude and manner. And no one would know if a merciful bullet had been put through his brain. Should he appeal to the Sergeant to do this ? No. . . . No appeals. . . . He'd fight.

Suddenly the Sergeant turned his head and shouted an order.

The troop broke into a trot, crossed the Bridge, and a few minutes later reached the rest-house.

That night, Henry Carthew slept well, his mind relieved of the hideous nightmare of the quick-sand that had haunted him.

But what did it mean ? Could it be possible that de Norhona's bark was worse than his bite ? That he was not as savagely vindictive as he seemed, and that, far from condemning Carthew to a horrible death, he was merely deporting him—setting him free, in fact, having decided that he had punished him sufficiently ?

Or had he Doña Guiomar to thank for this release ? That seemed more probable. Women were kind and gentle creatures, fundamentally. Or so he had always thought. On the other hand, there was the unpleasant theory about a woman scorned ; and it was quite possible that the Regent, failing to understand the utter impossibility of his living in luxury where his friend had crouched in a kennel and cringed under her whip, might consider his refusal scornful and insulting.

But his mind was running ahead too fast. The fact that he had crossed that terrible Bridge was no proof that he was going to be deported to Santa Cruz. De

Norhona doubtless had other ways of disposing of an enemy than throwing him alive into a quick-sand.

Next morning, soon after sunrise and an adequate meal, the cavalcade resumed its journey, and in a few hours reached the tiny embowered group of little Government buildings that sweltered beside the shallow creek and constituted the entire port of São Thomé. How terrific the heat seemed after the cool uplands of the great plateau, at the edge of which stood the town and Citadel of São Ildefonso.

Well! Thank God. He had misjudged de Norhona. Or else Doña Guiomar had ordered his deportation.

And there was the ocean. The blue sea that he had scarcely hoped ever to cross again. He could have cried aloud, " *Thalassa! Thalassa!* " but he was not given to crying aloud. And should his eyes, at the turn of the road, behold the Hadji's *dhow* lying at anchor, a few cables from the landing-stage, hope would become certainty, and a ray of positive happiness would lighten the darkness of the grief and horror through which he passed.

Arrived at Santa Cruz, he could feel that his mission and task were successfully accomplished. He had done what Antoinette had asked him to do. From Santa Cruz he could communicate with her, and tragic as his news would be, it would end suspense. A cable telling her that Reginald was dead would be a shock and a blow, but from these she would recover. It is uncertainty, anxiety and suspense that kill.

No. No sign of the *dhow*. But instead, a tiny armed steamer flying the flag of Portugal.

What was this?

In his eagerness, he turned for information to the Sergeant now riding beside him.

"That?" replied the worthy fellow. "That's our *dhow*-chaser. You're going for a trip on her."

"To Santa Cruz?"

"No. To our Leper Island."

XV

IT was Ensign Machado's not too painful duty to take delivery of the prisoner and of a letter addressed to him by His Excellency Dom Perez de Norhona in his own hand-writing. A *lettre de cachet*, in which the Secretary to the Council charged Ensign Machado, as he valued his life, to see that the prisoner was delivered safely and without delay at the Island of Todos los Santos. The use of the word " safely " in this connection struck the young officer as being a pleasing euphemism, and he wondered why His Excellency had not referred to the leper island by its popular name of the Health Resort.

Well, it's an ill wind and so forth, and though he could find it in his heart to be sorry for this fine fellow, it was indeed a fair wind that should blow a bored young officer far from these hot and malarious plains out on to the health-giving ocean. Unlucky prisoner. Lucky Ensign Machado. And perhaps on the voyage he'd be able to obtain information wherewith later to impress his superiors.

Thus it was that Carthew found himself pestered, bored and annoyed by the undesired company and conversation of a pleasant, olive-skinned, oily-haired youth who appeared anxious to practise his English.

As the young man was friendly and disposed to be sympathetic, Carthew bore with him until his inquisi-

365

tion became wearyingly persistent. If, thought Carthew, he had been condemned, and was on his way to receive his punishment, why should he be troubled by this gad-fly ? He had quite enough to bear.

So it came about that when Ensign Machado entered the bare and cell-like cabin allotted to Carthew, and after enquiring naïvely as to his health and happiness, began another unofficial examination of his prisoner, Carthew replied briefly, sarcastically and without his usual strict regard for truth.

" Now what really brought you to São Thomé ? " asked the intelligent and ambitious young officer.

" A *dhow*," growled Carthew.

" Yes, but why did you come ? "

" To see you."

This statement gave Ensign Machado pause. He realized that it was evasive, and tried to imitate the tone of the older man.

" Quite so," he agreed. " Now what else did you expect to see ? "

" My friend."

" His Excellency Dom Perez de Norhona ? " enquired the youth, smiling ironically.

" No. General Sir Reginald Jason."

Hullo! What was this ? Mr. Machado literally sat up and took particular notice. He was learning something. Thus do keen young officers gain promotion. Intelligence Department. Staff.

"Yes? " he said smoothly. "And did you see him? "

" I did."

" Met him ? Held communication with him ? "

" Yes."

" And having come all the way to São Thomé, and having actually found your friend here, what then ? "

" I murdered him."

366

Not so good. The man was endeavouring to deceive and mislead him. But stay. Might not this be a deeply interesting case of vendetta ?

The alleged friend had wronged him, had somehow heard of São Thomé as the remotest and most secret hiding-place in the world, and had fled thither ; this Kardieu, his enemy, had tracked him down, even to São Thomé, and had taken his revenge at last. Poisoned him, according to citadel gossip.

Rather nice.

But a disturbing thought that these two men should both have found their way to the hidden Island of the Blest.

" A woman in the case, of course," murmured Ensign Machado.

" Of course," agreed Carthew gravely, eyeing his persistent and irritating tormentor in a manner that the latter did not wholly like.

" Ah ! *Cherchez la femme !* " breathed the wise young man, exhibiting not only his knowledge of life but of three words of the French language.

Henry Carthew did nothing to break the ensuing period of silence, during which the amateur intelligence officer pondered the situation and the possibility of yet further enlightening, surprising and pleasing his superiors.

" It did, of course, come to my knowledge—in the course of my official investigations—that you also came to São Thomé to spy out the land, especially the mineral-bearing parts of the land."

" Did it really ? It never came to mine," murmured Carthew as he lay back wearily upon his wooden bunk.

" Strange," sneered the youth. " It was also reported to me that you hoped to obtain an incalculably valuable concession."

367

" No one reported it to me," whispered Carthew, closing his eyes.

" And I'll tell you for *what*," said Ensign Machado sharply.

" Do," sighed Carthew.

" Radium."

" What's that ? " asked Carthew, smothering a yawn.

Ah ! Contumacious. And silently the Lieutenant's lips moved as, in imagination, he wrote that part of his report. " *On being suddenly accused of being a concession-hunting radium-seeker, the prisoner showed signs of guilty confusion, even pretending not to know what radium is. . . .*"

§ 2

Just before dawn, Carthew was awakened from uneasy, nightmare-broken slumber, by the stopping of the noisy engines of the little wood-burning steamer. A few minutes later, a Corporal and a file of soldiers entered his cabin cell and bade him prepare at once to leave the ship.

Putting on what clothes he had removed, Carthew, escorted by the soldiers, went up on deck.

Saluting his prisoner, and speaking with kindly politeness, Machado expressed his regret that duty compelled him to disturb the Senhor so early. That he was about to abandon him for life on a tiny islet inhabited solely by lepers, did not appear an occasion for apology.

As the light increased, Carthew saw that they lay off the low sandy shore of an island as different from São Thomé as it was possible to be. A flat, lonely, gull-haunted pin-point on the face of the waters, that was probably unrecorded on any map and unknown to any man save the São Thoméan authorities and the wretched lepers whose dreadful home and grave-yard it was.

He was surprised to find how calm he was, how far from anything like terror. He decided that this state of quiet resignation to an appalling fate had little to do with courage, resolution or hope. Terror, horror, despair and madness would doubtless come later. At present he was stunned, from hope and fear set free. Too much had happened in too little time, and for the present he had ceased to feel.

" It is my painful duty, Senhor, to request you to descend into the boat. You will be rowed ashore," said Machado.

" Sharks abound in these waters," he added pensively.

Having thanked the Ensign for the courtesy and good treatment he had received, Carthew descended the short ladder and seated himself in the stern-sheets of the boat which was manned by four sailors and the boatswain. The Corporal and file of soldiers followed him, and the boat pushed off. A few minutes later, it grounded on the sandy beach, and the Corporal signed to him to get out.

" *Addios, Senhor,*" he smiled. " You are now free."

" You may be free yourself, some day perhaps," replied Carthew. " *Addios.*"

Hastily the man crossed himself and, with clenched fist and two extended fingers, made the sign which is well-known to be efficacious against the threat of evil.

Having waded ashore, Carthew seated himself on the sand and watched the boat as it was shoved off and rowed back to the ship. A few minutes later, the vessel raised anchor and began to move away. As she gathered speed, Carthew saw a puff of white steam

369

beside her stumpy funnel, and a second or two later, heard the sound of her siren.

How decent of Machado, or perhaps the Captain ! They were saluting him. Rising to his feet he bowed.

" *Moriturus te saluto !* " he said, and smiling grimly, turned and saw someone approaching him—a strange weird figure of a man who had neither fingers nor toes nor anything that could honestly be called a face.

Ashamed, but impelled by uncontrollable horror, Carthew turned and hurried away.

But the leper, in spite of his deformity, could travel across the sand-dunes as fast as Carthew, long practice having perfected his curious technique.

On and on, across patches of soft white sand, fine as dust, through thin wind-blown bents, up and down the little hills and dales of the dunes, pursued by the living Horror, that squeaked and gibbered as it followed. . . .

This was absurd. Cowardly. He was behaving like a frightened child. This was but one of his companions. This place was his new home, his long home. Here, with such people as this, he would live—until he died.

Halting, he turned about and faced the creature, who poured forth a torrent of whistling, gasping speech.

What was he trying to say ?

Something about priests ? Something about lepers ?

" What do you say ? " said Carthew sharply, scarcely conquering his repugnance. " Speak slowly."

Medieval Portuguese interlarded with Arabic and a Kanaka dialect, spoken by a toothless and almost mouthless man, is not easy to follow. The leper tried again, articulating slowly and deliberately.

" Who are you ? " he asked.

" I am a leper," replied Carthew.

" I see no signs."

" No, I'm a moral leper."

" What kind is that ? "

" The worst kind."

" Then you had better come to the Holy Fathers."

" Right. Will you show me the way ? "

As he strode along with the leper shambling beside him, Carthew questioned the man, and understood about half of what he said. He gathered that there was a small band of monastic Fathers who devoted their lives to endeavouring to ameliorate the lot of the living dead of this island graveyard, doubtless strengthening and saving their souls if they could do but little for their bodies.

If Carthew rightly understood his informant, the Fathers were a tiny community no member of which was ever allowed to leave the Island. When a São Thoméan priest elected to go to Leper Island, he went for life. When he died, he was buried in the grave-yard with the lepers, and there was a vacancy, quickly filled, for another obscure and nameless hero of the highest and noblest class.

" Do any of the priests themselves ever become lepers ? " Carthew enquired.

" Yes," replied the man. " Nearly all do, as they grow old, and then they leave the Priests' House and live as lepers in the leper village."

Carthew further understood that the Fathers taught the lepers to work, that they might not starve or go naked. They tilled the soil, cultivated fruit and reared goats. . . .

Had the Senhor's family refused to come with him ? piped the leper.

The Senhor had no family.

Ah, there the leper had the advantage of him. He

had a wife and daughter, and they had refused to be parted from him when he had been caught and deported.

" Caught ? "

Yes. When it was certain that he had contracted leprosy, he had gone and lived in the jungle. His wife had looked after the estate as well as she could, with the help of the bailiff, a faithful fellow who asked no questions and kept his own counsel. But they had not let even him know of his master's hiding-place. It had been his daughter who had brought him food and other necessities. It had been a very dreadful time for his wife and daughter. A time of anxiety, fear and grief. And at first he had been desperate at finding himself a leper. However, one gets used to things.

Carthew regarded the man who had got used to things, and wondered how long he himself would take to follow his example.

" But then misfortune befell us," he continued quaintly. " The Leper Inspector, a big and very important official, visited my property and enquired about me. He remembered that he had not seen me on his last tour. My wife said that I had gone to São Ildefonso on business. He asked how long I had been away, and though he tried to bully and trap her, and made further enquiries he never discovered the truth. But he fell in love with María who was a very beautiful girl. Still is. . . . He is a bad man and evil-looking, and has a wife and family. María feared and hated him. He made a suggestion to her, and when she said she would sooner die and very much sooner cause him to die, what do you think he did ? Denounced *her* as a leper, saying he would get her sent to Leper Island, if she did not give way. He did it too.

She said she'd much sooner go to Leper Island than to his bed, so he said very well she should, and reported to the Ministry of Health that María Garcia, daughter of José and Caterina Garcia of the village of Goncalo, was a leper, and obtained the usual form of expulsion to be enforced by the Police. Of course, I at once came out of hiding, denounced myself and accompanied her. My wife came too, as she refused to be parted from us.

" That's how I came to be caught. Funny, wasn't it ? "

" Very funny," agreed Carthew.

" That's the Priests' House," said the man as they topped another dune, and pointed to where a large hut, long and low, stood in the middle of well-tended gardens, and on the edge of a wide area of cultivated land.

XVI

CARTHEW'S arrival was obviously a cause for perturbation among the good Fathers. Evidently this man, simply flung ashore as the lepers were, must be some kind of a criminal, and an enemy and a danger to the State. As a public enemy he must be treated, since such he was ; on the other hand, he was a Christian, a man of culture and education, and a person of good-will. And moreover, he was a European of pure blood, and apparently what he professed to be, an Englishman.

Father Sebastien, who during his time in Europe had travelled widely and seen men and cities, said roundly that he was a *fidalgo caballero*, a gentleman. What else was a man who talked as he did, who behaved as he did, who knew English, French, Italian, Spanish and Portuguese—not to mention Arabic—as was quickly discovered by the five Fathers who, among them, professed these languages and two or three more.

Gentle and kindly questioning as to the cause of his summary and terrible punishment elicited only the statement that, having visited São Thomé in search of a friend, he had had the misfortune grievously to offend not only His Excellency Dom Perez de Norhona, but Her Highness, the Regent herself.

At this, the good Fathers left it. And on enquiry as to what Carthew wished to do, were delighted to learn that he wished to work in any way that might be helpful to them.   He, of course, had to earn his living, and if he could do it under the Fathers' direction, he would be only too pleased.

Wise Father Simão, who, preparatory to devoting his life to the lepers, had been allowed a year in Lisbon where he had learned English, decided to appoint him fisherman, to supply the House and such of the lepers as could not work, with food.

§ 2

One day, fishing in deep water from a flat rock, Henry Carthew suddenly realized that he was accepting life on Leper Island exactly as one accepts life in a dream, its incredibilities, incongruities and stark horrors.

The horrors were here provided by the lepers themselves, all too real and concrete spectres of the waking nightmare.

For the attitude of São Thomé to Leper Island was, as in most other matters, medieval, in other words, barbarous.   The leper was something to thrust from sight, to segregate, and to leave to perish miserably and horribly—and the sooner the better.

Thus it was that the Fathers, who devoted their lives to these grievously afflicted people, could devote little else, there being no official or other regular supplies from São Thomé, of medicines, surgical appliances, food, or anything whatsoever, wherewith to make and maintain the most elementary form of hospital.   Occasionally the Government *dhow*-chaser, which was also the leper boat, dumped a case of gifts from the monkish community at São Thomé, some charitable private person, or relative of one of the lepers.   But the boat came but seldom, and with

375

complete irregularity, and only for the bringing of a new victim of disease or injustice, and even among the religious, the charitable and the relatives, the opinion prevailed that lepers, like past sins, were best forgotten. In fact, a leper was a living sin, a warning against sin, and a walking example of punishment through the wrath of God.

" Have any of them ever escaped ? " Carthew enquired one day of gentle and innocent Father Simão.

" Escape ? " had been the reply. " It would be a long swim back to São Thomé, my son. And no leper or . . . other person . . . would find a welcome when he arrived. . . . Boat ? No. We monks are only allowed to come here on the clear understanding that we shall never build a boat or allow one to be made. Not so much as a raft. If we helped or willingly allowed anyone to leave the Island, we should be expelled, and the lepers would never have any friends or helpers again."

" And no one, leper or other, has *ever* escaped ? "

" Never. It is utterly impossible."

" Has no foreign ship ever called here and sent a boat ashore—for water or fruit or something ? "

" One did—some years ago. The men saw some of the lepers and rowed away even more quickly than they rowed ashore."

Carthew's heart sank, and he realized how much he had built on that foolish hope.

To live and to die on Leper Island !

To die a leper . . .

" And do any of the lepers ever recover ? "

" No. How should they ? "

" Has any non-leper escaped contagion ? "

" Only one."

That was something anyhow! Perhaps Henry Carthew would be the second.

" He committed suicide, poor fellow," continued Father Simão, " thinking that he had become a leper. But he was mistaken. Pure imagination. . . . It does prey on one's mind if one is not watchful."

Carthew admitted that it did. Then studying the Father's gentle, kindly and happy face—yes, actually serene and happy—he realized, with a sense of shame, that he had been thinking only of himself. This truly good man whose religion was one of works as well as faith, was in as great, or even greater danger than himself, and nearer to his horrible and inevitable end.

With what immeasurable calm courage had these men deliberately made their rendezvous with Death, in one of his most awful manifestations.

He must do more for them than he had. Work harder. Pull more than his own weight in this Charon's boat.

Fishing! Sitting on a flat rock in the sun!

Impatiently he rose to his feet. Who was this coming across the dunes? Garcia's daughter. María Garcia.

Aye. And there was another quarter in which a man could learn something about courage, unselfishness and practical piety.

This slip of a girl had shown a sustained and unflinching bravery of a higher kind than that which is rewarded with acclaim and decoration. If a middleaged soldier like himself shuddered at the sights he saw, and trembled at the thought that his own end must be such as that of those around him, what must be the feelings and fears of this girl, young, undeniably beautiful, and hitherto delicately nurtured in a home of gracious comfort ?

She could laugh. Sometimes even, she could sing. To-day, he noticed, she had put a scarlet flower in her hair above each ear.

And to Henry Carthew that was one of the most pathetic things he had ever seen.

On Leper Island. Tending people whom even to approach was an act of courage. Waiting for—no, he could not bear to think of it. . . .

And in such circumstances, she could put a flower in her hair, and come to greet him with a smile.

§ 3

The days and weeks and months drifted slowly by. Carthew made a garden about the hut he had built with the help of the monks ; worked as a field-labourer, a common carrier of burdens for the common good, a carpenter, cook, nurse, secretary, fuel-cutter and gatherer, washerman and general factotum to the Fathers—occupation his salvation.

In spite of restricted diet and the absence of almost everything that makes for mental and physical comfort and health, he kept well and, to his amazement, far from despair or chronic misery. He was not happy but he had happy hours—talking with María or the highly-educated priests, with some of whom conversation was a pleasure and a privilege.

Trying to copy them, however ineffectually, he sought the society of the lepers, came to know them all, to like many of them, and to find the majority admirable beyond words, for their courage and un-complaining fortitude. . . . Political " criminals" who watched daily, hourly almost, for the dreaded

378

spot which told them that their fate was sealed and that the death, which would take years to arrive, was now approaching. . . . Lepers who watched for this sign in wife and children who had accompanied them from their homes. . . . Women who watched and waited thus for the ineluctable signal to be shown by husband, son or daughter.

And His Excellency Dom Perez de Norhona, the Great Physician, sat over there in São Thomé and studied psycho-therapy, hypnotism, brain surgery and the perfecting of experiments in Permanent Hypnosis !

Why could he not study the cause and cure of leprosy, and stamp it out in São Thomé, instead of stamping the lepers out, and acquiescing in the horrors of this grave-yard of the living ?

Oh, to have him here ! To make him work among the lepers as the monks did, and to tell him he should go when the last leper was cured !

What was it that Carthew had once read about the discovery of some vegetable oil that was thought likely to cure leprosy if used in time ?

Since Norhona could get drugs and apparatus, surgical instruments and books from the best sources, could he not also get this oil ? If name and fame were what he wanted, surely here was a field wherein such could be found. The Man who conquered Leprosy ! Would not that be a finer title than The Man who achieved Permanent Hypnosis—at the cost of the destruction of human minds, bodies and souls ? And Henry Carthew dreamed foolishly of kidnapping de Norhona, with the Hadji's help, and bringing him to Leper Island to work out his own salvation by fasting, prayer and study, until he could fight a successful battle against the disease, cure the lepers, and earn remission of his punishment. . . .

Idle day-dreams.

And, meanwhile, the beautiful and wholly admirable María was daily risking infection—and worse than risking it. She was inevitably and certainly being infected ; and that lovely face and form would assuredly be, one day, as repulsive as those of any leper here.

XVII

SO Henry Carthew worked and dreamed, fought with Beasts of Despair, Fear, Horror and Hatred ; endured and endeavoured to imitate the Fathers, not only in their work and conduct, but in their serenity and peace of mind. At times his strength failed, horror overcame him as he thought of his inevitable end, and he remembered the man who was not a leper, and who " escaped." How had he done it ? An easy way would be to swim out to sea. Swim until one could swim no longer and then peacefully and thankfully drown.

Sharks. . . .

Cowardice would forbid that sudden death.

Did any of the Fathers ever think of suicide ? Did the girl María ? No. Nor would Henry Carthew.

But there were moments. There were dreams.

And one night, lying on the warm sand outside the crude hutch that was his home, he dreamed of the Hadji Abdulla of whom he so often thought. He dreamed that the Hadji was calling to him ; had seized his shoulder and was shaking him, and that suddenly he flashed a bright light into his face ; that he was saying, with amazing reality,

" Come on, Carthew. Quick. . . ."

Rising to his feet, he followed the Hadji as he turned and strode swiftly toward the water.

But was this the Hadji Abdulla ? He was different. But that had been his voice, most undoubtedly. Of course he was different. He was naked except for a loin-cloth, and bare-headed instead of wearing a turban.

Why? Had he swum ashore? No. There was the *toni* which was used as a dinghy for the *dhow*, drawn up at the edge of the water.

No. It must be because he did not wish to be recognized, if seen. That was it.

This was rescue!

The Hadji had heard of his fate, had sailed for Leper Island, had arrived under cover of darkness, had come ashore alone in the *toni*, and had sought until he found him. He would naturally expect to find a new hut somewhere near those of the Fathers. Dysart would not want to be seen and recognized, for if the news of what he had done ever reached His Excellency Dom Perez de Norhona, São Thomé would forthwith become a most unwholesome place for the Hadji Abdulla.

Yes, he was running a big risk. That of losing his valuable São Thomé business, and of finding, one day, that he was trapped in the Citadel to which smiling de Norhona had welcomed him once again.

What a wonderful fellow Brodie Dysart was. The perfect Hadji. The complete *dhow*-master. As genuine an Arab sailor as any *nakhuda* between Baghdad and Singapore, between Karachi and Cape Town. What a life he had led! And here he was, doing what. . . .

Suddenly a thought sharply struck Carthew's bemused and wandering mind. He couldn't go off like this—without a word to the Fathers. It seemed so ungrateful, so discourteous. It seemed like deserting comrades in distress.

And—*Maria!*

382

But he was dreaming of course.

His bare foot struck against a piece of stone and he swore mildly as he always did when he stubbed a toe.

No, he was not asleep and dreaming. . . . *Maria.* . . . He couldn't possibly . . .

" Dysart ! " he called.

" Shut up ! " was the peremptory reply. " We don't want to be seen off by a large crowd with a brass band. Come along, man."

" I must go back."

Poor fellow gone dotty already ? wondered Brodie Dysart.

" You're going back. To England. Come *on.*"

" Just a minute, Dysart," pleaded Carthew. " I really won't delay you for more than a few minutes. I can't go like this. Let me bring a friend."

" What ? A leper ? No, I can't do that. I've no . . ."

" She's not a leper," interrupted Carthew.

" Oh ! Like that, is it ? I see. H'm. I'll take your word, Carthew. And I'll give you ten minutes. I'll wait here, and if you're not back in that time, I *must* push off."

" Thank you, Dysart," said Carthew simply. As he turned and hurried away, Brodie Dysart stood in frowning thought.

Poor old chap !

Quite probably a leper himself by now, and had fallen in love with a leper girl. Well, the disease couldn't be sufficiently far advanced to be recognizable, or Carthew would not have given his word.

By the time that Dysart estimated a quarter of an hour had passed, Carthew came hurrying down to the water.

" Won't come," he said, and doubtless the queerness
of his voice was due to the fact that he had been
hurrying at top speed across loose sand.

" Won't come ? "

" No. . . . Parents. . . ."

" Sticking to them, eh ? "

" Yes."

" Are they bad ? "

" Father three parts dead.   Mother in early stages."

Dysart eyed Carthew's face, ghastly in the moonlight.

" Look here, Carthew," he said.   " Feel bad about
it ? "

" I'd as soon stay as go, if . . ."

" Look then.   I'll stretch a point.   If she'll come
away with the mother, I'll take them both, and for
the love of Allah, hurry."

With a word of thanks, Carthew ran back toward
the tiny settlement behind the little dune cliff.

He returned alone.

As Dysart looked up, Carthew shook his head.

" Come on, then."

Dysart pushed the *toni* well into the water, waded
after it, and balancing carefully, got into it and took
up the paddle.

Carthew followed him.

2

On the long voyage from Leper Island to Santa
Cruz, the seeds of a warm and strong friendship between Henry Carthew and Brodie Dysart, sown long
before, put forth shoots, took root and grew.   Instinc-
tively they had liked each other from the first, and
now Carthew's deep if mute gratitude, and Dysart's

384

admiration of this simple, brave and honourable man quickly turned liking into a sentiment much stronger.

Seated side by side on the high poop of the big *dhow*, they talked for most of the day and much of the night, Dysart giving Carthew news of São Thomé, Santa Cruz, of mutual acquaintances, and of the great world from which Carthew had for so long been cut off.

" How did you come to know that I was on Leper Island ? " asked Carthew one evening, as he watched the rising of the tropic moon.

" From the loquacious young gentleman who took you there," replied Dysart.

" Oh, yes. Of course. What's his name ? Machado."

" That's the lad. Small head, full of big ambitions—and nothing else. I don't know whether they employ him to give away State secrets that they want given away. If so, they've got the right man there. I suspect him of having spotted you as a European, and given us away intentionally or unintentionally. But how the devil he found out, I can't imagine. How should he know that you were a European disguised as an Arab, when hundreds of cleverer men than he never dreamt of such a thing ?

" Yes," continued Dysart, " he's one of the leakiest vessels that ever slopped all over everything, or else he's a very clever man—which I doubt."

" He didn't strike me as being a marvel of intelligence," agreed Carthew, " but I liked him. He treated me very decently. He mayn't be too bright, but he's a gentleman."

" Oh, quite," smiled Dysart. " I am sure that the worthy Palsover thought so. He talked with him a lot, I knew. . . . Nasty piece of work, Mr. Palsover.

385

I've seen as much as I want of him. Took him back to São Thomé twice. He didn't go ashore, but I got very tired of him on the *dhow*. Shan't take him again, whatever fare he offers to pay.

" By Allah ! " he interrupted himself, " could *he* have double-crossed us that time, and given you away ? "

" Good Lord, no," laughed Carthew. " Mr. Palsover never yet did anything against his own interest. He had absolutely fantastic hopes of making a fortune in São Thomé. Radium, I believe. Got hold of some wild story of the place being stiff with it. I never paid much attention. All I wanted was to find Jason. Besides, if he had told Machado that I was a European and that you were treasonably concealing the fact from the Government, wouldn't Palsover have been afraid of being arrested himself ? If he talked to Machado, he must have done so in English. Machado would have arrested him at once, surely. . . . Besides —the motive. Why on earth *should* he do a damn silly thing like that ? "

" It's a mystery," mused Dysart. " Hallo, though. Here's a point. Whether Palsover talked to Machado in English or not, Machado talked to him in English all right, which must have told even the brainy Machado that Palsover understood it."

" How d'you know ? " asked Carthew.

" Why, the excellent Palsover came to me with a cock-and-bull story that Machado had told him. Palsover said he now knew all about the fate of his great hero, General Jason. According to Machado, Jason had been imprisoned in the Citadel, then another British officer, Colonel Carthew, had gone there to do a deal with the Government, and, finding that the General had got there first and was going to get the concession,

386

he just up and killed him. Palsover was grinning like a dog. I daresay he did the same when Machado told him the yarn, for obviously Machado ' proved ' the truth of what he had been saying, by asking Palsover why else he supposed that the disguised Colonel Carthew had been sentenced to a lingering death on Leper Island. Which he had been, for had not he, the important Machado, been given charge of the prisoner ? "

Silence fell between the two men as Dysart stared toward the horizon and Henry Carthew sat with his hand across his eyes.

" Wonder whether Palsover invented the whole yarn for some excellent reason of his own ? " said Dysart suddenly. " I certainly took Jason to São Thomé, and I've never heard a word of him since.

" What a farrago of nonsense," he laughed. " Colonel Carthew found General Jason doing a deal and so did him in. Oh, yes," he added, " and there was a lovely lady in it too."

" Carthew," he said, and laid a large strong hand on Carthew's knee, " you and Jason were also rivals for the hand of Doña Guiomar. So what did you do but murder him ! All's fair in love and war, Carthew, but you shouldn't have poisoned him. For that's what you did do, according to either Palsover or Machado. One of those two lads has got a mind ! . . . My God, what a yarn ! "

Carthew raised his head.

" It's true," he said. " I did find Jason. I did poison him."

Dysart met the gaze of Carthew's tragic eyes, and made no reply.

3

When the *dhow* reached Santa Cruz, and the two went to the *Casa Real*, they found that Mr. Palsover had departed. According to his unsorrowing partner, he had taken ship for Belamu and England, promising to return when he had " done a bit o' business."

A day or two later, the *dhow* sailed again, and once more Carthew and Dysart sat and talked the long drowsy hours away. To Henry Carthew, it had seemed impossible for him to let the *dhow* go without him while he remained behind in that appalling place to await, perhaps for months, a visit of the Anglo-Portuguese coasting steamer. As Dysart was going, in any case, to Belamu, where Carthew could get a ship for England, the latter felt that his need for haste was not so urgent that he must miss this opportunity of exchanging lonely misery in Santa Cruz for the peace of the *dhow* and the comfort of Dysart's society.

On the first night out from Santa Cruz, as the beautiful boat slipped ghost-like through the sparkling phosphorescent water, Henry Carthew unburdened his soul of its load of grief and suffering, told Dysart the whole story of Jason's dreadful fate, and felt the better for the other man's deep silent sympathy.

" I should rather enjoy killing de Norhona," said Dysart. " Try an experiment of my own, on him."

" I suppose he thought he was justified," said Carthew. " If he really thought Jason was a German, a public danger to the peace and safety of the State of São Thomé. And I suppose he'd think almost any man who was a suitable subject for his experiment, ought to be proud of the honour of contributing to

388

the March of Science. . . . What's a life to a fanatical enthusiast like de Norhona ?

" And Jason never suffered," he added. And again as though to convince himself, to comfort himself and assuage an almost unbearable pain,

" No. No. He never suffered at all. He never knew. . . ."

On the second night, as they talked, Carthew suddenly remembered a matter that had occurred to him many times on Leper Island, as he sat and pondered the chain of events that had followed his encountering Palsover in Santa Cruz.

" That marvellous pearl," he said. " Did they return it to you when you left São Thomé—or when you went back ? "

" No," replied Dysart. " I never saw it again. Never shall, I imagine."

" Good Lord ! And you were never paid for it ? " exclaimed Carthew.

" Not a farthing."

" I *say*, Dysart. . . . Doesn't that mean a terrible financial blow. . . . I am sorry—and I feel that I . . ."

" I shall recover," smiled Dysart. " Blow not fatal."

" But, Dysart ! The value of that pearl must have been . . ."

" No. Not as much as all that, Carthew. It wasn't genuine, you know ! "

Carthew stared in amazement.

" Oh, no. When I've got something really good to sell, I don't let it go out of my hands until I've got the money. Once pearls go behind the purdah, for example, they are in no small danger of remaining there, and their substitutes coming forth—with polite regrets that the price is too high, or the pearl is not good enough. I've got some quite nice substitutes of substitutes," he smiled.

" Aren't you ever caught out ? "

" No. And if I were, I've only to explain that I never do the preliminary dealing with the genuine article, and that these pretty models are samples. One wouldn't attempt to play that fool game with experts, of course. But experts don't steal.

" From one another, I mean," he added.

" Aren't you sometimes tempted to sell a dud—to a person who has tried to swindle you, I mean ? "

" Sorely," laughed Dysart, " and I don't deny that I once sold a gentleman his very own substitutes at quite a good price—the price at which he himself had valued them as pearls, in point of fact. But I don't go about planting culture stuff on my honest clients, or on anyone who treats me fairly, when they want to buy a genuine pearl."

" No, I didn't suppose you did," replied Carthew.

" By the way," he asked, " what exactly would you do if Doña Guiomar or de Norhona offered to pay the price you asked for the big pearl ? "

" Take it and change the pearl. But I don't antici- pate that that will happen for some time. When de Norhona's suspicions are aroused, it's a devil of a job to allay them, and he definitely was suspicious that I knew more about you than I pretended. The tale was a bit thin, you know, and it was lucky for me that even de Norhona gets frightfully insular and provincial, not to say gullible. Out of touch with realities, and no wonder. As I daresay you noticed, he combines amazing scientific knowledge, wide and deep learn- ing, and superhuman cleverness with what one might call curious patches of unexpected ignorance. . . . Wonder what kind of places he thinks Bahrein and

Basra are, for example. Anyway, for all his science he does not know a pearl from a good fake."

"Another thing that occurs to me, Dysart," said Carthew, breaking a long meditative silence. "How long will it be before my escape from Leper Island is known. And won't you come under suspicion again ? "

"How long would it be before your escape from a churchyard would become known, if I came and snatched your body and left no traces ? "

"Never, I suppose," admitted Carthew.

"Same with that damned living grave-yard. Unless I or the *dhow* were seen and recognized by someone on the Island, why should I be suspected by the Fathers, or anyone on Leper Island ? And there's practically no communication between there and São Thomé. Next time the Government boat goes to the Island, it'll be to dump some poor devil at the water's edge, as they dumped you, and clear off again at once. At the most, they might put one or two boxes of food, or medical comforts on the beach, and it's an understood thing that neither monk nor leper goes anywhere near the sailors while they do that."

"Suppose there were a letter for the monks from their Father Superior ? "

"Oh, they just chuck it down and put a stone on it, or something."

"And if the monks wanted to write to him ? "

"They'd have to want," was the answer. "Absolutely nothing is allowed to go from Leper Island to São Thomé."

"And will you ever go back to São Thomé ? "

"Oh, yes. Rather. Most interesting place in the world. And my most lucrative place of call. I haven't missed a trip, you know, since someone gave you away and de Norhona blew up. I have to pretend to be very worried about the pearl, of course."

" Have you got the one of which he has the model ? "

" No. Wish I had. But there's a poor ragged old millionaire up the butt end of the Persian Gulf who has. If de Norhona thinks my services are worth retaining, he'll agree to the Regent buying the pearl."

Another silence.

" What made you take Palsover back again ? "

" Greed. . . . Amusement. . . . The human comedy. . . . And I'm not sure that there isn't a small touch of a faint malicious hope of seeing something of the human tragedy if that rascally humbug screws up his courage to go ashore and get taken up to the Capital— so that he can lay an attractive business proposition before the dazzled eyes of de Norhona and the Council of State. Give them a chance to put São Thomé on the map, and boost home industries.

" Wonder where he is now," he added.

" Probably ' interesting ' the financial magnates of the City of London," grinned Carthew.

In point of fact Mr. Palsover was at that moment seeking a good home for four hundred pounds, honourably forwarded to him by Lady Jason on receipt of Carthew's cablegram to the effect that he had found General Jason, and that he had since died.

XVIII

A T Belamu, Carthew said farewell to Brodie Dysart and exchanged the grateful peace, if narrow comfort, of the *dhow* for the bustle and luxurious amenities of the liner *Somali*, sister ship of that which had brought him thither on a day which seemed like one of a former life, decades ago.

He was amazed at the extreme reluctance with which he left the *dhow*, and concluded that it was the parting with Brodie Dysart that was the real cause of his depression.

Rarely in his life had he met a man whom he had liked so much in so short a time, admired so greatly or so completely trusted. In fact, next to Reginald Jason, this Sinclair Noel Brodie Dysart, ex-sailor, ex-soldier, ex-légionnaire, ex-member of a desert tribe, who had made the pilgrimage to Mecca and had travelled far and wide, seeing and doing things most rarely seen and done by white men—appealed to him more as a friend, than any other man whom he had ever met.

As, leaning on the rail, he looked down from the ship's deck at the *dhow* moored at a few cables' distance, he felt a sense of loss and loneliness that surprised him. It reminded him of that day at Sitabad when he had said farewell to Reginald and Antoinette, and their train had steamed out of the station, leaving him feeling like a small boy abandoned by a beloved Mother to the lonely terrors of the first day at school.

Yes. It was surprising. Amazing.

Positively he'd miss this chap Dysart as he had never missed any man since Reginald left the Regiment.

XIX

CARTHEW'S voyage from Belamu to England was not the happiest he had ever made.

On the contrary, it was probably the most miserable journey of his life. He thought constantly of the past horror and the future fear, the fear of his approaching interview with Antoinette. He could not and would not tell her the terrible and incredible truth, and he would tell her no lies. She would question him closely —she was that sort of woman—and before long she would have him tied in knots. At times, especially at about four o'clock in the mornings, as he lay awake thinking of Reginald, of the girl María, of the lepers, of the super-human men who voluntarily buried themselves alive with them, of Brodie Dysart, his courage would fail and he would decide to write to Antoinette.

Yes. He would go to his Club, sit himself down in the library, with reams of paper, and write a full and true account of it all, from the day he landed at Santa Cruz to the day on which he returned there. Then his mind would recoil from his own cowardice. How could he, for one moment, contemplate telling poor Antoinette the appalling truth about the man whom she adored, the man whom she had loved almost from childhood and with whom she had lived so many years. Reginald, her noble, dignified, stately husband, the finest figure of a man in the British Army, crawling about on all fours in a suit of shaggy skins, and behaving like the animal he thought himself to be.

No. That would be the ultimate cowardice. He must go straight to her, and just say that Reginald had died. . . .

And added to the terrors of the past and future was that of the present. The ever-present dread that he was, even now, himself—a leper.

Unclean ! . . . Unclean ! . . .

Had not Father Simão told him that not one of the monks had ever escaped, and that of the non-lepers who were sent to the Island, only one had ever done so, and that by committing suicide. Why should he not rise from his berth at once, make his way to the stern, dive overboard, and end his troubles in a few minutes ?

Why ?

An act of cowardice.

He had a duty to perform. He had promised Antoinette that he would do his utmost, and surely that included returning and telling her everything. . . . Nearly everything. Certainly he must *himself* give her his personal assurance that, of his own actual, indisputable, certain knowledge, Reginald was dead. He could assure her, on his word of honour, that he was dead, and buried in consecrated ground. Not only that, but in the precincts of a Cathedral.

Being a woman, that would in some curious way, comfort her.

Of course he must go home and face his painful duty. What was happening to him, that he should ever dream of shirking it ? Besides, wasn't he longing to see her ? What was there on earth that he desired more than to see Antoinette, whom he had always loved so deeply ?

Now that poor Reginald was gone, she was the greatest friend he had. Almost the only friend. Of course he must go straight to her, directly he landed, without wasting an hour.

But it would be a dreadful and a difficult interview.

It was.

Antoinette seemed changed.

She had always been a cool woman, inclined to irony and sarcasm, a trifle hard at times, and prone to say slightly bitter things, but he had never known her to be like this.

Even when she had first sent for him, told him all she could about Reginald, and begged him to go in search of the poor chap, she had not been like this. Distraught. . . . Off her balance. . . . And well . . . queer.

It was almost as though it was *his* fault that Reginald had wandered off. Got into trouble. Disappeared and never returned. Why did she take this line of knowing more than he told her? And why did she seem to take everything that he told her, as though with a grain of salt?

Could there have been some garbled account of the affair in the papers? Of course not.

Could the Hadji have written to . . .? Of course not. What a hopelessly idiotic idea.

Good Lord! Could that fellow Palsover have . . .? Even more utterly idiotic.

What he had been through must have affected his never too brilliant brain. Why should Palsover write to Lady Jason, or come here and . . .? Lunatic moonshine. For, in the first place, Palsover knew

397

nothing about what had really happened to Reginald. Did anybody in the world, except de Norhona, Dysart and himself know the truth about the death of General Jason ? Of course not.

Why, de Norhona himself didn't. What he knew, or thought he knew, was that the vile Colonel Kardieu had wrecked his marvellous experiment by killing a hypnotized adventurer who had come to the Island, guaranteed by Pereira himself to be a German named Fritz Schultz. De Norhona was not the man to take a stranger's verbal assurance against his own agent's written word. True, he had given poor Reginald the ' benefit of the doubt ' as he had said, and a Christian burial, but that in itself showed there was a doubt.

Anyhow, Palsover . . . No. Utterly impossible. . . . And yet . . . And yet . . . Who else could have betrayed them at São Thomé ?

Who but Palsover could have told Antoinette anything at all ? Palsover, according to his own story, had been associated with Reginald in the beginning, and up to the time the Hadji took him up to the Capital.

If it *were* Palsover . . .

" What did you say ? " asked Lady Jason sharply.

Carthew gave a guilty start. He must have been thinking aloud.

" Er—Palsover . . ."

" What ? "

" Excuse me, Antoinette. I'm even more stupid than usual to-day. Before we go any further, would you mind telling me whether you've had any sort or kind of communication from a man named Palsover."

" No. Never heard the name in my life," she answered somewhat curtly.

398

" Why ? " she asked.

" Well—er—it's a bit difficult to—what I mean is . . ." faltered Carthew. " Why—look here, Antoinette, I wouldn't dream . . . You seem to . . . I mean, I wouldn't dream of suggesting that you doubt my word, but we do seem to be at cross purposes. It's as though you had earlier and—er—better, wider, information . . . and . . . When I got to Santa Cruz I found a man there, a fellow of the name of Palsover, who used to be in the Regiment, years ago. Recognized each other at once, and when I asked him what on earth he was doing there in Santa Cruz, he said that Reginald had brought him with him. And he was just sitting there waiting for him to return."

" Are you sure his name wasn't Jones ? " Lady Jason asked coldly. " David Jones."

" Quite sure," replied Carthew quietly. " The man whom I saw at Santa Cruz, and who said he had come out from England with Reginald, was named Palsover."

" What sort of a man ? To look at, I mean. Could you describe him ? "

Carthew described Mr. Palsover in a manner that would have given that gentleman no satisfaction. It is doubtful whether he would have recognized the description as a picture that resembled him in the least. The last touches would have seemed ridiculous.

" And a plausible, lying, swindling rascal he is," concluded Carthew.

Lady Jason thought of her five hundred pounds, and seethed with rage. Normally a calm, even-tempered woman, when really angered she was apt to lose her admirable poise and self-control. She must hit out. Strike back. Punish someone.

" A man somewhat of that description, but of the name of Jones, did come to see me," she admitted.

" *Ah-h-h-h!* Now we're getting at it," said Carthew, and laughed a little drearily, perhaps a little unkindly.

" And what did he tell you ? " he asked, a contemptuous note creeping into his voice.

Lady Jason rose to her feet—the better, perhaps, to strike.

" Among other things, Henry, about a woman and a concession, he told me *that you killed Reginald!* "

And as one who, with a terrific effort, throws off a crushing burden, Henry Carthew, too, stood up.

" I did," he said.

There it was. It was out. It was off his mind.

Since Palsover had told her—and God alone knew how that fellow, Machado, had come to know of it—it was far better to admit the truth.

But . . . God grant that the unspeakable Palsover (and let him wait until Henry Carthew found him) had not told her the reason.

He couldn't have done so. No. He couldn't have done so. How could he possibly have known ? Poor, poor Antoinette. If Palsover . . .

She was speaking again.

" So he spoke the truth, did he ? And *you* killed Reginald ? "

" Yes."

" Why ? "

Turning away, the picture of guilt, Carthew walked to the window and stood looking out, seeing nothing.

" Why ? " came the inexorable question.

" I . . . I . . . He . . . he . . . he was better dead," he mumbled.

Henry Carthew heard a distant bell ring and the closing of the door, as Antoinette Jason walked out of the room.

XX

" COLONEL CARTHEW in the Club ? "

The hall-porter looked up from his desk and saw a remarkably sun-burned stranger, a very big man with piercing blue eyes, grim mouth and what the hall-porter was wont to term a sort of a kind of a *look* about him. Probably Admiral or Captain Somebody, R.N.

" Yes, Sir," replied the omniscient man promptly. " George, take this gentleman's card to Colonel Carthew in the library."

A minute or two later, Carthew entered the marble-flagged hall, beaming welcome.

" Good Lord, Dysart ! You ! I *am* glad to see you. What a surprise. Shock, in fact. The last man on this earth I should have expected to see here. You'll stay to lunch, of course. Come along."

And thus talking, for him, almost garrulously, and taking Dysart by the arm almost affectionately, he led the way to the vast and magnificent smoking-room in a deeply embayed window of which were two huge arm-chairs, a small table and complete privacy.

" Here we are. We can have a great *bukh* here, in peace. What will you have ? Nothing ? No one here watching to see if you break the laws of the Prophet, y'know. No ? Well . . . neither will I then. Sun not over the yard-arm yet. Smoke ? . . . Thought you weren't coming to England for years."

" So did I," replied Dysart, with a laugh. " But you never know, y'know, as those who know, say."

" Given up the sea ? "

" No. And shan't—until it gives me up."

" When the sea gives up its living, eh ? " smiled Carthew, briefly happy for the first time in a very long while.

" Or my living. No, it'll be the case of the sea giving up its dead before I quit it voluntarily. About the only clean and peaceful place left, nowadays.

" Not so peaceful either," he added. " Really what brings me home. I have found something I have been looking for. Been hunting it for a long time. Submarine base and depôt. Very neatly done. Just a poor little Arab fishing village. Reed huts. Stakes, nets and everything. Worthy of Wassmuss. So I've come home for a chat with a lad at the Admiralty who is deeply interested in that kind of thing."

He eyed Carthew narrowly as the latter stared gloomily at the thronged pedestrians and cars in busy Pall Mall.

Poor chap looked very ill. And most profoundly miserable. Was that ghastly Jason business preying on his mind ? One wouldn't have supposed so, for he was a brave man with a strong will and character.

" And what are you doing ? " he asked, breaking a silence that was growing over long.

" Nothing."

" It's not an amusing pursuit," hazarded Dysart.

" What isn't ? "

" Doing nothing."

" No."

" I daresay you'll excuse me if I have the impudence to butt in, Carthew, but you look to me as though you are doing something. Something damn bad for you."

" What's that ? "

" Brooding. Why don't you come back with me ? " he continued. " Finest life on earth—or water. I'll teach you the tricks of the trade and make you as good a *naukhada*—*dhow*-captain—as ever sailed out of the Persian Gulf. Teach you the pearl business, too, if you like. And later on you could buy a *dhow* of your own and make a fortune. Give you something to do."

" Most kind of you, Dysart. I should love it."

" Nothing to keep me in England," he added sadly, and a little bitterly.

Oh, that was how the land lay, was it ? Nothing to keep him in England. So he had been wrong in supposing Carthew was in love with this Lady Jason. As a rule, when a man refers to a woman as his best and dearest friend, he means something by it. And her husband had been as good as dead for years before he died. Something pretty wrong. That would account for his glumness and general air of depression.

Would he be putting his foot in it and stirring up horribly painful memories if he referred to that subject ?

No, quite obviously, by the look of him, the poor chap thought of nothing else. Absolutely getting him down. Do him a world of good to talk about it. Get it off his chest.

Carthew's next words gave Dysart the opportunity he desired.

" Heard no more of that infernal scoundrel, Palsover, I suppose ? " he said.

" Why, yes. He was back in Santa Cruz the last time I was there. Large as life. And sitting at the receipt of custom again at the *Casa Real*. Wonderful feller. He's going to make me a millionaire, this time.

All I've got to do is to interest de Norhona and the Council. They give me a concession. That's all I've got to do, to be let in on the ground floor. Mr. Palsover then goes to London, and approaches the necessary capitalists—once he's found a real gentleman to look after him and see he isn't swindled by the City sharks. I haven't the slightest doubt that that is the part poor Jason played ; and that is how he came to find himself in São Thomé."

"Good Lord!" ejaculated Henry Carthew. "I never thought of that. Even when he approached me . . . The lying scoundrel."

"Palsover! Palsover!" he said under his breath. And Dysart saw his knuckles whiten.

"Yes," said Dysart. "The death of General Jason. Your sojourn on Leper Island. And I haven't a shadow of a doubt that he had a hand, both hands, in that Pereira business."

"And another little item. Haven't told you about it yet," said Carthew.

"Palsover ? "

"Yes. He went to Lady Jason."

"What on earth for ? Make a touch of some sort, I suppose. Some form of blackmail . . ."

"And told her that Jason was dead, and that I had murdered him."

"Did he mention the reason ? "

"Oh, yes. We quarrelled about a concession."

"Lady Jason didn't believe a word of it, of course."

Carthew regarded his foot, swinging nervously, to and fro.

"You know what Palsover is. The most plausible rogue unhung."

"Yes," agreed Dysart. "The whitest sepulchre that ever covered corruption. You'd be ashamed to doubt him when he's telling the tale. Until you know what he is.

" But Lady Jason knows you, even if she doesn't know Palsover," Dysart continued. " She could not possibly, for one second, take his word against yours."

" No. . . . Not really. . . . But it was unfortunate," replied Carthew. " How was I to tell her what Reginald . . . was . . . when I found him ? How could I ? "

Carthew fell silent.

Dysart regarded him from beneath the hand with which he shaded his eyes.

" Suddenly she said," continued Carthew,

" ' *Is it true that you killed Reginald ?* '

' *Yes,*' I answered, and although her question nearly stunned me, I was almost thankful to know that she knew, and to get the confession off my mind.

" ' *Why ?* ' she asked. And there it was, Dysart. I felt dreadful . . . dreadful . . . for I could not and would not tell her the truth, and what was I to say ? I knew I should bungle it. . . . Make a mess of the whole thing. And I felt terribly constricted about the throat. And that was another shock. For that's how leprosy often begins to show. And when I could find my voice, and while I could find it, I just blurted out,

" ' *Because he was better dead.*' "

" And then, of course, you had to explain why he was better dead," observed Dysart.

" No, thank God. She just went out of the room.

" What on earth could Palsover have said to her ? " he continued on a note of pain and protest.

" Lord knows," mused Dysart. " But I'll bet he had a wonderful water-tight story, and no doubt, completely convincing proofs. Wonder if our friend

Palsover is a good forger ?   I should be very much surprised if he wasn't, and he must have had plenty of samples of Jason's hand-writing and signature.

"And by Allah !   That reminds me," he said, sitting up suddenly.   "Jason was frightfully upset when he was on my *dhow*, about a ring he had lost.   He was certain he had put it down on his bunk when he was getting a smear of caulking-pitch off his hand.   Quite likely Palsover pinched that, and one or two other things that helped to establish his *bona fides*."

"I think I'll take a trip to Santa Cruz on purpose to interview Mr. Palsover," said Carthew ominously. "I'd love a quiet talk with Samuel Palsover. . . .

"Was there any idea of his coming to Europe again, when you left ? " he asked.

"No.   Not at any early date, anyway.   He was going up-country to see a chief with whom he has dealings. . . .   Going to sell him a hundred-weight of lead razor-blades or dud electric-light bulbs, I expect."

"A pup of some sort, no doubt.   Probably gas-pipe guns and wood-alcohol."

The two men smoked in silence for a while, each following his own train of thought.

"Where's the *dhow* ? " asked Carthew suddenly.

"Belamu."

"When do you pick her up again ? "

"I'm sailing in the New Year ; probably first week in January."

"Shouldn't be surprised if we met at Liverpool Street."

"Why ?   Going to see me off ? "

"See each other off, Dysart.   I'm for Belamu too."

"What, coming *dhowing* ? "

"Dunno. But I've got to go to Santa Cruz again. I must have a quiet word with our Mr. Palsover."

"Well, combine business with pleasure. Come with me to Belamu and I'll run you down to Santa Cruz in the *dhow*. Bit slower than the Portuguese steamer, but you're in no hurry. More likelihood of Palsover being back by the time we arrive."

Silence again.

"What are you going to do with him?" asked Dysart, as he laid the ash of his cigar in the tray.

Personally he wouldn't care to be in Mr. Palsover's shoes if Henry Carthew were after him and feeling as he looked just at the moment.

"I don't know. Depends on what I can find out. . . . Whether he belied poor Jason to Machado, and so to Norhona. Whether it was he who betrayed us. Anyhow, I want a word with him about his visit to Lady Jason."

"Yes," agreed Dysart. "Personally I'd like to further his radium-concession scheme."

"You would? To make money, do you mean?" asked Carthew in great surprise.

"No. There's no money to be made in that direction. But I'd like to do exactly what he asks. Take him to de Norhona and let him tell his artless tale."

"Wonder what de Norhona would do to him?" mused Carthew.

"Wonder what de Norhona would do to me? That's more to the point," returned Dysart. "Do to him? . . . Do to him? . . . He'd either make him the subject of one of his Permanent Hypnotism experiments, or else dangle him up to the waist in the radium quick-sand, until his flesh rotted off his bones."

"Well—I don't want anything unpleasant to happen

407

to him," said Carthew gravely, " but I feel I must see
him once again.

" Once will be enough," he added.

§ 2

By the time he took his departure, Dysart was fully
convinced that Carthew, whom more than ever he liked
and admired, was in a thoroughly bad way. His
morbid, hurt, unhappy mind grievously afflicted his
body, and caused the insomnia, lack of appetite, and
general feeling of indefinable illness of which he com-
plained.

Also that the causes of his mental trouble were
partly incurable and to be ameliorated only by the
passage of time ; partly curable and needing a cure
which he, Brodie Dysart, could at any rate endeavour
to perform.

In the first place, he was suffering from the loss, and
still more from the manner of the loss, of his great and
life-long friend, General Jason.

In the second place, he was naturally and inevitably
suffering from a terrible fear of becoming a leper.
Quite obviously, although he said nothing about it, he
had handled them, tended them, worked with them
and for them, as freely and fearlessly as the Fathers did.

And what made this even more cruel still, was the
fact that he was in love with this woman, and now that
he was at last free to hope that she might marry him,
here was this new and insurmountable obstacle. He
might be a leper.

Of course, he had admitted nothing of the sort, but
from the way he spoke of her it was as clear as daylight
that he was not only in love with her, but had been in
love with her all his life.

His oldest and dearest friend. . . . His best and kindest friend. . . . The woman for whom he had undertaken this quest for her missing husband. Of course he was in love with her. And of course Carthew, being Carthew, had not spoken up for himself. Had not given her the faintest idea of the tremendous moral and physical courage that had been called for. . . . The devotion. . . .

Well, here was a chance to befriend Carthew. Fools rush in ? Might be cases where the fool had more pluck than the angel. He hated butting in, and minding other people's business, but Carthew was a sick man, and this might be by far the biggest cause of the misery and unhappiness that were turning him so morbid.

Why, if she were worth her salt, she'd jump at the chance of making some amends, some return for all that he had done for her.

Once she knew the truth, surely she wouldn't be put off by the fact that he might possibly have contracted leprosy. She ought to be given the chance, anyhow. And she should be. It was only fair to her as well as to Carthew.

Poor devil ! Sitting there, day after day, in that gloomy Club library, writing letters to her and tearing them up—because he was unable to explain why he had killed Jason.

Well, things couldn't be worse, and he'd have a damn good shot at making them better : and if he failed to help him in that direction, he'd get him aboard the *dhow*—and keep him there.

Sunshine and salt sea air. Take him to Santa Cruz and let him have his " word " with Palsover, if that would make him feel better, and then he'd take him as far as a *dhow* could go. Show him some of the

409

loveliest places in the whole wide world. Places to which this blight called Civilization, this curse called Progress, had even yet not penetrated.

And in all pure selfishness too, for the one thing he lacked in life was a man of his own kind with whom to talk.

XXI

L ADY JASON was more than a little surprised, and read the card once again.

Sir Sinclair Brodie Dysart ?

The name was absolutely unfamiliar to her.

Travellers' Club ? Some friend of poor Reginald's ? He had never mentioned the man so far as she could remember. . . . Some business acquaintance ? Lady Jason inclined her head in assent, and the butler, returning to the hall, informed Dysart that Her Ladyship was at home.

" Sir Sinclair Dysart, my Lady," he announced, and softly closed the door.

Yes. A complete stranger, thought Lady Jason, and also noted that the stranger was a remarkably personable figure of a man. Looked like something from the bridge of a battle-ship.

" Good afternoon, Lady Jason," he said. " I would apologize for this intrusion, but for the fact that I hope and believe that you'll be glad that I came, when you've heard what I have to say."

" I'm sure I shall. Do sit down," smiled Lady Jason, quite prepared to forgive the intrusion, whatever this attractive visitor might have on his mind, provided it was neither silk stockings nor a vacuum-cleaner.

" It's about your late husband."

A mask seemed to settle over Lady Jason's face.

411

" And Colonel Carthew."

" Do you come from him ? " she asked, in a cold and level voice.

" Most definitely I do not. Let us have that absolutely clear from the beginning. I am prepared to find him extremely angry and resentful when he hears that I have been to see you—about this tragic business."

Lady Jason leant back in her chair and, without reply, prepared to listen.

Then succinctly, clearly and convincingly, Brodie Dysart told Antoinette Jason the story of the disappearance of General Jason; of his evil genius, Palsover; of the still unexplained mystery of his being taken for a Nazi German emissary; and of his fate at the hands of a Government to whom such people were anathema.

Sparing her feelings as much as possible, he told her the plain unvarnished truth. Told her of the state in which Carthew found her husband, and endeavoured to make her realize that the only thing that Jason's truest friend could do, was what his friend did do.

Nor did Brodie Dysart fail to impress upon his hearer that he had done his utmost to prevent Carthew from venturing into the place where he believed General Jason to be, for his going there was inevitably fraught with the greatest danger.

" So I felt sure, Lady Jason," concluded Dysart, " that you would like me to come and tell you all I know about the matter, and particularly to tell you all that Carthew—being Carthew—was bound to leave unsaid."

For a few moments he eyed her in silence.

" A man of marvellous moral courage as well as physical courage," he mused aloud.

412

Lady Jason appeared to have no comment to make on that subject.

" Not that you'd ever dream that he had run any particular risks, nor had had to make a decision of a kind which few men have ever been called upon to make."

" All he said to me was that he had killed my husband because he thought he was better dead," said Lady Jason.

" He would," observed Dysart. " Knowing Carthew, didn't you question him further ? " he asked.

" No. He had come to tell me everything—and that was all he had to say."

It would be a bit difficult to say more after you had marched out of the room, thought Dysart.

" M-m-m. Yes," he said. " Well, that is why I came. He's a dumb fish, isn't he ? Not much better with a pen. I believe he has made a few score efforts to write to you about it."

" Why didn't he, then ? "

" Didn't want to give you unnecessary pain. More delicate-minded than I am. I'm afraid, Lady Jason. No doubt he thought you'd understand, and find it quite enough, when he said that it was the best thing to do—or he wouldn't have done it.

" Incidentally," he asked, as he rose to say farewell, " he didn't mention, I suppose, that in trying to serve you and General Jason, he has probably contracted leprosy."

" *What ?* "

Ah ! That penetrated. That was a genuine look of horror.

" Yes. He was arrested and imprisoned, and condemned to death. The slowest and one of the most dreadful deaths conceivable—confinement on a tiny

413

leper-island, already over-crowded. He naturally thinks that he has contracted leprosy—as he may have done. And it hasn't done him any good, I assure you. He sits and broods, and watches for the first sign. What he needs, beyond anything, is company, friendship, sympathy."

Before Dysart's level gaze, Lady Jason's eyes fell.

"Poor Henry," she murmured. "Poor Henry. . . . I didn't dream . . . I'll write to him."

"I'm sure it would do him a lot of good," said Dysart crisply. "And I'm sure when you've thought it over and grasped the situation, you'll get him down here, and—er—look after him. Enough to drive him mad, sitting in a Club bedroom, expecting the worst, and waiting for it. And it's not only that, you know. He took a most frightful knock over General Jason, his life-long friend. Imagine what it was to a man like Carthew, to find him in that state, and then to do what he felt was his duty.

"Can't you understand how he sits and chews that over? While he waits to find that he is a leper."

"Oh, *don't!* Don't tell me any more. I'll write to him. I'll write . . ." said Lady Jason.

"Well, as I've said before, I hate butting in, but I do feel that it is up to you—to save him. And you can, you know," and, as he extended his hand, he added, "I wish you could hear how he speaks of you."

Poor old Carthew, he thought as he left the house.

Still, I'm glad I've seen her, and so long as he thinks she is what she certainly isn't, well . . .

XXII

CARTHEW sat at the window of his Club bed-room and gazed, unseeing, across the tree-tops, visualizing as now he so often did, a lonely islet, a pin-point speck upon the face of the illimitable waters, the haunt only of sea-birds and lepers.

What he saw, as he sat staring, was not the London scene of blackening trees or reeking chimney-pots, but white sand and waving bents, and a blue sea that lapped gently with soft susurrus on a lonely beach, and coming across the dunes down to the water's edge, a girl. A girl who, living in the midst of horror, pain and privation, lacking almost everything that is dear to the heart of a girl, could still place a flower in her hair and sing as she walked.

That was a girl of courage. A fine spirit.

But what was this, her singing and her poor little effort at personal adornment, beside the splendour and nobility of her act of renunciation and self-denial—when he came to her in the early dawn and offered her escape, freedom?

If he lived to be a hundred he would never forget those painful minutes while he did his utmost to fight against her unselfishness, her sense of duty, her love for her father and mother. It had been truly dreadful. The girl longing, with all her heart and soul, to get away from that abominable prison and return to a way of life that was worth living.

But the teaching of the Fathers, the innate loyalty, sense of duty, and simple filial piety had conquered; and, as she cast herself down upon the sand, tears streaming from her eyes while she begged him to return, he himself had faltered, half tempted to stay.

But he had given his word to Antoinette that he would find Reginald or discover beyond shadow of a doubt what had happened to him, and that he would himself give her his personal assurance of the truth and certainty of what he had to tell.

Besides, what folly. What quixotry run mad. Dysart was waiting and running a risk on his behalf.

Curious how frequently that picture of the Island now occupied his mind. How constantly he thought of those wretched lepers, those noble Fathers, and of María—a heroine as deserving of a niche in the temple of fame as was any Joan of Arc or Florence Nightingale. . . .

He looked at his watch. Good Lord, he had been mooning here since breakfast, and had missed lunch. He must really take himself in hand and conquer this miserable morbid mooning, this day-dreaming . . . looking back at São Thomé with horror, the Leper Island with regret and to the future with fear.

The future! What should he do if the worst happened?

A leper!

Well, time he was getting along to the School of Tropical Diseases again.

Wonderful chaps those research men. And very comforting and reassuring. God grant they were right but . . .

No. He could stand it no longer. No sign from Antoinette. It had been most exceedingly kind of Dysart to go and see her and tell her all that he himself had left untold. Had it been cowardice that had kept him from doing as Dysart had done? He didn't think so. He had honestly wished to spare her, and there had really not been the slightest reason why she should ever have known the real facts, but for that unspeakable hound, Palsover. She need never have known that Reginald had not died a natural death. . . . malaria . . . dysentery . . . cholera; or met with an accident, exploring, big-game shooting.

Still, as it was, she at any rate knew from Dysart's independent testimony that Reginald was dead, and that, however bizarre and dreadful his end, he had suffered nothing at all.

But it was strange that she had never written.

Suddenly Carthew, who was walking up and down his room, stopped.

Good Lord! Could it be—could it possibly be because Dysart had told her about Leper Island? Could *that* be the reason why . . .?

It was the reason.

Lady Jason, like most other people, had a great horror of leprosy and lepers.

She had seen them in India.

§ 3

No. He neither could nor would stand it any longer. It was bad enough now, while Brodie Dysart was in England and they were able to meet quite frequently.

What it would be like after the New Year he did not care to contemplate. There was not a soul in England with whom he could sit and talk about what filled his mind. Or better still, sit in companionable silence and refrain from talking about it. More and more, his mind dwelt on the thought of going with Dysart to Belamu, joining him on the *dhow*, and sailing once more for Santa Cruz.

What would happen there was on the knees of the gods, but his resolution as to what should happen when he reached that accursed place was crystallizing out, was hardening fast. Each time that he and Dysart met, he parted from him with increased determination, increased longing—*longing*, could that be possible ?—to see Leper Island again.

No, it must be for the *dhow*, the sunny peaceful days and glorious tropic nights that he was longing. Surely not for a lost island over which the sea-birds screamed in thousands, where one of the noblest and bravest bands of men worked and waited, and Death brooded.

XXIII

L ADY JASON sat at her desk, the one at which poor Reginald had worked so hard in those last days before he went away for ever.

A difficult letter to write.

Poor dear Henry. It was of course splendid news. She had always been under the impression that *that* was absolutely incurable. Was it possible that he could be mistaken ? No. He wasn't the sort of man to make a mistake of that kind. And if he were, those oriental-disease specialists were not.

Poor darling, what a fright he had had ! Now that it was all right again, she must try and make it up to him.

A pity he was so over-modest and diffident. She would positively have to make the running.

She had always been fond of Henry, from the time he was a scrubby untidy subaltern. Such a contrast to poor dear Reginald. Ordinary-looking, where Reginald was so amazingly handsome ; insignificant, where Reginald had such a magnificent presence and such a dignity of bearing ; rather stupid, as compared with Reginald's brilliance—and so dreadfully *dull*. *Dreadfully* dull.

But then again, he was a contrast to Reginald in other ways, she must remember.

Reginald had never really loved her, whereas Henry adored her. From the very beginning, Reginald had

419

put his career first and his wife a bad second. With Henry, it would be Antoinette first and everything else nowhere . . . nowhere. So faithful, so unswervingly devoted to her all these years.

Yes, and she must remember the tale of the years if she were going to marry again, which she most certainly was. Dear Henry. Dear dull Henry. But so faithful. So unswervingly faithful. So obedient too. And a woman who had been married to Reginald Jason could appreciate that.

Lady Jason's eye wandered from the letter in her hand to the window and her beautiful garden beyond. Why were good obedient children always so boring ?

Well, better a little peaceful boredom than the worry and anxiety of the last three or four years. Love (even with Henry) . . . Peace . . . Security after this damned mess that Reginald had gone off and left her in. Just like the man. . . .

Lady Jason, after one or two efforts that she found unsatisfactory, wrote Henry Carthew a letter that should surely have brought that humbly-devoted and single-hearted man hastening to her side.

That it did not do so must be considered as largely due to the fact that he never received it.

" Where do Colonel Carthew want his letters addressed to ? " enquired the desk under-porter of the Hall Porter as he sorted the members' letters.

" Nowhere I shouldn't think," was the reply. " I asked him, and he just smiled sad and sarcastic and said,

' No fixed abode, John, and no visible means of support.'

" Better keep 'em all," he added, and Lady Jason's very beautifully worded letter was accordingly kept.

" Well, well," smiled Brodie Dysart warmly, as he came face to face with Carthew on Liverpool Street platform, and wrung his hand. " Allah be praised."

This was good. This was splendid. It wasn't often that one could combine the purest selfishness with one's good deed for the day—or for the year. For many years, he hoped. It would make all the difference, having this good chap with him. One of the most lovable men he had ever come across. Just such another as Dacre Blount had been ; such a deeply interesting mind, well-stored, judgmatical, and clever in the best sense of the word. A man with a fine and a high philosophy of life. Most attractive. Never a dull moment in his company, and yet a man with whom one could sit in absolute silence and enjoy the quiet communion as much as the long, long conversations about every interesting thing on earth. A man after one's own heart, of one's own sort and kind, with similar likes and dislikes, and who spoke the same language.

Well, there was one thing. Once aboard the lugger he'd not part with him lightly or easily. Thank God he had been mistaken about him and Lady Jason. Brittle as well as hard, that woman. Shallow as well as deep.

Still, he was glad he had done what he had conceived to be his duty in the matter. For he had most firmly believed that Carthew's future happiness was bound up in her—" the very best and dearest friend he had ever had."

And he wasn't sorry that he had let her know what sort of a chap Carthew really was, and what he had done and suffered for her and her Reginald. Though that was beyond her knowing. Nor could he suppose that Carthew, as soon as he knew for certain that he had escaped leprosy, had proposed and been rejected. He had none of the air of a rejected lover. On the contrary, his health and spirits had seemed to improve from the very day that he had rung him up and, with an unmistakable note of satisfaction and cheerfulness, if not joy, said,

" I have decided, Dysart. I am coming with you on the *Ceylon* to Belamu. Does your offer hold, to run me down to Santa Cruz ? "

And when he had laughed and replied that nothing on earth would suit him better than to have Carthew as a passenger, the funny old chap had said,

" Ah, but I want to take a frightful lot of stuff. How much could you manage ? "

And when he had replied,

" Oh, say a hundred tons or so," Carthew's laugh had been positively merry.

He had wondered why the devil he wanted to take a lot of stuff down that way. Not Bond Street creations for the belles of Belamu. And it wouldn't be " trade " either. Carthew wouldn't have the slightest idea as to what sort of goods would be profitable.

Besides, he'd leave that side of it to him, the owner of the *dhow*, naturally.

§ 3

On the way to Belamu, as they walked the deck or reclined in long chairs, Brodie Dysart did his best to paint in radiant hues the picture of the life that he himself so loved. A life of the uttermost freedom known to civilized man. A life of simple joys, rude health, constant change and activity. A life of the deepest interest and one not closed to modest ambition and reasonable financial success.

To be one's own master. To be like the wind that bloweth whither it listeth, and to be constantly in a sufficiency of danger to give life that savour without which it must be dull, even if profitable.

Yes, he must convert Carthew from soldiering to sailoring, teach him all he himself knew, and sweeten his veins with the salt of the sea.

§ 4

At Belamu he was, in spite of what he had said, a little surprised at the number, weight and bulk of Carthew's packages, and deeply disappointed to learn of his plans.

He realized that this feeling was purely personal and wholly selfish, fought against it manfully, and strove entirely to conceal it.

For, as they stood in the heat and glare of the white stone quay, between the great ovens that were the corrugated-iron Customs sheds, Carthew asked him if the *dhow* could not only carry the lot to Santa Cruz, but on from there to Leper Island.

" O-oh, I see. Stuff for the Fathers. And medical comforts and so on, for the lepers, eh ? Yes. I'll dump them there for you, Carthew. Of course I will. Only too delighted. You'll come too, naturally."

" Oh, rather. I want you to dump me likewise."

And it was then that Dysart's heart sank. He might have known it. The sort of thing this noble lunatic would do.

" Not for six months, surely," he said, conscious of a sense of shame in saying even so much in discouragement. Too well he knew that nothing that he could say would deter Carthew, but he might at least have the grace to refrain from the attempt. But no, it wasn't wholly selfish. One should, one must, do something to prevent such a man as this from such a fearful form of suicide. He was not a dedicated priest, a super-human being who had renounced Life and offered himself to Death·that he might do a little doubtful good among men whom God had stricken.

No. But he was of the stuff of which such men are made.

Could it be that Jason woman, after all ? Had he so loved her that he had now no further wish to live—with such memories ?

" Yes, I'll take you, Carthew," he said. " And I shall come again for you at the end of six months."

Carthew smiled his thanks.

§ 5

At Santa Cruz, Carthew learnt with regret that Mr. Palsover had not yet returned from his up-country trek to the territory governed by the paramount Chief Poaha, a man who inclined to drastic measures, arbitrary methods and power politics.

Felice Diego, Mr. Palsover's partner, in the owner-ship of the *Casa Real* and other less obvious business ventures, was indeed of opinion that it would be quite a long while, a very very long while, before Mr. Palsover returned to Santa Cruz and the circle of friends who undoubtedly missed him.

" Why ? " asked Carthew, seated in an uncertain long chair on the unsafe verandah, together with the Hadji Abdulla, who in turban, robes and cotton

424

silham, sat cross-legged on an unworthy mattress, supported by what Senhor Diego described as cushions.

" It's that Poaha, Sah," explained the Goanese. " That man, Sah. Blaming Palsover Sahib about dem shields."

" What shields ? "

" King Poaha's. All him warriors have big ox-hide shields, Sah. Brown for one *pultan*, brown and white for another, black for another, but best of all, King's own bodyguard must have black-and-white. Very few black-and-white cattles in King Poaha's country. So he send messengers to King Loratu offering to buy all black-and-white ox-skins he got, because King Loratu's people live by keeping cattles and drinking their milk. Got *lakhs* and *lakhs* of cattles.

" But King Loratu not liking King Poaha for always shooting him up and playing the other mischiefs, says, ' *You get to Hell outa this,*' and cuts off their heads.

" Just then Palsover Sahib goes up to Poaha's country with Best Bombay Spirits and things."

" Trade gin and gas-pipe guns," murmured Carthew. " Yes ? "

" And he does big deal with Poaha for black-an-white hides to make shields for number one *pultan*. Very clever man," sniggered Senhor Diego. " He go to India *ek dum*, and buy all white ox-hides, black ox-hides and black-and-white ox-hides. Municipal Slaughterhouse, Karachi, Bombay, Madras, Calcutta. All places. Also makes advertisements wanting black, white, and black-and-white hides. Then he ships whole lots to Santa Cruz and we sort them out."

" Smelt nice, didn't they ? " enquired Carthew, visualizing vast stacks of raw hides in the sweltering heat of the *Casa Real* go-downs.

" Nossir," contradicted Mr. Felice Diego. " Not so

425

very nice. Then Palsover Sahib takes up big waggon-load of black-and-white hides which pleases King Poaha very good. And while Palsover Sahib gone, I have to dye black patches on white hides, and have to paint white patches on black hides.

" Then Palsover Sahib comes back, and we send up the rest with Toto."

" Who's he ? "

" Bar-man, Sah. Man Hadji Sahib beat up, for bumping little *chokri*[1] with bottle."

" Oh, that swine."

" Yessah. Then Chief Poaha, very big *bahadur* now he got brown shield regiment, brown-and-white shield regiment and what he think very good best of all, real black-and-white King's Regiment. So he tells his regiments to sharpen their spears, because he go for make war on King Loratu.

" Then, after big barley-beer drinking and war-dance, he sends more messengers with rude words to King Loratu. He leads out his fine army to invade country. In front goes Royal Regiment with black-and-white shields. Very proud, pomptious and con-temptious. But suddenly it becomes rain like Hell. And black dye on white shields runs over all shield, making it black and drips off.

" Then King Poaha shout, ' *Oh, my goddam. Oh, my blast it all.*' His heart break and he go home. Royal Regiment coming last, not cockahooping, but all drooping and gone to damn, so that the women laugh. Then King Poaha sit down and think up something good for Palsover Sahib. But he can't think up nut-ting better than old country custom.

" So he send for Toto still waiting there for payment for the hides.

[1] Girl.

" ' *Get you up, oh man,*' he say to Toto. ' *Harness your oxen to your waggon and go you back.*'

' *Without payment ?* '

' *Sure,*' says Chief Poaha, ' *an' you go quick unless I alter my mind and pay you. Go before the sun sets, and go to your master an' tell him to come here to me, to King Poaha. And I will pay him for his hides and for something else.*'

" And from the way King Poaha speak, Toto don't think King Poaha like Palsover Sahib so much no more. Toto think King Poaha's country damn bad place for Palsover Sahib, so he come back quick an' tell Palsover Sahib that King Poaha very pleased, very glad. Want more hides same black-and-white. Pay more for nex' lot. And if Palsover Sahib come up now, he pay him for first lot and make agreement about new lot."

" And he went, eh ? " asked Carthew softly.

" Yes, Sah. Palsover Sahib go *ek dum.*"

" I gather that—er—Toto was not very fond of Mr. Palsover ? "

" No, Sah. Not so much. Palsover Sahib beating him up and cutting pay."

" And you've heard nothing more of Mr. Palsover ? "

" No, Sah. Only his boots, and they all gnawed about."

§ 6

It was, as Mr. Felice Diego had said, an Old Country Custom of the dwellers in the Santa Cruz hinterland, and a very unpleasant one, final in its effects on those to whom it was applied, and deterrent to others contemplating similar malefaction.

Descending from his waggon, Mr. Palsover had

thrown the reins to his giant factotum and strode across to the royal village, before the largest house of which sat King Poaha, who, long before, had been notified of the approach of the mule-drawn cart.

" Greeting," said King Poaha, rising from the royal stool.

" Greeting," replied Palsover, extending the right hand of honest friendship.

This the King did not grasp, but raised his spear aloft with a royally dramatc gesture.

But not to strike. The spear-blade pointed to the sky and, as though conjured from the earth, stalwart unarmed men stepped forth from within and behind the huts, and from the shelter of rock and bush and tree.

Mr. Palsover gazed about him in some anxiety as the great silent crowd closed in about him. This was not the manner in which he was accustomed to be received by Poaha or any other dirty native. This was something new and uncomfortable-like. Had the words ' sinister ' and ' minatory ' formed part of Mr. Palsover's vocabulary, he would have found appropriate use for them now.

The point of Chief Poaha's spear fell. His men crowded yet closer about Mr. Palsover and suddenly he was seized from behind. A stout thong of plaited leather was tied about his waist, and to this his right hand was firmly lashed behind him.

" 'Ere, wot's the game ? " shouted Mr. Palsover in good honest English.

In his own deplorable tongue King Poaha offered apology. He greatly regretted that the funeral baked meat was not quite ready. The cook was doing his best.

From the Chief's brief and polite speech, Mr. Palsover garnered only the words, ' meat ' and ' cook,' and failed to connect the cooking of meat with this unseemly fastening of the cord about his middle, and the firm attachment of his right hand thereto.

However, King Poaha continued to the effect that the provision of meat should be made forthwith, in order that his honoured guest should be in no danger of starving.

" No," pondered King Poaha aloud, as grimly he eyed the large and paling countenance of Mr. Palsover. He did not think there would be any danger of hunger.

Mr. Palsover understood the word ' hunger,' and was the less amazed when, from the King's own hut, emerged a fat perspiring man who bore in his greasy grasp what Mr. Palsover recognized as a nicely roasted goat. Done to a turn. Beautifully browned.

Rather reassuring, but undoubtedly a rum go. Meat. Cook. Hunger.

And here was a very nice bit of posho. But why had he got to eat it there and then, standing up, and with only his left hand to use ?

Some blooming native custom, no doubt.

Puzzling. Very puzzling. And increasingly so when his other arm was seized and the savoury roast was not merely tied, but firmly lashed, to his hand and fore-arm.

What was the game ? . . . What the Hell ? . . . And 'ere, what was this ? . . . This 'ere goat.

They were tethering a live goat to him. Actually. What did they think he was ? A perishin' post in a bloody farmyard ?

Native custom ? Well, he had never ate a damn great joint tied on to his fist yet, and he wasn't going to start now, custom or no blasted custom. He'd bloomin' well . . .

Again King Poaha raised his hand, and the men

429

crowding about him fell away, ran from him as though he were stricken with pestilence.

Then Mr. Palsover saw that some thirty paces in front of him, a line of young warriors, each bearing a white shield badly stained with an unstable black dye, held their throwing spears aloft.

As one, the sinewy arms went back behind the shoulders and,

" *Run!* " shouted Chief Poaha.

With a swift glance behind him, Mr. Palsover saw that the way was clear, for the crowd had formed a double line, a lane through which he could escape. . . . And scarcely had the Chief uttered his one word of good advice, than Mr. Palsover was running as he had never run since, as a young recruit, he had entered for the hundred yards event in the annual sports-meeting of the Wessex Fusiliers.

Behind him leapt and cavorted the goat, swiftly realizing that its immediate future was bound up with that of Mr. Palsover.

A great spear passed over his head and embedded itself in a tree-trunk just ahead of him. But he could not increase his speed. As he dashed past it, the haft still quivered and swung. Could be possibly reach the cart before a spear like that struck between his shoulder-blades, impaling him as, when a boy, he had impaled flies upon a pin.

If he fell . . .

If he fell . . .

This cursed goat . . .

This weight upon his arm . . .

How could he run straight . . . keep his balance . . . one hand tied behind him ?

The damned cowards ! That swindling, lying swine of a Poaha ! Let him wait till . . .

God! That was a near one. And he had nearly fallen.

When would he reach the cart?

Where in Hell? Why . . .

And with a terrible sense of defenceless nakedness, he realized that the cart was not there, that he must have passed, far back, the place where he had left it. That, had it been here, right in front of him, without the use of his hands it would have been utterly impossible to climb into it, snatch the reins and start the mules.

But Toto? He had left Toto there. The swine had deserted him . . . betrayed him. Or else Poaha's devils had killed him. He hoped they had.

His breath came in painful gasps and, from time to time, he stumbled, staggered and almost fell.

Were the sounds of pursuit growing fainter?

Yes. Thank God.

He had shaken them off. He had beaten them. Fooled them. Escaped from them.

He had—by reason of King Poaha's strict order to his young men that not a hair of Mr. Palsover's head should be hurt.

Soon he fell into a jog-trot. Into a shuffle. A walk. And, before long, sank exhausted to the ground. The goat, nothing loth, rose on its hind legs and began to sup upon the succulent young leaves of the bush beneath which Mr. Palsover lay and fought for breath.

When, at length, the sobbing of his labouring lungs grew quieter, the man sat up and took stock of his position.

Unhurt. Night coming on. A hundred miles from home. A damn good supper tied to his left arm and

431

beginning to weigh like a half hundred-weight sack of potatoes.

A perfectly good goat tied to his backside.

What a B.F. he'd look, walking down the Avenida at Santa Cruz.

Got to get there first though. Take him four days, with luck.

He'd come back and drive Poaha over the same course with a rhinoceros-hide whip. Yes. Harness him beside the mules. He'd teach the tricky swine something about mule-skinning. Skin him alive, he would.

Ah ! And take more than four days over it too.

But why had the beggar given him this roast meat ? Just to make him last the longer ? That was it. Wanted to spin out his sufferings, knowing it would be just about damn-all he'd find to eat between Poaha's country and Santa Cruz.

Dirty swine.

Yes. That was the only reason why he had given him the food. And he had tied it on to his fist so he shouldn't drop it when he bolted from those murderin' savages with the spears.

That was why he had tied this roasted meat on to him, but why the Hell had he sent the goat along ?

Suddenly Mr. Palsover's question was answered in the wide deep silence of the night.

For, from either near or far, from either the east or the west, or perchance from the north or the south, came the terrible cry of the hungry, questing beast.

Mr. Palsover leapt to his feet.

Which way ? Which way ?

Could he climb a tree ? Of course not.

Where could he hide ? Where could he run ?

432

The frightened goat uttered a loud and piteous bleat.
" Shut up, you — — —," hissed Mr. Palsover, fiercely
yet ludicrously.

Again the terrible cry, as the great beast, on the
strong scent of its prey, drew rapidly towards it.

Blindly, Mr. Palsover ran with all his ebbing strength.
Dashed into dark shadows in search of safety. Dashed
into a tree and fell to the ground, winded and half
stunned.

Again the terrible cry that made his blood run cold.

Looking up, he gazed wildly about and saw, or
thought he saw, the moonlight glinting upon two
terrible eyes.

A great crouching form. . . .

And again, with a superhuman effort, he rose to
his feet and fled.

The last sound ever uttered by the plausible and
persuasively garrulous Samuel Palsover was a long
scream—suddenly cut off.

XXIV

SO Henry Carthew failed to have his quiet " word " with Mr. Palsover, but bore with fortitude the news, brought by Toto, that he had been able, beyond peradventure of a doubt, to identify his late and deeply-lamented master by his boots—both of which had frequently kicked him.

And when his business in Santa Cruz was completed, his *dh ʾw* provisioned and her cargo bestowed, the Hadji Abdulla informed his admired passenger that he would sail, an hour before dawn; would make land-fall at Leper Island; disembark him and his baggage on the beach at another dawn, and then weigh anchor for São Thomé and what might then befall.

" Why not land the stuff and leave it, Carthew ? " he said, as they sat on the verandah. " *Do*. Be sensible. You've escaped once. The leprosy, I mean."

" The Fathers . . ." began Carthew.   .

" Think of the joyous amazement of the Fathers when they find the Island smothered in good things. They'll think it's direct answer to prayer—and you'll have founded or fathered another indisputable miracle. Everything they'd been praying for. Parcels from Heaven. Carriage paid. Why, they'll . . ."

" The Fathers, I was going to say," interrupted

434

arthew, " will be rather glad to see me. And to know that I'm going to carry on with the bit of work I was doing."

" They'll be damned sorry to see you—committing suicide by leprosy."

" It's what they are doing."

" Well—it's their job. I mean they've made it their job."

" Can't I ? "

" They've renounced the world."

" Not sure that I haven't."

" Don't be a fool. Excuse me ; I didn't mean to say that. You've no right to do such a . . ."

" I promised. I ought to have told you."

" *Promised ?* The Fathers ? "

" She just sank down on the sand in such an agony of grief as I could not bear to see. It was like murdering a child that trusts you utterly. And when she sobbed ' *Come back !* *Come back again !* ' I stooped and stroked her hair and said ' *Yes. I will* . . . *I'll come back, Maria.*' And she sprang up and threw her arms about my neck—and then thrust me from her. She wouldn't leave her father and mother, Dysart, and I am going back."

" Of course," said Brodie Dysart.

§ 2

On the voyage to Leper Island, Dysart did his utmost to dissuade Carthew from taking any irrevocable step, such as solemnly dedicating himself to the service of the Fathers as a lay-brother and helper in their life-work of succouring the lepers.

" I don't know," was the only reply that he could get. " It depends—to some extent."

Dysart could make an accurate guess at what it depended upon.

"But why not take her away from the Island?" he expostulated. "Now. This voyage. I'll take you both straight back to Santa Cruz. I'll take you to Belamu if you like—or anywhere else."

Carthew put his hand on Dysart's shoulder, for him a very rare gesture. Scarcely had he made it a dozen times to Reginald Jason, his life-long and only friend till now.

"Extraordinarily good of you, my dear chap," he said. "She wouldn't come while her parents are alive."

"Suppose they're dead?"

"Suppose she's a leper?"

"Suppose she's not," countered Dysart.

"Well, if her parents are both dead, and she has, so far, no sign of being a leper—and cannot of course return to her home—what should I do with her? Supposing she were willing to leave the Island."

"'*Willing*' to leave the Island!" repeated Dysart in tones of amazed incredulity.

"Yes . . . The Fathers, you know. They get a wonderful hold of you. They did of me. How much more so of an impressionable young girl. And she's of that type—the born devotee. Yes. They get a wonderful hold of you," mused Carthew.

"Not intentionally, of course," he continued. "But you can't live with them, watch them, know them, without—oh, you know what I mean. They radiate the sort of thing from which the hardest cases aren't immune. She'd want to stay with them."

Dysart eyed his friend, and smiled.

"She would, eh?"

"Yes. And if she wouldn't, what could I do with

436

her at Santa Cruz, or Belamu, or even Portugal if I took her there ? "

" Marry her," replied Dysart succinctly.

" My dear chap!" expostulated Carthew, and also smiled.

And Dysart found that, for all his quietness, gentleness and apparent meekness, his passenger was a man firm of purpose, immovable as a rock, when once his mind was made up, his goal before him, and his duty clear.

The utmost concession that Dysart could wring from him was the promise that he would " look out " for him, daily, at dawn, for a week or so, some six months hence ; and that until he had pondered the matter for that period, he would give his promise to no one that he would remain permanently on the Island.

" And if you do tell me any nonsense of that sort when we meet, I'll bring every one of my crew ashore, armed to the teeth, and kidnap you, my son. I will. And then how will you find your way back again ? " he asked.

A day or two later, just as the moon and stars began to pale, and a faint new light to tint the eastern horizon, Dysart roused Carthew from his mattress on the high poop deck.

A bad moment.

Bad as when he left the *Valkyrie*.

Bad as when he realized he had lost Dacre Blount.

Bad as when he knew that never again would he see his leader, Walter Manny Chandos.

Almost as bad as that day in Luong-Tam-Ky's tent.

This man whom he had come to love so well, was going to his death.

And what a death !

No. He shouldn't. He shouldn't, if Brodie Dysart could prevent him.

Six months hence he must . . .

Carthew sat up.

" Just over there," said Dysart, pointing to the bows. " A couple of cables."

" Thanks."

Carthew went forward to where the short bow-sprit pointed him his way.

Would she come running across the dunes, the sunlight of the fresh sweet morning gilding her lovely face ?

Would she have a flower in her hair ? A song on her lips ?

A song in her heart, to answer his ?

Yes. It would be like that.

He and she, alone by the kindly sea, between the golden sands and the azure sky.

And afterwards ?

TOM STACEY REPRINTS

This series makes available again some of the best books by the best authors of our time, priced at £1.95 each except where stated otherwise. Already published are:

ROMANCE and ADVENTURE

Gerfalcon
by Leslie Barringer

Tarzan's Quest
by Edgar Rice Burroughs

Jungle Girl
by Edgar Rice Burroughs

Monsieur Blackshirt
by David Graeme

The Sword of Monsieur Blackshirt
by David Graeme

The Vengeance of Monsieur Blackshirt
by David Graeme

The Ancient Allan
by H. Rider Haggard

The Ghost Kings
by H. Rider Haggard

Morning Star
by H. Rider Haggard

Pearl-Maiden
by H. Rider Haggard

Red Eve
by H. Rider Haggard

Swallow
by H. Rider Haggard
(£2.50)

The Wanderer's Necklace
by H. Rider Haggard

The Yellow God
by H. Rider Haggard

The Heart of Princess Osra
by Anthony Hope

Phroso
by Anthony Hope

The King of the Via Veneto
by Ronald Kirkbride

Clementina
by A. E. W. Mason

The Courtship of Morrice Buckler
by A. E. W. Mason (£2.25)

Fire Over England
by A. E. W. Mason

Bluefeather
by Laurence Meynell

King of the Khyber Rifles
by Talbot Mundy

The Man in Grey
by Lady Eleanor Smith

Tzigane
by Lady Eleanor Smith

Bosambo of the River
by Edgar Wallace

The Keepers of the King's Peace
by Edgar Wallace

Lieutenant Bones
by Edgar Wallace

Sanders
by Edgar Wallace

Sanders of the River
by Edgar Wallace

Sandi the King-Maker
by Edgar Wallace

Action and Passion
by P. C. Wren (£2.25)

Fort in the Jungle
by P. C. Wren

Spanish Maine
by P. C. Wren

Port O' Missing Men
by P. C. Wren (£2.50)

The Siege of Malta
by S. Fowler Wright
(£3.50)

Blind Corner
by Dornford Yates

She Painted Her Face
by Dornford Yates

MYSTERY and DETECTION

Dead Man's Shoes
by H. C. Bailey

Slippery Ann
by H. C. Bailey

The Sullen Sky Mystery
by H. C. Bailey

The Big Fish
by Francis Beeding

The League of Discontent
by Francis Beeding

Behind That Curtain
by Earl Derr Biggers

Charlie Chan Carries On
by Earl Derr Biggers

The Chinese Parrot
by Earl Derr Biggers

Keeper of the Keys
by Earl Derr Biggers

Enter Sir John
by Clemence Dane and Helen Simpson

Below Suspicion
by John Dickson Carr

The Four False Weapons
by John Dickson Carr

To Wake the Dead
by John Dickson Carr

The Judas Window
by Carter Dickson

Murder in the Submarine Zone
by Carter Dickson

She Died a Lady
by Carter Dickson

The Ten Teacups
by Carter Dickson

The Unicorn Murders
by Carter Dickson

The Benson Murder Case
by S. S. Van Dine

Bulldog Drummond on Dartmoor
by Gerard Fairlie
following Sapper

Holiday Express
by J. Jefferson Farjeon

The Case of the Sulky Girl
by Erle Stanley Gardner

The Case of the Velvet Claws
by Erle Stanley Gardner

Fatal Friday
by Francis Gérard

Secret Sceptre
by Francis Gérard

Murder in the Rue Royale
by Michael Harrison
(£2.00)

Cork in Bottle
by Macdonald Hastings

Cork in the Doghouse
by Macdonald Hastings

Cork on the Water
by Macdonald Hastings

Phantom Lady
by William Irish

The Norths Meet Murder
by Frances and Richard
Lockridge

Last Laugh, Mr. Moto
by John P. Marquand

Stopover: Tokyo
by John P. Marquand

Thank You, Mr. Moto
by John P. Marquand

Two-Thirds of a Ghost
by Helen McCloy

Here Comes a Chopper
by Gladys Mitchell

Laurels are Poison
by Gladys Mitchell

The Rising of the Moon
by Gladys Mitchell

St. Peter's Finger
by Gladys Mitchell

The Adventures of
Jimmie Dale
by Frank L. Packard
(£2.00)

The Puzzle of the
Briar Pipe
by Stuart Palmer

Uncle Abner
by Melville Davisson Post

Death From A Top Hat
by Clayton Rawson

No Coffin for the Corpse
by Clayton Rawson

The Devil Doctor
by Sax Rohmer

The Golden Scorpion
by Sax Rohmer

The Mystery of
Dr. Fu Manchu
by Sax Rohmer

The Si-Fan Mysteries
by Sax Rohmer

The Yellow Claw
by Sax Rohmer

The Wrath of Fu Manchu
by Sax Rohmer (£2.00)

Crime on Her Hands
by Rex Stout

More Deaths Than One
by Rex Stout

Red Threads
by Rex Stout

The Second Confession
by Rex Stout

The Silent Speaker
by Rex Stout

Some Buried Caesar
by Rex Stout

Where There's a Will
by Rex Stout

Too Many Cooks
by Rex Stout

Rim of the Pit
by Hake Talbot

Run For Cover
by John Welcome

GENERAL FICTION

These Charming People
by Michael Arlen

Miss Hargreaves
by Frank Baker

The Carved Cartoon
by Austin Clare

Cimarron
by Edna Ferber

Show Boat
by Edna Ferber

Death of a Gentleman
by Christopher Hollis

Jenny Wren
by Ronald Kirkbride

Still the Heart Sings
by Ronald Kirkbride

Greenery Street
by Denis Mackail

The Late George Apley
by John P. Marquand

The Hole in the Wall
by Arthur Morrison

Crouchback
by Carola Oman

The Fortnight in
September
by R. C. Sherriff

Greengates
by R. C. Sherriff

Under Capricorn
by Helen Simpson

French Leave
by E. Œ. Somerville and
Martin Ross

One Foot in Heaven
by Hartzell Spence

The Young Matriarch
by G. B. Stern (£2.50)

State Fair
by Phil Stong

Young Blood
by Annie S. Swan

The Headmistress
by Angela Thirkell

Love Among the Ruins
by Angela Thirkell

The Old Bank House
by Angela Thirkell
(£2.00)

The Gate of Happy
Sparrows
by Daniele Vare

The Maker of Heavenly
Trousers
by Daniele Varè

The Balliols
by Alec Waugh

Jill Somerset
by Alec Waugh (£2.00)

Unknown to History
by Charlotte M. Yonge
(£2.20)

NON-FICTION

Danton
by Hilaire Belloc (£2.50)

The Four Men
by Hilaire Belloc

The Siege at Peking
by Peter Fleming

Thank You for Having Me
by C. A. Lejeune

Eating and Drinking in
France Today
by Pamela Vandyke Price
(£2.80)

FANTASY and
WEIRD TALES

The Human Chord
by Algernon Blackwood

Planet of the Apes
by Pierre Boulle

At the Earth's Core
by Edgar Rice Burroughs

The Land That
Time Forgot
by Edgar Rice Burroughs

The Moon Maid
by Edgar Rice Burroughs

Pellucidar
by Edgar Rice Burroughs

The Slayer of Souls
by Robert Chambers

The Sorceress in
Stained Glass
A new collection of
Ghost Stories edited
by Richard Dalby (£2.00)

The King of
Elfland's Daughter
by Lord Dunsany

The Lost Stradivarius
by John Meade Falkner

Carnacki, The Ghost Finder
by William Hope Hodgson

The Kingdom That Was
by John Lambourne

Burn Witch Burn
by A. Merritt

Creep Shadow Creep
by A. Merritt

The Ship of Ishtar
by A. Merritt

Land of Unreason
by Fletcher Pratt and
L. Sprague de Camp

Brood of the Witch-Queen
by Sax Rohmer

WESTERNS

Silvertip
by Max Brand

Silvertip's Strike
by Max Brand

Silvertip's Trap
by Max Brand

Apache Devil
by Edgar Rice Burroughs

The War Chief
by Edgar Rice Burroughs

Gunsight Trail
by Alan Le May

Bar-20
by Clarence E. Mulford

The Bar-20 Three
by Clarence E. Mulford

The Coming of Cassidy
by Clarence E. Mulford

Hopalong Cassidy
by Clarence E. Mulford

Johnny Nelson
by Clarence E. Mulford

Mesquite Jenkins,
Tumbleweed
by Clarence E. Mulford

Hell and High Water
by William MacLeod
Raine

The Outlaw Trail
by William MacLeod Raine

Man of the West
by Philip Yordan

CHILDREN

Master Skylark
by John Bennett (£1.80)

Mother West Wind's
Children
by Thornton W. Burgess
(£1.70)

Old Mother West Wind
by Thornton W. Burgess
(£1.70)

The Cozy Lion
by Frances Hodgson
Burnett (£1.30)

Racketty-Packetty House
by Frances Hodgson
Burnett (£1.30)

The Spring Cleaning
by Frances Hodgson
Burnett (£1.00)

The Tapestry Room
by Mrs. Molesworth
(£1.50)

The Merry Adventures of
Robin Hood
by Howard Pyle (£2.25)

The Pelican and the
Kangaroo
by E. M. Silvanus (£1.80)

The Ugly Dachshund
by G. B. Stern (£1.20)

The Hired Man's Elephant
by Phil Stong (£1.40)

Knock Three Times!
by Marion St John Webb
(£1.75)

Tom Stacey Reprints Ltd
28–29 Maiden Lane, London WC2E 7JP